THE TRYSTAN TRILOGY
VOLUME 1

THE WOLF IN WINTER

BARBARA LENNOX

Copyright © 2021 Barbara Lennox

Barbaralennox.com

Barbara Lennox has asserted her moral right under the Copyright, Designs and Patents Act 1988 to be identified as the author of this work.

All rights reserved. Printed in the United Kingdom. No part of this publication may be used or reproduced in any manner whatsoever without written permission, except in the case of brief quotations embodied in critical articles or reviews.

This book is a works of fiction. Names, characters, places, events and incidents, although at times based on historical figures and events, are the product of the author's imagination or are used fictitiously. Any resemblance to actual persons, living or dead, events or locales is co-incidental.

Book and cover design, and maps © B Lennox, incorporating images used under licence from Shutterstock, images made available by Jean-Pierre Pellissier and Jeremy Lefaivre from Pixabay, and battlefield symbol by Pethrus, Public domain, via Wikimedia Commons.

ISBN 979-8-5489-8083-0

1st edition November 2021
10..9..8..7..6..5..4..3..2..1

DEDICATION

To my late parents, who gave me that greatest of gifts,
a love of reading.

CHARACTERS AND SETTINGS

CHARACTERS

(Principal characters in bold)

In Lothian:

Corwynal – half-Caledonian son of the King of Lothian
Trystan – King of Lothian's son, Corwynal's half-brother
Rifallyn – King of Lothian
Blaize – half-brother to Rifallyn, Corwynal's uncle, also half-Caledonian
Ealhith – Corwynal's Angle slave
Aelfric – Angle from Bernicia
Heilyn – Dunpeldyr's Chamberlain
Madawg – Leader of Lothian's war-band
Tegid – Galloway guard in Corwynal's troop
Blodwen – Dunpeldyr goose-girl
Arawn – Dunpeldyr's huntsman
Clust – Man of Dunpeldyr
Elphin – Man of Dunpeldyr
Rhun – Man of Dunpeldyr
Conaire – Former member of the war-band, a Scot

Wulfric – Angle raider
Janthe – Corwynal's mare
Rhydian – Trystan's stallion

In Gododdin:

Lot – King of Gododdin, Overlord of Lothian and Manau, Duke of the Britons
Gaheris – Lot's third son, twin to Garwth
Gawain – Lot's eldest son, leader of Gododdin's war-band
Agrafayne – Lot's second son
Garwth – Lot's fourth son, twin to Gaheris

In Manau:

Gwenhwyvar – Queen of Western Manau, daughter of the late King, Ogryfan
Caw – King of Eastern Manau, brother of Ogryfan
Heuil – Caw's eldest son

In Selgovia:

Hoel – King Consort of Selgovia
Essylt – His daughter
Kaerherdin – His illegitimate son

In Galloway:

Marc – King of Galloway
Gwenllian – Marc's sister, Trystan's mother
Andrydd – War-band leader of Galloway
Dynas – Steward of Galloway
Vran – Galloway trooper
Daere – Member of Galloway's war-band
Llwyd – Captain of Gwenllian's bodyguard

In Strathclyde:

Dumnagual – King of Strathclyde

In Dalriada:

Feargus – King of Dalriada
Ferdiad – Dalriada's Fili
Loarn – Feargus' foster brother, Lord of Dunolly
Oengus – Feargus' foster brother, Lord of The Isle
The Morholt – Dalriada's Champion, brother in marriage to Feargus
Dhearghal – Dalriad spearman
Lugh – God of skills and the arts
Manannán – God of the sea

In Caledonia:

Arddu – God of the forests
Broichan – son of Ciniod, King of Atholl
Domech – Archdruid of Atholl
Camulos – God of war
Taranis – God of thunder
Ase – God of death

Others:

Arthyr – Mercenary from Gwynedd
Bedwyr – Arthyr's friend and kinsman
Maredydd – trader from Rheged
Sigeweard – Angle pirate chieftain of Dun Guayrdi
Woden – Angle God
Thunor – Angle God

SETTINGS

Lothian:

Dunpeldyr – Principal stronghold (Traprain Law)
Trimontium – former Roman settlement and fort on the border between Gododdin, Lothian and Selgovia (Newstead, near Melrose)

Selgovia:

Meldon – Principal stronghold (Black Meldon Hill Fort near Peebles)

Manau:

Dun Eidyn – Principal stronghold, Eastern Manau (Edinburgh)
Iuddeu – Principal stronghold, Western Manau (Stirling)

Galloway:

The Mote – Principal stronghold (The Mote of Mark, near Rockcliffe)
Trystan's fort – Hill fort in Galloway (Trusty's fort, near Gatehouse of Fleet)
Loch Ryan – Harbour of Galloway's war-fleet (Stranraer)
The Rhinns – Andrydd's lands in Galloway (The Rhinns of Galloway)
Carraig Ealasaid, the Rock (Ailsa Craig)

Gododdin:

Ad Gefryn – Principal stronghold (Yeavering Bell)

Strathclyde:

Alcluid – Principal stronghold, on the River Cluta (Dumbarton on the Clyde)

Dalriada:

Dunadd – Principal stronghold of Feargus (Dunadd fort in Kilmartin Glen)
Dunollie – Principal stronghold of Loarn (Dunollie castle, near Oban)
The Isle – Principal holding of Oenghus (Islay)
Ceann Tire (Kintyre)
Crionan – western port for Dunadd (Crinan)
Loch Gair – eastern port for Dunadd (Loch Gair on Loch Fyne)
Arainn (The Island of Arran)
Ulaid (Ulster)
Hibernia (The Island of Ireland)

Bernicia:

Dun Guayrdi – Angle pirate stronghold (Bamburgh)
Gyrwum – Angle stronghold in Bernicia (Jarrow)

Caledonia:

Atholl – Caledonian Kingdom (roughly Perthshire)
Circind – Caledonian Kingdom (roughly Angus)
Fife – Caledonian Kingdom (Fife)

Other locations:

Caer Lual – Principal stronghold of Rheged (Carlisle)
Glannaventa – Port in Rheged (Ravenglass)
Llyn Llumonwy – The Beacon Loch (Loch Lomond)
The Gwerid (The River Forth)
The Tava (The River Tay)
Tuaidh Water (The River Tweed)
Gwynedd (North Wales)

TRIBES AND NATIONS

The Britons:

The Kingdom of Gododdin (Votadinae tribe)
The Kingdom of Lothian (Votadinae tribe)
The Kingdom of Manau (Votadinae tribe)
The Kingdom of Galloway (Novantae tribe)
The Kingdom of Strathclyde (Dumnonae tribe)
The Kingdom of Selgovia (Selgovae tribe)
The Kingdom of Rheged (Carvetii tribe and others)

The Scots:

The Kingdom of Dalriada (The Dal Riata tribe, originally from the north of Ireland, Ulaid (Ulster) but who've expanded north into Western Argyll)
Various tribes of the mainland of Ireland (not mentioned)

The Caledonians (a generic term for all 'Pictish' tribes):

The Kingdom of Atholl (Caledonian tribe)
The Kingdom of Circind (Venicon tribe)
The Kingdom of Fife (Venicon tribe)
Other kingdoms/tribes in the 'Caledonian Confederacy' (not mentioned) – Taexels, Vacomagi
Other Caledonian tribes – Creonn, Carnonacs

The Anglo-Saxons (Germanic tribes from the continent):

The Angles – Originally from Denmark, now occupying Northumbria and spreading into lowland Scotland
The Saex – Originally from Saxony, occupying lands to the south of Northumbria
The Jutes (not mentioned) – Originally from Denmark

MAPS

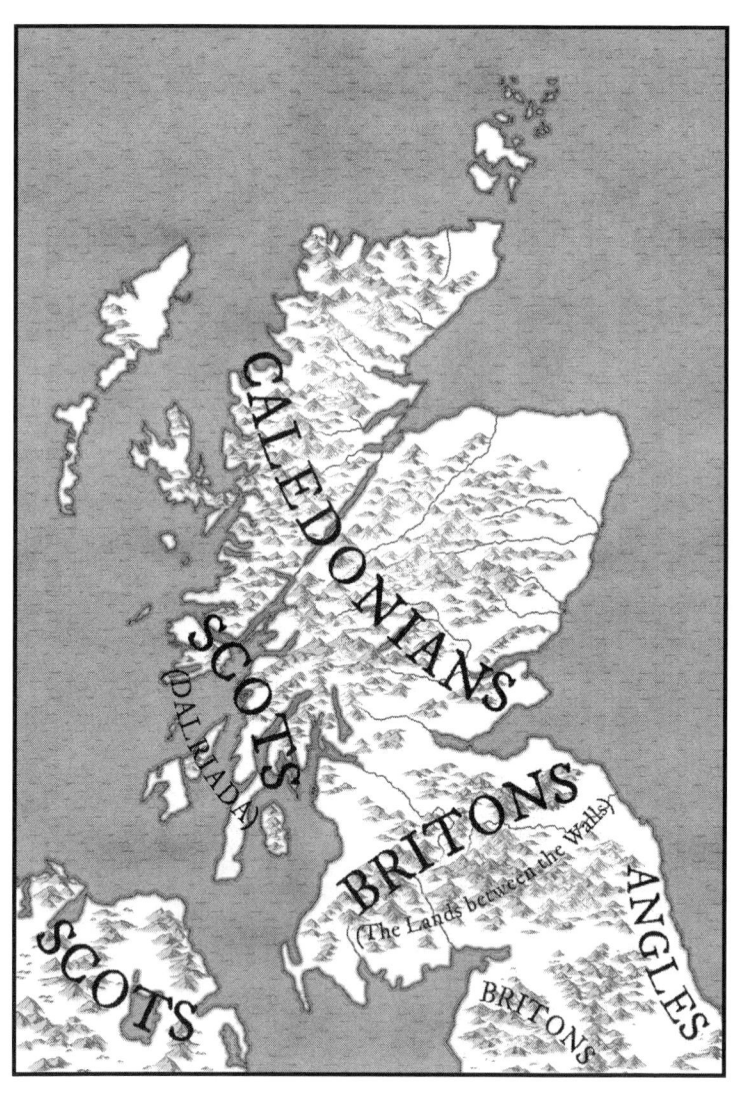

THE FOUR PEOPLES OF *THE WOLF IN WINTER*

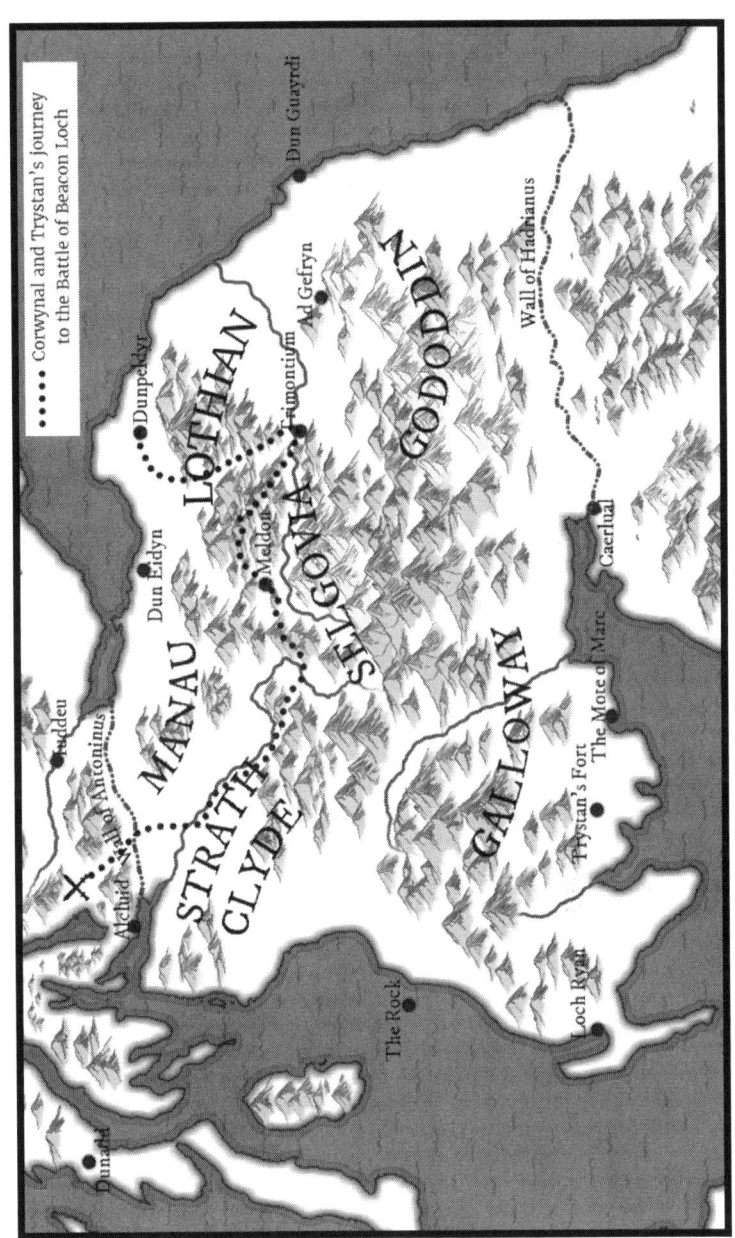

THE LANDS BETWEEN THE WALLS

THE TRYSTAN TRILOGY

ENDING AND BEGINNING

Dunpeldyr in Lothian

Spring 491 AD

Tomorrow, I will burn my father.

Tomorrow, I'll set flame to his pyre and send the smoke of his burning high into the sky. Men will see that smoke from Dun Eidyn in the west to the eastern lands the Angles have taken for their own, and know he's dead, the man who ruled Lothian for over thirty years. But Lothian won't remain unruled for long. Tomorrow, once the fire has burned away to ash, the Chieftains will gather in Dunpeldyr's hall to choose another king. They'll argue and bicker, remember old feuds and settle new scores, debate the rights of this one or that, declaim their qualities and ancestry. Yet I will say nothing and none will speak my name. I'll sit in the chair that stands beside my father's, the one I've made my own, and let his ashes sift through my fingers until they've talked themselves into a decision. For they have little choice and I will have none.

So, tomorrow, I will be King, but tonight I'm free. Tonight, I'll pace Dunpeldyr's ramparts and watch the sun bleed behind the sloe-black peaks of Manau until all light and warmth have vanished from the world. Tonight, in the cold and dark, I'll tell myself the story of everything that has led me here, before that too vanishes. Already my tale is that of a man I no longer know, a man whose name, amongst others, was Corwynal of Lothian. Tomorrow, that man will step over the threshold the fickle gods have forced him to cross. But tonight he'll remember the night of Imbolc more than a score of years before when he made a choice of his own and stepped over another threshold. So that's where he'll begin – on a Night of Thresholds when he still had a father, but not yet a brother.

Or a son.

THE WOLF IN WINTER
PART I

LOTHIAN

IMBOLC, 468 AD

AND SPRING, 485 AD

PROLOGUE

Dunpeldyr in Lothian

Imbolc 468 AD, twenty-three years earlier

A DEATH AND A BIRTH

Corwynal flinched as yet another scream knifed through Dunpeldyr's empty hall. The cry shrieked up into the smoke-stained rafters, before dwindling to a low moaning echo that trickled away to dusty silence. Eventually, however, other sounds slipped back into the hall; snow creaked on the thatch, women murmured anxiously in the chamber at the end of the hall, and, in the distance, borne on the wintry east wind, the sounds of celebration rose from the lambing fields.

Corwynal should have been down in those fields with the rest of the men of Dunpeldyr, for it was the night of Imbolc, the night that marked the end of winter. Instead, he was listening to a woman scream in a cold hall lit only by a handful of little lamps, though, in truth, he had no choice. He was Captain of the woman's guard, and his duty was to protect her, although, right then, he couldn't guard her from what was happening beyond the leather hangings at the end of the hall because no-one could. And now it had begun to seem as if he was no longer there to witness the birth he'd expected, but the death he feared. Night edged its way toward dawn, and each scream was weaker than the last, each silence longer, until it was the silence rather than the screams that burned through his blood and bones.

If he'd been alone, he would have raised his fists to shake them at the gods and demand they do something for once. He might even have begged. But he wasn't alone. His men waited with him, men with more right than him to guard the woman, for they, like her, were from Galloway. They were hard, these men, their faces scarred and evil, their weapons honed to a gleam. They lived and breathed battle, laughed at its bowel-churning terror, yet still they flinched at a woman's screams.

Corwynal, as their leader, had to be harder than any of them. He had to hold his stance, head back, feet apart, one hand clenched so tightly on the pommel of his sword his nails had driven into his flesh, leaving his palm sticky with blood. He had to pretend this meant nothing to him, and so he gripped his expression just as fiercely. Perhaps he fooled his men, for none of them spoke, though he felt their breath pluming on the back of his neck as they muttered curses or prayers. He heard them move restlessly behind him as if they too wished they were far away, down by the Imbolc fires, drinking and feasting to drive away the dark.

In Lothian, as in all the Lands between the Walls, Imbolc, the Night of Thresholds, was a night for men to sing and shout and stagger back to the arms of their women in the bitter dawn of the first day of spring. But the Galloway men didn't complain. Instead, they waited, bracing themselves for each scream to rise out of the anxious murmur of the woman's attendants, until Tegid, the youngest, unable to bear it any longer, whimpered in distress, and Corwynal came at last to a decision.

'This can't go on.' He turned to face his men for the first time that night and jerked his head at Tegid. 'Fetch Blaize.'

The Galloway men exchanged glances, and in the dim light of the flickering Imbolc lamps Corwynal saw Tegid pale.

'But where? And what—?'

'Just find him!' Corwynal's voice began to crack open, but he caught and held it.

Tell him She's dying. 'She.' That was how he thought of her. She needed no other name, though of course she had one. His men would have called her Princess Gwenllian, the Fair Flower of Galloway, for she was sister to Marc, Galloway's King. But she was Queen of Lothian now and soon to give birth to its heir, for she was wed to the King – who was Corwynal's father.

Time passed, then more time, as he waited for Blaize to come and wondered if he'd done the right thing in sending for his uncle. A birth was a women's battle to fight, and Blaize had little patience with women. But, after a day and night of screaming, Blaize, with healing skills, might be her only hope.

The embers in the firepit dwindled to a smoor of ruddy ash that gave little light and no warmth at all. Some of the Imbolc lamps guttered and died and sent greasy smoke spiralling into the rafters. The stench of mutton-fat merged with the stink of stale rushes and the harsher, acrid smell of whatever was happening at the other end of the hall. Somewhere, a shutter banged as the wind rose, and within the hall the wall-hangings stirred in the draughts, setting the woven wolves, Lothian's symbol, slinking through the shadows as if they were alive, their jewelled eyes glinting balefully. The remaining Imbolc lamps flickered and waned but, like Corwynal's hopes, couldn't quite be extinguished. As long as he waited, witnessing her pain, she wouldn't die, *couldn't* die. Not when she was only eighteen, a bride of a mere eight months.

It was close to dawn when Tegid returned, slipping back to take his place with the others and throwing Corwynal a guilty, apprehensive glance as he did so. Behind him the door crashed open, and snow plumed into the hall on a blast of icy Imbolc air that smelled of pine and heather. The wind drove back the stench of smoke and rushes, and most of the lamps blew out, turning the man who stood in the doorway into a hard-edged silhouette set against the streaming torchlight of the courtyard. Corwynal's heart began to thud, for he knew that silhouette all too well. It wasn't Blaize who'd come, but another man entirely.

Rifallyn, King of Lothian, his father and Blaize's half-brother, ordered his men to wait outside, then slammed the door behind him and strode over to the firepit, stripping off his gloves as he did so to thrust his hands out to the faintly glowing ash. The Galloway men straightened and stared into the middle distance, hoping to make themselves invisible. Perhaps they succeeded, for the King ignored them and gazed down into the fire, a tall man, broad across the shoulders, his bulk accentuated by a shrouding cloak of wolf-skin.

'Well?' he asked, lifting his head. His tone was mild, but his expression mirrored that of the snarling wolf's head on his gold-embroidered tunic. More gold glinted from his wrists and neck, from the grip of his sword and the jewelled brooch on his shoulder. Yet none of these could compete with the glitter of his amber wolf's eyes. 'Well, Corwynal?' he repeated, his voice not quite steady, and Corwynal began to be afraid, and not just for himself.

'The Queen is come early to the birth,' he replied as evenly as he could, with a deliberate glance at his men to remind his father of what was at stake. 'But her women say it goes badly.'

The sound of the women was louder now, and one of them was sobbing noisily. His father turned and spat into the fire. 'Women!' He threw his gloves to the floor and, thrusting aside one of the Galloway men, strode over to Corwynal and loomed over him. 'What do they know? What do *you* know? Tell me that!' He took Corwynal's upper arm in a painful grip, his fingers digging into the flesh above his bronze armband. 'What has any of this to do with *me?*'

'Rather a lot, I would have thought,' said a voice from behind them.

The Galloway men, who hadn't noticed Blaize come into the hall, hissed and backed away, though, to Corwynal's eyes, the man who strolled towards them looked harmless enough. He was of medium height and of middle years, with a northern look to him, for, like Corwynal, he was half-Caledonian. His long greying dark hair was pulled back into a silver ring and he was dressed in a none-too-clean habit such as those worn by the priests of Chrystos, though he didn't follow that god. Blaize served older gods; around his neck hung an oak-leaf medallion, and his forehead bore the faded mark of the druids. Corwynal's men believed him to be a Caledonian sorcerer, but he thought of his uncle as a friend, one of the few he had.

'You married the girl,' Blaize reminded his half-brother. 'You wanted her to give you a son, and so . . .' He shrugged. 'So, here we are . . .'

'Indeed!' Rifallyn snarled, but he slackened his grip on Corwynal's arm. 'Well then, since you've chosen to interfere, you can see that she does.'

Blaize held the King's eyes for a moment, then smiled his wintry smile, loosened the knife in the sheath at his waist, walked to the end of the hall and pushed aside the hangings that barred the entrance to the women's chambers. Moments later, three of the Queen's attendants came stumbling out to throw themselves at Rifallyn's feet, sobbing and begging for his protection from the druid priest, and reaching up to touch his tunic in entreaty, their hands slick with blood and mucus.

'Get out!' the King snapped, stepping back sharply, his voice thick with disgust, and the women scuttled off into the night, keening as they went. *Is She dead?* There was no longer any sound from the bedchamber where a woman had been screaming; all Corwynal could hear was the ragged breathing of his men and his own heart thudding in his chest. Then a fresh cry came from beyond the hangings, and his heart stopped entirely. It wasn't the scream he'd braced himself for, nor the lasting silence he dreaded more.

It was the faint, querulous wail of an infant.

The Galloway men muttered, but Rifallyn quelled them with a glance and turned to Corwynal, eyes boring into his.

'She's borne a child then,' he said tonelessly.

'She's borne *you* a child, Sire,' Corwynal replied with equal lack of expression.

His father might have accepted it then. He might have played his part in the game of kings and kingdoms, and nothing of what followed would have happened. But it was Imbolc, the Night of Thresholds, when gods meddle in the affairs of men and force them to choose. And so She cried out once more, no longer in pain, but still in fear – of darkness and endings and all the things a woman might be afraid of in the hour that comes before the dawn. She called out a name that went running like fire and ice through his whole body. It could have been a memory or an accusation, a plea or a denial – any or all of these things. Or none. But no-one would ever know, for the cry faded to a sighing whimper that merged briefly with the wails of the child, then fell away to nothing. And so she died, the laughing girl who'd thought the world created for her own enchantment, dying with the wrong man's name on her lips.

His own.

Corwynal began to tremble, for that cry changed everything, and he could tell from his men's appalled expressions that they understood it too. The King would need to blame someone for the death of a queen and the birth of a child who might not be his own. Why not Galloway, who'd sent her this woman? Why not her guards? They looked at Corwynal anxiously, wordlessly demanding he say something to save their lives. But he couldn't meet their eyes and nor could he look at his father, for he knew what he'd see in his face.

Someone would have to take the blame for this, and, for the sake of everything he valued, he knew it had to be him. There was more at stake here than the lives of a few men. He'd have to bear his father's anger until it cooled and the King understood he mustn't kill everyone who'd heard Corwynal's name echoing from the rafters. For if he killed the Galloway guards there would be war, a war Lothian couldn't afford. A threshold loomed and, by his refusal to defend himself, Corwynal chose to cross it.

Only then did he look up at his father and see everything he'd feared – accusation and betrayal. But there was also a grief that surprised him. After a moment, however, the grief vanished, leaving nothing behind but the need for retribution. Rifallyn turned away, barked out a word of command, and some of his war-band stamped into the hall and ranged themselves around the walls, loosening their swords as they did so. Cursing, Corwynal's men formed a line and tightened their grip on their spears.

'No!' he shouted, but they ignored him and hefted their weapons.

'Don't be fools!' Blaize threw back the door hangings and emerged from the women's quarters. He'd cast off his priest's habit and was bare-chested now, his tattooed markings black against his pale skin. His arms were gory to the elbows, and there were spatters of blood on his chest and neck. He crossed the hall to the fire pit, reached into the fading embers, plucked out a handful of still-warm ash and walked towards the Galloway men.

Moments before, they'd been prepared to fight twice their number. Now, faced with one man armed only with a handful of ash, they edged together as cattle do when wolves gather. Blaize circled them, murmuring under his breath and blowing into each man's face from a dusty, bloody palm. They shook their heads as if they were dizzy and let their spears fall to knuckle their eyes free of the stinging ash.

'Send them back to Galloway.' Blaize suggested, turning to the King. 'Let them take the body of their Princess back to Marc. Have them tell her brother how much you grieve.'

Rifallyn's right hand clenched on the grip of his sword and a muscle in his cheek flickered, but he nodded and jerked his head at one of his war-band.

'Do as he says. Give them horses and wagons, but make sure they leave today.'

Relieved, Corwynal moved to follow his men, but his father reached out to grip him by the arm.

'Not you.' He jerked him around and saw the tears he was

trying to hide. 'Why do you weep?' he asked softly in the tone Corwynal had learned to fear.

'For your loss, Sire,' he replied, struggling to speak through his clogged-up throat. He meant it; his tears were for more than his father's loss of a queen. There were other losses here, not least the trust that had begun to grow between them, a trust destroyed by that dying cry. He opened his mouth to say something – anything – but Blaize, who was idly fingering patterns in the ashes of the fire, rose to his feet and made for the doorway that led to the private chambers of the Queen. 'Come,' he said. 'Both of you.' And so they followed him to the women's quarters at the back of the hall.

Corwynal was young in those days, barely twenty, but he'd been fighting since he'd turned fourteen. He was used to the blood of men he'd killed, of comrades whose wounds he'd staunched, and his own, as borne out by the scars on his body. He was used to birth too, for there was no man of Lothian who didn't help with the lambing, and few who hadn't birthed a foal or a calf, and he thought he understood birth and blood, that he was hardened to both. His father, veteran of a generation of civil wars, was just as familiar with blood and pain, yet both recoiled from what they found in the small bedchamber.

She was spread-eagled on the bed, the lower half of her body sheeted in blood, the bedcovers soaked black with it. Her skin was almost as pale as the stained sheets on which she lay, and her fair hair was dark with sweat. Her eyes, in death, were open, a vivid astonishing blue in a room that otherwise was black and white, and very, very red. The King went over to her and looked down at this ruin of a woman.

'Such a pretty thing,' he murmured, touching the eyelids to close her eyes. 'Marc worshipped her, you know. They all worshipped her. They all loved her . . .'

He snatched his hand away and glowered at Corwynal. 'Didn't they?'

He refused to look at his father and couldn't bear to look at the woman lying on the bed. Instead, he fixed his gaze on the bloody scrap of an infant, a boy, who lay beside her, his legs kicking feebly, and wondered how such a little thing could have caused such a death.

'Yes, they loved her,' he said tiredly. 'But not in the way you mean.'

'She was a whore!' Rifallyn snarled. 'And her child's a bastard!'

'That child is your *heir!*' he snarled back at him, and they glared at one another through all the years of bitterness that lay between them, not king and vassal, but a man and his son. In that moment, he saw in his father the man he might become. And perhaps Rifallyn had the same searing vision of the son Corwynal might have been. Both held the other's eyes, only vaguely aware that Blaize was still in the room, his arms folded across his chest, tutting irritably.

'Is he?' His father rounded on Blaize.

'He is, if you say he is. But that isn't what you're asking. At the very least, he's heir to Galloway until Marc has sons of his own.'

'Will he live?'

Blaize shrugged himself into his threadbare habit. 'Marc, or the child? Are you asking me for prophecy?' He shook his head impatiently. 'Very well. He'll die. All men die.'

'Then let him die now.'

Rifallyn turned away from the bed and made for the door.

'You can't let Her child die!' Corwynal protested.

The King turned back, his face rigid with anger.

'She was my wife. *Mine*. And if that child's my heir he's mine to do with as I wish. I could kill him now if I wanted to.' His hand moved to the hilt of his sword, and he leant towards Corwynal, his voice a hiss of icy breath. 'Unless you were thinking of trying to stop me?'

He was twice Corwynal's age, but still strong and skilful. Seeing him hesitate, Rifallyn grinned without humour, a wolf's smile in his dark face. 'You imagine I might shrink from killing a child?' The smile faded, and his voice dropped to a whisper. 'Why should I when I killed my own father?'

With those words, the past reared into life. Years before, Rifallyn had rebelled against and killed his father, a crime for which he expected to be punished. And who better to wield the blade than the only son to live to manhood, the unwanted son of a cast-off Caledonian war hostage, the son he'd sent away as a boy, but who'd come back a man? Now, in every-thing Corwynal did, his father saw the workings of the reckoning he half-feared, half-longed for. Even now he was taunting him to fight and, despite his resolve never to do so, Corwynal's hand drifted to the hilt of his own sword.

'Stop this, both of you.' Blaize stepped between them. 'Think like a King, Rifallyn. There are more important matters to consider than this old history. You know you can't afford Marc's anger, so take your queen down to her women and let them see you grieve. Her men will tell her brother she died in childbirth and won't mention the name she called out. One by one they'll forget until there's no-one who remembers what happened here, or what was said, except the three of us.'

'What of the child?' The King's eyes narrowed in calculation.

'That child is the one consolation for the death of your beloved queen. He'll remain in Lothian, in the care of the only man of Lothian Marc trusts . . .'

'No!' Corwynal protested, for Blaize meant himself.

'Please . . . not that!'

The King smiled. His teeth were white and sharp, his smile a wolf's grin, his eyes glittering with satisfaction.

'Why not? Why shouldn't I give his life into your hands? If you value your freedom, you can let him die. But if you choose otherwise, you'll be his nursemaid until he's old enough for you to be his tutor: woman's work for a man who enjoys the company of women!'

He threw his head back, laughed loudly, a wolf's howl in the night, gathered the body of his queen in the blood-soaked sheets and carried her out to the hall, leaving Blaize and Corwynal alone with the wailing infant.

'I sent for you to save her, not kill her!'

Blaize stepped back sharply, as if he feared Corwynal might strike him. 'I didn't kill her!' he protested. 'She would have died whether you'd sent for me or not. I can't work miracles – unlike that god my brother worships these days. She wasn't built for childbirth; any fool could have seen that. But I managed to save the child. Would you rather I'd let him die?'

'He killed her.' Corwynal jerked his chin at the child, grizzling and kicking feebly on the stained mattress, the infant who'd just changed everything.

But Blaize shook his head. 'He, at least, is innocent. The person you should blame is the man who got her with child.'

Guilt settled, with a dull thud, on Corwynal's soul, and all the blood drained from his face to pool queasily in his stomach. He had reason enough for guilt, but, even so, he didn't think he deserved his father's punishment, the one Blaize had suggested.

'You didn't have to sacrifice me.'

'I sacrificed you to save your life! What do you think would have happened if I hadn't given your father a reason to let you live?'

Blaize cocked his head to one side and eyed him narrowly. '*Are* you the boy's father?'

'I . . . I don't know.'

His uncle snorted in disbelief, but Corwynal couldn't be certain, one way or the other. Can any man? The child could well be his, and yet he was small for a new-born. Might he really be an eight-month child and so his father's? Or the son of someone in Galloway, someone whose name he didn't know or care to guess at?

'You think I should take him.' He frowned down at the child who was to be his punishment for a crime he might not have committed.

'Should? Perhaps not. Will? Yes, I believe you will. Because, despite all the evidence to the contrary, you're no more of an idiot than your father. You know Lothian can't afford war with Galloway. And because, like your father, you understand the subtleties of retribution.' Blaize looked down at the stained mattress that still bore the impression of the body of a queen and shook his head. 'She was foolish and has been punished. But you were foolish too and your punishment has only just begun. Your father won't make it easy for you, yet you'll accept it.'

But Corwynal made no move to pick up the child. 'I'm a swordsman, not a nursemaid. I have a troop, men who trust me to lead them. I have reputation, honour. I have a *future!*'

'We all have futures. Yours is different now, that's all. You've made choices before, good ones and bad ones. They all change the future. In this case, however, unless you're willing to let the boy die – Gwenllian's child, no matter who his father is – you have no choice.'

No choice... Corwynal felt the fetters of an altered future grip him and bind him fast. Blaize was right; he couldn't let Her child die. So, one by one, he let his dreams wither and die, like autumn leaves shrivelling in the first frosts of winter. Then, taking a breath to give himself courage, he picked the grizzling infant up and held him awkwardly as he wrapped a corner of his cloak around his naked, blood-streaked body.

'Good lad,' Blaize said, patting him on the arm. Together, they left the stained and bloodied chamber where a queen had died and left behind the stink of smoke and blood. They passed through the empty hall and out into air that caught at the throat and made Corwynal's teeth ache but smelled, blessedly, of nothing. It had stopped snowing, and the sky to the east was beginning to pale, but the stronghold of Dunpeldyr was still in darkness except for the pinpricks of light from the Imbolc lamps the women had set at each door to light their men home. All over Lothian, in fort and homestead, the little Imbolc lamps were burning, lighting the land with a glitter of stars that rivalled the night sky itself, a sight intended to placate the gods.

'Foolish men with their little lamps!' Blaize muttered sourly. 'As if it makes a difference. As if the gods care for anything but their own amusement.'

Corwynal shivered, for on this, the Night of Thresholds, he felt the touch of those gods.

'You spoke of futures. What of the child's?'

'His? I imagine you'll turn him into the warrior you were, the leader you could have become, and the king you might have been.'

'You *imagine?* Can't you *see?*'

Blaize scowled at him. 'I'm not a seer, you know,' he said tartly. 'Or the sorcerer everyone assumes I am. That business with the ash didn't mean anything, even if those Galloway idiots thought it did. Anyway, it isn't a good thing for men to know their fate. If they did, they wouldn't struggle, and what is life if not struggling against a half-imagined fate? It's best not to know the future. Not that I do,' he added quickly.

Corwynal didn't believe him. Prophecy was in Blaize's Caledonian blood, honed by his druid training, as it was, weakly, in his own.

'Tell me,' he insisted. 'Give me something to make all this worthwhile. Surely a child born on The Night of Thresholds has a future worth me giving up my own future for?'

Blaize grunted irritably, but reached out to touch a finger to the forehead of the whimpering infant, his eyes darkening with foresight. After only a moment, however, he shook himself out of his vision.

'He'll be a great warrior, a great lover of women, and a great singer of songs,' he said, as if none of these things were desirable. 'Now, come along. We'd better find him a wet-nurse or he'll have no future at all. And I suppose, since my brother declined to do so, we ought to give him a name, something suitable for the heir to two kingdoms.' He reached out to stroke the cheek of the grizzling infant. 'Drustan,' he suggested.

'A Caledonian name?' Corwynal asked uneasily, knowing how it would be interpreted.

'Why not?'

'You know why not. I don't belong there any longer. I *chose* to be a Briton, not a Caledonian. You might think that a bad choice, but it's the choice I made.' Corwynal looked down at the child, who stared back at him with unfocussed blue eyes. He didn't want a son – he didn't even know if he *was* his son – but if he was to give up his life to play the part of his father, he'd have the naming of him.

'Trystan,' he said, giving the child a name that meant the same as Blaize's suggestion. 'I'm going to call him Trystan.'

Lothian, Spring 485 AD

Seventeen years later

THE FIRST NOTES OF WAR

He's watching Trystan die. Gulls are crying and water is beating on shingle. The air is sharp with the salt-smell of kelp and sour with the reek of blood.

The man who's killing Trystan is a giant. He wears the symbol of a ship on his tunic and on the helmet that obscures his features, and the banner flying from a pole thrust roughly into the sand bears the same symbol. But where the banner shows a black ship on a white ground, the man's tunic is more red than white, for a slash in his neck has soaked it with blood. The giant is hurt and tiring, but so is Trystan, and Corwynal watches the final moments of a fight that has already gone on too long.

Trystan's limping, and there's a gash in his sword arm. It isn't a serious wound, but blood has run down his arm and slicked his palm. He parries the next blow, but his sword slips in his grip, leaving nothing between him and the absurdly fast return. Corwynal watches the other man's weapon bite deep *below Trystan's ribs, the blade shattering on bone as it does so. He watches him stagger, a hand go to his side, blood spurt between his fingers. He watches him fall to his knees and bow his head. He watches and watches and does nothing...*

Iron touched his throat and, in the way of dreams, the sounds and smells of the sea vanished. Corwynal found himself in a wood, lying on a patch of grass in a slant of sunlight, the scent of moss and leaf-mould all about him. A thrush was singing from the treetops.

'Shall I kill you?'

A shadow moved across the sun and the metal bit deeper. This was no longer a dream, but he didn't know where he was or why he'd been asleep. Then it came back to him: the ride to the farm in the valley, the usual argument about the tribute, the shortcut he'd taken on the way back to Dunpeldyr, the grassy glade with its inviting patch of sunshine, a warmth in the air for the first time that spring. He'd been tired, he recalled. He'd only lain down for a moment. Lothian was at peace, so it should have been safe.

He squinted along the length of the blade at someone taller than he was and broader across the shoulders, and whose long braided hair was as amber pale as that of the Angles. The boy was less than half Corwynal's age but, right then, he felt old indeed, for he prided himself on his instinct for danger yet hadn't heard him coming. He flicked a glance around the clearing, but the boy seemed to be alone. The only movement was that of Corwynal's mare, Janthe, hobbled at the edge of the trees and snorting as she tore at the new spring grass. His sword hung from her saddle, and the only weapon he had on him was the skinning knife strapped to his thigh.

'Shall I?' the boy repeated.

'Why would you want to?'

'Vengeance. For years I've planned this.' The blade pressed harder. 'I could kill you like a dog, but I'm feeling generous today, so I'll give you the chance to fight me.'

'You consider that generous?' Corwynal asked, hoping to distract the boy from the slow slide of his right hand towards the knife. But the boy stepped forward, one foot pinning Corwynal's hand to the ground.

'Fight me,' he insisted.

Corwynal sighed. 'Get off my hand, Trys, and I'll think about it.'

Trystan grinned and stepped back, but, as he did so, Corwynal grasped him by the ankle and jerked hard, throwing him off-balance. He crashed to the ground, and his sword flew off to one side. Corwynal rolled away, unsheathing his knife, and then he was on top of him, his knee in Trystan's stomach, one hand twisted in his hair, the other holding the knife at his throat. Trystan swore softly and fluently.

'Vengeance, is it?' Corwynal asked. 'For all those thrashings, I imagine, though they were well-deserved, every one of them.' He let him go and sheathed the knife. Trystan sat up, brushed grass from his riding leathers, and laughed ruefully. Corwynal smiled back at the son of the woman he'd loved, and his heart turned over as it always did when he saw her in Trystan. He had her eyes, her hair, her singing voice, her sunny disposition, and the same profound belief in his own immortality.

Is he my son? From time to time, the question rose to the surface of his mind, but, for the most part, he was able to ignore it. For both their sakes, it was best if he – and the world – believed Trystan to be the son of the King. So Corwynal treated him like the man everyone believed him to be – Trystan's older brother, his guardian and tutor, the man who beat him when he deserved a beating, praised him when he deserved praise, bound up his wounds when he was hurt, answered his questions when he knew the answers, and listened to his dreams when he had the patience.

'Why are you looking at me like that?'

Because he'd just seen Trystan, barely older than he was now, fall beneath a broken blade on a wave-racked shore. Corwynal had dreamt that dream so many times he knew that one day it would come true. It was the shadow that lay over his present and Trystan's future, the fate he'd do anything to prevent. But he couldn't tell Trystan about his fears, and so, because the boy needed an answer, he let his expression sharpen into its usual critical regard.

'Because you told me you were going hunting today, yet here you are, far from our hunting runs, disturbing a tired old man who rarely gets the chance to sleep in the sun.'

'You're not old.' Trystan shook his head impatiently. 'And if you're tired, it's your own fault. No-one asked you to become Lothian's Steward. You should be in the war-band with the rest of us.'

Corwynal lay back on the grass, laced his hands behind his head and sighed, because this was an old argument. He'd been Trystan's guardian since the hour of his birth, his tutor from the day he could talk, but once Trystan had reached his fourteenth year, three years before, he'd joined the war-band and Corwynal's roles of tutor and guardian had formally ended. So he'd looked for other ways to protect him, and that had meant becoming Steward of Lothian, a position of immense power but strangely little status, a role that Trystan, not understanding his reasons, resented on his behalf. It was an argument they'd had many times before, so Trystan didn't really expect an answer now, and he lay down beside Corwynal in the patch of sun to peer through the purpling branches of an oak at a spring sky that was as blue as the harebells that fill the meadows in summer. It wasn't the end of the matter though, and, after a moment, Trystan turned on his side and propped his head on one hand, his eyes glittering with mischief.

'Especially now there's going to be war.'

A cloud drifted across the sun, an eider-down wisp of white. In its shadow, the air still held the chill of winter, for it was only a few days past the spring equinox. Corwynal shivered, the vague foreboding he'd felt all winter hardening to a stone beneath his heart. *War.* Once he'd longed for war, but now he saw the world differently. He was Lothian's Steward, the man who tried to keep Lothian safe to ensure the one person who mattered would be safe too. But there would be no safety for anyone if Lothian went to war.

'There's no reason for war,' he said. 'Lot beat the Angles last year and drove them south of Gododdin.'

'But that's *why* there will be war!' Trystan sat up and wrapped his arms around his knees. 'Lot will want to follow up on his victory and force the Angles south of the Wall. But he can't do it on his own. He'll need men from all his client kingdoms.'

Corwynal's foreboding returned, heavier than ever. Trystan was right; Lot, King of Gododdin and overlord of Lothian and Manau, wouldn't waste this opportunity, and that meant, come the summer, there would indeed be war. And if Lothian was to be part of it, Trystan would want to be part of it too. He was in the war-band and, like any boy of his age, desperate to prove himself in a proper battle. Even Corwynal felt something he'd thought long dead begin to sing through his veins, but the song was quickly swamped by a dry hiss of fear. If war took Trystan from Lothian, then somewhere, sometime, he'd meet the man who bore the sign of the black ship – and Corwynal couldn't let that happen. 'There isn't going to be war,' he insisted. *Not for you, Trystan. Nor for me.*

'No?' Trystan raised an eyebrow but couldn't suppress a grin of triumph. 'Then why has Lot come to Dunpeldyr?'

Corwynal sat up in alarm and began to scramble to his feet. 'Gods, Trys! Why didn't you tell me?'

'I'm telling you now. But he won't have arrived yet. He sent word ahead he'd reach the fort by nightfall. So I came to find you.' He grasped Corwynal's arm to stop him from getting up. 'Wait! I need to talk to you.'

'There's no time.' Corwynal knew where this conversation would lead. It would flow out of his grasp as a mountain stream, swollen with rain, plunges down the hillside. He tried to pull away, but Trystan's grip was surprisingly firm. 'I'm Steward, Trys, whether you like it or not. I have to be in Dunpeldyr to greet Lot when he arrives.'

Trystan didn't ease his grip even a fraction. 'I'll let you go when you promise to speak to the King,' he said. 'Because if Lot's come for Lothian's war-band, I want to go with them. I *have* to go. You understand that, don't you?'

But the only thing Corwynal understood was that he had to keep Trystan in Lothian where he was safe, as he'd done since the dream had begun, three years before.

'I'm seventeen,' Trystan complained. 'Yet what have I done? What have I seen of the world? When you were my age, you were fighting the Scots in Galloway with a troop of your own. But what do I have? Permission to ride with the war-band as long as it doesn't leave Lothian? Skirmishes with Angles as likely to run for their boats as stand and fight? Where's the glory in that?' He let Corwynal go and began to tug at a clump of grass. 'For the whole of my life, I've never been allowed outside Lothian, not even to be fostered. It was as if the King was afraid for me, but why should he be? He's never liked me. So why won't he let me go?'

'You're Lothian's heir, Trys, whether he likes you or not. He doesn't want to risk the succession.'

'You're his son too. You could succeed him.'

'No, I couldn't,' Corwynal said curtly, for they'd had this argument before also. 'Even if my father named me heir – which he wouldn't – the Council of Chieftains would never agree to someone with Caledonian blood taking the throne, no matter who my father is. Come, Trys. The King won't live forever. Be patient.'

'I can't be patient! I want to live, to see the world, to make a name for myself. I want to be someone people sing songs about. Can't you understand that?'

Of course I do! Corwynal thought bitterly, for once he'd wanted the same things for himself and believed he could have had them. *The leader you could have become,* Blaize had said on that Night of Thresholds seventeen years before. The future he'd sacrificed for a new-born child.

'I'm serious,' Trystan went on. 'If there's to be war, I'm not staying here. If the King doesn't let me go with the war-band, I'll go anyway. He can't stop me. I'm heir to Galloway too, so I could go there. Or I could raise my own war-band and fight under my own banner.' He smiled at Corwynal's appalled expression, a wide affectionate smile, his mother's smile. 'Come with me! Let's go to war, you and I! Give up being a Steward and come adventuring with me!'

For a moment the challenge rang through Corwynal's blood like a horn calling to hounds, but the sound of horns was drowned by the surge of water on shingle as he remembered where adventuring would take Trystan.

'I can't do that, Trys—'

'Then I'll go alone.'

This was Corwynal's deepest fear, the one threat he didn't know how to counter. The only weapon he had was Trystan's affection for the man he believed to be his brother.

'Promise me you won't!' He reached out and gripped Trystan's arm. 'Promise me!'

Trystan narrowed his eyes and tilted his head in a way Corwynal knew meant trouble.

'You could earn that promise . . .'

Corwynal groaned because he knew what was coming.

'Fight me,' Trystan insisted. 'Single combat. And if you beat me, I'll promise anything you want. But if I win, I want you to speak to the King.'

'You know I don't play those games.' Corwynal got to his feet, went over to Janthe, and began untying her hobble.

'Why not?' Trystan got up and followed him. 'I want to be the best. I've beaten everyone in Dunpeldyr except for you, so give me a chance! And I really do want revenge for all the times you thrashed me!'

'All well-deserved thrashings! And what triumph would there be in beating a man twice your age?'

Trystan just laughed and drew his sword. 'Come on!'

But he didn't really expect Corwynal to take up the challenge, for he knew how much he disapproved of the cult of single combat, so he was still laughing when Corwynal reached for the saddle horns to pull himself up.

But instead of kicking up, he kicked back, lashing out with his booted feet. Trystan jerked out of reach with an oath as Corwynal spun around, drawing his own sword free as he did so. Trystan was off balance now, so, instead of bringing his blade down, Corwynal swept it across in a slashing backhand that Trystan blocked awkwardly. His sword grated along the length of Trystan's and crashed against his wrist-guard. Only the strength of the muscles in Trystan's forearm prevented his weapon from being torn from his grasp.

'You devious bastard!'

'It's not a game! It's *never* a game!' Corwynal needed Trystan's promise too badly for it to be a game. This was going to be a fight.

He stepped back, and Trystan's return blow came in hard. His blade was slammed to one side, and he was forced further back. He'd never had Trystan's sort of strength. Instead, he relied on speed and was forced to use it now as he sidestepped each blow Trystan expected him to parry. Trystan wanted to use the power of his shoulders to beat the sword from Corwynal's grip, but he wouldn't meet him, and, time after time, he forced Trystan to swerve and recover his balance as he backed slowly up the slope and into the trees. Then, just when Trystan expected him to avoid the next blow, as he had all the others, he met it instead and leapt forwards in a stabbing attack not much used in the practice ring. Trystan fell back, swearing under his breath, flicked his hair back and blinked sweat out of his eyes.

It was warm in the spring sunshine, but Corwynal wasn't sweating. He'd gone cold as he always did when he fought, and everything slowed as he watched each of Trystan's lunges come sweeping towards him. It was as if he stood outside himself, admiring the parabola of sun on steel, the curve of a wrist, the fluid dance of the swordsman. Time slowed, but his mind raced ahead of it, rushing into the future, and before he'd completed one movement the next crystallised ahead of him. All he had to do was step inside its pattern. It was a gift he had, one that came to him at need and not desire, and he'd never sought to teach it to Trystan. At first Trystan tried to meet this, as he met all challenges, by using his power and speed to beat down his opponent, but he was failing because Corwynal wasn't letting him fight in the way he wanted. Nevertheless, he was grinning, his face alight with pleasure, and Corwynal began to find the same joy in the dance, and the growing certainty he would win, because each of Trystan's parries was a fraction late, each blow less powerful than the last. It was then, just as Corwynal was certain of victory, that Trystan reached for something more, and he found himself fighting someone better than the boy he'd trained. Gradually he was beaten back as his every move was met almost as it formed in his mind, each lunge blocked and swept aside in a shiver of steel. The prospect of winning receded, and he began to contemplate defeat. That was when he heard the music.

Gods, not now!

Drums were beating out a rhythm in time to the thud of blood in his ears. Horns brayed out, echoing as if from walls of rock, and each step and slide, each curve of his blade, began to fall into the rhythm of the music in his head. Here, in a wood in Lothian, Corwynal was back among his mother's kin where he'd learned to fight to the sound of drums echoing from the mountains. He felt the breath of the gods in his throat, their powers thrilling in his nerves and sinews, their sweet unstoppable savagery in his blood.

Please, not now!

He tried to drive the music from him, to allow Trystan to

beat him, but something that had been born in those stony places drove him now. He stepped back unevenly, letting Trystan think he'd stumbled, then lunged forward once more and slammed his sword down towards Trystan's neck. Trystan parried the blow, but the force of it drove him to his knees, and his eyes widened with shock. The music fled, but Corwynal's strange chilling vision continued, and he saw what would have happened if Trystan hadn't parried that blow. He saw his sword biting down into Trystan's shoulder, smashing through the collar bone and driving deep into his chest. He fell back, appalled, and let the point of his sword drop. Trystan remained on one knee, a hand on the ground for balance, and Corwynal thought they'd end it there, but Trystan flung a handful of earth in his face, surged to his feet and aimed a low slash at Corwynal's legs. He twisted desperately to one side, crashed into a tree, and his sword flew from his hand.

Trystan laughed. 'You'd better yield before we kill each other by mistake!'

Even then, Corwynal couldn't yield so lightly. There was too much at stake. His sword lay, hilt down, in a patch of blaeberries a few strides away on a slight downward slope. He checked the ground between – tussocks of grass and the brown fronds of last year's bracken – and estimated his chances of picking it up on the roll. Trystan, closer but downhill, made the same calculation, and they both dived for the weapon.

Both missed. Trystan slid on a patch of mud, and Corwynal discovered that the grass concealed a tree-stump that threw him off balance. He crashed into Trystan, who was still recovering from his slip, and brought him down. Trystan's own sword slithered out of his grasp as they both tumbled down the rest of the slope to end up sprawled, weaponless now, in the sunlit patch of grass where the whole episode had begun.

Trystan, unaware of how close to death he'd come, began to laugh.

'Shall we call it a draw?' he suggested, getting to his feet. 'I give you my word I won't leave Lothian on my own. But you have to speak to the King for me.' He held out a hand to pull Corwynal up. 'Well? Shouldn't the Steward of Lothian be getting back to Dunpeldyr? Why don't I race you there? And if I win—'

'No, you impossible boy! I'm not ruining Janthe's wind chasing after that bad-tempered stallion of yours. Go ahead. Tell them I'm on my way.'

By the time he'd pulled himself into the saddle, Trystan was a distant drumming of hooves on the track below the woods, but Corwynal didn't follow him. Instead, he stared down at his hands and watched them shake as he thought about how close he'd come to killing the boy he'd always tried to protect. Had he meant it? Unbidden, Blaize's words of the Night of Thresholds came back to him. *The king you might have been.* Blaize hadn't meant King of Lothian, of course, but Corwynal couldn't deny that ruling Lothian had once been his dream. No longer, though. In time, Trystan would become King and, with Corwynal as his Steward, they'd turn Lothian into the land it deserved to be, peaceful and prosperous.

All he needed to do was keep Trystan in Lothian until the danger of the black ship had passed. But if war was coming, he'd have a fight on his hands – not just with Trystan, but with the man he'd never been able to defeat.

His father.

※

'Ealhith? Ealhith! Have you heard?' Heilyn was panting as he threw back the door to Corwynal's quarters, partly because the stairs up from the stables were steep, but mostly because he was in a panic. 'What are we going to do?'

Ealhith looked up from her task of searching through one of Corwynal's chests and regarded Dunpeldyr's aged Chamberlain with the usual mixture of exasperation and affection. As the fort's Chamberlain, Heilyn was responsible for all the arrangements required by the impending arrival of their overlord, King Lot: accommodation for an unknown number of men and horses, and a feast every night for an unknown length of time. But, being notoriously indecisive, Heilyn rarely did anything without consulting Corwynal first. And so, in the Lord Steward's absence, it was to Ealhith he turned, Ealhith who was only sixteen, an Angle and a slave.

'It's all right,' she said, not for Heilyn's sake but for her master's. 'I'll deal with it.'

She went to the hall and calmly directed the cooks, the stable-hands, and the chamber servants – men and women far older than her, Britons and freedmen for the most part – and quickly had them running to her bidding simply because she spoke in Corwynal's name.

They were all afraid of him, for the half-Caledonian Steward of Lothian, the man responsible for taxes, tributes and treaties for the whole of the Kingdom, as well as entertaining passing overlords, was demanding and short-tempered, and didn't suffer fools gladly. Those who failed to meet his exacting standards soon caught the edge of a cuttingly sarcastic tongue, and he frequently reduced grown men and women to tears, which generally made things worse because the Lord Steward of Lothian had little patience with tears.

No-one envied Ealhith her position as his slave, nor the role they all assumed she also fulfilled, as his woman. She might not be pretty, but she was young and what, after all, was the point of a man having a slave if not to warm his bed? Why else would she share his sleeping quarters above one of the stables? Few, however, knew that a door separated the main room from the tiny storeroom in which she slept. No-one would imagine a slave might have a room of her own, or that the Lord Steward might have fixed a bolt on the door, on Ealhith's side. And no-one, not even Corwynal, knew how long it had been since Ealhith had slid the bolt to, and how often she'd lain awake, listening to him crying out in the night of a ship, a boy, a death. Often, he'd wake from such nightmares to pace the main room, and she prayed to Freya that once, just once, he might push her door open. But he never had.

Ealhith couldn't really blame him. She was nothing more than a slave and an Angle, and the Steward of Lothian could have anyone he wanted. Not that he seemed interested in the sort of girl the son of a king, even a bastard one, might take as his woman. And when he went down to the rabble of huts beyond the walls where there were taverns and prostitutes, he always came back in a foul temper. He didn't like women much, Ealhith concluded, and he tolerated her presence only because she was quiet and efficient and very nearly invisible.

Maybe that's for the best, she thought, with the pragmatism she'd cultivated during her years as a slave, and abandoned her musings to give her full attention to the arrangements necessary for King Lot's arrival. Eventually she was able to leave the hall, confident everything Corwynal would expect to be done was already being carried out, and returned to his quarters above the stables. He could have slept in the hall with the warriors and other men of rank, but he preferred the relative peace of the room above the stable, even though it was cold in winter and hot in summer. Ealhith, liking having him to herself, preferred it too.

He'd need his best tunic, she decided, and unearthed it from his largest trunk and held it against her cheek. The dark wool was thick and soft and smelled of the herbs that kept it free of moth. She allowed herself only a moment before shaking out the creases and filling the room with the scent of thyme and mugwort that almost banished the stink of horses from the stable below. Then she laid the tunic out on his sleeping pallet and got out the battered disk of silver Corwynal used on the rare occasions he wanted to shave properly. It was badly tarnished, so she polished it with a scrap of leather, trying not to see her own reflection as she did so. But it couldn't be avoided. There she was, and this was how he saw her – a slightly built girl, more child than woman, with the washed-out blue eyes and mouse-fair hair of the Angles. She wore her hair loose, but it failed to hide the livid purple scar that ran from eye to jaw down her left cheek. That wound had brought her to him, and maybe it was the scar that kept her there.

She'd been a slave since she was thirteen, when the Angle ship on which she'd been travelling had been wrecked in a storm on Lothian's rocky coast. She'd been taken by the Britons who'd come to plunder the wreck and brought to Dunpeldyr where she was put to work in the kitchens. The work had been hard but not intolerable, and the people, though strange, hadn't been unkind to the little Angle girl who seemed so strangely indifferent to becoming a slave of her people's enemies. She'd quickly learned the language and made herself useful, and had even begun to think she'd made a life for herself.

Then one night one of the warriors had seen her not as a child to be tolerated but as a woman to be taken. She'd managed to fight him off, but the man, surprised and furious, had slashed her face open and probably would have killed her if the

Lord Steward hadn't intervened. He'd beaten the man, leaving him with a broken nose and a bloody mouth. His own knuckles had been grazed, but he'd ignored them as he'd salved and bound the wound in her face. She was safe now, he'd told her. The man would be leaving Dunpeldyr, and she was now the Lord Steward's personal slave. But he hadn't looked pleased about it, and nor had he been pleased when her wound had failed to heal properly, leaving her with a scar that made him flinch every time he noticed it. It was why he'd never touched her. It was why he'd never open her door.

Ealhith took one last look at her reflection and didn't blame him. But there was little point in mourning the loss of a beauty she'd probably never have possessed, not when there were other things to worry about, especially the impending arrival of King Lot and what it might mean.

There had been rumours all winter, ever since news had come from the south of a battle in which the Angles had been defeated. Not that she cared much about that defeat, because she didn't think of them as her people anymore. There was only one person from her old life she cared about, and he was far away. What troubled her was Corwynal's increasingly grim expression. She could read his face as well as she could now read the Latin script in which he recorded the tributes due to the King. He was worried because it meant war, and war, to Ealhith, meant hostages taken and exchanged, Angle slaves freed in exchange for Briton prisoners. It might mean one Angle slave in particular being sent back to the fate she'd avoided, a fate even more intolerable now, for that would mean leaving the only man, except for one, that she could ever love.

'Must you dress like a peasant?'

Corwynal had barely had time to stable Janthe before being summoned to the King's private chamber at the back of Dunpeldyr's great hall. It was a strangely warm room for a man as cold as his father, and too bright with firelight for someone who gathered shadows around himself as if they were a cloak. Rifallyn of Lothian was sitting in a high-backed chair pulled up to a brazier, one gnarled hand resting on the carved wolf's head of the armrest, the other on the narrow head of the deerhound that crouched beside him. The King had been brooding into the shifting flames, but he looked up as Corwynal entered and frowned as he noticed his stained riding leathers, mud-spattered boots and torn and bloodied shirt.

'Can't that woman of yours sew?'

Corwynal might have pointed out that he would have changed his clothes had the King not summoned him so urgently. Or that Ealhith could indeed sew, but she wasn't his woman. He had no woman as other men did, no-one he cared for, no-one who might die. But this wasn't a conversation he could ever have with his father, so he returned the older man's critical regard in silence.

The King was wearing a long robe of fine black wool, on the breast of which lay a heavy gold cross set with blue and red enamel, for he followed the god Chrystos, as did so many now in the Lands between the Walls. On one hand he wore an amber ring that gleamed like a wolf's eye in the firelight, like his own eyes. Over the years Rifallyn had become more like a wolf himself, a gaunt, emaciated wolf perhaps, but still with the patience of a predator that waits and watches. He was watching Corwynal now, irritated by his refusal to rise to his taunt.

'So, what does Lot want?'

Lot had not yet arrived, much to Corwynal's relief, for when he did, the meeting between Overlord and King would be an uneasy one. Both would remember the reasons each of them held their rank, Lot having been instrumental in the uprising against the last High King, while Rifallyn, siding with Lot's faction, had killed his own father in the final battle. The years that lay between these old betrayals and the present day had given neither cause to trust the other.

'What brings him here in person for the first time in ... what is it ... ?'

'Eighteen years.'

'Quite.'

Rifallyn poured wine from a flagon that stood by the fire and handed Corwynal a goblet. The scent of spices rose from the steaming liquid and the fumes mixed pleasantly with the tang of apple wood smoke from the fire. But Corwynal took only one sip of the wine before setting the goblet down. One needed a clear head to deal with the Old Wolf of Lothian.

'I've no idea why he's here. His business will be with Lothian's King, I assume, not its Steward.' He folded his arms across his chest and leant back against the door.

Rifallyn grunted, convinced Lot's visit was the result of some treachery hatched between him and Corwynal eighteen years before. It had been Lot, after all, who'd brokered the marriage that had sealed a treaty between Lothian and Galloway. His father didn't forget or forgive things like that.

'Oh, sit down, for God's sake!' he muttered testily. 'And pour more wine.' Corwynal crouched down to refill his father's goblet and winced as a spasm of pain shot around his side. Had he cracked a rib?

'What's wrong with you? Fall off your horse?'

Corwynal rose to lean against the door once more and held

his father's scornful gaze until the King looked away. A conversation with his father was noted more for the texture of its silences than the words they used, and this was no exception.

'I was sparring with Trystan.'

'Beat you, did he?'

'No.'

Rifallyn grunted. 'I thought you'd taught him to fight? You can't have taught him very well if a young man of— How old is he now?'

'Seventeen.' They both knew to the day, the hour.

'—if a young man of seventeen can't beat someone twice his age.'

'More than twice his age,' Corwynal pointed out. 'I taught him well, but he's with the war-band now, and Madawg's idea of training is somewhat different from mine.'

His father smiled thinly.

'You don't think much of my war-band or my war-band leader, do you?'

'They're adequate for the tasks you set them,' he replied with a shrug. But instead of taking offence, his father gave a snort of amusement.

'Good enough for hunting, eh? Good enough for raiding?'

'Good enough for brawling and drinking and wenching their way through the winter!'

His father raised an eyebrow in mock surprise. 'But that's what war-bands do, though you've never understood that. You've never been one for brawling or drinking, have you?'

The unspoken word 'wenching' hung in the air between them. Corwynal could hardly be accused of that these days, but his father had a long memory.

'They're lazy and complacent. If it ever comes to war—'

'Is that it?' Rifallyn's eyes sharpened. 'Is that why Lot's coming here?'

'It seems likely.'

His father turned back to the fire, nodding his head as if something long hoped for or long feared had come to pass. But when he spoke, it was with his usual scorn, his voice sharp and acidic.

'You expect me to believe that's all he's coming for?'

'All? Isn't it enough?'

'Not for Lot. Nothing's ever enough for Lot. So why has he come himself? I doubt it's for the pleasure of my company.'

Corwynal looked at his father warily. Age had stiffened the old man's body, but it hadn't blunted his mind, and it didn't surprise him that his father's first question was of Lot's motives in coming in person. But his next question was quite unexpected.

'It's you, isn't it? He's here for you.'

'Me?'

'Come, Corwynal. I know you don't lie to me – you're far too clever for that – but I know when you keep your silences. I know what you want and what you feel you're owed. He was your friend once, but he left you here in Lothian and didn't ask for Trystan to be fostered in Gododdin and for you to go with him. Not that I would have let either of you go, but he could have asked, couldn't he? It must have hurt when he didn't. Ah, yes! I can see it did!' His father smiled his wolf's smile. 'Lot was always one to make sure of his own advantage first, but now he's come to make recompense and give you another chance at the old glories. That's what you want, isn't it?'

'Hardly, Sire. I'm rather too old for glory.'

'Really? Well, I hope you remember that when he asks you. And I'm sure you'll disabuse him of the notion that you might leave Lothian. I didn't ask you to be my Steward, but since you have somehow acquired that position, I would find it... inconvenient... to have to find another. I imagine Lot knows how difficult it would be for me to mount and supply a war-band in the absence of an efficient Steward.'

'Mounting and supplying the war-band is the responsibility of Lothian's war-band leader, not its Steward.'

'True, but Madawg, like the war-band, is— how did you put it? —lazy and complacent, qualities that won't, I feel, escape Lot for very long.'

Rifallyn rose to his feet, leaning heavily on the arm rests as he did so, and looked down at Corwynal, for he was the taller man. The shadows gathered themselves around him as they always did, and his voice seemed to come from a place of cold stone rather than the room of firelight, spiced wine and wood smoke.

'You will stay in Lothian.'

'Of course, Sire. But I assume Trystan will be going?' He spoke lightly as if he didn't care one way or the other, for this was part of the game they played. Corwynal sought ever to hide his desires, his father always to discover and thwart them.

'You assume a great deal,' Rifallyn replied, telling him nothing, but Corwynal had expected little more, so he just nodded. His father, perhaps hoping for more of a reaction, flicked an angry glance at him. 'Well? Don't we expect guests? Isn't there something the self-appointed Steward of Lothian ought to be doing?'

He waved a hand in irritated yet weary dismissal. Their audience was at an end, and, as usual, nothing had been resolved. The games they played never had a resolution, only the constant wearing down of one another, as a weapon-smith will grind a blade until it shatters. Suddenly, Corwynal was tired of it all. They were similar men, but couldn't find a way to approach one another. Yet there were times when he longed to tell his father what was in his heart, so when Rifallyn said his name softly as Corwynal put his hand to the door, he turned back gladly, but only to see that his father's pretence at weariness had vanished entirely.

'Get that woman of yours to sew your shirt.'

'She's not—' he began but managed to stop himself. Despair washed around his heart.

'—very pretty, is she?' Rifallyn's voice dropped a register to freeze the air between them. It was the voice of a man betrayed. 'I thought you liked them pretty.'

Some things, Corwynal understood, would never be forgiven.

'Ealhith? Ealhith!'

She'd been busy with the swine-keeper, selecting a pig for the feast and watching it being dispatched and butchered. Once she'd seen it turning on the spit, she'd sprinted back to the stable, only to find Corwynal shouting for her, and it didn't sound as if he was in a very good mood. She ran up the short flight of stairs, a dozen excuses and questions on her lips, then came to an abrupt halt, heat washing into her face. He'd stripped off his shirt and stood with his back to her, rummaging through one of the smaller chests.

'Where in the five hells is that salve Blaize left?'

The light from the door threw the patterns on his back into sharp relief, dark blue against his winter-pale skin. She could make out a half-moon, a broken spear, a fish rippling across his ribs and a stag on his shoulder. She'd seen the patterns before, but only fleetingly, for he usually kept them hidden. Now, hearing her come in, he glanced over his shoulder and frowned when he saw her staring.

'Well? Where is it?'

Only then did she notice the flesh around his ribs was torn and bleeding and already purpling into a bruise.

'Here, Lord,' she said, retrieving the little pot from a high shelf and holding it out to him.

'Don't be a fool, girl. I can't reach. You put it on.' She hesitated, and his frown deepened. 'The markings don't bite, you idiot. Get on with it.'

The tattooed animals might not bite, but the salve did. He gasped at her first touch, and it masked her own intake of breath at the feel of his skin beneath her fingers. The heat in her face spread through her whole body as she smoothed the salve into the grazes, the scents of mint and valerian mixing with the scent of his skin. She longed to lean closer, to breathe in the smell of horses and sweat, moss and bracken, to trace the patterns on his back, to have him turn to her and . . .

Ealhith tried to force her thoughts in another direction, but all that came to mind were her fears of the war that might send her away from him, and tears welled in her eyes. She sniffed the tears away as quietly as she could, but not quietly enough.

'What is it now?' He turned to take the pot of salve from her suddenly nerveless fingers and frowned down at her. She knew better than to lie.

'They're saying a war is coming. Is it true?'

'You shouldn't listen to rumours.'

'I know, Lord. But . . . but if there is, it will be against the Angles, won't it? And then there might be hostages.' She hesitated, half-reaching out a hand to him. 'You wouldn't send me back, would you?'

His expression sharpened into suspicion, and Ealhith's stomach plummeted.

'You're not important enough to be ransomed. You were only a servant, weren't you?'

She nodded, not meeting his eyes, afraid he might see the one lie she'd told.

'Then don't be ridiculous. Now where's my best shirt?'

She handed it to him and watched as he shrugged it over his shoulders, tied the laces, and pulled his tunic on top, wincing as he did so.

'You won't fight, will you?' The words were out of her mouth before she could stop them. 'If there's a war, you won't go?'

'Why shouldn't I?' he snapped. 'You think I'm too old?'

'No . . .' With this new, unlooked-for fear of losing him in a different way, her tears welled in earnest.

'Oh, for the gods' sake, Ealhith! You—'

She was saved from whatever cutting remark he'd been about to make by the sound of horns at the gate in challenge and response.

'That'll be Lot!' His relief at the distraction was all too evident. He turned to the door, flung it open and clattered down the stairs. Ealhith watched him stride across the courtyard towards the group of riders who'd ridden through the gates.

One of them, a grizzled grey-haired, heavily built man, slid down from his horse and threw out his arms. She watched as the Steward of Lothian who, despite being a king's son, had always borne himself as if he was of little account, stepped forward into those open arms and allowed himself to be embraced like a brother by Lothian's Overlord.

Above the two men flew a standard she'd never seen before, a black boar on a red background, which must be Lot of

Gododdin's personal symbol. She thought about the pig she'd picked out to be slaughtered to welcome this man to Dunpeldyr, an innocent mild-tempered creature very different from the beast that snapped in the wind. This one looked powerful, intelligent and distinctly dangerous, and Ealhith wondered if Lot of Gododdin was like his sign.

She thought it likely, very likely indeed.

2

A BLOOD-FLETCHED ARROW

Lot was rather proud of his map, though he wouldn't dream of saying so. It was a copy of an old Roman itinerary that showed their roads and marching camps, watchtowers and waystations. Most of these had vanished, but the Walls of Hadrian and Antoninus still stood, and it was at a point close to the eastern end of the southern Wall that he pointed.

'That's where we beat the Angles, at the fording of the River Glein.'

'A great victory!' Madawg declared. 'Would that the men of Lothian had been there to share it!'

Lot glanced sharply at Lothian's war-band leader. Was the man drunk or just a fool?

'Gododdin didn't need Lothian's aid,' Rifallyn explained for Madawg's benefit. 'Nevertheless, it was indeed, I believe, a great victory.'

Lot shifted his gaze to the King of Lothian, who was neither drunk nor a fool, as he knew to his cost. The old bastard was being sarcastic, since everyone – apart from Madawg apparently – would have heard the rumours that the victory at the Glein had been snatched from the jaws of defeat by a certain mercenary captain from Gwynedd, a man he'd employed for the season. A man called Arthyr.

Lot glanced at Corwynal, who was leaning against the door, his face in shadow, and wondered how much the man knew of what had happened, or guessed what would come of it. Rather too much, Lot reckoned, judging by his stony expression.

Curse Blaize! Why did he have to disappear just when I actually needed him? If anyone could persuade Corwynal to do something he didn't want to do, or his father to listen to what Lot had to say, it was Blaize, Lot's advisor. But the sodding man had run off to investigate some rumour or other, leaving him to deal with Lothian on his own.

So there were only four of them in Rifallyn's private chamber, where they'd retired after the interminable feast of welcome. The food had been excellent – Lot was fond of roast pork – and the ale acceptable, but the singing had threatened to go on all night. Even the boy Trystan had sung, and to great acclaim, so Lot assumed he was good at it. But he'd never had an ear for music, so when the song was over, he'd hoped that would be the end of it. Sadly, not. Rifallyn's own bard had taken the floor and proceeded to twang his way through one ballad after another, each extolling the Old Wolf's deeds in campaigns in which Lot had played no part and therefore had no interest.

'Enough of these old battles!' Lot had jumped up at the end of one particular dirge before the cursed bard could draw breath to launch himself into another. 'It's of battles as yet unfought I've come to speak!'

'But not, I think, in public,' Rifallyn said, rising to his feet.

'Your war-band leader should hear what I have to say. And your Steward.'

'My Steward? What have battles to do with Stewards?'

'An army needs weapons and provisions.'

Corwynal had frowned at Lot's use of the word 'army' as opposed to 'war-band', so now, in Rifallyn's over-warm chamber that smelled of apple-wood smoke and wet dog, it was to the Steward of Lothian that he looked.

'It was a victory,' Lot said, for the outcome was all that mattered. 'It will keep the Angles in check for this season at least. And that means we can turn our attention to the north.'

Lot was sweating in the heat of the room, but he noticed Corwynal shiver as if a cold draught had swept through the chamber.

'North? You mean against the Caledonians? But—'

'*We*, you said, Lot,' Rifallyn cut in. 'Who exactly do you mean by *we*?'

'I mean all of us. All the Britons between the Walls – Gododdin and Lothian and what's left of Manau.' Lot stabbed a finger down on the map as he did so, indicating the eastern lands that owed him allegiance, then gestured casually at those in the west. 'And Galloway and Strathclyde.'

The King of Lothian scowled at the mention of Galloway. 'Ambitious,' he murmured, with some justice, for Galloway and Strathclyde owed Lot nothing. 'One wonders what lies behind such ambition.'

A log settled in the brazier with a hiss and a flare of blue flame that cast harsh shadows up into Rifallyn's face, and, for a moment, he looked like one of those ancient forest carvings, dark-eyed and malevolent.

Bloody man! Lot thought. There were times when the King of Lothian could be too astute. Rifallyn meant the High Kingship of course, Lot's long-held ambition. Not that he intended to make his move until he had a victory in the north, but Arthyr had persuaded him that victory could be won, and now, with the map spread out on a trestle table in Rifallyn's room, Lot showed them how.

'We need to retake Iuddeu,' he said, pointing at the old fort that commanded the crossing of the River Gwerid and had once controlled the old Briton lands of Western Manau, now in the hands of the Caledonians, lands Lot was determined to recover. 'Then we'll sweep north, drive the Caledonians back into the hills and re-garrison the old glen-forts so we can keep them there.'

'Ambitious indeed!' Rifallyn said dryly. 'Such a plan would unite all the tribes in the Caledonian Confederacy against us, something that hasn't happened in generations. Have we far-from-united Britons the numbers to stand against them?'

Trust the old bastard to go right to the heart of the problem! Lot, aware that Corwynal's mother's tribe of Atholl was the mainstay of the Confederacy, felt Corwynal's eyes bore into him, but he refused to meet that all too perceptive gaze.

'We will have,' he declared airily, making the sign for luck behind his back. 'I've two thousand of my own men, plus five hundred mercenaries from Gwynedd. I'll expect a thousand each from Galloway and Strathclyde, and I'll get five hundred, if not more, from Eastern Manau.' He paused, aware the numbers weren't compelling, and that Rifallyn was only interested in one thing. 'So I'll just need five hundred from Lothian,' he said casually, as if this was a small thing.

'Five hundred!?' For once, Rifallyn was shocked out of his urbane cynicism. Even Madawg looked surprised. Corwynal just looked sick, for five hundred men would mean three times as many horses, supplies for both horses and men, wagons, tents, armour, weapons, and a multitude of other things even an efficient Steward would struggle to lay his hands on. And it would also mean raising the levy since Lothian's war-band numbered only one hundred. It meant that every man in Lothian who could wield a sword or hold a spear would be summoned to war.

'Yes, and I need them quickly,' Lot went on. 'I've sent to Galloway and Strathclyde, and the war-branch has already gone out to summon Gododdin and Manau. I came myself to Lothian.'

'Now why is that, I wonder?' Rifallyn asked. It was a question Lot had no intention, right then, of answering, and silence fell, broken only by the crackle of fire in the brazier and Madawg's noisy swallow as he knocked back the dregs of his ale. Apart from Lothian's war-band leader, they were all looking down at the map. Even in the shifting torchlight and flicker of the burning logs, the difficulties of their situation were all too clear.

They were surrounded by enemies. In the north, past the Wall of Antoninus, lay the tribal lands of the Caledonians. To the south-east, beyond the southern Wall, the Angles were pushing north into Lot's own kingdom of Gododdin. In the west, the Scots, pirates to a man, had staked their claim to the sea-lochs and islands of the western seaboard. How long would it be before the Britons of the Lands between the Walls were crushed by all these enemies? Britons who, as Rifallyn had pointed out, were far from united?

Gododdin and Lot's client kingdoms, Manau and Lothian, in the east, could be relied upon, but Galloway and Strathclyde in the west were less dependable. The two kingdoms had hated one another for generations, and getting them to agree to be part of the same army had forced Lot to make promises he wasn't sure he could keep. Even so, Galloway and Strathclyde weren't his main concern.

Lot frowned down at the map and drummed his fingers on

the table as he regarded the one Briton kingdom he hadn't yet named, a place of high moors and forests, dark and secretive, a land surrounded by all the others, yet friendly with none. The Kingdom of the Selgovae, a bitter people, locked in the past, wasn't exactly an enemy, not these days, but they couldn't be said to be friends either, despite Corwynal having negotiated a trading treaty with them the previous year. But if Lot's plan was to succeed, he was going to need more than a trading treaty. It was one of the reasons he'd come to Lothian himself.

But just as he was trying to frame a request he was almost certain would be refused, Rifallyn rose to his feet.

'Five hundred men. If that's what you want – and you're quite sure that's all? – I suppose I'll have to see how to get them for you. Or at least my war-band leader and Steward will do so.'

Lot nodded, relieved not to have to bring up that other matter just yet. He moved to leave the room, dropping his hand to Corwynal's shoulder as he passed. The man had been his captain once, a man he'd relied on and then betrayed, but needed to rely on once more. 'I need those men,' he said softly, knowing it was Corwynal and not Madawg who'd find them.

Corwynal made to follow Lot and Madawg from the room, but his father called him back and waved him to a chair. The King poured wine for them both, pushed a goblet towards him, and sat back in his chair, his fingers steepled together.

'So, Lot's war is to be against the Caledonians. Is that going to be a difficulty?'

'For them? For Lot?'

'For you.'

I chose to be a Briton. That was what he'd told Blaize all those years before, though both knew loyalties were never that simple. So when Corwynal had understood what Lot was planning, a tremor of unease and something like guilt had run through his veins. But he'd shaken off his apprehension; he wasn't going to be fighting anyone, Angles, Britons, or Caledonians.

'No,' he said flatly.

His father regarded him thoughtfully for a moment, then nodded. 'Good. So, shall we address the practicalities? The five hundred men Lot wants . . . Can we find them?'

'You should ask your war-band leader. It's his responsibility.'

'Madawg's drunk and he's not ready for war. You know better than him. So, tell me.'

Corwynal rested his chin on one hand and stared at the map, looking at Lothian and its borders, the hills and forts that were its strength, the open shores and river channels that were its weakness, its neighbours who protected them, its enemies who threatened them. Normally the first strong south-easterly of spring would bring the Angles to Lothian's shores from their coastal stronghold of Dun Guayrdi that lay in the south of Gododdin. But if Lot was right, they wouldn't trouble them this year and perhaps the treaty with Selgovia would hold. So if they called on the men who were stationed on the coast and along the Selgovian border . . .

'Perhaps,' he said, thinking through the possibilities.

Corwynal could see his father make the same judgements, for he was a king who knew his country and his people, and Corwynal was conscious once more that, beneath their old resentments, their games and bitter warfare, they were two men with the same thoughts. And so his father would have taken one important factor into consideration, one that had to be discussed.

'Five hundred men means the entire war-band and the levy,' Corwynal pointed out. 'And that includes Trystan.'

Rifallyn rose from his chair, stepped over to the brazier and leant over it, his gnarled hands held out to the warmth, the flickering glow from the logs burnishing his face in shifting bars of light. The haze of smoke made it impossible to read his expression.

'I'm aware of that.'

Corwynal had to tread carefully here. If he was to keep Trystan safe in Lothian, he had – somehow – to persuade his father to forbid him from going to war. But simple persuasion rarely worked with the Old Wolf of Lothian. What he had to do was make his father believe it was Corwynal's wish that Trystan should go, and rely on the King's desire ever to thwart his wishes.

'Lot will want Trystan in the war-band, if only to reinforce Lothian's support of Lot's ambitions, whatever they might be.'

'I'm aware of that also. But it's for me to say who goes, not Lot.'

'True. But Lot might make concessions in return for Trystan. Men and supplies we don't have to give him.'

'So that's your advice to me in this matter?' His father took up his goblet and swirled the dregs around its base.

Corwynal hesitated, choosing his words carefully, like a man picking his way through a thicket of gorse.

'As your Steward, I'd recommend agreeing to Lot's requests.'

'And as Trystan's guardian?'

'I'm no longer his guardian. He's in the war-band now.'

'A life you trained him for. The life you gave up.'

'The life you *made* me give up.'

'No, Corwynal. You had a choice—'

'It was no *choice!*'

His father shrugged. 'Other men would have seen it as such. And chosen accordingly.'

'Then I'm not as other men.'

'I know that,' Rifallyn said softly. He set his goblet on the table and sat down once more. 'So, what do you suggest I do with Trystan?'

Corwynal's fingers were clenched around his goblet, but he forced himself to loosen his grip. 'Trystan's ready for war. He's a good fighter and a natural leader. Yes, there are dangers, but I believe he deserves the chance to make a name for himself.'

'Once, rather a long time ago now, you went to fight the Scots in Galloway because *you* wanted to make a name for yourself.' *And look what came of that.* The words remained unspoken, but they both heard them, and Corwynal couldn't stop himself from looking down at the map once more and tracing the route he'd taken to Galloway over eighteen years before, and the route by which he'd returned, escorting a Princess. Unbidden, a single shining memory escaped the bonds he'd placed on it. A May dawn, a newly risen sun sparkling on the dew, footsteps followed to the river, a pool fringed by willows, and then the woman, rising naked from the water like a spirit of the forest. She'd beckoned and he'd gone, betraying his father, his friend and his own honour. *And look what came of that.*

He crushed the memory back into the place in which he kept it, but knew he'd have to use his father's mistrust of Galloway if he was to keep Trystan safe.

'This is different,' he said. 'The heir to Lothian is *expected* to make a name for himself. As is the heir to Galloway.'

Predictably, his father's expression darkened, and his brows snapped together.

'You realise that's why Lot's here?' Corwynal went on. 'Strathclyde's troubled by Caledonians on its northern border, but Galloway has no reason to join Lot's war – unless Marc's been offered something. It could be Trystan.'

'I will not have him go to Galloway! I will not have him consort with that drunken degenerate!'

'He's still his uncle.'

'And you'd approve, I suppose,' his father said waspishly. 'Because Marc was your friend once. *That's* why you want me to let Trystan go to war.'

'I'm not suggesting he go to Galloway. But if he were to meet Marc under Lot's protection, I believe it would do him no harm.'

His father's hands tightened on the carved arm rests of his chair, and he leant towards him.

'That's your advice, is it?'

Corwynal nodded. 'I think, on balance, it would be for the best.'

'For Trystan? Or for you?'

'For Lothian.'

'Ah! For Lothian!' His father leant back in his chair, a thin smile on his lips. 'No-one asked you to be Steward, but you took the role in your bid for power. Now you think to ingratiate yourself with Lot and Marc, so you advise me to let Trystan go with the war-band, hoping he'll never return. Because then your way would be open to the position you've always craved. Mine.'

The king you might have been . . .

No. That dream had died seventeen years before. Nevertheless, this wasn't the first time the accusation had been made, so he should, as on every other occasion, have smiled and let his father think whatever he wanted. But this time he couldn't.

'That's not true!'

'But it is. I know what you want, for once I wanted the same thing. So, let me tell you why I killed my father. Because I thought he was wrong and I was right. Because he'd given me reason enough. But largely because I wanted Lothian. I wanted it with the sort of desire I've never felt for a woman, not even for—' Even after all these years his father couldn't bring himself to say Gwenllian's name. 'I've seen the same desire in you,' Rifallyn went on. 'One day it will grow beyond your control and you'll take Lothian from me, as I've always known you would, even before I sent you back to Caledonia with your mother. You came back, Corwynal, and it was for a purpose, one you've not yet fulfilled. I've *dreamt* it.'

'You're wrong!' Corwynal jumped to his feet, knocked over his goblet of wine and spilled the dregs over the map that lay between them. 'You judge me always by a dream – a dream that lies!'

'Some dreams, whether we like it or not, are true. It was also your mother's prophecy. Was *she* wrong? Did *she* lie? How could such a thing be *wrong*?!'

They stared at one another across the spreading stain of wine, as dark as blood in the firelight, across a waste of bitter years. For a moment, Corwynal saw his father as he'd been thirty years before, a man who'd taken his own father's crown, a man who'd furthered his ambitions and expected to pay the price. He looked at his father with the eyes of a boy, barely seven years old, who was to be sent with his mother, the warhostage from Atholl, away from the only home he'd ever known into a land of strangers.

'– and I won't come back until you beg me!' his mother had hissed at Rifallyn as they'd parted at the gate, accepting the freedom she'd long dreamt of but no longer wanted. 'But your

son will.' She'd turned back one last time, dragging Corwynal around to face his father. The new King of Lothian was standing alone beneath the gateway, his face as hard and unyielding as the stones of Dunpeldyr's walls, his eyes as cold. 'One day your son will come back and he will kill you!'

'You came back as she promised you would,' his father said softly, as if he too heard those words echoing through the years. 'Why else if not to fulfil your fate?' He'd been leaning across the table, but now he eased himself back into his chair, weariness in every line of his body, his voice thin and reedy, his expression darkening into shadow. 'You can't avoid your fate, Corwynal. No-one can. It runs in a man's veins.'

'You're wrong!' Corwynal slammed his hand down on the table, on the map. Lothian lay between them, stained with wine as if with blood, and the symbolism of that escaped neither of them. 'If I'd wanted to kill you I've had over twenty years of opportunity! So why haven't I done it? And, if you really believe it, why keep me in Lothian? Why not send me away again?'

His father laughed. 'Why haven't you killed me? Why do I keep you here? Don't you understand it yet? Because it's a game, this life of ours! And neither of us have tired of it yet. You won't move against me until the time is right, and it amuses me to watch you. But I won't help you. I'm minded to keep Trystan in Lothian, so you'll stay also.' His father smiled his wintry smile once more. 'You and I, we understand punishment. Perhaps you think death would be too easy a punishment for me, and perhaps I agree. But, in the end, you will be my retribution, so I rather think I must be yours.'

Corwynal stared at him, but no longer with the eyes of a boy. Two women stood between them – the woman his father had sent away, and the woman who'd borne the child who could as well have been Corwynal's as his father's, an act of betrayal

Rifallyn had convinced himself was Corwynal's revenge for sending him to Caledonia all those years before. Sometimes, in his darkest moments, he wondered if his father was right.

'You're wrong,' he whispered, unsure if he was speaking to his father, the gods, or just himself. 'And I will prove it.'

He dreams that night, but not of Trystan, not to begin with. Instead, this is his oldest nightmare, a dream of falling, of rock closing in on him, of a tomb from which there's no escape, of being alone in the dark. Then he's alone no longer. A boy is there, but it's not Trystan. He's not sure who he is. Perhaps the boy is himself. Then, abruptly, in the way of dreams, he's no longer entombed. He's lying on a mountain in Atholl, windswept and bitter beneath the stars. He dreams of drums beating between walls of rock, the smoke of campfires and the wolf-dances of Imbolc, music so sweet it strips his soul bare, and blue dye being pricked into his skin. He's in a place he's begun, against his will, to love. And so he dreams of why he left. That same mountain crowded with people, a single impossible demand, one body falling, then another, a voice yelling at him to run, dogs howling on the hunt and voices screaming from the hills behind him as he gasps his way to freedom. Kinslayer!

Then he's back in Lothian and his father is waiting at Dunpeldyr's gates, a hand held out in welcome. But Corwynal has no word of greeting for him. He has nothing but a dagger in his fist, nothing in his mind but surprise at how warm his father's blood is as if flows over his hand. Kinslayer!

Then he's fighting Trystan once more, but they're no longer alone. Others are watching, his father among them, all of them watching as his blade bites deep into Trystan's chest, all watching in silence as Trystan smiles up at his killer – his own brother, his own father. Kinslayer!

And when he looks down, he sees on his tunic, in place of the wolf emblem of Lothian, the sign of a black ship . . .

⁂

The hunting the next day was disappointing, but, uncharacteristically, Lot decided not to blame Arawn, Rifallyn's chief huntsman. Game had been thin on the ground in all the Lands between the Walls for the whole of the winter. The day wasn't a complete waste of time, however. Rifallyn's boy, Trystan, with the doubtful assistance of Gaheris, one of Lot's own sons, had run down a big stag. Trystan, it seemed, was as good at hunting as he was at everything else. He was only seventeen, and yet men already spoke of his prowess with weapons. He also, by all accounts, sang and played the harp well enough to have been a bard. Gaheris, in contrast, could barely speak, far less sing. Still, inarticulate though he was, Gaheris appeared to have made friends with the boy, and that might prove useful.

Trystan was one of the few good things to have come out of Lot's visit to Lothian. The boy was clever, seemed to have the makings of a warrior, and, to crown it all, was charming and good-looking. Yes, Trystan would do very nicely for the part Lot wanted him to play. There was only one problem. Well, two really – Rifallyn and Corwynal – neither to be discounted, especially if they acted together. But that was unlikely.

'Where's that brother of yours?' he demanded of Trystan later that day. There were a fair number out hunting, his own men, Lothian's war-band with that fool Madawg in charge, and Rifallyn with some of his attendants. He'd assumed Corwynal would be among them, but hadn't seen him.

'He's coming later. Right now, he's back at the fort sorting out the levy,' Trystan said with a derisive glance at Madawg. 'Corwynal will do it better, and quicker, than Madawg. But it's not his job. He shouldn't be Steward at all, especially if there's to be war. There is, isn't there, Sire? And if there is—'

'Trystan, dear boy...' A voice intruded into their conversation. 'Please be so good as to find out from Arawn where, exactly, he's taking us.'

Trystan jumped, and Lot, to his annoyance, jumped too. How did Rifallyn do it? Sneak up on a man like that? He'd been looking forward to a private talk with Trystan. The boy was clearly desperate to go to war, so much so he might be prepared to play the part Lot had in mind for him. After that, Lot had intended speaking to Corwynal to persuade him to play his own part. Lot didn't want to talk to Rifallyn. But once Trystan had consulted the huntsman, the King sent him off with Gaheris, leaving Rifallyn and Lot alone.

'Those five hundred men...' Rifallyn began. 'Corwynal believes we can provide them, but they won't include Trystan.'

'Why not? He wants to go.'

'His wants are of no interest to me. He's my heir. You have... how many sons? Four, is it? Or five? You can afford to lose a couple.'

I could certainly afford to lose Gaheris, Lot thought. 'You have two sons. And they say you've no fondness for either.'

Rifallyn's eyes flashed and Lot wondered if he'd gone too far. 'Trystan will stay in Lothian,' Rifallyn said coldly.

The King of Lothian reined his horse in, heeled it in the flank, and began to move down through the trees, but turned in the saddle before disappearing behind a stand of hawthorn. 'And if you've any plans for Corwynal, you may disabuse yourself of them. He will be staying in Lothian also.'

Wonderful! Lot thought as he too made his way down through the woods, heading for the clearing at the foot of the valley where the slaughtermen had arrived with carts to take the spoils of the hunt back to the fort. Corwynal had come with them but didn't appear to be in a very welcoming mood. There might be a number of reasons for that, Lot's failure to visit Dunpeldyr for eighteen years being one of them. The man very likely had a complaint or two to get off his chest. *Oh well*, Lot thought, *best get it over with.*

'Thought you were back at the fort,' he said airily, having trotted over to where Corwynal was sitting on a fallen tree-trunk at the edge of the clearing.

'I was.' *Raising the levy for your war.* Lot chose to ignore the unspoken accusation. 'But now I'm here, waiting for Trystan.'

Corwynal didn't get up, didn't call him 'Sire', he noticed. No cursed respect.

'He went off with Gaheris. They took down a nice stag and went after another.' Lot waved a hand at the woods to the north. 'Never mind Trystan. It's you I was looking for.'

'You can't have looked very hard. I've been in Lothian for the last eighteen years.'

No hesitation. Straight to the heart. Typical!

'Still hold it against me? That I didn't offer to foster the boy in Gododdin and you with him? But think about it, man! Marc needed to know his nephew was in your care, safer with you than in Galloway. And Rifallyn wanted Marc's nephew as hostage. So everyone was happy.'

'Including me? Was I supposed to be happy too? Mouldering my life away as a nursemaid and tutor until I was too old to do anything?'

So Corwynal thought he was too old, did he? Lot might be able to use that.

'Ride with me,' he said. 'I want to talk to you.'

Corwynal scowled at him but got up, mounted a neat little chestnut mare, and followed him up through the woods. The trees thinned up on the ridge, oak giving way to birch, then pines and a low scrub of juniper, with the occasional wind-stunted rowan clinging to the rocks. A deer track led up to the crest of the ridge and from there they could hear the sound of the hunt in the woods below them rising up on the still air –the shouting of men, the barking of dogs and, once, the coughing roar of a stag. Mist lingered on the slopes and drifted through the pines, but up on the heights a breeze had swept the moorland free of cloud, and they could see as far as the firth in the north, as iron-grey as the sky, and south to the heather-dark hills beyond which lay the land-locked Kingdom of Selgovia.

'The thing is, Corwynal, I need more men. A levy from Lothian and what's left of Manau isn't going to be enough. I need all of Galloway and Strathclyde's fighting men, and they won't give me them if they're worried about the Selgovae raiding them when they're away in the north. So I want you to go and talk to the Selgovae, get them to stop all this raiding, and join us in the fight against the Caledonians.'

Corwynal just laughed. 'Join us? Are you mad? Many of the Selgovae have Caledonian blood. Given the choice, who do you think they'd fight for?'

'I don't want Caledonians in Selgovia threatening Manau. So you'll have to convince the Selgovae to make the right choice. You need to remind them who they are – Britons who speak our language and worship the same gods—'

'No they don't. They worship the old gods, while you, by all accounts, follow Chrystos and his priests. Like my father.'

Lot scowled at the younger man. He worshipped whichever god was appropriate to the season and paid as little attention to their priests as he could get away with. Didn't everyone?

'You follow the old gods, don't you? Well, then, my point stands. I don't want them harbouring our enemies at a time like this. I need their neutrality, if not their active support.'

'You're not likely to get either. Do you know how difficult it was negotiating a simple trading treaty with them?'

'But you *did* it!' Lot slammed a fist into the palm of his other hand for emphasis. 'That's why I want you to go. I need someone I can trust, someone they can trust too. I want you to go and offer them an alliance with Gododdin, an alliance of marriage. Hoel has a daughter but no sons. I'm offering them Gaheris.'

'Gaheris! Your own son?'

'Why not? It shows I'm serious. Come on, man! All you need do is go and see how the proposal's received. Tell them that unless they accept Gaheris for the daughter, give me a troop of men, and stop plotting with the Caledonians, I'll come and personally tear them limb from limb. You'd have to put it more tactfully than that, of course.'

Corwynal stared at him. 'So, let me get this clear,' he said. 'You want me to offer them Gaheris then threaten them if they turn him down?'

'Exactly!' Lot beamed at Corwynal's ready understanding. 'So, you'll do it?'

'Of course not! I've no desire to find myself hanging from one of their death-trees!'

'God's blood, man! You're just as pig-headed as your father! Do you know what he just told me? That Trystan's not going to war. What a cursed waste! The boy's made for it. And he told me you're staying in Lothian too. But you can't want to. Come on, man, where's your sense of duty?'

Corwynal began to smile and Lot thought he'd convinced

him, but after a moment the bloody man shook his head.

'I'm not going to Selgovia. And that's my final word.'

※

Trystan's not going to war. Corwynal felt dizzy with relief. Until Lot told him, he hadn't been certain he'd succeeded in manipulating his father into that decision. And if Trystan wasn't going to war, then neither was he. So it was easy to refuse to go to Selgovia for Lot and to keep on refusing all the way back to the clearing. Lot had tried to make him change his mind, of course, appealing to his loyalty and pride, but he hadn't weakened, and in the end Lot gave up and rode off in a temper.

It was only then that his relief began to ebb away. He knew his father would make him break the news to Trystan, and he wasn't looking forward to that. He'd promised Trystan he'd speak to the King, and Trystan had trusted him to succeed. Corwynal had broken that trust, so there was a danger Trystan might break his own promise and go off on his own, and he knew no way of stopping him. He couldn't even tell him about the dream, couldn't warn him of the man who wore the sign of the black ship because, far from being afraid, Trystan would run towards that fate like a man might to a lover, convinced that, by his skill, he could overturn it. The dream had to remain Corwynal's secret fear.

He waited in the clearing for some time, both hoping for and fearing Trystan's return, but eventually he gave up. If Trystan had gone after another stag with Gaheris, there was no telling when he'd get back. So he got to his feet, took his bow and quiver from Janthe's saddle, and wandered into the trees in the hope of a little belated sport.

He wasn't in the mood for hunting, however, and, in any case, the wood seemed unnaturally still. No bird sang, and nothing moved in the undergrowth. Even the sound of the men in the clearing behind him was swiftly muffled by a watchful, listening silence. Corwynal walked on into the trees with the unnerving feeling that, rather than being the hunter here, he was the hunted. A path was being chosen for him, and he was more conscious than usual that there were gods here, as there were gods everywhere, not only the little gods of stream and spring, but the greater gods of war and death. Those gods liked to watch a man struggle against his fate but, if asked in the right way, might intervene in his affairs. And, right then, Corwynal needed their help.

He was deep in the wood when he came to the glade, an open space beneath the spreading branches of a great oak. In summer it would be a pool of shadows, but now, in spring, before the leaves unfurled themselves, it was shot through with a thin misty light. A stream ran to one side of the glade and a stand of blackthorn edged the other, the creamy blossoms trembling a little as if something moved in the depths of the thicket. A smell hung about the place, pungent and feral. The sense of presence was stronger here, a presence he hadn't felt in over twenty years, and his heart began to thud. When he'd abandoned Atholl, he'd thought its god, Arddu, had abandoned him in his turn. But perhaps he'd only been biding his time until he was needed.

Corwynal knelt by the little stream to cup water in one palm. It tasted of moss and fern and was cold enough to make his teeth ache. Quickly, while his hand was still numb, he drew the edge of his skinning knife across his palm and watched the blood pool, then dipped the white fletching of an arrow into the blood until the feathers were red, nocked the arrow to the bow and drew it back.

A question could be asked and an answer might be given, though he'd need skill to interpret it. The muscles in his shoulder quivered as he held the bow taut, uncertain which question to ask since he had so many. *Who bears the sign of the black ship? How do I keep Trystan safe in Lothian?* In the end he asked the one he'd ignored for seventeen years, the one that made no difference. *Is Trystan my son?* Then he loosed the arrow.

The wind caught the shaft, tugged it eastwards, and a flash of sun flared the blood-soaked feathers to crimson as it fell back into the wood. He'd have to search for it and hope its place of landing would give him an answer, but first he crouched down to wash the blood from his hand.

'Corwynal!'

He turned at the scream and saw a blur of movement, pale hair flying, a flash of metal and a spear raised in one hand, drawn back then hurtling towards him. He threw himself aside, heard the spear whirr past him and grunted with pain as he crashed into the bole of a tree. At the same time there was a squeal of pain and fury as something flew past him, hooves churning the ground – a heavy grey body with mad red eyes and a blood-fletched arrow buried in its haunch. The boar was already swerving away from him as it went past and so missed him by a hairsbreadth. Blood sprayed his face from a wound in the beast's shoulder where that flung spear had struck a glancing blow, diverting the animal in its course. Now the boar was charging with renewed ferocity towards the man who'd flung that spear and who was yelling from the other side of the clearing. Trystan.

Time slowed as it did when Corwynal fought, and he watched for what seemed like an eternity as the maddened animal thundered towards Trystan. The ground shook and clods of earth flew from the boar's hooves. He could smell its rank sour stench, could see in impossible detail the leaves that clung to its bristles, the dried mud streaked along its flanks. He saw how white its tusks were and how they gleamed like blades. Trystan's eyes were wide, his teeth bared in a feral grin, his feet braced for balance, a short stabbing spear, his only weapon, gripped tightly in his hands.

Corwynal stood there, unable to move, as the great grey body with its razor-sharp tusks churned towards Trystan. And still he stood, immobile, when the animal crashed into Trystan and brought him down in a writhe of bodies and blood. He carried on standing, listening to Trystan scream, to the boar squealing, until all sound fell away into a yawning void of silence.

Time, which had slowed and stopped, rushed ahead once more, and yet Corwynal remained as motionless as the body beneath the boar. Trystan's hair was spread out on the ground, no longer amber-pale but red, and his face was masked with blood. On the night Trystan had been born there had been so much blood, so perhaps it wasn't so surprising there was this much at the end. Corwynal shook his head, confused by this double vision. The past, the present, dream, reality. In his dream Trystan had been cut down by iron, not tusks, and had been standing on the edge of the sea far from the world he knew. But this had happened in the heart of Lothian where Corwynal had believed him to be safe.

You ask if he is your son, but you will not let him live. What father would deny his son the chance to live? You sent me an arrow to ask a question. This is your answer.

Corwynal's heart stopped as the dry voice hissed inside his head.

'Lord?' His voice came out as a croak. 'Arddu?'

Arddu, God of the Caledonians, Lord of the forests and empty places, was standing between two trees on the far side of the glade, his naked body patterned with beasts, his great sweep of antlers lifting, a smile flickering across his lips as he watched Corwynal fall to his knees. Then the God rippled, his shape shifting until he was in his wolf-form, his yellow eyes implacable.

You had to choose between life and death, and you chose death.

The words were the rustle of autumn leaves in Corwynal's mind, but he was listening to another voice.

I'm seventeen, but what have I done? This was his answer. He hadn't let Trystan live, so the God had taken him, as he takes all men. Corwynal had chosen death, but not for himself. *How can I keep Trystan safe in Lothian?* He couldn't, for there was no safety anywhere in the world. *Who bears the sign of the black ship?* That no longer mattered. Even so, remembering his nightmare, he glanced down at his tunic, but he bore the sign of the wolf as he'd always done. *Is he my son?* He should never have asked that question, for it no longer mattered. Not now Trystan was dead.

'Corwynal?' He'd thought he was alone in the clearing, but a crowd of men had gathered, Lot and Rifallyn on their horses. Lot slid down to come over and put a hand on his shoulder. Perhaps he spoke some words of comfort, but Corwynal didn't hear them, for he was reaching for the God.

Please, Lord, I beg you . . . Let him live! Demand anything of me – but let him live!

The God was already turning away, disappearing into the dappled shadows between the trees, but now he paused and turned back. *Anything?*

Anything!

The God lifted up his muzzle and howled, but no-one else heard him. Then he vanished, and there was a long moment of stillness in the little glade. It was Gaheris who broke the immobility of the watching men as he pushed his way through them and went across to the body of the boy he'd come to regard as a friend.

'T-T-Trystan?' Gaheris crouched down, and in the silence of the wood Corwynal heard hissing as the boar's bladder emptied itself.

'Get this bloody pig off me!' Trystan said distinctly. With a cry of astonishment, Lot strode forward to help Gaheris pull the boar to one side, and Trystan, freed of its weight, groaned and rolled over but got to his feet unaided. He straightened carefully, testing the functions of his body, wiped the blood out of his eyes, and looked up.

'Corwynal?'

His frozen immobility gave way to a hot fierce need for action. He walked over to Trystan and hit him hard across the face.

'You idiot! If you aim at something, you should hit it!'

Trystan's face crumpled. 'It was heading for you. I . . . I thought it would kill you!'

With a sob, Corwynal flung his arms around Trystan and held him hard against his chest. 'I thought you were dead!' he whispered, closing his eyes to feel the beat of Trystan's heart against his own. *I thought I'd killed you!* 'I thought you were dead.'

'So did I!' Trystan began to shake, and he clung to Corwynal, laughing weakly, until Lot put a hand on both their shoulders.

'So, the Boar yields to the Wolf, does it?'

Lot's men laughed, lightening the mood in the clearing, and everyone cheered. Trystan freed himself from Corwynal's embrace and turned to grin at them before bending down to examine his kill.

But Corwynal was aware, as he'd been all along, of a dark presence behind him, and he turned reluctantly, convinced the God was still there watching him. But it was his father, still mounted on his horse, looking down at the scene in the clearing, his face expressionless. Then he twitched his reins and, without a word, slowly walked away.

3

A MAN FROM THE SOUTH

There was a great deal of singing that night, some of it very bad. Both Lot's men and Lothian's war-band had an inexhaustible store of vulgar songs, and it wasn't long before they were yelling out the choruses and stamping their feet until the whole hall shuddered. Everyone was in high spirits after Trystan's killing of the boar, and the boar itself formed a major part of the feast. The rich red smell of roast pork filled the hall, but Corwynal couldn't eat anything, far less the flesh of the animal that had almost killed Trystan. So he stared into his cup of ale, reliving over and over that moment of stillness when he'd been certain Trystan was dead. He *had* been dead, but the God had given back his life and now he would exact his price.

Anything! It had been a foolish thing to promise, but he knew what Arddu would want of him. *You had to choose between life and death, and you chose death.* The God was right; keeping Trystan in Lothian was a living death for a boy desperate to fly free. So, no matter what dangers lay ahead, Corwynal would no longer try to keep him in Lothian. He had to set him loose to live the life he'd trained him for. But not alone. He knew that, one day, Trystan would meet the giant from his dream, but maybe Corwynal could change that dream. If, as the God maintained, he'd chosen death, need it be Trystan's? Why shouldn't he fight the man himself? He'd always protected Trystan, so why not in this way?

But that was for the future. For the present, there was the war Lot had brought them, a war with Corwynal's mother's people, Arddu's people, and Corwynal would be expected to play his own part. What that might mean, he had no way of guessing, but if he was to win freedom for Trystan and go to war himself, he'd have to do the one thing he'd never managed to accomplish. He had to get his father to change his mind.

'Please, Sire. I have to speak to you.'

'Not now, Corwynal. I'm listening to the . . . entertainment.'

His father scowled as the singing, led by Madawg, reached previously untapped depths of vulgarity.

'I need to talk to you about Trystan.' Corwynal glanced across the hall. Trystan was sitting with Gaheris, laughing at the singing but, tactfully, not joining in.

'Oh, very well.' His father pushed away his platter and cup, got to his feet and led the way to his chamber.

The brazier wasn't lit, so the place was cold and musty; a single lamp cast uneasy flickers of light around a room full of clinging shadows. Lot's map was lying on the table and though the spilled wine had dried, it had left a blood-red stain across Lothian. His father sat down and gestured at the stool on the other side of the table. His expression wasn't encouraging and Corwynal wasn't sure what he could tell him, other than the truth – or as much as he thought his father could stomach.

'Trystan almost died today,' he said.

'I'm aware of that.'

'And he hasn't lived, not really. Please, Sire, let him go to war and—'

'Correct me if I'm wrong, but I believe we've already had this conversation.'

'Yes, I know, but... but you decided to keep him here for reasons that had nothing to do with Trystan and – I confess it – I wanted him to stay.'

'Then why did you urge me to let him go to your friend Marc?'

'Because I knew you'd refuse.'

The King looked at Corwynal with neither surprise nor emotion. 'I see,' he said. 'And what's made you change your mind?'

'I thought Trystan was dead today, and I understood how wrong I'd been to try to keep him in Lothian.'

His father regarded him steadily, his expression unreadable. Then he picked up a small bell, rang it to summon a servant and told him to fetch Trystan who, perhaps expecting the summons, came quicker than Corwynal expected. He was smiling faintly, his eyes alight with excitement – and Corwynal couldn't bear it, for he knew that whatever his father intended, it wouldn't be to give Trystan what he deserved.

'I've decided to give you a troop of your own, Trystan. Fifty men. Discuss it with Madawg when he's sober.'

Corwynal stared at his father, unable to believe this capitulation, but Trystan's eyes gleamed and he threw Corwynal a look of gratitude he knew he didn't deserve.

'I've been giving thought to the defence of Lothian in the war-band's absence,' the King went on. 'We need a small mobile troop, and someone with the imagination and energy to lead them.' He paused, then smiled his wolf-smile. 'So, Trystan – do you think you're up to it?'

The sparkle left Trystan's eyes, and his hands curled into fists. A muscle flickered in his jaw, but when he spoke his voice was steadier than Corwynal expected.

'So when the war-band leaves, I'm not to go with them?'

'I almost lost my son today – both my sons. Indulge a father's weakness,' the King said, still smiling. 'I don't consider I can do without either of you for the foreseeable future. That is all, Trystan. You may go. No, Corwynal, I'd like you to stay.'

Trystan, unable to speak, nodded in assent, but his expression, when he glanced at Corwynal, was full of disappointment, hurt and accusation. He slammed the door behind him, leaving Corwynal and his father alone in a silence solid enough to be cut by a blade.

'A father's weakness!?' Corwynal jumped to his feet as soon as Trystan's footsteps had faded into the distance. 'When have you ever shown a father's weakness to either of us? What has Trystan done that you should treat him this way?'

'It's what he *is* that matters – heir to Lothian. And how have I treated him badly? How have I treated *you* badly? It's what you wanted, whatever you may claim now, whatever scheme you've hatched with Lot. Oh, yes, I know Lot wants Trystan, but no matter what he's promised you, he isn't going to get either of you. You're both mine to do with as I like. Trystan will stay in Lothian, and you'll stay to ensure he doesn't leave. So make this very clear to him; if he leaves without my permission, I will disinherit him and find myself another heir. And as for you—' His father's face was as unyielding as the carved stones of the northlands. 'If you help him leave Lothian, you will leave also and never return. Do you understand me?'

They stared at one another, the Old Wolf and the Young. *I killed my father because he'd given me reason enough.* Was this reason enough? Fury seared through Corwynal's veins and he reached for his dagger, but, after a moment's quivering hesitation, he let his hand drop.

'I understand you,' he said tonelessly and turned for the door, but his father reached out, grasped his left hand and twisted it over to reveal the shallow cut that sliced across the palm.

'You think I didn't notice?' he hissed, letting Corwynal's hand fall with a snort of disgust. 'The arrow, red with blood, buried in the boar's haunch? You think I didn't hear what no-one else heard – a wolf howling in the forest? Well understand me in this also – there can only be one wolf in Lothian and, for the moment, it is I.'

※

The door to Trystan's room, in the annexe to the hall, opened just as Corwynal reached it, and a girl, only partly clad, shot past him. It was early the following morning and, while the girl's appearance didn't surprise him, it drove the carefully prepared arguments from his mind.

'Who was she?' he asked. The room was the usual mess of gear, clothes, and half-eaten food. A hound, curled up in a corner, opened one eye to look up at him, but Trystan, lying sprawled on the bed, half-covered by a blanket, didn't open either of his.

'You might knock,' he muttered.

'I was about to. So, who was she?'

'What did she look like?'

'Small, dark-haired, plump. Pretty, I suppose.' They were always pretty.

'Then that would be Branwen or Blodwen – something like that. She looks after the geese.'

'You might at least know their names, Trys!'

Trystan opened his eyes, then narrowed them at the light coming in the door. They were bloodshot and rimmed with red, the probable cause a cup by his bed, an overturned flagon, wine-stains in the rushes. The place stank of stale wine, stale rushes, male sweat and, faintly, of goose-shit.

'Oh, don't start!' Trystan scowled at Corwynal's expression. 'What else is there to do but drink and wench? What else is there going to be to do? *Fifty men. The defence of Lothian.*' He mimicked the King's words with cruel accuracy. 'And for a moment, last night, I thought . . .' He closed his eyes again, squeezing them shut on tears of disappointment and fury, but when he opened them once more, all that remained was accusation. 'You said you'd speak to him. You *promised!*'

'I *did* speak to him, but he wouldn't listen.'

'How strange, when you're able to persuade him of anything else you really want him to do – oh, yes, I've seen you in action. I know how you manipulate him. So why couldn't you persuade him to let me go? Did you even try?'

'Trys, listen.' Corwynal crouched down beside him. 'I *did* try, but the King refused. What's worse, he told me he'll disinherit you if you leave without his permission. You can't do that – you'd be landless and lordless, and few captains would be willing to take someone like that into their company, no matter how well they fought. I understand how much you want to go, but the King's made you a good offer. It means you'd have charge of Lothian's defences. Fifty men is only a start. You could train more. And who's to say Lot will be successful? War might come south, or the Angles might raid us in spite of what Lot believes – and you'll have all the glory you crave.' But Corwynal believed none of this and knew it wasn't what he'd promised the God, or himself.

'Then I'll go to my uncle in Galloway,' Trystan said, sending a cold wash of fear through Corwynal's veins, for Marc's court was riven by factions.

'No! Let me try again. One way or the other, I'll get the King to agree, and I promise that when the war-band rides, you'll be riding with them. I *promise* you!'

Trystan eyed him sceptically. 'Why does he hate you so much? I thought it was me he disliked, but he doesn't care about me one way or the other. It's you he hates. It's you he wants to keep in Lothian, and that's why he keeps me here. He thinks you want to go to war, but you don't, because you're afraid to fight the Caledonians.'

Corwynal stared at him, his skin prickling as the blood drained from his face, even as it mounted in Trystan's.

'Get up!' He jerked Trystan's blanket away to reveal a purpling mass of bruises, one of them a shadow across his cheekbone where Corwynal had struck him. But, right then, he was too angry to apologise for that. 'How dare you! I can fight the Caledonians as well as I can fight anyone else. I made a choice, a long time ago, and I chose to be a Briton.'

Did you? The God's voice murmured through him, stirring up all his old doubts.

'I made a choice,' he insisted. 'If you knew—' He stopped himself just in time.

'But I *don't!*' Trystan exclaimed. 'You never talk about them. Everything I know of Caledonia I've learned from Blaize, not you. Why won't you tell me?'

Kinslayer! Corwynal could still hear the insult echoing across the empty moors from the part of his life he'd shut away, even from himself. Except in dreams. But now the memories coiled through him like the smoke from a smoored fire as the past tried to break free. *Kinslayer!* It was an old story, a shame he had to live with, but he couldn't tell Trystan, because, once he began, where would he stop? And so he said nothing and watched Trystan's face stiffen.

'I'm going hunting.' Trystan turned away, pulled on his leggings and reached for his tunic. 'I can still do that, I suppose, while I wait for the King to die.'

But he wouldn't meet Corwynal's eyes and he knew Trystan was neither resigned to staying in Lothian, nor convinced by Corwynal's promise. *When the war-band rides, you'll be riding too.* And perhaps he was right to doubt him, for Corwynal didn't know how to fulfil either that promise or the other – the pledge he'd made to a god.

'Woden's balls!'

Aelfric of Gyrwum, son of Herewulf, lately of Bernicia, waded ashore from the last long-boat to land, saw the smoke plume up from the fishing village and gave vent to his feelings in a flood of oaths in Angle, Jute and Saxon. 'You complete *prick*, Wulfric! You motherless son of a goat, you arse-licking polecat!'

The motherless son of a goat in question emerged from one of the hovels down by the shore. He was dragging a screaming woman by the hair but let her go when Aelfric strode up to him, grasped his tunic with one hand and dragged him up until his face was on a level with Aelfric's own. The man's feet dangled well above the ground, since Aelfric was an uncommonly tall and powerful man.

'This isn't what we agreed!'

'Fuck what we agreed! These are easy pickings, man!'

'These peasants? There's nothing here but slaves, and puny

ones at that! We agreed we'd go straight to Dunpeldyr.'

'It's a fucking fort!'

'I know that, you cretin! And now, because of your mindless stupidity, they'll have closed the fucking gates!' And if the gates were closed, this whole expedition would be a waste of time.

The smoke was denser now, the thatch on the torched buildings burning in greasy billows about the village. Women were screaming somewhere in the chaos, children were crying and cattle bawling, but the men who'd been shouting before had fallen silent. For the most part, they were either dead or wishing they were. The wind was picking up now, a blustery south-easterly that had driven their three ships swiftly from Dun Guayrdi. Getting back would be more difficult, especially if they were loaded down with slaves and cattle, but Aelfric seemed to be the only one who'd thought about that.

'Gold, Wulfric – that's what we came for.' Aelfric let the man go with a snarl of disgust. He really did stink like a goat, and his breath was unspeakable. 'Dunpeldyr's a King's fort. There'll be gold there, jewelled cups, pearls, beautiful women.' Wulfric's piggy eyes gleamed with a foul mixture of avarice and lust at Aelfric's string of lies. The man really was a moron, something Aelfric had been relying on, but this torching of the village had gone beyond stupidity. 'Come on, you thick fucker, call your men off and get the fires doused before they see the smoke from the fort.'

It took time, of course. Fires light easy enough but putting them out's another matter. Then the captured cattle had to be slaughtered and the best parts of the carcasses loaded on the ships. Which still left the peasants to deal with since they could hardly be turned loose. So they were roped up, taken to the ships and left under guard. Which meant that when the Angles finally headed inland, there were less of them than Aelfric had counted on. They'd just have to hope they didn't run into any Britons before reaching the fort. When they got there, all Wulfric's men had to do was create a diversion. They'd probably all be killed, but Aelfric didn't care about that. He despised the lot of them – pirate scum, not real men at all. All that mattered was for Aelfric to get into that fort and recover what he'd come for. Not gold or jewels or beautiful women, but a single slave, an Angle girl who'd never shown any promise of beauty.

'I'm coming to get you, Ealhith,' he promised her as the raiding party headed inland, making for Dunpeldyr. He'd been promising that ever since he'd learned what had happened to her. 'I'll get you back, love. I'll take you away from him.'

For he was going to Dunpeldyr for one other reason – to find the man whose slave she'd become.

'And then I'll kill him,' he promised himself. 'Corwynal of Lothian, I'm going to fucking kill you!'

Corwynal's argument with Trystan began what turned out to be a very bad morning. The men had begun to arrive to join the levy and, though it was Madawg's responsibility to see to their accommodation and stabling for their mounts, Madawg and the war-band had decided to go hunting with Lot and his men, leaving Corwynal to deal with his responsibilities as well as his own. And not for the first time.

By the middle of the morning his temper was worse than usual, and he was in danger of offending the very people whose help he needed, so he escaped to the ramparts to try to master his ill-humour. Normally the sight of the hills to the south, their tree-lined slopes greening in the late spring, restored his equanimity, but he hadn't been there for long before he heard a voice shouting for Madawg and demanding to know where the war-band was. Moments later, someone clattered up the stairs and sprinted along the walkway.

'Where's that pack of useless bastards?' A hand caught him by the elbow and jerked him around. 'Where's the war-band, you idiot?'

The man, stinking of human and horse sweat, was so liberally spattered with mud that he was unrecognisable. But only two men had ever risked calling Corwynal an idiot to his face, and this wasn't his father.

'Blaize? What—?'

'Just answer the sodding question! Where's the war-band?!'

'Gone hunting with Lot's men.'

'All of them?' Blaize pushed past him, jumped up to the lookout post and peered into the north. 'In the name of all the gods! Can't Madawg even be bothered to post a look-out! Look! Smoke down at the coast!'

Corwynal leapt up to join him, and a knot formed in his stomach when he saw a smudge of thick smoke purpling the horizon like a bruise. In spite of Lot's glib assurances of a season of peace, the Angles had come after all.

'I've been in Dun Guayrdi,' his uncle said, naming the Angle pirate stronghold on Gododdin's coast. Blaize sagged against the rampart; beneath the filth he was pale with exhaustion. 'I heard a rumour the Angles were planning something, so I went to find out what it was. Someone's persuaded those Dun Guayrdi bastards to make up a raiding party, and they're heading for Dunpeldyr. Three keels – that's fifty, maybe sixty men. Some of them must have turned aside to raid the villages on the coast.' He rubbed a hand down his face. 'I came as quickly as I could, killed one horse under me, but the winds have favoured them. Curse it to the five hells, we need the war-band!'

Corwynal stared at the distant smoke and wondered how long the settlements had been burning. He thought of distances and timings, of fifty Angles heading for Dunpeldyr. They'd have to cross the river north of the fort and the waters were still running high from the night's rain, so if they could be held at the ford for long enough . . .

'Come with me!' Corwynal dragged Blaize with him down the rampart steps, across the muddy courtyard and into the hall in search of his father, but the King just listened with maddening calm as his half-brother summarised the situation.

'Really, Blaize, do you never wash? Very well, Corwynal, have a rider go after the war-band, then order the gates shut until they're in sight.'

'But if we take what men we have, we can hold them at the ford and—'

'No! I forbid it! We'll shut the gates and wait.'

'If the gates are shut, they'll know we expect them. They'll slip away, go back to their boats and harry the coast until they're bored or loaded down with plunder. We need to stop them now!'

'It's not your place to advise me on such matters! It's your place to stay here!'

'Corwynal's plan's a good one,' Blaize insisted. 'I'll get a fresh horse and go after the war-band.'

'No. Let the Angles come here if they wish. They're in no position to mount a siege.'

'That isn't the point!' Corwynal exclaimed. Surely his father could see the Angles were taking a gamble. If it paid off, they'd sack Dunpeldyr. If not, they'd raid the countryside instead. They had to be stopped, not on the open ground before the fort where they could form a shield-wall, but down by the ford, where they'd be vulnerable to horsemen. But his father wasn't thinking about the Angles at all.

'I know what the point is!' He turned on Corwynal. '*Your* point! You won't wait for the war-band because you want the glory for yourself. You can't bear for Trystan to beat you in this, can you? That's why you tried to persuade me to keep him here. So he couldn't compete with you!'

The unfairness of this took Corwynal's breath away.

'That's unworthy, Rifallyn, even of you,' Blaize said coldly, turned and walked away.

'At the ford, Blaize!' Corwynal called after him. Blaize lifted a hand in assent as he reached the door.

'Are you defying me?' the King demanded, but Corwynal just smiled back at him with the wolf-smile they shared.

'Yes, I'm defying you!'

⛬

He rode hard across the muddy fields, heading for the ford. There were twelve of them, himself, nine men who'd ridden in to join the levy, and a couple from the fort. Blaize had headed for the hunting runs to the south. Behind them, Dunpeldyr stood on its crag, pennants flying, the gate fully open. Rifallyn hadn't ordered it shut after all. Looking back, Corwynal saw his father standing on the rampart, watching them go, raising a hand in ... what? Dismissal, blessing, or curse? It didn't matter. He was going to prove him wrong – about everything.

His old mail-shirt was chafing his shoulders, and his bruised ribs were aching, but these discomforts served only to spur him on. He'd stood by, helpless, while the boar had charged Trystan, but he wasn't going to stand helpless behind Dunpeldyr's walls watching the war-band fight the Angles on the killing ground outside the fort – Angles forewarned and with the advantage of the higher ground, Angles who might, for all he knew, bear the sign of the black ship. This way was safer for the one member of the war-band who mattered.

He lashed Janthe, and she leapt forward with a scream as they dropped down to the river. They were not a moment too soon, for the Angles had already reached the far bank, a mass of men among the trees, forty or fifty strong, the wan sun glittering on mail and helms and spears. They wore dark surcoats, most bearing the axe symbol of the pirates of Dun Guayrdi. At least half were helmed, but those who weren't had limed their hair into jagged, frightening shapes. They'd limed their shields too, and some had been daubed with an axe, painted with fresh blood. All of them, like most Angles, were armed with spears.

'Clust, go back up the track! Keep a look-out for the war-band! You two – spread out!' Corwynal tossed Rhun his quiver of arrows, and he and his cousin Elphin spurred off along the banks of the river. They were the best bowmen amongst them, and in a few moments there were angry cries from the Angles as the cousins' arrows found their marks. Unsettled, the raiders edged back from the fast-flowing, thigh-deep water. Only nine Britons faced them on the other side of the river. Nevertheless, the Angles were on the verge of breaking, afraid not so much of the water and the spirits who dwelled there, but of the killing hooves of the Britons' battle-trained mounts. Their leader, aware of his men's reluctance, just watched and waited, giving no command.

In truth, there was little Corwynal and his men could do. The Angles were out of spear-range, and they'd edged together behind shields to avoid Rhun and Elphin's remaining arrows. Each side waited for the other to make a move. If the Angles retreated, the Britons wouldn't risk following them, and they knew it. Yet, if the Angles found the courage to cross the ford, nine men wouldn't be able to hold them back.

For a long moment, only the voice of the river broke the silence. Nothing moved but the wind in the trees and a kingfisher, flashing blue as it darted upriver. Then a single man pushed his way to the front, the biggest man Corwynal had ever seen, as big as the giant in his dream. But the black token embroidered on his tunic wasn't a ship; it was a bear.

The Angle warrior spat his derision at the Dun Guayrdi pirates, and angry words were exchanged. He turned his back on them, plunged into the river and thrust through the water, a few men close behind him. Corwynal gave the command, and the Britons' spears flew, but most fell short or struck the Angles' shields. His own thudded deep into the warrior's shield, but the man jerked it out as if it had wedged in butter and flung it back at him. It buried itself in the ground at Janthe's feet, setting her rearing and screaming out her own challenge.

'Back!' Corwynal yelled, and the Britons retreated up the slope. The Angles jeered and several pushed forward, but the leader of the pirates waved them back. No doubt he was waiting to see what happened to the big Angle who wore the sign of the bear before committing his own men.

'They're coming!' Clust was shouting from the head of the track. 'The war-band's coming!'

Thanks to the gods! But Corwynal still had to stop the warrior and his companions. If they reached the near bank. the other Angles would follow, and the Britons would lose the little advantage they had. *Let the war-band come soon, or my father will be right!* He lashed Janthe into a temper and plunged back down the slope. The others followed a heartbeat later, and the Angles' spears began to fly. One splintered through the edge of Corwynal's shield and lodged by its barbs. The weight dragged the shield down so he flung it away, catching one of the Angles in the face. To his right a horse screamed as it went down, then everything was a chaos of water and men and horses, mounts whinnying and men yelling, himself among them.

His blood chilled as it always did when he fought, and it was as if he stood outside his body watching himself fight, seeing his sword hacking and slashing independently of his will. He was guiding Janthe with his knees as she kicked out and bit, as much of a weapon as the sword he swung with such singing joy. Beside him, the rest of the men were also using their mounts to ride down the Angles in the river, but the footing was poor after the winter rains, and another horse went down in a welter of foam, its rider splashing into the river. On the far side of the bank the remaining mass of Angles surged forward into the current.

'Back!' Corwynal yelled once more, jerking at Janthe's reins, afraid they'd lose the horses. She tossed her head and screamed as a blade sliced through her shoulder. He caught a glimpse of a snarling face, blond hair streaming from below a helm with a crest of bear's fur and saw the blade of an axe slicing up at him. He blocked the blow, twisted in the saddle, and hacked his sword down at that grinning face. But the big Angle caught it on his shield and thrust hard against Janthe's wounded shoulder. She screamed again, lost her footing and fell, throwing Corwynal into the river. He came close to being pinned down by her weight but managed to roll out of the saddle and into the shallows.

'Get down, you stupid bastard!' He was forced to duck as a roan stallion flew over him, and he flattened himself against the bank as the war-band galloped over him, streamed across the ford and rode down the packed mass of Angles who'd edged into the water. The river was a confusion of yelling men and screaming horses, and the water ran red until the Angles broke and fled back into the forest, the Lothian war-band in close pursuit. Corwynal gave a silent prayer of thanks to the gods of the waters as the last of the war-band rode over him, then got to his knees. His clothes were sodden, his mail shirt heavier than ever, and he was shivering from his immersion in the bitterly cold water.

'Look out!'

An axe flashed down at him but was blocked on the shield of the man who'd shouted. Corwynal rolled away as the shield splintered under the force of the blow. The axe, deflected, thudded into the bank a hairsbreadth from his shoulder. He scrambled to his feet and turned to see that the big Angle, who must also have taken refuge under the bank, had surged to his feet and was fighting the boy who'd saved Corwynal's life for the second time in two days. The axe whirled towards Trystan, and he raised his damaged shield.

'No!' Perhaps Trystan heard him, or maybe his own instincts took over. Instead of trying to block the heavy weapon, he ducked, and the axe whirled over his head. Trystan struck out with his sword, but it met chain mail on a thigh that must have been made of iron, belonging to a man a good foot taller than him who was wielding the heavy axe as if it weighed nothing at all.

Trystan twisted away, but in doing so he exposed himself on the left. The Angle smashed in with his iron-bossed steel-rimmed shield, caught Trystan on the arm and tumbled him into the water. The axe rose and Corwynal's frozen immobility melted into action. He threw himself forward, his full weight crashing into the warrior. The man's axe fell away, and both of them went down into the swollen river.

The Angle was the first to find his feet, and he dragged his sword from its scabbard. Corwynal saw it flare against the sky and begin to descend towards him in a bludgeon of steel. It never reached him; the Angle's sword met Trystan's, the two weapons shivering together in a crash of iron on iron. The Angle stumbled backwards and Trystan stepped towards him but lost his balance in the silt of the river-bed and would have fallen if Corwynal hadn't reached out to catch him by the shoulder and pull him back. They both stumbled into the shallows, dashing water from their eyes, then, breathing heavily, turned to watch the Angle make his escape across the river.

Instead of escaping, however, the cursed man bent down to recover his axe, threw away his shield and, armed with both sword and axe, waded towards them. Trystan swore and glanced at Corwynal. *What do we do now?* He wasn't entirely sure. He'd trained Trystan to fight with either hand, to fight without a shield when necessary, to fight on horseback and on foot. He hadn't trained him to fight in a river against a man armed with both axe and sword. Not one the size of this one. Nevertheless, Trystan appeared to find the whole situation amusing, for he began to laugh.

'Careful!' Corwynal said, edging backwards, away from Trystan, luring the Angle towards himself.

'Careful yourself!' Trystan snorted.

'We do this together,' Corwynal said, making it sound as if they were on the training ground. 'Move to the right. Then do what I tell you.'

The Angle flicked a glance between the two of them as they separated, unsettled by their speech and Trystan's laughter.

'*He* isn't going to!'

Trystan was right; the Angle didn't. Nor did Trystan do what Corwynal told him, but it didn't matter. The Angle charged at

Trystan, slashing from the right with his sword. Corwynal closed in on the left, only to fall back a moment later as, impossibly, the axe whistled in a backhand that almost took him in the stomach. Trystan, who'd blocked the first blow, thrust forwards but met mail and stepped back, almost as if they'd agreed in advance, to let Corwynal hammer down at the Angle's neck. But the man's axe was as much a shield as a weapon. The broad head blocked Corwynal's blow, and he was forced to fall back himself and allow Trystan to make the next move.

So it went on, their dance by the river. Time slowed as it always did, each move being plucked out of the future as he and Trystan flowed into the pattern laid out before them. It was as if they were the same person fighting one man. But it couldn't go on forever.

Distantly, through the drumming rhythm of their fight, Corwynal was aware of horsemen behind them on the track down to the river but didn't have time to look because Trystan had swerved to the left to come in behind the big Angle. The man spun, his axe outstretched. It slammed into Trystan's sword –which shattered in his hand.

The world stopped, but only for a second. Then time ran on, fast and breathless once more, as the Angle half-turned in his direction, expecting him to take Trystan's place, and smiling broadly as Corwynal raised his sword. Almost without thinking, he threw his blade to Trystan, who caught it deftly, twisted it in the air and hammered it down on the Angle's mail-clad arm before the man could turn to face this new threat. The man grunted with pain and fell back but recovered faster than Corwynal expected. He threw his axe at Trystan and, though the head missed Trystan's shoulder, the haft knocked him off balance and sent him sprawling into the river. Corwynal's heart stopped, as it had in the glade, when he saw what would happen – the Angle's blade stabbing down at the defenceless boy at his feet. But the man stepped over Trystan and came straight for Corwynal, who, weaponless now, backed out of the river until a tree brought him to a halt. The Angle brought up his sword, levelled it at Corwynal's heart, and grinned.

'I'm going to kill you, Caledonian,' the Angle said in perfect, if accented, Briton.

Corwynal believed him. He could see it in the man's eyes, in the set of his shoulders and the half-smile on his lips. *Arddu?* he breathed, with little confidence that the God would listen. He didn't want to die. Not here, not now, not before he'd lived. He remembered someone else saying that.

That someone surged out of the water with Corwynal's sword in his hands, a sword he pressed to the Angle's throat.

'Touch my brother and you're dead,' Trystan said.

The Angle flicked a glance at Trystan, then ignored him, his muscles bunching as he readied himself to drive his blade into Corwynal's chest.

Then something whined past him and a black dart buried itself in the Angle's shoulder, driving right through the man's mail, the force of it knocking him backwards. Corwynal kicked the man's sword-hand and his weapon slipped from his grip as Trystan crashed into the Angle and brought him to the ground. Both of them piled on top of the man, but he threw them off, one after the other, until someone shouldered Trystan aside and pressed a wooden object into the Angle's chest.

'I could pin your heart to the ground, and let the ravens feed on your rotting body,' Blaize said in a conversational tone.

Corwynal got to his feet, breathing hard, his knees trembling with reaction. Trystan, however, showed no such weakness and levelled Corwynal's sword at the man's throat once more.

'You tried to kill my brother,' he said.

'I am Aelfric of Gyrwum, son of Herewulf,' the Angle said. 'I have come to Lothian to kill this man.' He glanced at Corwynal, his lip curling in contempt. 'I am sworn to it.'

'Give me back my sword, Trys.' Corwynal sighed and held out his hand. 'He won't make a useful slave. Best I kill him now.'

'No. He's mine.'

Corwynal hesitated and glanced at Blaize, but Blaize just shrugged. It was all very well killing a man in the heat of battle, but rather harder when he was sprawled on the earth and at your mercy. Yet this was something Trystan would have to learn to do, though Corwynal didn't like it.

Aelfric of Bernicia was clearly a man of pride and lineage, a man who possessed immense skill but very little sense since he should have run away with the others. 'Let him get up first,' he said. 'Let him die on his feet.'

The Angle stared at Corwynal, his expression unreadable. It wasn't gratitude or surprise or even hatred, but something more complex than any of those.

Trystan lowered the sword and stepped back, but Blaize kept his crossbow trained on the Angle. The man got to his feet without assistance despite the dart in his shoulder, took off his helmet and shook out his braided blonde hair. He was younger than Corwynal had thought, in his middle-twenties perhaps, with the pale blue eyes of the Angle nation. Behind them, on the track, some stragglers from Dunpeldyr arrived, saw what was happening and moved closer, murmuring at the size of the man. Trystan spoke with two of them and, before the Angle realised what was happening, they'd grabbed him from behind, tied his wrists with leather straps and kicked his legs from beneath him so they could tie his ankles too.

'What are you doing, Trys? This is no way to kill the man!'

'I'm not going to kill him,' Trystan said, handing Corwynal his sword. 'You have an Angle slave. I've a fancy to have one myself.' The men jeered their approval.

'No!' The Angle struggled violently until someone had the presence of mind to knock him unconscious with the flat of a sword.

'You won't be able to make a slave of him.'

'Perhaps not, but I still want him,' Trystan said with decision. 'I want to know why a man from Bernicia speaks Briton. I want to know why a man who's never set foot in Lothian until today wants to kill you.' He grinned at Corwynal. 'And I want him to show me how to fight a man with an axe, because that's something you forgot to teach me!'

They argued about the Angle most of the way back to the fort. Lot caught up with them with the news that most of the Angles had fled, and Madawg, with Lothian's war-band, was pursuing them. Of the men Corwynal had taken to the riverbank, only one was dead, though some of the others were wounded. Blaize rode on ahead, for his healing skills would be needed, but Corwynal decided to walk back to the fort since Janthe's shoulder was still bleeding. Trystan, leading his grey stallion Rhydian, insisted on walking with him through the steadily darkening woods. Eventually their arguments tailed off, and they lapsed into silence. The sun was smouldering on the horizon, but from the east, borne on the sea-wolf wind, slate-blue clouds brought a flurry of stinging rain that strengthened to a downpour. But it wasn't the weather that darkened Trystan's mood.

'I can't stay in Lothian,' he said. 'Not after today. You understand that, don't you? Today was what you trained me for, what I was born for – what we were *both* born for. That's why I have to leave. I'm not in love with Lothian as you are. Maybe one day I will be, but not yet. Not before I've lived!'

They'd reached the edge of the woods by then, and, as they emerged from the shelter of the trees, the setting sun broke through the clouds to the west and gleamed through the rain. In that vivid glowing light Trystan was incandescent, his eyes shining, and Corwynal thought how like his mother he was in that moment, so vibrant, so mortal.

'We were alive today,' Trystan insisted. 'Together, fighting that Angle, just a breath away from death. That was life!' Then something of his brightness began to fade. 'Are you listening to me?'

But Corwynal was listening to other voices. He was hearing himself trying to persuade Trystan to stay in Lothian, trying to persuade his father to keep him there, trying to make him change his mind and failing. He was listening to himself accept his father's compromise, then trying to persuade Trystan to accept it too. All of that had been wrong because of the promise he'd made to a god.

Anything!

Trystan was frowning at his failure to reply, but Corwynal had turned his gaze to the countryside, to the fields and copses, to the haze of smoke from settlements, to the rock of Dunpeldyr with its ramparts, black against the sunset. He was hearing, once more, his father's threat. *You will leave Lothian and never return.* Now he knew what his promise really meant.

Trystan was right. He *did* love Lothian, and what else would satisfy a god but the sacrifice of the one thing he loved only a little less than Trystan?

'You *will* leave, and in honour, with the war-band,' he promised, and this time he really meant it. 'You'll go to war, Trys. Both of us, we'll go to war.'

So Corwynal would go to fight the Caledonians, his mother's people, because he'd made a choice years before.

And because he'd just made another.

4

EVERYONE HAS SECRETS

Rumours ran around the fort long before the men returned. A battle against Angles, they said. A battle lost – or won – or lost. Men had been wounded, men killed, all of them slaughtered, not a man of them touched. Victory. Defeat. No-one knew for certain, so everyone had an opinion, but Ealhith cared about one thing only; Corwynal hadn't come back.

She'd seen him up on the rampart earlier that day, then later, crossing the courtyard with another man, heading for the hall. Not long afterwards, a rider had galloped through the gates, dark hair streaming behind him. She'd run up to the walkway over the gate and watched the rider make for the hills, but if it was Corwynal he wasn't riding Janthe. Not long afterwards, other horsemen left the fort and rode north, but she couldn't be sure he was among them. All she knew was that he'd vanished, leaving a dagger of fear in her stomach that wasn't for herself.

And so, despite everything she ought to be doing, she hung about the gate in the rain, hoping for news. By late afternoon, riders began to return, men from the levy to begin with, then a few of the war-band. Some were wounded and there was at least one body, but it wasn't Corwynal's. The men spoke of victory by a ford against pirates from Dun Guayrdi; some of the Angles had been killed, but the rest had fled back to their boats, pursued by the war-band.

'But where's the Lord Steward . . . ?'

'Beat a big Angle warrior, him and Prince Trystan,' one of the returning riders told her. 'Took him captive – at least the Prince did. The Steward wanted to kill the bastard. But see for yourself, lass. They're bringing him in now.'

A cart was moving through the gates, a cart carrying only one man, a big man, still wearing chain-mail, his wrists and ankles lashed to the uprights of the cart. His back was to her, and she could see blood matting the back of his head, darkening his fair hair. As the cart passed into the courtyard, the men who'd gathered by the gate jeered, and the prisoner turned and glared at them. Then his eyes shifted and went straight to hers, like an arrow out of the dark. She felt it as a blow, not the sharp pain of the dagger of fear twisting in her stomach, but as if something had been torn out of her chest and rammed back in again.

All the strength flowed out of her legs and she sagged against the wall, staring at the captive and wondering if this was some waking nightmare. But it was no dream. This was as real as the sign of the bear on the man's blood-stained tunic, as real as the black dart in the man's shoulder, as real as the face she knew better than her own, though it was older now, as she was older.

'Aelfric,' she murmured, and saw his lips move in the shape of her own name. 'Oh, Aelfric . . . !'

'What's all this nonsense I've been hearing about a boar and an arrow?' Blaize burst into Corwynal's quarters above the stable where, in the annoying absence of Ealhith, he'd been trying to bind a gash in his arm. 'And that Trystan's not going with the war-band? Why not? He's a warrior. You made him into a warrior. He ought to be going to war. You can't protect him forever, you know.'

Corwynal scowled at Blaize, for his uncle had a talent for seeing just what one most wanted to hide. But he was the only man to whom Corwynal could open his heart and, since he badly needed to talk, he told him everything – Trystan's threat to leave, their fight, how Corwynal had almost killed him, Lot's arrival, the arguments with his father, his dream of the black ship—

'That bloody dream!' Blaize snatched the strips of linen from him, took a cursory look at the gash, and began to bind his arm. 'So that's why you're keeping him here! Curse it, man, why won't you listen to me? Dreams rarely mean what you think. This place you've convinced yourself is anywhere but Lothian probably doesn't exist. And I'm tired of asking everywhere I go if anyone knows this black ship symbol of yours. Red ships, blue ships, green ships – those I can find, but not black. And the man, this giant, he's not real either. None of it is *real!*'

Corwynal shook his head, then yelped as Blaize tied a knot in the linen and tugged it to make sure it would hold. 'The dream *is* real. But I should never have tried to keep Trystan in Lothian because of it. Arddu made me understand that.'

'Arddu?' Blaize sat down on Corwynal's pallet and leant back against the wall. 'I thought he'd left you.'

'He's returned.' Corwynal frowned down at his uncle. 'It's because of Lot's war against the Caledonians, I suppose. Arddu doubts the choice I made. Even Trystan asked me if I was afraid to fight my mother's people. Is that what everyone thinks? But why should they? You have as much Caledonian blood as me and no-one doubts *your* loyalties.'

Blaize shrugged. 'I'm Lot's advisor, not a warrior, but you are – or were – and people remember that. They know Caledonians are reluctant to fight men of their own tribe.'

'So you doubt me too! Have you forgotten why I left?'

'Hardly! An archdruid murdered, your own grandfather. And—' He stopped abruptly.

And the child, Corwynal thought, with a surge of old guilt. Was that what Blaize had been about to say?

'—and you barely out of manhood,' Blaize went on as if he hadn't hesitated. 'How can I forget when it was me who had to get you out of Atholl? At no small price to myself, I might add. I've never been able to go back there, you know. I doubt I ever will be.'

'Nor me.'

'That's less certain. One day, you'll have to go back – and part of you wants to. You can't stay in Lothian for ever. Trystan's a man now. He doesn't need you, dream or no dream, and you don't need him. It's time you began living for yourself, and you can't do that until you face up to your past. I remember a time when you loved Atholl.'

'I did, once.' It was true; he'd loved the high hills and the deep secret lochs, the drums and horns and the fierce people. 'But not anymore.' Not now he was a Kinslayer. 'And I loved Lothian long before I went to Atholl. I chose to be a Briton then, and that's what I am now, no matter what everyone thinks. As for my place, it's by Trystan's side, wherever he is, whoever he faces, and if that turns out to be Caledonians, I can fight them just as well as I can fight anyone. I'm not afraid of them. That isn't why I wanted to stay in Lothian.'

Blaize snorted in exasperation. 'Whatever your reason, you've got your wish, because if my cold-hearted bastard of a brother's made a decision, he won't change his mind. It's as well to ask the sun to rise in the west.'

'He *will* change his mind. I'll make him. He'll let Trystan go with the war-band, and me with him.' He eyed Blaize sourly. 'North with the war-band, Blaize. Not to Selgovia.'

'Ah . . .' Blaize's eyes slid away.

'So it *was* your idea!'

'All good ideas are mine! We need Selgovia and you're the one man they might listen to.'

'They barely listened to me the last time.'

'Barely or not, you achieved what no-one else has.'

'I achieved very little, and my father's still complaining about it.'

'Well, this is your chance to show what you're capable of, with Lot backing you up. No-one's been to Selgovia save for a few traders. Imagine riding into Meldon with a company at your back. Better still, imagine riding out again with a troop of their archers behind you. You're the one man who could do it.'

For a moment, Corwynal was tempted. Blaize's appeal had touched him as Lot's had not. Perhaps his days as a warrior were over, but this was something he could do. He saw himself riding into Meldon, the secret stronghold of a secret kingdom, and making them listen. After a moment, however, he shook his head; that was all just wishful thinking.

'No, Blaize. I'm not going to Selgovia, no matter what scheme you and Lot have come up with. I'm not a fool, you know. This isn't about the war, not entirely. It's about the High Kingship, isn't it?'

'Listen, Corwynal,' Blaize said, leaning forward. 'Dark times are coming. We Britons between the Walls need to be united if we're not to be swept away. This war will bind us together, and after the war a High King will keep us bound. It needn't be Lot, though I can't, at the moment, think of anyone else who could do it.' He got to his feet. 'But that's a long way in the future. For the moment there's a feast in the hall to celebrate our 'victory', and I, for one, am hungry.'

They left Corwynal's quarters and headed for the hall. The great doors stood open, spilling torchlight across the rain-washed courtyard. The air was heady with the smell of freshly baked bannocks, roasted meat and rich red ale, and Corwynal realised he was hungry too. But as they crossed the courtyard Blaize grasped his arm and pulled him into the shadows of the granary.

'Look!' He jerked his head at a girl who'd slipped from the side-door of the hall and made her way to one of the store-rooms. A guard stood outside, but after a brief exchange with the girl he left, and she slipped into the building.

Corwynal and Blaize exchanged a look before making for the storeroom themselves. They'd both recognised the girl and knew what was behind that door. *This*, Corwynal thought, *could be interesting.*

༝

'You fool! Oh, you *fool!* Why did you have to come to Lothian?'

Aelfric was chained by wrists and ankles to the central upright of the building. The door had been guarded, but Ealhith had convinced the man he was wanted in the hall. She ought to be there herself, helping serve the ale or, at the very least, helping Corwynal organise the feast. He'd been shouting for her earlier, but for once she hadn't run to his call. She had to see Aelfric and make him promise to keep her secrets, but the sight of him in the storeroom, chained like a beast, hurt but still defiant, just made her want to shake him.

'I came to rescue you, you idiot!' he complained.

'They said you were dead.'

'Me? Dead? And you believed it?'

'You didn't come back, Aelfric. You promised you'd come back!'

'I *did* come back!' A little colour washed into his face. 'Alright, I was away longer than I said. But I thought you'd wait for me.'

'I did wait. But then they said you were dead, and I had no choice but to accept—'

'No choice? An Angle woman always has a choice. In the law—'

'Oh, don't speak to me of the law! The law's made by men for men. I was alone, Aelfric. I tell you, I had no choice!'

Aelfric's face flushed a deeper pink, and Ealhith knew he blamed himself. He'd gone to the old country to make a name for himself and, being Aelfric, would have enjoyed himself so much he'd pushed his promise to return within the year to the back of his mind. *Ealhith will be all right*, he'd have told himself. *Ealhith will wait.*

'I thought you were dead,' she whispered, remembering how her kinfolk had used her grief to persuade her into a marriage that would have been distasteful to any right-thinking woman. But she hadn't been a woman; she'd been a child.

'I thought *you* were dead.' He slid down the upright to which he was chained and sat on the floor in the straw and dust. Only now did he seem to understand the seriousness of his situation – chained in a leaky storeroom that stank of stale straw and mouldy grain. The dart protruded obscenely from his shoulder, the wound still oozing blood.

'I'll fetch the fort's healer.'

'No, wait,' he said, as she turned for the door. 'Tell me what happened. They said the ship taking you north vanished in a storm, that there were no survivors. I *mourned* you, Ealhith.'

She shivered, imagining offerings made in groves for her. But why not? The girl she'd been in Bernicia was dead. Her life was in Dunpeldyr now, with Corwynal.

'I mourned you too.' She sat down beside him, grateful for the warmth of his thigh against hers, the sheer living solidity of him. How could she have believed him to be dead? He was alive, and she was no longer alone. The Prince, she'd heard, had taken Aelfric as a slave, which meant they'd be prisoners together. The thought gladdened her heart, but only for a moment. For Aelfric, slavery would be a living death. 'How did you know I was here?'

'A trader passed this way at the end of last year, ended up in Bernicia, mentioned an Angle slave with your name, slave to a painted Caledonian devil. I didn't believe it at first because I thought you'd drowned. Anyway, how could you be a slave? You should have been ransomed. There was gold enough. You must have known that.'

'They didn't think I was worth anything. I said I was a servant.'

'Why, in Thunor's name?'

'You know why! That ship was taking me to Dun Guayrdi to marry Sigeweard, and I didn't want to go. The storm drove us north and forced the ship ashore. I jumped off before it struck the rocks, so I survived when the others didn't.' She shivered at the memory. She still dreamt of the screaming of wind and timbers, the icy shock of the sea, the water closing over her head, the relief as she'd crashed into and clung to an empty barrel that had washed towards the shore, taking her with it, the welcome solidity of sand, rock-hard, beneath her body. 'I didn't want to be ransomed – they'd only have sent me back to Sigeweard – so I didn't say who I was. And now it's too late.'

'It's not too late. I'll tell them who you are and wergild will be paid—'

'Who by? You? Look at you!' She gestured at his shoulder, the chains holding him prisoner. 'And no-one else is going to, especially Sigeweard.' She'd kept her left side in shadow until then, but now she turned her face so he could see her clearly. 'Look at me, Aelfric. Who'd pay for this?'

She flinched as his shock changed to fury. His hands gripped the chains, and she felt the building tremble as he jerked at them, but they held fast and the manacles just cut into his wrists. 'I'll kill him! I'll fucking kill that fucking Caledonian!'

'No! It wasn't him who did this. He's been kind to me.'

'Kind?! You're his *slave!* I'm going to kill him for that alone. I'll kill anyone who's touched you.'

'He hasn't touched me, not . . . not in that way.' She dropped her eyes for fear he'd see her shame, her longing, and her despair.

'Boy-lover, is he?' There was derision in his voice.

'No. He just . . . doesn't want me.' She began to cry, and turned to him, wrapped her arms around his waist and sobbed with the relief at being able to tell someone what was in her heart. 'But I want *him*. I'm sorry, but I can't help it. I love him. That's why I have to stay. I don't want to be ransomed.'

She was sobbing so hard she didn't hear the door creak open, but she couldn't miss the voice.

'How very touching!' The voice was accented with the northern lilt of the Caledonians, but it spoke in the Angle tongue.

Aelfric surged to his feet and pushed Ealhith behind him. It was the man who'd shot him, the man he'd heard the guards talk about, not realising Aelfric could understand their tongue. The man's name was Blaize, and he was a Caledonian and a druid, which was some sort of spell-weaver. The Britons were afraid of him. Now this spell-weaver was leaning against the doorpost, his arms folded, a self-satisfied smirk on his face. He must have been there for some time, listening to everything he and Ealhith had been saying.

'What's this, then? A reunion of childhood sweethearts?' The druid was talking in Briton now for the benefit of someone standing just behind him, a man who moved into the light and revealed himself to be the Caledonian Aelfric had come to kill, the man who considered himself Ealhith's master. Aelfric had failed to kill him earlier that day, but it wasn't too late. He launched himself at the bastard, but the chains brought him up short a pace away from the other man. The Caledonian's eyes blazed and his hands curled into fists as he stepped towards Aelfric, but Ealhith jumped between them.

'Don't you hurt him,' she hissed, looking from Aelfric to the Caledonian and back again. 'Don't you dare hurt him!' Who was she speaking to? Him or the Caledonian?

'How's the shoulder?' the druid asked. 'I'm afraid I forgot all about you, but I'll take a look at it now . . .' He gestured the Caledonian over. 'Help me get this dart out of his shoulder. It's ruining that rather fine mail coat.' He snapped his fingers at Ealhith. 'Fetch warm water and bandages. Go on, girl,' he added when Ealhith made no move to obey him. 'I'm not going to hurt him.' He chuckled to himself, a far from reassuring sound, but still Ealhith made no move to leave.

'Do as you're told!' the Caledonian snarled. 'And be quick about it!'

How dare he speak to her like that!

'You half-breed bastard!' Aelfric surged forward, but, once more, the chains jerked him back. 'You're not fit to touch her, you painted spawn of a demon! She's so far above you, you—'

'Please Aelfric, don't,' Ealhith whispered. *Don't give me away!*

With an effort, Aelfric bit back what he'd been about to say, and the druid gave a short bark of laughter.

'Painted spawn of a demon! And I thought the Angles had no poetry! I congratulate you on your rather surprising grasp of our language.'

Aelfric drew himself up to his considerable height. 'I had Briton slaves. Many, many Briton slaves.'

'And now you're a slave yourself. But a slave with a dart in his shoulder is no use to anyone.' He stepped closer to examine the wound, but Aelfric jerked away. He didn't want a Briton spell-weaver touching him, even though his shoulder hurt like hell.

The Druid shrugged. 'It's just a flesh wound but it will fester if I don't remove it, and you'll die, quite unpleasantly, I expect. But it's your choice.'

'Don't be so stubborn, Aelfric,' Ealhith urged. 'You're no good to me dead.'

Aelfric wrestled with that truth for a moment. 'All right,' he spat at the druid. 'Take it out.'

'Ealhith, fetch water and bandages as Blaize told you,' the Caledonian said, but still Ealhith hesitated. 'Do as I say! You've wasted enough time over this cursed Angle already. I had to look for you when I got back. Where in the five hells were you? Here, I suppose!'

'Don't you shout at her, you fucking worm, you—'

The Caledonian advanced on him once more, but the druid put a hand on his chest. 'Just ignore him,' he advised the man, then turned to Ealhith. 'Go on, girl. I won't hurt him.'

She glanced at Aelfric, made a gesture half of appeal, half of apology, then ran off, leaving him alone with the druid and the Caledonian.

'I lied,' the druid said, unsheathing a short, sharp-looking dagger. Aelfric stepped back until the post was at his back. 'Hold him.' The Caledonian grabbed Aelfric's wrists and dragged his arms behind him, wrenching his shoulder open. Pain blossomed and he couldn't stop himself from gasping, but the druid just smiled as he grasped the stump of the dart. 'I lied because it *is* going to hurt. Rather a lot, I'm afraid.'

It did. It fucking did. But Aelfric didn't scream. He clenched his jaws so hard together he thought his teeth were going to shatter. He felt the dart suck itself out of his shoulder, tearing the flesh as it did so. Then everything went black.

⁂

By the time Ealhith got back, it was all over. Aelfric lay on his back in the straw, his eyes closed, but still breathing. The dart had gone and his shoulder was bleeding freely as Blaize crouched over him and probed at the wound with a fine pair of pincers.

'Got it!' he said with a crow of satisfaction, waving the pincers at her. Between their jaws was a broken ring from Aelfric's mail shirt. 'It's the things left in a wound that cause the problems,' Blaize said. 'Our ancestors knew what they were doing when they went into battle naked.' He nodded wisely, then turned to Corwynal. 'Go on to the hall. Ealhith can help me clean up the wound...' Blaize smiled at her, a serpent's smile. '...and we'll have a nice little talk while we're about it, won't we?'

Corwynal left without protest, much to Ealhith's relief. Her life was shaped by the texture of his moods, and she knew he was angry about something, and not just with her. She wasn't afraid he'd beat her, even if she deserved it, because he'd never beaten her, but his tongue could be sharper than a whip. She was dreading what he might say to her when they were alone, especially if Blaize told him what he'd overheard.

'So, you're in love with my foolish nephew, are you?' he said as he crumbled dried leaves into the bowl of water she'd brought. The scents of woundwort and rosemary rose in pungent clouds.

Ealhith said nothing as she worked to loosen the fastenings of Aelfric's mail coat, but Blaize took her silence for confirmation. 'You aren't the first and won't be the last.' He took hold of the loosened mail, hauled it off the still unconscious Aelfric and cut away his under-tunic to lay bare the wound in his shoulder. 'Nor will you be the first, or last, to be disappointed.' Taking the basin from her, he washed out the wound. 'Hold that there, will you?' He showed her how to press down on the pad of linen he laid on Aelfric's shoulder. 'My nephew doesn't believe in love,' he said, tearing the rest of the linen into strips. 'That isn't to say he doesn't believe in the act of love, though he wouldn't call it that, or think the two things were related.' He tilted his head thoughtfully. 'Maybe he's right.'

Aelfric began to stir and Blaize lifted one of his eyelids and grunted in satisfaction. 'He's coming round.' He cocked his head at her. 'I assume he's here for you? Is it love again?'

Ealhith shrugged. She had no intention of telling Blaize any more than she needed to, though she had the unnerving conviction he already knew too much. 'Yes, he loves me, and I him. Not that it matters.'

'Ah, but it does. Does he love you enough to keep your secrets?'

'I don't have secrets,' she replied woodenly, but Blaize just tutted.

'Everyone has secrets. Little ones, big ones, silly ones, unspeakable ones. It's what makes us what we are, Ealhith. I have a bit of a weakness for other people's secrets. You could say it's my profession, the gathering and using of secrets. But don't worry that I might know yours, for I see no immediate way of using them. Now run along, there's a good girl. Go and enjoy yourself in the hall. It sounds as if everyone else is . . .'

***

The hall stank of roasting meat and spilled ale, wet dogs and stale sweat. Someone had taken it upon themselves to open one of the barrels of imported wine, and the noise, when Corwynal entered, hit him like a hammer. Piecing together the shouted boasts and claims, he gathered that few of the Angles had got away and that their own losses had been light. Lot had decided to head west in the morning, together with Lothian's war-band. The levy was to follow in four or five days, with the spare horses and the bulk of the supplies. Everyone was in high spirits. Lot, drunk enough to be tolerant, was talking over the day's events with Madawg. Gaheris and the rest of Lot's men were laughing and boasting, but Trystan, sitting with them, was noticeably despondent. Despite Corwynal's promise, he knew it was over for him. The glory had lasted less than an hour, and all he had to show for it were bruises, a broken sword, and a slave who'd almost certainly turn out to be a mistake.

Corwynal glanced at his father, who was sitting at the head of the hall, listening with ill-concealed contempt to the shouts and boasts echoing about the room. He saw Corwynal enter and scowled, so Corwynal made his way to a bench as far away from him as possible, then picked at a bowl of stew, poured wine into his cup, and took a deep swallow. It was stronger than he expected and swirled pleasantly in his stomach, spreading warmth through his whole body. But it didn't lighten his mood. Like Trystan, he had nothing to show for the day except for his father's anger at his defiance. Like Trystan, Corwynal had tasted the joy of battle, and one taste wasn't enough. He was Lothian's Steward and that part of him wanted to stay in Lothian, but another part of him longed to go to war, to be the warrior he'd always meant to be. To be valued by his peers, by the war-band, by Lot. And by his father.

Why didn't you stay in Atholl? Why did you come back?

Because I thought you loved me. But that was a lie, wasn't it? Because when I came back you hated and feared me long before I'd given you cause. So I took Her from you before you even knew you wanted Her.

'Well, that was interesting, wasn't it?' Blaize said, shaking rain from his cloak and sliding into the place beside him. He dragged Corwynal's barely touched dish towards him, spooned the stew into his mouth and began to talk about the Angle. But, seeing Corwynal wasn't listening, he laid his spoon down and eyed him critically. 'Are you drinking?'

'Why shouldn't I be drinking?' He reached for the flagon and shook Blaize off when he tried to stop him from pouring more wine into his cup.

'Because you can't handle it. You start by getting reckless, then turn maudlin, and end up remembering nothing. It won't be pretty and you'll regret it in the morning.'

He'd probably regret a great deal more than the wine. *Reckless*, Blaize had said. Yes, that was what he had to be, and the wine would help, so he reached for the flagon once more.

'Do you remember what happened seventeen years ago?' he asked.

Blaize glanced around, but no-one was listening. Nevertheless, he dropped his voice. 'Of course I remember, you bloody idiot!'

'I hated him.' Corwynal nodded at his father. 'I hated you too. And Her. I hated Her for dying. I hated Trystan too, more than anyone.'

He'd been full of hate in those early days, most of it directed at himself. Then one night, when Trystan was almost two years old, he'd had a fever, and Corwynal had thought he would die. For the whole of that long winter's night, he'd watched the child toss and turn. He'd tried to make him drink the bitter liquids one of the women had given him, but Trystan spat them out and wept for the comfort of someone two years' dead. Corwynal began to weep too, then picked Trystan up and held him as he'd stubbornly refused to do since the night he'd been born. His touch seemed to soothe the child, so he lay down, holding him against his chest. During the night Trystan's fever broke, and they both fell asleep, and in the morning Corwynal found Trystan lying against his heart, a thumb in his mouth, his fever burned away. Corwynal's hatred had burned away too, and from its ashes had arisen a terrifying love and the determination to protect Trystan from anything and anyone who might try to harm him. But in doing so, he'd stopped Trystan from living.

What father would deny his son the chance to live?

Corwynal looked up, but the voice, that familiar dry rustle, was inside him. He felt the pulse of the God's presence at the base of his nerves, but Arddu himself was standing on the other side of the hall, his antlers sweeping the rafters. Then, between one moment and the next, the God vanished.

'Where are you going?' Blaize demanded as Corwynal got to his feet.

'To get some justice,' he said, pushing Blaize aside. He negotiated the bench, walked between the tables into the centre of the hall, and waited for everyone to fall silent.

'You want to say something, Corwynal?' his father asked with a jerk of his chin.

'I want to say something that needs to be said.' He spoke slowly and carefully, and felt cold and clear and very certain. 'Trystan's been in the war-band for three years now. He's beaten everyone in single combat. He's the best fighter Lothian has.' There was a cheer from around the hall. This was what the war-band liked, simple statements they could agree with. 'Yesterday, he killed a boar marked by the gods. He saved my life at the risk of his own. He almost died, but he has the favour of the gods. Few men have that.' The war-band shouted and banged on the tables, and Corwynal, carried away by his own eloquence, raised his voice. 'Today he fought a warrior of the Angle nation, one that few men would care to fight. He bested him and made him his slave. He's proved himself as a warrior and a leader of men. Who here can deny that?'

No-one did. They banged on the tables once more, stamping their feet until the whole hall shook. 'Trystan! Trystan! Trystan!' But Trystan just stared at Corwynal as if he'd gone mad, then turned his eyes to the King. Reluctantly, Corwynal did so also, for though he knew his father could no longer deny Trystan the right to leave with the war-band, he'd never forgive Corwynal for publicly forcing him to do so.

Rifallyn stood up. He didn't say anything, but his presence was such that the whole hall fell silent.

'Trystan!' he barked. Trystan eyed Corwynal uneasily, but came to stand beside him before the King. 'Everyone seems to think that today has earned you your place in the war-band,' Rifallyn looked at Trystan for a long time, his face grim with displeasure. 'Go then. Go to war if that's what you want to do.' He sat down, half-turned to Lot, then glanced back at Trystan, who hadn't spoken.

'Well? Is it? Got a tongue in your head?'

'Yes, Sire. It's what I want. Thank you. But —'

Corwynal groaned. *Just say yes and sit down, Trys!* Trystan glanced at him and Corwynal nodded, thinking he'd understood. But he hadn't.

'Forgive me, Sire, but if I've earned my place in the war-band today, then so has Corwynal.'

'Corwynal?' Predictably, his father's face darkened. *Don't anger him Trys. Let me do that. Let me be the one to bear his displeasure.* 'Has he indeed!' His father turned to him, his eyes cold, his lips thinned in disapproval, and when he spoke his voice was as soft as sifting ash in an empty grate. Nevertheless it carried to every corner of the hall. 'Do you think that by defying me and riding off with a band of peasants, foolishly trying to hold an impossible position and having to be rescued by the war-band gives you the right to a place with Trystan and the others?'

'That's not fair!' Trystan objected.

'Be silent!' The King rose to his feet once more and turned back to Corwynal. 'Do you?'

He held his father's eyes and said nothing but had little hope of being let off so lightly.

'Do you want to leave Lothian?'

Say no, he thought. *Convince him you want to stay and he'll send you away.* But he wasn't there for that sort of deception. He was there for justice.

'Yes,' he said.

His father looked at him long and hard, his expression unreadable.

'Go then.' He took his seat once more and waved a hand in weary dismissal. Despite himself, Corwynal's heart lifted. Was it over then, his punishment? Was his father giving him his freedom, and with honour? But of course he wasn't. 'However, I'm afraid I can't allow you to join Lothian's war-band,' his father continued. 'You're not fit to join them. Look at you – an old man, well past your prime.'

'That's not fair!' Trystan repeated, but Corwynal gripped his arm to silence him.

'I'll go with the levy then,' he said bitterly. 'Lothian needs all the men it can get, even those past their prime.'

But his father still wasn't satisfied.

'No. The levy won't leave for several days. If you want to leave Lothian, you go tomorrow. Perhaps Lot would allow you to join his war-band?' He turned to Lot with a smile of quite malicious sweetness. 'Will you take him, for what's he's worth?'

Lot scratched at his beard, irritated at being put in this position.

'Thing is, Corwynal, we're going to fight the Caledonians . . .'

Something red flared behind Corwynal's eyes. 'You doubt my loyalty?!'

'No, but —'

'Does anyone here—' He turned to face the hall, his voice rising to a shout. '—doubt – my – *loyalty?!*'

No-one said anything, but all around the hall men he knew wouldn't meet his eyes. Even Blaize had his hands over his face and was shaking his head in despair.

'I don't,' Trystan said staunchly, and somehow his support just made it worse.

'Listen, man,' Lot hissed at Corwynal. 'I need that levy. I need you to arm and provision them.' He needed Corwynal to back down.

'But my dear Lot, you mustn't be concerned about the levy!' Rifallyn said in apparent surprise. 'Do you imagine that if you take Corwynal you won't get it? Nothing could be further from the truth. My Steward will arrange it for you. My new Steward. Corwynal ceased to hold that position as of this morning when he defied me.'

The silence grew even heavier.

'May I enquire, Rifallyn, as to the identity of your new Steward?' Lot asked carefully.

The King smiled and looked around the room, letting his gaze fall first on one and then another. All paled and shifted nervously. 'I haven't decided yet,' he said, amused at having caused so much disquiet.

'You can't do this!' Trystan protested.

'Can't, Trystan?' Rifallyn said in silkily dangerous tones. 'Believe me when I tell you that I can.'

'But it's not fair! What has Corwynal done? What is his crime? To ask if I can go with the war-band? Well, if that's his crime, it's mine too. All I wanted was to share what I thought you'd given me. But if you grudge me that then I'll share his punishment too. I'll stay here in Lothian. But please, for Lothian's sake, keep Corwynal as Steward!'

Oh, Trystan! Corwynal thought, his eyes blurring.

His father turned to him. 'Is that what you want? To be Steward? But I thought you wanted to go to war. Do make up your mind.'

Choose! he was saying. *Choose between us. Choose between two fates; watch Trystan die in battle while you stand helplessly by, or stay in Lothian and kill an old man who's given you every reason to do so, and who's giving you reason even now. There is no compromise. Even for you, whose whole life has been a compromise. Choose, Corwynal!* But he'd already chosen. He'd come for justice, and not only for Trystan. He'd come for himself. If he was to leave Lothian, he was going to leave with as much honour as he could scrape together.

He walked towards his father, placed his fists on the table in front of him and leant forward. He spoke softly, as his father had done, but the whole hall heard what he said for no-one spoke and no-one moved.

'I don't want to be your Steward. But I'm still Lothian's Steward until you replace me. Lot wants his levy and I'll give it to him. He wants to leave tomorrow. He can do that too, with five hundred men, horses, arms and supplies. By tomorrow.'

'Steady on, Corwynal!' Lot exclaimed. 'You can't do it by tomorrow!'

'I can do it, Lot. Give me until nightfall.' Right then it seemed the easiest thing in the world. 'Then accept me into your war-band.'

'We had a conversation the other day,' Lot reminded him. 'About something I wanted you to do first . . .'

'I'll do it,' Corwynal said, without hesitation. *Anything*, he'd promised a god. 'I'll go to Selgovia.'

A slow smile of satisfaction spread over Lot's face.

'Until nightfall then.' Lot got to his feet and left the hall. Only when he'd done so did Corwynal look at his father.

'Selgovia?' For a moment Corwynal thought he heard confusion and concern in his father's voice. But no, he must be mistaken. He had to be mistaken or else he wouldn't be able to say the thing that had to be said to fulfil his promises both to a god and to Trystan.

'Why not? Why should you care where I go? You're sending me away, as you did once before, but this time I won't come back.'

He looked around the hall, in defiance, in pride, and in farewell. He'd made the sacrifice now, and given up Lothian. In the shadows near the door an antlered head nodded in satisfaction. Then the God vanished once more. Corwynal knew it wouldn't be long before the pain began, but the wine dulled his senses. Perhaps that's why what he'd said didn't seem to be enough. He looked at his father and knew they'd never be reconciled now. That had always been a foolish hope. And so he sacrificed that too.

'I won't come back to Lothian until you beg me.' The colour drained from his father's face as Corwynal repeated his mother's words of thirty years before. He leant forward until his face was close to his father's. 'Not until you *beg* me!'

5

FIVE HUNDRED MEN BY NIGHTFALL

Ealhith didn't go to the hall. The smell of meat and ale made her stomach turn. Instead, she went to Corwynal's quarters above the stables, lay down on the pallet in her little room and wept until she felt sick. Too much had happened to her that day: seeing Aelfric again after believing him to be dead, Corwynal shouting at her, and finally what Blaize had said. *You won't be the first, or last, to be disappointed.* She understood now how foolish her hope had been and could see, all too clearly, her life stretching out before her, the years passing one by one as that tiny flame of hope flickered and died. Corwynal would never open that door, would never turn to her.

But a girl can't cry forever, no matter how badly her heart's broken, so she sniffed back her tears and wiped her face. The shouting from the hall had ceased, she noticed. Puzzled, she raised her head to listen and heard a pulse of voices as if the hall doors had briefly opened. A few moments later, someone stumbled up the stairs, someone who tried to mount them and failed, someone who was drunk and therefore dangerous. She scrambled to her feet and reached for the bolt on her door. Then she heard his voice.

'Ealhith? Ealhith!' His voice was slurred and distorted, but only one man said her name in just that way.

'My Lord...?' She found him sitting on the bottom step, rain dripping from his hair, his head between his hands. Abruptly, he lurched forward and threw up a sour liquid that reeked of wine. *He's drunk*, she thought, astonished. Unlike the war-band, he drank rarely and then sparingly. Wine merely sharpened his tongue and made his early morning surliness worse than usual. But this went far beyond that. She held him as he retched, one hand on his forehead, her other arm around his shoulders, until it was over. He leant back, sagged against her, and buried his head in the crook of her neck, sobs shaking his whole body.

'Come, my Lord.' She coaxed him to his feet and got him up the stairs, then persuaded him to sit down and drink some water. She even managed to get his wine-stained shirt and tunic off before he collapsed. Then she pulled off his boots and covered him with a blanket. 'Sleep now.' She drew back to allow him to do so, but he reached out and caught her wrist.

'I'm sorry I shouted at you,' he said, his voice still slurred. 'I'm sorry about the Angle. I'm sorry about everything.'

'It doesn't matter.'

'You're a good girl really,' he told her. 'Not pretty, of course. But good.'

It was the most praise she'd ever had from him, and she fought back tears as she tried to unwind his fingers from her wrist. His grip, however, was surprisingly firm.

'I always make you cry, don't I? Why is that? Is it because I said you weren't pretty?' He peered up at her and frowned as tears spilled down her cheeks. 'Don't cry, Ealhith.' He pulled her down to sit beside him. 'I'll need you tomorrow.'

'Why, Lord?'

He frowned, as if struggling to chase down a thought, then shrugged. 'Don't remember. Just something I have to do tomorrow. It can wait. Everything can wait . . .'

He let go of her wrist, but only to slide his hand up her arm. Her heart thudded hard and fast behind her breastbone as she saw something change in his eyes. His fingers gripped her shoulder and pulled her closer.

His mouth tasted of sickness, his breath of sour wine, but Ealhith didn't care. He was kissing her, one hand moving to twist itself in her hair, the other sliding across her back to pull her closer still. His tongue probed her mouth and his teeth bit her lips as urgency grew in him. He needed her now, not tomorrow, and now might be the only time she'd ever have.

He wasn't gentle, but she didn't care about that either. All that mattered was his skin on hers, his hands awakening the strangest of sensations, her own fingers tracing his patterns as she'd always longed to do. His urgency roused something inside her she'd never expected to feel. Indeed, nothing about this was as she'd expected, being neither as painful nor as pleasurable as they said. There was pain, true, but it was brief, and it seemed to Ealhith that her body welcomed it, that she melted towards him, enclosed him within herself to give him the oblivion he needed. Not tomorrow, but now. Blaize was both right and wrong, she thought at the end, when the man she loved cried out and shuddered against her, then grew still, his breathing easing into sleep, one arm pinning her down. She hadn't been the last to be disappointed. She hadn't been disappointed at all.

⸙

Corwynal woke with a sense of well-being, a feeling that he'd slept properly for once and, judging by the angle of sunlight coming through the slats in the door, for longer than usual. He lay still, his body heavy and his mind sluggish, and watched motes of dust dance in the shafts of light. Gradually, however, he was overcome by the growing and unsettling conviction that the lateness of the morning was not a good thing. There was something he ought to be doing, though he couldn't think what it was. Then, in a strident echo, he heard his own voice ringing in his ears.

Five hundred men, horses, arms and supplies. By nightfall.

His sense of well-being fled. His head began to pound, and his stomach swirled as he tasted bile at the back of his throat. He groaned, fighting nausea, as the room spun in dizzy spirals.

'What's the matter, Lord?'

Someone sat down beside him, shutting out the sunlight for a moment. Soft hair brushed against his cheek and the voice was soft too. But even a soft voice thundered in his pounding head.

'What have I done!?' he muttered.

He felt a hand on his shoulder and realised it was only his slave, Ealhith. 'It wasn't what you think,' she said. 'You didn't—'

He groaned again, remembering. 'I did. I promised to find five hundred men, and to arm, mount and supply them by nightfall.'

She sat back, her hand falling away. 'Is that all you remember?'

I will never come back to Lothian until you beg me. He remembered that too. It hurt now, quite badly.

'Is there something else I should remember?'

Ealhith didn't answer immediately, but when she did, her voice was no longer soft. 'No, nothing else, Lord. You argued with the King and then you came here. You were ill.'

'I'm still ill.'

Corwynal closed his eyes. Had he really promised to supply the levy in a day? It would take three days at least. He tried to work out how much he could get done by nightfall and what corners he could cut, but the immensity of the task made him dizzy. His stomach began to force its way up his throat.

'Get out!' he gasped. 'Right now!'

Ealhith ran off, slamming the door behind her, and he was violently sick, retching up a sour flood of wine until his stomach was painfully empty. He was still retching weakly when the door opened once more.

'Charming!' Blaize said, tutting in disgust. 'But you'll feel better when you've had some breakfast.' He held out a dish that reeked, to Corwynal's newly fastidious nose, of rotting fish.

Corwynal groaned and turned his head away. 'Just let me die.'

'Nonsense! They're all waiting to be told what to do. Come on. You need to get up.'

His head was still pounding, but he forced himself into a sitting position and eyed, with a nauseous tightening of his throat, the reeking mess in the dish Blaize was waving under his nose. For reasons Corwynal could no longer remember, he'd taken off all his clothes before falling asleep. Now, with considerable disquiet, he contemplated the effort it would take to put them on again.

Five hundred men, horses, arms and supplies. By nightfall. Right at that moment, he couldn't even put on his clothes. But he was going to have to. Slowly, aware of the aches of the previous day joining the new ones in his head, he pulled on the breeches that were lying on the floor and took the dish from Blaize. It was some sort of green porridge and tasted foul. He could only keep it from coming up again by gulping down the cup of water Blaize handed him. It was cold and seemed to clear his head a little, so he drank another and braced himself to face the day.

They were indeed waiting for him. Trystan was sitting on the edge of the horse trough, Madawg standing next to him, leaning on a spear.

'You look terrible!' Trystan observed with a frown, but Blaize just laughed.

'Have you never seen your brother with a hangover?'

'Hangover? You weren't drunk, were you?' In other circumstances, Trystan's dawning comprehension and disappointment might have been comical. 'Is that why you—?'

'Trystan!' Blaize snapped, and Trystan closed his lips on whatever he'd been about to say, but he looked embarrassed, and no wonder. Corwynal had made a fool of himself by drunkenly promising something that was impossible. Somehow Trystan's embarrassment was harder to bear than his father's contempt. But he'd show them, all of them.

'It *can* be done,' Corwynal insisted, because it *had* to be done. 'But I'll need your help, Trys. I'll need everyone's help.

᯼

Corwynal worked like a slave for the rest of that all-too-short day, and made everyone else work like a slave too, even Madawg, who wasn't used to work. His head was aching, his stomach sour, and his temper as brittle as a shard of ice. Eventually, however, whatever Blaize had put in that green mess took effect, and by late afternoon he felt more like himself. Or perhaps it was simply that by then he'd begun to believe it really was possible – men, horses, arms and supplies for them all, for an unknown length of time, in unknown territory, in unknown conditions. And that meant milled grain and sacks to hold it, wagons to transport the sacks and horses to pull the wagons, then feed for the horses, for it was too early in the year for forage. He needed men to care for the horses, drive the wagons, mill the grain, and make the sacks. All that was just for the grain to feed the men. There were also tents and weapons and mounts and remounts to be found . . .

He made enemies that day and lost the few friends he'd had. He used all the little charm he possessed, and when that ran out, he unleashed his temper and shouted until he got what he wanted. Not everything, of course. Despite his ridiculous promise, it wouldn't be perfect, but by the end of the afternoon he had most of the men, with more on their way, at least half the supplies and horses, and pledges for the rest.

'You'll have to make sure it all gets sent on,' he told Ealhith when he returned to his room to collect his gear. It was only then he remembered he'd be leaving Dunpeldyr that night and never coming back, and that there were a great many people he wouldn't have time to say goodbye to. Perhaps that was for the best, but this particular parting was one he couldn't avoid.

Ealhith was folding one of his shirts with deft flicks of her wrists and smoothing the creases from the linen with the backs of her fingers. She had her back to him, and there was an odd rigidity to the curve of her spine. He saw a tear splash onto the shirt and considered pretending he'd forgotten something and leaving. But he doubted if he could have achieved what he'd done that day without her help, so he owed her a little kindness.

'What's wrong?'

'Nothing,' she said, still with her back to him.

Corwynal ran a hand through his hair in frustration. He didn't have time for this. 'Is it the Angle?' Girls, in his limited experience, cried over men, children and small animals. 'Were you really childhood sweethearts?'

She turned, dashing tears from her face with the back of one hand. 'Is that what you think?'

In truth, he hadn't given it any thought. 'It seems unlikely, since you were a servant and he was a warrior.'

'Can't a warrior feel affection for a servant?' She looked up at him without dropping her gaze for once. 'Even a servant might mean something to someone,' she said as she turned back to her packing. 'But not to you. You'll hand me on to the next Steward like a sack of grain.'

'Ealhith . . .' Corwynal sighed. This was exactly the sort of scene he'd wanted to avoid. Yet she was right. He hadn't thought about what would happen to her when he left. 'I'm sorry about the Angle, if you care for him. I'm sorry he was captured, but there's little I can do about it now. He's Trystan's slave, not mine.'

'Prince Trystan listens to you,' she said, turning back to him.

Corwynal smiled wryly, wishing he did, and his smile encouraged her to move closer and put a hand on his arm.

'Please, Lord – take Aelfric with you.'

He stared at her. 'Have you lost your mind?'

'He's a warrior. He can fight for you.'

'Fight for me? An Angle? A man sworn to kill me? Although what he thinks I've done, I can't imagine.'

'It's because of me,' she began, her face colouring. 'Because you have me as your slave and he thinks you—'

Feet clattered up the stairs and the door burst open.

'Lot wants to speak to you,' Trystan announced.

Corwynal didn't want to speak to Lot, but he grasped at this opportunity to escape and, with a gesture intended to convey to Ealhith both apology and farewell, he hefted his gear and followed Trystan down the stairs.

'Why was she crying?' Trystan asked as they threaded their way through the muddy confusion of men and horses and carts in the courtyard.

'Ealhith? Oh, some stupid notion that I might take the Angle with us.'

Trystan stopped and looked at him as if this wasn't an entirely insane idea.

'I guess you said no . . . ?'

'Of course I said no!' He wondered what Trystan intended to do with the man, but only briefly. There were more important things to worry about. 'What does Lot want?'

'Oh, some question about the delegation to Selgovia,' Trystan said airily.

'Why? Who's going?'

'You are, of course!' Trystan turned to him with a frown. 'You said you would – last night. Were you really so drunk you don't remember?'

Five hundred men, horses, arms and supplies. By nightfall. He remembered that. What else had he promised? Dimly, something came back to him. *Does anyone here doubt my loyalty?* He thought he'd dreamt that, and that he'd dreamt the other thing too. *I'll go to Selgovia.* Had he really been that stupid?

'You don't remember,' Trystan concluded bitterly, observing Corwynal's growing horror. 'And I thought you meant it. I thought you wanted to prove something.'

'I don't need to prove anything, and if I did, I'd prove it by going with Lot's war-band to fight the Caledonians.'

'Anyone can do that,' Trystan said with a dismissive wave of a hand. 'This is something only you can do.' Corwynal heard an echo of Blaize's arguments in his words. 'Go on. Lot wants to go over the details.' Trystan nodded towards the hall but didn't go in with him. It wasn't until later that Corwynal understood why not.

※

The hall was virtually empty, though a few slaves were scuttling about, clearing up the mess of the previous evening's feast. Lot was sitting at the high table with the wine-stained map spread out before him. Standing behind Lot, like a shadow, was the man Corwynal had both hoped and feared never to see again.

'Well, Corwynal,' his father said mildly. 'Ready to leave, are you?' There was no mention of the fact that he'd raised the supplies for the levy in a day. No expression of surprise or pleasure or pride. No regret that his son was leaving Dunpeldyr and never coming back. Nothing. But what else had he expected?

'Yes, but not to go to Selgovia.'

Lot jumped to his feet, smashed his fist on the table, and glared at him.

'That was the deal! Maybe you were drunk, but you said you'd go! Everyone heard you. If you want to ride with my war-band, you go to Selgovia first!'

'No. I'm going north with Trystan.'

Lot glanced at Rifallyn, and it was he who answered.

'Trystan's not going north. He's going to Selgovia himself,' his father said with a thin smile.

'What?! Whose idea was this?!'

'Trystan's,' Lot said.

'But he wanted to go with the war-band!' But even as Corwynal protested, he understood what Lot and Blaize had done. They'd told Trystan what they hoped to gain – a war-band of Selgovian archers – and implied they'd be Trystan's to command, his very own war-band. They wouldn't have told him of the dangers, of the Selgovians' death-trees and their Caledonian allies, but, even if they had, it wouldn't have altered Trystan's determination to go. What astonished him was that Lot and Blaize had convinced his father to grant Trystan's wish.

'You agreed to this?'

'I agreed,' Rifallyn said with a shrug. 'Lot tells me this venture is a matter of diplomacy rather than force of arms, and it seems to me that diplomacy is something you've yet to teach Trystan. This little expedition might be instructive for the future King of Lothian.'

'A little expedition? Instructive? Surely you realise how dangerous it will be?'

'I'm sure you'll be able to protect him,' his father said. 'Or he you, given that he's saved your life twice in as many days. As for the Selgovae, they're stubborn, quick to take offence, and with more pride than is warranted, but these are qualities with which you must surely be familiar. So, what are you afraid of? Can it be that you don't wish to meet their allies, the Caledonians? Is that it? Better to meet them in Selgovia, Corwynal, than in the heart of a battle in Manau, because there you really would have to make a decision.'

And so he had no choice. *Anything!* the God reminded him. Corwynal glanced around the hall and heard the rustle of wings high in the rafters, but it was only a pigeon dropping to the floor to peck in the rushes. Nevertheless, he was certain Arddu was laughing at him as he turned to Lot, who couldn't prevent himself from smirking at his own cleverness.

'All right,' Corwynal agreed sourly. 'But you'd better tell me how I'm supposed to speak to them. It took me months to arrange a meeting last year, and I've no desire to find myself strung up on one of their death trees because I've strayed across their border without permission.'

'Oh, that's all been arranged,' Lot said with maddening, and probably misplaced, confidence. 'A guide will meet you in Trimontium, at the old Roman Mansio by the western gate. He'll make himself known to you and your party. Only a small one, I'm afraid. Just you, Trystan and Gaheris; I can't spare any more men at the moment.'

'Blaize . . . ?'

'No. I need him with me in the north.' Lot glanced down at the map. 'Here,' he said, pointing to the fort at the east end of the northern Wall. 'Camelon. That's where the war-bands are to muster. We'll move west from there after the Beltein truce, so you have a month to take care of this Selgovian business. Until then we'll be raiding in Fife. We need to get control of the grain-lands, and it's a good way to blood the men and get them working together . . .'

It made sense, Corwynal supposed. Whenever there was a war, both sides sought to control the rich farmlands of the Caledonian kingdom of Fife, and its people would end up paying tribute to whoever won. This had been going on for so many generations that the farmers just sighed and gave in, so there wouldn't be that much fighting. Selgovia, however, was a different matter, the wild piece in the game of kingdoms that he had to turn to Lot's advantage. It would be a difficult and dangerous fight with a difficult and dangerous people but, now he'd resigned himself to going, he craved the challenge almost as much as Trystan craved battle. Perhaps he did indeed have something to prove, and perhaps Selgovia was the place to prove it – landlocked Selgovia, a land with no coast, no shingle beach, nowhere waves could break. No black ship. That realisation stripped away the last of his doubts, and, for a moment, while the elation lasted, he forgot he was leaving Lothian forever.

Aelfric could smell it. It was stronger than his own sweat, stronger than the reek of the salve on his shoulder. He could hear it in the shouts of men, their boasts and nervous laughter, the whine of the whetstone, and the creaking of wagons as they were loaded up with stores. Lothian was going to war and Aelfric, warrior of Bernicia, a man made for war, was a prisoner and a slave.

He jerked at the chains in frustration, but there were no weaknesses in the chains or the manacles, or in the post to which they were fastened. He'd have to rely on the weakness of men if he was going to get out of this fucking storeroom. But no-one came in, and the guard on the door refused to talk to him. He had orders not to, he'd said resentfully, as if, given the choice, he would happily have sat down with Aelfric and debated the issues of the day with him. The Britons were like that, Aelfric reflected, with a mixture of contempt and exasperation. Dreamers, the lot of them, but not as weak as he'd thought.

He'd been a hot-headed fool, and he understood it now. He should never have come to Dunpeldyr in the way he had. But he'd been bored in Bernicia, so when the news came that Ealhith was alive – Ealhith, whose loss had been a great hole in his heart – he'd grasped the opportunity with both of his extremely capable hands. He'd been angry, naturally, given her circumstances – slave to a painted savage of a Caledonian – so it wasn't surprising he'd sworn that very public oath. There was a lot he regretted now: his haste, hiring those pirate scum, his plan to storm Dunpeldyr and somehow find one girl among hundreds. But he didn't regret that oath, especially now he'd seen the man. He must be a spell-weaver, like the druid, because why else would Ealhith imagine she was in love with him? The Caledonian was twice her age at least, and far from handsome, being slight and dark, with a proud face and cursed cold eyes. Now, if it had been the boy, the one Aelfric still couldn't believe had beaten him, he might have understood it...

'How's the shoulder?' The voice snapped Aelfric out of his reverie. He jumped to his feet and lunged forward, but the boy – for it was him – stood just outside the reach of his chains. 'It won't heal if you do that,' he pointed out.

'What do you care?' Aelfric growled, retreating to the post. He leant back against it with his arms folded across his chest, and regarded the boy uneasily, not because he'd beaten him, but because when he'd first seen him, surging out of that cursed river with a sword in his hand, Aelfric had thought he must be an elf. Didn't they say the lands of the Britons were full of spirits, elves, wights and ghosts? It had put Aelfric off his stride, and that was doubtless why the boy, together with that Caledonian bastard, had been able to beat him. But, though the boy was pretty enough to be an elf, he was a bit too solid to be a spirit and was finding all this a little too amusing for Aelfric's liking.

'I care because a man with a ruined shoulder's no use to me.'

'I've no wish to be of use to you – or that Caledonian bastard.'

'You mean my brother, I assume?' the boy said, his eyes sharpening.

'Brother?' He remembered now that the boy had claimed it by the ford.

'Half-brother. Didn't Blaize explain? No? I suppose not. My uncle likes to be mysterious.'

'Uncle?'

'Blaize is half-brother to the King,' the boy said in an off-hand manner, as if this would explain everything, but it didn't.

'King?'

The boy threw his head back and laughed. 'You don't know who any of us are, do you?'

'I don't care who you are, boy! Now tell me what you want with me and be done with it!'

The boy carried on laughing, but after a moment he sobered and leant forward.

'I want you to join my war-band.'

Now it was Aelfric's turn to laugh. 'Are you mad? You expect me to fight for you against my own people? I don't know how it is in Lothian, but in Bernicia slaves don't fight, especially when they're in chains. And how does a boy of your age come to have a war-band?'

'I'm seventeen, old enough for a lot of things. Did you fight at the Glein?'

Aelfric didn't see what that had to do with anything, but he nodded. It had been a good fight. They should have won.

'Then you would have seen Arthyr. The bear's his symbol, as yours is. One day I'll have a war-band like Arthyr's – men who choose to fight for me, with no allegiance to country or people. I already have the beginnings of my war-band; two princes of the Briton lands ride with me, and we're riding to war.' He cocked his head at the noises outside. 'Do you hear that? The war-band leaves tonight,' the boy told him. 'But not to fight your people, at least not yet. They're riding north, against the Caledonians.'

'And what use would a war-band of Princes have for a chained and weaponless slave?' Aelfric asked, trying to hide his growing excitement. 'And why would you trust me not to stab you in the back whenever I get the chance?'

'Why would I trust you?' The boy smiled. 'Because I'm a good judge of character? Because I like taking risks? Both these reasons. But mainly because I know a bit more about you now.'

Ealhith! Aelfric concluded. *What has she told him?*

The boy's smile widened, as if he'd seen into Aelfric's thoughts. 'You like adventure, by all accounts, Aelfric of Gyrwum, and that's what I'm offering you. Given the choice between living for the rest of your life as a slave in Dunpeldyr, and coming with me, I know what I'd choose if I were you. But you'll have to swear an oath.'

'An oath?'

'Swear to serve me and protect all who ride with me.'

So this was the catch. Aelfric tried to tell himself he'd seen it coming. 'I've already sworn an oath. I can't swear another.'

'Why not, if the second oath doesn't conflict with the first?'

'I've sworn to kill your brother.' Then he understood. 'You want me to go with you so that Caledonian bastard will be safe, skulking here in Dunpeldyr like the coward he is!'

The boy was a blur of movement, light catching on iron. A hand gripped Aelfric's throat, forcing his head back, and a dagger pricked into the soft flesh of his neck. He was held as much by the cold, hard gaze of the boy's no longer laughing eyes as by his impossibly strong fingers.

'You can try to kill my brother, but I won't let you insult him! He's not afraid of you, chained or not, and never will be. You call him a coward, but a coward would have knifed you in the night, and yet you've spent that night under his protection. Who do you think arranged all this?' He let Aelfric go and gestured at the fresh straw, the blanket, the food – which hadn't been bad – the pitcher of water, and the bucket that served as a latrine. 'Who helped Blaize treat your wound? Who placed a guard on the door, not to stop you escaping, but to protect you from those with reason to hate all Angles? Not me, who should have thought of these things, but my brother. So don't speak of him like that again or I'll leave you here, chained like a bear, to work the fields by day and amuse the men in the hall by night.'

'No! Not that! Please, my Lord . . .'

Aelfric could tell the boy meant it, and for one horrific moment he thought it was himself pleading for mercy. But it was Ealhith. She'd burst into the stable, past the guard, and fallen at the boy's feet. 'Please, Lord . . .'

'I told you to wait outside,' the boy said, then turned to the guard who'd followed her in. 'No, it's all right, she can stay.' He gestured for the man to leave.

'Aelfric doesn't understand, Lord,' Ealhith explained. Which was a masterly piece of understatement.

'Then I must make him,' the boy said. 'So, understand this, Aelfric of Bernicia. My brother isn't afraid of you, and if you were to fight once more, he'd defeat you. But I won't let you fight him, and I won't let him fight you. Try to kill him and you'll find me standing between you. And you won't defeat me either.'

'I won't be foresworn!'

'Oh, you and your stupid oath!' Ealhith burst out. 'Is that all that matters to you? What about a promise? You said you'd come back, but you didn't. You broke that promise, Aelfric. So you owe *me* an oath!'

And Aelfric knew what that oath would be. 'I've sworn to kill Corwynal of Lothian,' he insisted. 'I'm going to fight him, man to man, and this time I'll win, and I *will* kill him. I won't be foresworn.'

'When?' the boy asked.

'When what?'

'When did you say you'd kill him?'

'I . . . I didn't say.'

'Then you needn't fight him straight away. Not that I'm going to let you kill him, in a fight or otherwise. I'm just pointing out that your two oaths needn't conflict. Swear and your chains will be removed.'

Aelfric's immediate reaction was to refuse. An oath was an oath, not something hedged about by conditions like a lawspeaker's judgement. It was a pledge to the gods. A day's reflection, however, had taught him the value of thinking things through. He'd come to kill one man, but, chained as he was, had no prospect of doing so. The fulfilment of his oath might, of necessity, be delayed, possibly indefinitely. He needed to get himself free and his weapons back, so, right then, he was willing to consider anything.

Serve me and protect all who ride with me. Aelfric didn't like the idea, but the boy hadn't said for how long and, anyway, it made sense to wait until his shoulder had healed before fighting the Caledonian once more. Because, oath or no oath, that was what he was going to do, and this time he'd beat the man. He had to, if only for the sake of his own reputation. No-one was going to be able to claim that Aelfric of Gyrwum had been defeated by a painted Caledonian bastard well past his prime. If that meant swearing the boy's oath, he'd just have to do it.

Ealhith was a difficulty, however, because she'd want him to promise not to kill the man. But she was going to be disappointed in that. *I will fight and kill Corwynal of Lothian – one day, when my shoulder has healed.* It didn't sound quite right, and Aelfric suspected the gods would agree, because oaths were supposed to be simple. But nothing in life, he'd discovered, was ever as simple as it ought to be.

'Decide quickly,' the boy said. 'I'm leaving at sunset, with or without you.'

'Very well,' Aelfric said heavily. 'I swear to serve you and protect all who ride with you. But one day I'll fight and kill your brother.'

The boy nodded. 'You can try. Now swear an oath to Ealhith.'

Aelfric turned to her, bracing himself to refuse her.

'Bring him back,' she said. 'Protect him and bring him back to Dunpeldyr.'

'Who?' Aelfric was confused once more. Did she mean the boy? Was it him she was in love with after all?

'Corwynal. I need you to promise to bring him back to Dunpeldyr. Alive and unharmed.'

'But—'

'My brother's going with us,' the boy said, his eyes glinting with delight at having tricked Aelfric so cleverly. 'He's part of my war-band, and you've just sworn to serve me and protect all who ride with me. In fact, I want you to be his personal bodyguard.'

'No!'

'You swore.'

'You bastard! You jumped up little—'

Ealhith gasped, but the boy just smiled. 'No, actually,' he said coolly. 'Neither a bastard, nor a jumped up anything. I'm Trystan, Prince of Lothian, heir to the throne.'

Which explained a lot, Aelfric thought sourly. But not everything. Then the pieces of the puzzle began to slot together. *Brother, half-brother, uncle, King...*

'Yes,' the boy added, his smile broadening to a grin. 'My brother is Prince Corwynal and, regrettably, *is* a bastard, though I don't advise you to call him that in my hearing. You probably thought the Steward of Lothian was a freedman of no account. Well, he's not, though that's irrelevant. You swore an oath to me. Now swear one to Ealhith.'

This one was harder, now he knew the facts. He'd have to protect the bloody man when all he wanted to do was kill him. Ealhith wanted him to bring the Caledonian back to Dunpeldyr, alive and unharmed – but she hadn't said willingly. She hadn't said free. *I'll bring him back in fucking chains*, Aelfric decided, his spirits lifting.

'I swear,' he said. 'No man but me is getting to kill him. So I'll bring him back, alive – but then he'll be mine.' By which time whatever enchantment he'd put on Ealhith would have worn off and she'd be glad to see the man dead, glad to return to Bernicia where she and Aelfric belonged.

The boy Trystan nodded his assent and Aelfric grinned. He was free, and he was going to war. Once he got his weapons back, he was going to kill not just one Caledonian, but tens, maybe hundreds. Then he'd have the pleasure of dragging the one Caledonian he wasn't allowed to kill back to Dunpeldyr and forcing him to fight. Life, suddenly, was full of promise.

※

'What's he doing there?' Corwynal demanded of Trystan, as their pathetically small party got ready to leave, a party that had, unexpectedly, increased to four.

'Him?' Trystan eyed the Angle perched awkwardly on the back of a big roan gelding. 'Trying to stay on that horse, I reckon.' He grinned at Corwynal's expression. 'He's coming with us. Ealhith came to see me after you'd turned her down and, to be honest, I wasn't sure what else to do with him.' His grin broadened. 'Don't worry! He won't run away or try to kill us all in the night. I made him swear an oath, and the Angles take their oaths seriously. He's promised not to kill you, not yet anyway, so I've made him your bodyguard.'

'My bodyguard?! What do you take me for?'

'A stubborn pig-headed Caledonian! He's mine. He goes with us.'

And so Corwynal acquired an Angle bodyguard, a man he suspected would be a thorn in his flesh for a very long time to come.

The sun had set before everything was ready. Sacrifices were made to the gods, and those men of Dunpeldyr who followed Chrystos were blessed by their priests. Nevertheless, there was still light in the sky as Corwynal watched Lot lead his men, Lothian's war-band, and the levy, out through the main gate and down the track to the foot of the hill. The sky was a jumbled mass of slate-grey clouds, but to the west the air was clear, and the sun was setting in a long line of brilliant light that cast a golden glow over Dunpeldyr and burnished the thatch of the huts and stables to gleaming bronze. Torchlight caught on spear-blades and burned in the amber eyes of Lothian's wolf that was straining on the standards in a rising wind. A night and a day would bring the men beneath the looming mass of Dun Eidyn, principal stronghold of Eastern Manau, and from there they'd head west for Camelon. Corwynal's route lay in the other direction, south-west across the hills to strike the road that ran at their foot, and thence to the old Roman settlement of Trimontium where they were to meet the man who was to guide them to into Selgovia. Then, no doubt, they'd follow the Tuaidh Water upstream to Meldon, the principal Selgovian stronghold.

Corwynal had hoped to slip away without being noticed, but his father was waiting by the gate as they came to leave, and he braced himself for a final meeting that would be a parting also.

Rifallyn exchanged a few words with Trystan who nodded and trotted down the track with Gaheris and the Angle, and Corwynal nudged Janthe to follow them.

'Wait.' His father stepped into his path.

'There's nothing more to be said between us.'

Rifallyn shook his head. 'I wonder if you'll ever understand why I've done this in the way I have?'

'I doubt it. I've never understood why you hate me so much, and why you made me hate you in return.'

'Hate...' his father murmured. 'Such a straightforward emotion. So much safer! But I don't delay you to talk of you and I, Corwynal. I merely ask you to be careful in Selgovia.'

'How can you say that when it was you who gave Trystan permission to go?'

'Have you not always tried to protect him? Was that not your duty? But now your roles have reversed, and he's afraid for you. It seemed a kindness to let him go.' He smiled thinly. 'You accused me of showing no kindness to either of you. In this, perhaps, I've made amends, at least to Trystan.'

'But not to me.'

His father sighed. 'No, not to you. It's not what you want. What you want isn't in me to give.'

'You sent me away thirty years ago, and I came back. This time I won't.'

Corwynal gathered the reins in his hands, but, before he could nudge Janthe into motion, someone darted forward and grasped the bridle.

'Don't say that, Lord!' Ealhith begged. 'You *will* come back!'

To his annoyance and shame, Corwynal realised he still hadn't made provision for her future. But the solution came from an unlikely source.

'Give her to me,' his father said. 'She could be useful to me once you're gone.'

'Useful?'

The King raised an eyebrow at his tone. 'Oh, not in the way you so clearly imagine! I meant that, as your slave, Ealhith knows how this kingdom runs, and I've always been of the opinion that knowledge is better used than squandered. And, in case you're concerned, I'll be kind to her, kinder perhaps than you have been.'

What did his father mean? Hadn't he rescued Ealhith from that warrior, taken her as his own slave when he hadn't wanted a slave, given her a room of her own and even fitted a bolt on her door? Not only had he never touched her himself, he'd made sure no-one else did either – all of which was a great deal more than any slave had the right to expect. Even so, he felt she ought to have the choice of her next master.

'Is this what you want, Ealhith?'

She nodded, and, when Rifallyn held out an imperious hand, she went to him without hesitation. Corwynal was conscious of a strange regret and an even stranger anger. He'd grown fond of the girl. Why did his father have to take everything of which he was fond?

'Very well,' he said, because he had no choice, and the King put a hand on Ealhith's shoulder, claiming ownership. She yielded but bore the weight. Beneath her slight frame she was a strong woman. She'd need to be. 'Goodbye, Sire.' He refused to call him Father.

'Goodbye, Corwynal. Go wherever your fate takes you, but always remember whose son you are.'

Corwynal kicked Janthe into a trot and rode through the gate, his eyes blurring in the smoke from the torches. He told himself he wouldn't look back but couldn't stop himself from doing so at the first turning of the track. They'd already turned away, his father leaning heavily on Ealhith's shoulder. But, as he watched, it seemed as if it was his father who supported Ealhith, and then, as they disappeared into the shadows of the gate, that the two of them supported one another.

PART II

SELGOVIA

SPRING 485 AD

6

THE BLACK WOODS OF SELGOVIA

Corwynal's party reached Trimontium after two nights on the road and two days of slate-grey palls of rain shot through with brilliant washes of light, strangely moody weather that had swung between the threat of winter and the promise of spring. His own mood, however, had remained wintry as they'd ridden further and further from Dunpeldyr, and he'd found he was homesick for a place to which he'd vowed never to return. But as they approached the town, his spirits began to lift. Leaving Lothian, he decided, was the best thing he could have done. Not for himself, but for the land of his birth. One day, Trystan would be King, and Corwynal owed it to Lothian that he prepare him as well as he could for that role. This journey was part of that preparation, and at least he and Trystan were together, which had to count for something.

Trimontium was a sprawl of buildings that had grown up in the shadow of the old Roman fortress. A faint echo of the town's past could be seen in the remains of the fort's ramparts, the squared terraces and buildings of dressed stone. For the most part, however, it was just like any other Briton settlement: a jumble of alleyways that led nowhere. A shroud of smoke hung over the place from the smokeries near the meat market and the smithies close to the walls, and there was a stench of ordure from the slaughterhouse, of urine from the tanneries, and the usual reek of any town: rotting vegetables, broiling meat and unwashed people.

The inhabitants themselves were oddly disappointing. The blood of Roman soldiers must still flow in the veins of the men and women who lived there, but there was little sign of it. In reality, Aelfric and Corwynal, with their foreign blood, were more exotic than anyone, and they attracted a fair amount of suspicious interest, particularly once they neared the Mansio that stood close by the western gate.

'In the name of all the Saints, will you get that beast under control!'

A young priest of Chrystos, judging by his habit, and a Scot, judging by his accent, had been riding ahead of them as they'd approached the gate. He too appeared to be making for the Mansio, but the narrow streets of the town were no place for someone like Aelfric who couldn't master his horse. The big roan took exception to a woman throwing a bucket of slops out of a doorway, and plunged forward, shouldering the Scot's sway-backed dun gelding to one side and crushing the man against the wall of a tannery.

'I thought you were keeping an eye on that cursed Angle,' Corwynal complained to Trystan, for this wasn't the first time Aelfric had lost control of his mount. But Trystan was too busy staring at the first Roman town he'd ever seen, and it was Gaheris who grabbed Aelfric's reins and dragged the roan away from the gelding, leaving Corwynal to apologise to the Scot.

'Sure, there's no harm done,' the young man said with a smile, for Corwynal had spoken in his own tongue, picked up years before when he'd fought Scots raiders in Galloway and acquired a couple of Scots slaves. Not that he intended mentioning this particular detail. They exchanged a few further words, and the Scot coaxed his nervous horse on down the alley. Trystan followed, but Corwynal held back, aware that someone was watching them.

A tall man in patched and faded hunting leathers was standing in the shelter of the gable end of a brewery. He was eying them intently, or possibly their horses, for Trystan's Rhydian, a grey stallion with a deep chest, strong hocks and an evil temper, always attracted attention, as did Corwynal's Janthe. The man appeared to be a huntsman; a quiver of arrows hung from one shoulder, an unstrung bow from the other, and a long-sheathed skinning knife was strapped to his thigh. He had a hunter's stealth too, for, between one moment and the next, he vanished, slipping like a lynx into the deeper shadows of the alleyway next to the brewery.

Corwynal dismissed the man as merely curious and caught up with the others, concerned that the Angle might cause further trouble. However, they stabled their horses without incident, hired a room for the night and went to join the company for the evening meal. The common room was almost full, but they found a table at which only one man sat, the young Scot they'd met in the alley. He'd thrown back the hood of his habit to reveal dark unruly hair and a pleasant, wind-beaten face. He looked to be only a couple of years older than Trystan.

Corwynal had little love for the priests of Chrystos, especially the ones who dripped poison into his father's ears, but those, for the most part, were from the lands of the Britons. The priests of the West, from the Island of Hibernia and the Scots' lands further north, were a different matter. These men avoided courts and kings and were more often to be found travelling the smaller roads and trackways, telling their stories to the folk of the countryside, and this young priest, judging by his dusty threadbare habit and half-starved appearance, was one of them.

He was a pleasant young man who made light of the incident outside, and was happy – enthusiastic, even – to share their meal of mutton stew and fresh barley bread, then to indulge Trystan's desire to practice the Scots' tongue that he'd also picked up.

'Conaire,' Trystan said in answer to Corwynal's raised eyebrow, naming a Scots warrior who'd joined Lothian's warband for a season some years before. 'I didn't just learn spearwork from him.' It wasn't long before he was plaguing the Scot for stories of his homeland. But other than saying he was from Dalriada, the Scots' lands that lay to the west of Galloway and Strathclyde, the priest said little about what had brought him east, and eventually he got up from the table and felt in the pocket of his habit for a few coins.

'I'm off to see if I can earn the cost of a bed.' He nodded across the room where a game of dice was in progress and went to join in.

'Aren't the S-S-Scots our enemies?' Gaheris asked once the Scot was out of earshot.

Corwynal shrugged. 'If you live in Galloway or Strathclyde and are raided all the time, perhaps, but here in the east we've no quarrel with them.' In truth, he'd liked most of the Scots he'd met, even the ones trying to kill him.

'He's not my enemy,' Trystan said with decision. 'Come on, Gaheris, let's go and see how he gets on.' They walked off to the other side of the room to watch the dice game, leaving Corwynal with Aelfric.

'Go after Trystan,' he told the Angle.

'What? How much trouble can he get into watching a dice game?'

But Corwynal knew Trystan better than anyone. 'Just do it.'

'I thought I was your bodyguard, Caledonian, not his,' the Angle grumbled, before getting up to follow the younger men.

Corwynal watched from a distance, but the game seemed amicable enough. The tall huntsman he'd seen outside the Mansio played briefly and badly, threw his dice to the floor in annoyance, then picked them up and gave up his place to the Scot. Various other men were knocked out by unlucky throws until only two were left, the Scot and a heavily built man who appeared to be a miller since his clothes and hair were liberally sprinkled with flour. At this point, Corwynal lost interest in the game and abandoned the table where they'd eaten in favour of a bench against the wall, away from the noise and heat.

'Games for children!' said the huntsman, emerging from the shadows to take a place on the bench beside him.

He was a man of between twenty and thirty years old, with a long, serious face. His braided dark brown hair was decorated with carved wooden rings, and he was dressed in a patched deerskin tunic. He looked out of place within the walls of a town, but Trimontium attracted many strange people.

'You're a Caledonian?' the man asked.

'I'm from Lothian.' Corwynal indicated the wolf embroidered on his tunic. 'We're all from Lothian.'

'Indeed?' The man seemed to doubt it. 'The younger ones have the look of Gododdin and the west. And the big one . . . I've heard tell of Angles.'

'He's a slave, taken in a raid.'

'*He* doesn't think he's a slave,' the huntsman said, nodding at Aelfric, who was still watching the game, and where an argument had broken out. Then a roar of disbelief greeted the next throw of the dice.

'You're cheating, you Scots bastard!' the miller shouted.

'No, he's not.' Trystan's voice rang out over the baying of the crowd.

Then all five hells broke loose.

Fuck horses, Aelfric had been thinking, as he'd walked across the room to watch the dice game. *Fuck Britons who won't walk when they can ride.* They must have arses of leather, he'd concluded. His own felt like one massive blister, and, from what the boy Trystan had told him, there was still a long way to go before they got to wherever it was they were going, all of it further and further from the sea. That had made Aelfric distinctly nervous, as had the woods they'd travelled through – dark woods, peopled by Thunor knew what creatures, all determined, Aelfric was convinced, to suck his courage away. That oath had been a big mistake. *Fight for me*, the boy had said. He hadn't said anything about fucking riding through fucking ghost-infested woods. First chance he got, Aelfric would be off, oath or no oath. And his gods must have been on his side for once, because it wasn't long before he got his chance.

'You're cheating, you Scots bastard!' The miller leant across the board to grasp the tunic of the Scots boy who'd shared their meal, the one Aelfric's Woden-cursed horse had crushed against a wall.

'No, he's not,' Trystan insisted, and, before Aelfric knew what was happening, the miller let the boy go, surged to his feet and grasped Trystan's expensive-looking tunic in a very large hand.

'Who're you to say he isn't, you cocky little lordling?!'

Trystan reached for his knife, but another man grabbed him by the arms and twisted them behind his back. The miller whipped out his own knife and pricked it at Trystan's throat, forcing his head back. The Caledonian, seeing this argument, leapt over benches and tables from the far side of the room, grabbed the weapons they'd been made to leave by the door, drew his sword and pulled Gaheris away, then tossed the Gododdin boy his own weapon, before edging back, looking for space. But the place was too crowded for a swordfight, and there wasn't much either of them could do as long as that knife was at Trystan's throat.

'No fighting!' The landlord rushed in, waving his arms. 'It's not allowed!'

No-one paid him any attention. A few of the men in the room made their escape, but others, companions of the miller, went for their own weapons and waited for some sign from their friend.

'The Scots bastard was cheating, and this young lord is going to say so, aren't you?' He thrust the knife up into the hollow below Trystan's jaw, forcing his head further back, but the boy met his eyes unflinchingly. The Scot was kneeling on the floor, feverishly gathering up the stake from the game that had been swept off the table, and stuffing rings and bent silver coins into a pouch at his waist. He ignored the bloodshed threatening to break out over his head until one of the miller's companions hauled him to his feet.

'I wasn't cheating, you godless ignorant pig!'

This is my chance! The miller had lowered his knife a fraction, and the Caledonian leapt into action. His weapon twisted in the air, catching the light, ready to smash down into the arm holding the knife. *Any moment now!* There would be so much blood and confusion it would be easy to slip away. The Caledonian brought his sword down hard, but it whistled through empty space, just past Aelfric's ear, to splinter the floorboards because, instead of stepping back into the shadows as he'd intended, Aelfric launched himself at the miller, punching his shoulder into the man's chest and driving him to the ground. The miller's knife spun harmlessly away, and Trystan, free of the man's grip, kicked out and sent the miller rolling across the floor to trip up his friends, who ended up in a pile on top of him. The Caledonian tossed Trystan his own scabbarded sword, and the boy drew it with a hiss of steel and backed towards the older man and Gaheris until at the three of them formed a shield-wall.

No chance! Aelfric thought. The three Britons were outnumbered by the miller's friends who'd picked themselves up and bunched together, forming a line between the Britons and the door. There was only one thing to be done. Aelfric roared and threw himself at the miller, his fists coming up. *Fight for me*, the boy had said. Right then, though, Aelfric was fighting for himself. *Fucking Britons*, he thought as he smashed his fist into the man's mouth with a satisfyingly wet splat, imagining as he did so that it was the Caledonian's teeth shattering beneath his knuckles. He slammed the miller in the stomach, leaving him gasping, and in Aelfric's mind it was the Caledonian he'd robbed of breath. Then he drove his knee up into the man's groin and the miller fell to his knees, clutching himself and squealing with pain and outrage. Aelfric stepped back, breathing hard, but it wasn't over. Behind him, Trystan, Gaheris and the Caledonian were backing towards a door at the rear of the room, but the miller's friends, realising they might escape, began to push forwards.

A lamp flew through the air and smashed on the floor right

in front of the miller's friends, sending shards of pottery and splashes of oil everywhere, and flame sprang up as the oil took light.

'Run!' someone yelled.

'Run!' The Caledonian echoed the shout and sprinted for the door. Trystan and Gaheris were already moving. Aelfric reached down, hauled the miller to his feet and tossed him through the blazing oil to crash into the mass of men who were coming for them. The Scot had vanished.

'Gaheris, get our gear! Trys, the horses!' They burst through the door and slammed it behind them. 'Come on, man!' the Caledonian yelled at him, but Aelfric had noticed a heavy oak dresser just behind the door and stopped to heave it away from the wall and send it crashing to the floor to block the corridor. *That'll hold them up!* Then, forgetting he was supposed to be escaping from his captors, forgetting the blisters on his arse, Aelfric ran after the others, out of the inn and towards the stable. Gaheris swerved into the sleeping place to collect their gear, and Trystan feverishly saddled both his own horse and the fucking roan, while the Caledonian saddled his chestnut and Gaheris' black. Behind them in the inn there was yelling and screaming as more of the common room took light, and men and women came streaming out of other buildings to see what was happening. By the time the miller's friends realised they were escaping, all four of them had mounted up and were riding hard, heading for the gate.

'That way!' Corwynal pointed down an alleyway, hoping he was right.

'They're coming after us!' Trystan yelled as they burst out of the alleyway. Ahead of them was the western gate, still open, thanks be to the gods. They thundered through the gateway and out into the darkness beyond.

'Which way?' Gaheris wanted to know, reining in his horse as they reached a crossroads. To the north, across the bridge, lay Lothian and safety. To the south-east were Lot's lands of Gododdin.

'This way!' Corwynal kicked Janthe on, heading west, skirting the hill and making for the woods that clung to its lower slopes, black against the last embers of the sunset. It wasn't long before they were riding between trees and the track had dwindled to a path. Night seemed to rush out of the forest, and they slowed first to a canter, then a trot, until finally they were picking their way through the trees. The sounds of pursuit faded behind them, as Corwynal had hoped, for few would willingly enter woods that led to Selgovia, not after nightfall.

'Are we in Selgovia now?' Trystan asked when they reached a clearing deep in the woods.

The rain clouds of earlier had moved off to the north, and the sky to the west was clear and still held a little ruddy light. To the east, the moon was rising, and the two lights, red and silver, mingled strangely among the trees. A little breeze was making the trees move and whisper, bringing with it the smell of the deep forest – fox and moss, pine-needles and leaf-mould. But strongest of all was the sweet-sour reek of something that had nothing to do with woods or trees. It was the stink of corruption. A great oak stood on the western side of the clearing, and as the moon lifted in the sky its light slanted down to illuminate an object that hung from the lower branches, something with legs and arms.

'Arddu!' Corwynal murmured as he took in the full horror of what hung there. A man, dead a month or more, was hanging from a hook slung through his shoulder.

'Woden's balls, where's his head?' Aelfric whispered.

'There,' Trystan said, swallowing hard, nodding at a smaller object that hung by its hair from another branch, a face with crow-pecked pits for eyes and a mouth that still screamed.

'Unsettling, isn't it?' said an amused voice.

Corwynal's hands tightened involuntarily on the reins and Janthe backed into Aelfric's roan, which reared, nearly unseating the Angle. In a gap in the trees behind them, silhouetted against the moon-washed sky, a man was mounted on a rough-coated pony and laughing softly at their nervous confusion. His arms were crossed loosely across the saddle-horns, and he gave the distinct impression that he'd been waiting for some time. Yet he couldn't have been, because the last time Corwynal had heard that voice had been in the Mansio in Trimontium. *Run!* he'd yelled.

'What are you doing here?' he demanded of the huntsman.

'How did you get here?' Trystan asked more practically.

'I rode,' the man replied with a shrug. 'There's more than one way into the lands of the Selgovae, and, in answer to your question, you're not in Selgovia. Not yet.' He nodded at the oak with its horrifying fruit. 'That tree marks the border, and it serves as a warning. So, bearing in mind that warning, do you still want to go to Meldon?'

Corwynal hesitated, unnerved by the forest and his conviction that beyond the body, swaying in the breeze, lay a threshold he didn't want to cross.

'We were to meet a guide in Trimontium,' he said, having no desire to go into Selgovia without protection.

'Perhaps this is your guide,' the huntsman said, cocking an ear to the east. Faintly, but coming closer, they could hear a single horse picking its way through the trees. Then someone rode into the clearing and stopped abruptly at the sight of the body hanging from the oak.

'In the name of the Good Lord and all his Blessed Saints!'

'What are you doing here?' Trystan asked the Scot from the Mansio.

'Escaping,' the young man said curtly, once he was able to tear his appalled gaze from the corpse. 'If I'd stayed in Trimontium, the miller and his friends would have found me, taken my winnings and beaten me to a pulp. So I followed you, and now – since you owe me protection – I'm coming with you.'

'No, you're not,' Corwynal said. 'We don't owe you anything. It's you who was cheating at dice.'

'I wasn't cheating! I was playing with loaded dice.'

'Exactly!'

'But they weren't mine. I was given them. That's the other reason I followed you. I wanted to know why.' And with that, he turned to the huntsman. 'Well?'

The man smiled thinly. 'I was curious to see what you would do.'

'Curious!?' Corwynal exclaimed. 'You almost got us killed!'

'It was a test,' the huntsman said coolly. 'I wanted to know what sort of men you were, whether you'd protect a companion, whether you'd fight for one another.'

'The Scot's not our companion.'

The huntsman shrugged. 'He arrived with you. He ate with you.'

'He's not going with us. He's a priest of Chrystos and your people have no fondness for priests.'

'I'm not a priest, actually,' the Scot said. 'I was kicked out of the seminary in Galloway for . . . for reasons that need not concern you. So now I'm just a wandering healer. My name's Ninian,' he added.

'You're a healer?' Trystan exclaimed. 'A Scot's healer? But they're famous! So why—?'

'Is he coming with you, or not?'

'Yes,' Trystan stated before Corwynal could object. 'But what's it to you who goes with us or not? What gives you the right to test us? We're supposed to be guests of Selgovia, not enemies. We have safe conduct. Who are you to threaten us?'

The huntsman drew himself up in the saddle and kicked his horse forward into the moonlight. 'Right? I had need, not right. As to who I am, I'm Kaerherdin, your guide to Meldon. You and your companions are guests of King Hoel, but there are others who don't want you in Selgovia. I'm not one of them, however, so I'm not threatening you. But I *am* warning you; there will be dangers on this journey. So, if you still want to go, and if I'm to guide you, you'll go where I say and do what I tell you.' He smiled faintly at Trystan's mulish expression, then nodded at the darkness that lay beyond the oak, the threshold that was marked with death. 'Well, shall we . . . ?'

☙

They made camp when they were barely an hour's ride from the glade with the oak tree, down near the River Tuaidh, in a clearing normally used by charcoal-burners.

'Can't we carry on?' Trystan asked, for the moon, almost at the full, was high in the sky, the track by the river easy enough to follow.

'No,' Kaerherdin said.

'Why not?'

'Because one of you is hurt and one of your horses is weary.'

Trystan flushed darkly and looked over at Aelfric. His left eye had swollen closed, and his nose was encrusted with blood.

A dark stain at his shoulder suggested his wound had opened up.

'I'll deal with it.' Ninian slid from the saddle of his drooping horse. 'Perhaps that will earn me my place,' he added with a sideways glance at Corwynal, because he and Trystan had argued about him earlier.

'I need a healer for my war-band,' Trystan had insisted.

'You don't have a war-band'.

'Not yet,' Trystan had agreed. 'But one day I will.'

Trystan had refused to back down, and eventually Kaerherdin hissed them to silence. But Trystan could never be silent for long.

'Where are we?' he asked, looking about the clearing and the track that headed upstream. 'How far are we from Meldon?'

Kaerherdin shrugged. 'By this track? A day. By the way I'll take you, perhaps two.'

'Why take the longer route?'

'Because I say so,' Kaerherdin said curtly, rolling himself in his blanket as far away from the rest of them as possible. 'Now, get some sleep. Tomorrow will be a long day.'

⛦

He was right. The following morning they turned off the track by the river and took to the woods. The trail, in places little more than a deer track, wound past deep-bedded streams, climbed to skirt hillsides, then plunged down rocky steps beside torrents that rushed into yet another valley. They had to lead the horses for part of the way, for this land was seamed with water and hidden gorges, thick with a forest even denser than the black woods of Atholl in the north, and filled with a faint mist that gradually thickened to a blur of green-tinged drizzle.

Corwynal's disquiet deepened as the day wore on. He became convinced they were being watched, for he kept imagining movement at the edges of his vision, and occasionally thought he saw the gleam of eyes in the undergrowth. Once he heard a cry on the wind, a sparrowhawk calling to its mate perhaps, but here in Selgovia the cry seemed to hold some deeper message. This forest was older than others he'd known, and there would be gods here, the little gods of stream and oak who were rarely welcoming to men. He said nothing of his fears, however, but edged closer to the others.

Trystan and Gaheris were at the back, each vying to prove their courage to one another by bringing up the rear. Even Ninian, who, like so many Scots, loved to talk, was beaten into silence by the woods. He rode close to Aelfric, who clung grimly to his saddle and peered nervously between the trees, unnerved, Corwynal thought, by the lack of a horizon. The Angle was a sea-bred creature, and Corwynal could imagine the man's discomfort in these enclosed and breathless tunnels of forest, for he felt the same discomfort. But Kaerherdin led them on without hesitation, answering questions with a grunt or a shrug or, when he was feeling loquacious, with a monosyllabic yes or no.

It wasn't until dusk was falling that the track climbed out of the woods and headed for the crest of a moor where rocks broke through the thin soil to form an outcrop. They dismounted in the shelter of the rocks to let the horses crop the coarse grasses that grew between the heather, while they ate a frugal meal of dry oatcakes and hard cheese washed down with water from a spring flowing from the base of the outcrop.

Once he'd finished eating, Corwynal clambered up the outcrop to look out over Selgovia in the last of the light, for the earlier drizzle had eased off, and the clouds had lifted. To the west, the land fell away to a wooded valley before rising once more to a more distant moorland whose summit was crowned by a fort surrounded by wooden palisades. But no smoke rose from behind the walls and the fort seemed as empty as the land itself, for they'd seen little sign of habitation other than the occasional smear of smoke from charcoal-burners in the forest.

'What a country!' Trystan said, coming to join him, impressed and intrigued by the novelty of Selgovia. 'You realise we're being followed?' he added, lowering his voice.

Corwynal nodded. 'By people who don't want us here.'

'Caledonians?'

'Or those that support them. That'll be why Kaerherdin's taken us by this route.'

'He knows we're being followed,' Trystan said. 'And I think he knows who by.'

But the night they spent camped below the rocks passed uneventfully, though once, when he woke, Corwynal saw Kaerherdin silhouetted against the stars as he stood guard over them, and it was barely dawn when he shook them awake and told them to get moving.

The clouds were lower that day, the drizzle heavier, but Kaerherdin led them unerringly across the cloud-wreathed moor and down into the wooded glen Corwynal had seen from the heights, where a river ran noisily as it headed north past reedy meadows that might once have been pasture. Down in the woods, the sensation of being watched was stronger, and more than once he heard the cry of a bird he knew only from the north. Perhaps Kaerherdin recognised it too, for his expression grew grimmer, and he began to push the pace. The track headed along the river until they reached a confluence of two streams. There they left the track and crossed the river to pick up a faint path that rose steeply through dense forest past a stand of holly that hid them from the valley below.

'Wait here,' Kaerherdin said, reining his mount around to ride back down the path.

'Why?' Corwynal asked.

'Do as I say! If you want to reach Meldon, do *exactly* as I say!'

'An ambush?' Trystan asked, but the Selgovian didn't reply, and he vanished into the trees with the skill of an experienced hunter, moving silently on his shaggy little horse. The rest of them waited and listened and, though they heard nothing, he, Trystan, and Gaheris all loosened their swords in their scabbards.

'Give me my weapons!' Aelfric growled. 'That man is as faithless as all you Britons!'

Corwynal shook his head and glanced at Trystan, who nodded his agreement. Nevertheless, Trystan adjusted his pack so Aelfric's weapons and shield might come easily to hand.

'Listen! H-h-horses!' Gaheris ignored Corwynal's hissed command to get back before he was seen, slipped from his horse and ran a little way down the path to where he'd have a view of the river. Corwynal could hear the jingle of harness as riders trotted up the track the Britons had just ridden along, but when they reached the place Corwynal and the others had turned off, the riders carried on upstream, and he was able to breathe once more. But not for long.

'He's w-w-with them!' Gaheris ran back, leapt into the saddle, and jerked his horse around. 'K-K-Kaerherdin! He's leading them!' Then he was gone, riding on up the track, Ninian following. Corwynal smothered a curse, for surely Gaheris had misread the situation. Kaerherdin would be leading their pursuers away. But, with Gaheris and Ninian vanishing up the hillside, they could do little else but follow them. He glanced at Trystan, who nodded and turned to Aelfric.

'Stay on that horse and you'll get your weapons back,' he said. 'Fall off and we leave you. Come on!'

The path broadened as the wood thinned, then climbed up to higher ground. Once they'd left the trees, the gradient eased and the horses, which had stumbled and jibbed all the way up the hillside, stretched out their necks as they were urged into a canter. Corwynal, having caught up with Gaheris and Ninian, glanced behind him; Aelfric was clinging desperately to his mount, Trystan riding beside him. Then Kaerherdin burst from the woods a little way off and angled towards them, his horse swift and sure-footed among the tussocks and peat-hags of the moor.

'Head for the fort!' He gestured ahead of them, and when they crested a rise, Corwynal could make out, through the swirling cloud, the palisaded fort he'd seen the previous night.

'Who *are* those men!?' he demanded when Kaerherdin caught up with them. The Selgovian looked over his shoulder, swore, and kicked his mount into a gallop. Whoever they were, the riders had followed him up from the valley. Their horses were bigger than Kaerherdin's but less suited to the rough terrain, and the Britons were outpacing them on the smoother track that led towards the fort. Corwynal glanced back, counted ten or twelve men. *There are five of us . . .* The odds could have been worse.

They reached the lower slopes of the rise on which the fort stood and headed for the entrance, then pounded up the inclined track and burst through the gateway. And into nothing.

Beyond the gateway there was no settlement and no gates, only a ruined wall on which stood the remains of a rampart. A few buildings huddled against the walls, empty and roofless, and on the far side of the fort the rampart had burned down and there was a great gash in the wall. This place wasn't the refuge he'd hoped for. It was a trap.

'Kaerherdin!' The Selgovian had already gone and was galloping away from the fort, heading west. He shouted something in reply, but his voice was lost on the wind.

Only four of us now.

'Ninian, get the horses together!' Corwynal dropped to the ground, unstrapped his weapons, and tossed the boy a spear. The Scot caught it, hesitated for a moment, his face as white as twice-skimmed milk, then let it fall.

'I don't fight,' he said, reaching out to take Janthe's reins. 'I'm a healer.'

Corwynal swore. *Three then, to fight a dozen or more. Unless...*

'You have to give me my weapons now, you whore-poxed Caledonian!'

They had little choice. Trystan tossed Aelfric his sword, axe and shield, and a broad grin split the Angle's face. For good or ill, the man was armed once more, but at least there were four of them now.

They scrambled up the broken walls to where the rampart still stood. The riders were circling the fort, looking for a place to attack. Pennants flew from iron-tipped lances, but Corwynal couldn't make out their device. There was no flutter of cloaks from their shoulders, no flash of body armour. Their shields were square, their swords in shoulder scabbards, and they bore long flame-headed war-spears. One whistled over the remains of the ramparts to fall harmlessly among the jumbled stones of the wall.

It was then that he heard the first notes of music. But this time it wasn't in his head. It came from the beating of hollow skin-clad drums that hung from the riders' saddles, and from the throats of those riders themselves. He didn't need to see that the war-spear was girdled with herons' feathers and painted with symbols he alone could read to know who, or what, they were.

Caledonians. From Atholl.

7

A GIRL WITH WHITE HANDS

Aelfric felt good. He wasn't on that fucking horse for a start. And he was out of those black woods with their malevolent sprites and spirits. Best of all, he had his weapons back. His shield was strapped to his arm, the hilt of his sword was in his right fist, the haft of his axe in the other, all of them as deeply and warmly familiar as a woman. He was Aelfric of Gyrwum once more, and he was ready for a fight. He didn't care who their attackers were or why they were there. All that mattered was that there were plenty of them. He could take them all on single-handed – and it looked as if he might be doing just that, because the cursed Caledonian was staring at the spear that had come over the wall, as white as if he'd seen a ghost. Like the coward he was.

'Corwynal?' Trystan frowned at his brother's ashen face. 'Who are they?'

'Caledonians,' the man said.

Caledonians? A burst of anticipation ran through Aelfric like a draught of ale. *Excellent!* It was almost worth having managed to stay on that fucking horse to have this chance, though he might not have them all to himself. Trystan raised his bow, nocked an arrow to the string, took careful aim, and fired. He struck a horse in the hindquarters and it went down, but the rider slipped away from the thrashing beast and swung up behind a companion. The two Caledonians rode off and waved the others out of range. Gaheris, beside Trystan, waited patiently, his bow half-drawn, steady and unafraid. Trystan was assessing the terrain, his eyes gleaming, his expression cool and controlled. *Those lads'll do all right*, Aelfric thought approvingly. They might even bag a couple of Caledonians between them. But that would still leave the rest for Aelfric, though he might have to share those too, since the Caledonian had torn his gaze from the spear and appeared to have found a little courage.

'Trys, you'll have to hold this breach with Gaheris. Ninian will look after the horses.' Then he turned to Aelfric. 'You and I have to stop them getting through the gateway. If we don't, we're all dead. You wanted to fight, didn't you? Now's your chance.'

'It's you I want to fight, not them.' But Aelfric knew it made sense. The riders had split up; some had slipped off their horses and were advancing towards the breach through the jumble of the fallen wall. The rest were circling the fort, and it wouldn't be long before they found the open gateway on the far side.

The Caledonian beat him to the gap, but only by a stride. There was no sign of their attackers yet, and Aelfric crouched, weapons at the ready, waiting for them to appear. But instead of doing likewise, the Caledonian threw down his sword and shield, stripped off his tunic and shirt and tugged away the leather strip that bound his hair back. Aelfric stared at him. *What's the bloody man playing at?* Then he stared some more because the man's chest, back and arms were painted with beasts. He'd always known Caledonians were patterned, but only now did he appreciate just what that meant.

'Give me your sword,' the man said, picking up his own.

What?! 'Fuck that!' No-one was going to take his weapons away from him ever again.

'Come on! Give me your sword!' The Caledonian kicked Aelfric in the shins and dragged it from his hand. 'Now attack me! Defend the gateway. Make it look convincing, then fall back. *Now*, you Angle bastard!'

The Caledonian lunged at him, and Aelfric's instincts took over. He blocked the blow on his shield and his axe whistled over the man's head, just as two of their attackers appeared. Then Aelfric understood. The two men would see them fighting, would see someone who was painted as they were, fighting with two swords in the way the Caledonians fought, and assume the cursed man was one of their own. The Caledonian yelled at them in foreign, and they fell for it.

Aelfric was enjoying himself now, slashing his axe at the man, who struggled to parry it with the twin swords. He was good, though, even if Aelfric's weapon was too long for him, and their fight must have looked convincing enough because their attackers ran to help him.

'Fall back now!' the Caledonian hissed.

Aelfric staggered back in response to a low feint from the other man, then, pretending he'd been struck, fell face-down on the ground. A blade plunged into the earth so close to his head it must have looked as if the Caledonian was finishing him off. And it worked. Out of the corner of his eye, Aelfric saw the two men breasting the rise. The Caledonian bent over to lean on one of his swords as if he was winded, allowing his loosened hair to obscure his face. He shouted something else in foreign and waved the men on in the direction of the fort. They fell for that too.

'Now!'

Aelfric surged to his feet, yelling out his war cry. His axe took one in the spine. The man arched backwards with a cry that halted the second in his tracks. He looked back, confused, just as the Caledonian tossed Aelfric his sword. The second man died in that moment of confusion, beaten down by a blow of Aelfric's blade that half-severed his neck. *Two to me, none to the Caledonian.*

He grinned and tugged his axe from the body of the first one. The blow hadn't killed the man, and he was lying on his side, one hand clutching feebly at the heather. The Caledonian crouched down, drew his hunting knife, murmured some words, and cut the man's throat, but not before he muttered something that made the Caledonian grunt, as if in pain. Then he turned him over and stumbled back, his face drained of colour. The dead man was also patterned with beasts, and some of them looked the same as the ones the Caledonian bore. Perhaps he'd just slit the throat of a man of his own tribe. Not that Aelfric cared one way or the other.

'They're easy to kill, these painted men.'

'You know nothing about it!' the Caledonian snarled. He got up and sheathed his knife, but Aelfric could see his hands shaking.

'How does it feel killing your own people?'

'You killed them, not me!' But it had been the Caledonian's ruse that had led them to their deaths, and the man knew it. Aelfric regarded him with pitying scorn for a moment but was distracted by movement further down the hill. Other men were among the rocks, and they wouldn't be fooled so easily.

'I'll deal with them,' he said. 'Since you don't have the stomach for it.'

The Caledonian swore at him, using words Aelfric didn't

understand, but was determined to learn once this was over. They moved back to the gateway, the Caledonian murmuring under his breath, doubtless some prayer to his gods for courage.

There were four of them, armed with spears and shields. A spear's a thrusting weapon, lethal at the charge or against horsemen, but less so in a standing fight, and Aelfric and the Caledonian held the slightly higher ground. By unspoken assent, they took their stance in the narrow opening of the gateway where they couldn't be flanked. And perhaps for this reason, the warriors seemed reluctant to attack. Or maybe they were waiting for reinforcements.

Fuck that! Aelfric thought and launched himself at them with a yell loud enough to turn the blood in their veins to water. 'I'm Aelfric of Gyrwum! Come and get me!'

He killed one outright. *Three to me, none to the Caledonian!* It unnerved the others, but only for a moment, then all three attacked at once. Aelfric feinted to the right with his sword, then swung his axe, driving it deep into the man's breastbone, splitting the symbol of a wolf in two. *Four to me.* Beside him the Caledonian was fighting another, but badly, which was odd, for when Aelfric had fought him at the ford he'd been a man worth fighting. Now he was lunging and parrying and grunting with the effort. He was sweating too and looked pale, as if he was afraid. Yet the man he was fighting seemed afraid too. He couldn't keep his eyes off the symbols on the Caledonian's body and kept glancing towards his companions to see if they were coming to his aid. They weren't. Aelfric hammered his sword down, slicing deep into the neck of his remaining opponent. *Five to me.* This was too easy. Only one was left, the man fighting the Caledonian, but both appeared reluctant to finish it.

Then, from the other side of the fort, Aelfric heard cries and the clash of metal on shield. The breach hadn't held as long as they'd hoped. The Caledonian lifted his head, and maybe his opponent saw something in his face, for he let his guard slip. All it would take was one thrust, but still the bloody man hesitated, and it was Aelfric's blade that drove deep beneath the man's ribs. *Six to me. None to the Caledonian.* Aelfric let out a blood-curdling yell, waved his axe over his head, and grinned at the Caledonian.

'Well? Are you coming or not?!'

They ran, the other man, with his shorter stride, falling back a little, so when they reached the breach Aelfric was in the lead. One of men from the other group of attackers had broken through, and Trystan was fighting him in the jumble of the broken wall. Gaheris was up on the rampart, still with a bow in his hands, firing down at the others. As Aelfric and the Caledonian ran for the breach, Gaheris nocked an arrow and aimed over the wall but, distracted by the sight of two men running towards him from inside the fort, turned towards them. It must have looked as if Aelfric was being pursued by an enemy warrior, so Gaheris did the only sensible thing in the circumstances.

He shot the Caledonian.

⸙

Corwynal felt a sharp tug at his side, an impact that made him stagger. The shaft of an arrow penetrated his body just above the hip, and when he reached for it, blood welled through his fingers. He had a momentary desire to laugh at the ridiculousness of the situation, but then the pain began, wave on wave of it, robbing him of breath. His legs folded beneath him, and he dropped to his knees.

'Corwynal!?' Gaheris jumped down from the ramparts, sprinted over, skidded to a stop and crouched down beside him, his face reddening then draining of colour. 'I didn't recognise you! G-g-god's blood! T-T-Trystan will k-k-kill me!'

Corwynal thought it very likely.

'Trystan? *I'm* going to fucking kill you!' Aelfric yelled at Gaheris. 'This Caledonian's mine!'

'Get back to the wall!' Corwynal gasped as Ninian ran over. 'Help Trystan.'

'Leave Corwynal to me.' Ninian sounded calm and confident, and the others ran off. The Scot prised Corwynal's fingers away from the agony in his side and probed the wound. 'It's just a flesh wound,' he said. 'But it's bleeding badly.' He guided Corwynal's fingers to where the arrow emerged from his back, got him to hold it still, then snapped the shaft. He almost blacked out at the pain and then, as Ninian poured some burning liquid over the wound and drew the broken arrow from his side, he did so in earnest. When he came to once more, his waist was bound so tightly he could barely breathe. 'Lie still or you'll bleed to death,' the Scot said. 'Lie still! They don't need you.'

They don't need a Kinslayer. That was what the man had called him – the warrior marked as being of Atholl by the wolf on his chest, his rank and lineage by the other symbols. It had been a bad moment when he'd realised who'd come – his own people, who wanted him dead.

It had always been a possibility, for the tribal lands closest to Selgovia were those of Atholl, but he'd persuaded himself that any dealings the Selgovae had with Caledonians would be with other tribes, those of Fife, perhaps, or Circind. In his heart, however, he'd known he was wrong, and so it had proved. He'd prayed to Arddu, but there had been no answer, and he hadn't expected one, for why should Arddu help him fight his own kinsmen? For the first time in his life, the world hadn't changed as it always did when he fought. Nor had the music come. He'd tried to find something else, but all he'd found was fear. And so he'd fought badly. Instead of the cold clear dance of metal and muscle he was used to, the fight had been a scrabbling scuffle of sweat and rasping lungs, and the only cold thing inside him had been the dread in his bowels. He'd never felt fear like that before, raw and terrifying. This, he understood, was what most men felt most of the time. Even Gaheris was fighting better than he had.

Lot's son was up on the breach, engaging a spearman, but he was blocking well, his blows precise and careful. Some men fight better when they're afraid, and Gaheris was terrified of Trystan's anger. His fear fuelled a ferocity Corwynal hadn't imagined the boy possessed, but if he fought like a demon and Aelfric like the savage he was, Trystan, silhouetted against the blaze of a low turbulent sunset, fought like a god, singing as he did so. Corwynal knew no-one could withstand him that day, that perhaps no-one ever would withstand him – not until the island with its wheeling gulls where a man wearing the symbol of the black ship would bring him to his knees. But that wasn't going to be today and, as he watched, Trystan killed his opponent with a precise thrust to the throat. He stepped back from the gout of blood, then looked up, his eye caught by something out on the moor. 'Riders! More of them!'

Ignoring Ninian's protests, Corwynal struggled to his feet, pulled his cloak from Janthe's saddle, wrapped it around his shoulders, and limped to where he could look out. Sure enough, there were horses heading towards them, dark shapes emerging out of the low cloud. Then a horn sounded from somewhere below him, and the man fighting Gaheris broke and ran. He jumped down the rubble of the broken wall, but Aelfric flung a spear after him and the force of the throw slammed it straight through his body. The man ran on for a few paces, clutching the spear at his chest, before tumbling down into the rocks.

'Back to the rampart!' Trystan shouted. The riders were closer now, so Aelfric and Gaheris headed back to the relative safety of the wall, but Trystan lingered, and so both he and Corwynal heard the movement among the boulders at the base of the wall. One of the Caledonians was still there.

'Come on!' Trystan leapt down the rocks. Corwynal followed as carefully as he could, pressing his hand to his wound. The bandage was soaked, and blood was oozing down his side. The man they'd heard emerged from the boulders, scrambled down the last section of scree and began to run, but he couldn't outrun Trystan, who reached him in a few strides and cried out some challenge. Snarling a reply, the man drew his twin swords and crouched. But, to Corwynal's surprise, Trystan stepped back and made a gesture of dismissal. The man stared at him for a moment, before slipping into the shelter of a peat-hag and disappearing.

'Why did you let him go?' Corwynal asked when he reached Trystan. 'He'll just join the others.'

'I was tired of killing.' Trystan sheathed his sword and turned to climb back up to the fort. Then a gust of wind tugged Corwynal's cloak aside to reveal the bandage and the blood. 'You're hurt!'

'It's nothing. I'll be fine.' Corwynal waved him away. 'Get back to the walls.'

'Don't be stupid. Can you walk? We'll go and meet them.' He laughed at Corwynal's confusion. 'Did you think those riders were more Caledonians? No, it's Kaerherdin. Didn't you hear him shout that he was going for help? I wondered when he'd get here, but he's too late now. He's missed all the fun!'

Corwynal groped for a boulder and sat down heavily, cursing. If he'd heard what Kaerherdin had shouted, he would have insisted everyone hide in the fort until re-enforcements arrived to chase off the Caledonians. He needn't have fought his kinfolk or exposed himself to Gaheris' well-meaning attempt to save Aelfric's life, the life of a man who'd sworn to take his. Indeed, the whole thing was so ridiculous that he began to laugh weakly and was still laughing when the others joined them. From their vantage point on the rampart, they too had seen that the riders were Selgovae, and that Kaerherdin rode ahead of them on his shaggy horse. Corwynal laughed even harder when Gaheris took Trystan to one side and confessed what he'd done.

'You *what!?* Trystan punched him in the face and Gaheris' head snapped back.

'I'm s-s-sorry, T-T-Trys,' he said miserably, blood pouring from his nose as Trystan grasped him by the shoulders and shook him.

'Don't try to kill my brother again or I'll be *really* angry!'

'I won't.' Trystan grinned at him, then at Aelfric and Ninian. A moment later, all five of them were pounding each other on the back.

And so the Selgovae found them laughing like madmen, having killed a troop of Caledonians. The only hurt any of them had taken had been inflicted by their own side. But Corwynal didn't know what happened after that because the laughter made him dizzy, and the darkness that had been hovering at the edges of his vision crept inward. All he could see was a rider dismounting, and all he could hear was a dry, amused voice bidding them welcome to Selgovia.

Then he fainted clean away.

He woke to see stars caught in a net of branches, lights that swung and swayed as if he was being borne on a river, and yet he could smell horses and hear the sound of their hooves. Then there was darkness again, the scent of flowers, drums beating through the earth, his own blood pounding in his ears. He woke once more to bitter liquid spilling into his mouth and hands forcing his jaws open when he tried to turn away. He was hot, then cold, then hot. His throat was sore and arid, his body slick with sweat, and a fire burned behind his eyes. From time to time, the darkness lifted and faces peered down at him. Then night would close in again, along with the walls. He woke screaming because he thought he was alone and trapped in a dark place of stone. But he wasn't alone. There were voices – angry voices, quiet voices, men's voices, women's voices. He began to pick one out, a woman speaking Briton but with a sweet Caledonian lilt like his mother's, a voice that took on shape and colour in his dreams. Dark blue the eyes would be, dark the hair. It was his own face softened into that of a woman's, his mother's face . . .

When Corwynal finally came to, he found himself in the small dark space of his nightmare. He sat up in panic and felt something pull in his side. Then light began to gather, first around a small brazier burning apple-wood, then from the doorway where a skin hanging had been pulled back to let in light and air. Outside he could see the moss-covered wall of an enclosure and, above it, a grey sky from which rain fell steadily. But it was the interior of the hut that caught Corwynal's eye, for he was surrounded by beasts. On every surface, on each upright, on the door lintel, on the legs and seat of a stool, even on the pallet on which he lay, were carved every manner of animal. There were stags and salmon, wolves and serpents, horses and dogs, all of them entwined with flowers and faces, each carving flowing into the next so that flowers became beasts, beasts men, men flowers. The designs drew his gaze up into the smoke-stained rafters from which were suspended strange pale objects that swayed gently in the draught from the door. He watched them idly for a while, wondering what they could be. Then he knew, and his understanding sent him gasping into reality. They were the bleached skulls of men.

'You must get used to such things,' said the voice from his dreams. 'You're in Selgovia now.'

He turned his head, a more difficult task than he'd anticipated. Someone was sitting on a stool beside him. His dreams had been so vivid he'd expected his mother to be there or, at the very least, someone who resembled her. But though the eyes that looked gravely down at him were blue, they weren't the slate-blue of his mother's eyes, and nor were they the eyes of a woman. A girl of maybe fourteen or fifteen was sitting beside him, a pale little thing with small features in a long face, fine fly-away mouse-fair hair, and eyes the colour of melt water. A servant, he decided, judging by her plain, neatly darned clothing.

'Where . . . ?' He tried to speak, but nothing more emerged.

'You're in Meldon,' the girl said. 'You've been ill for many days. There was fever from your wound. No, don't touch it!' she said as he reached for the place that ached and throbbed. 'It's healing well.'

His waist was bound with a bandage, but, other than that, he was naked beneath the blanket.

'You... you cared for me?'

The girl nodded without embarrassment. 'Ninian treated your wound, but I have a knowledge of herbs, and it was my medicine that cured your fever.'

Ninian? It was a moment before Corwynal remembered the Scots healer who'd refused to fight at the fort. Then the fight came back to him too – the Caledonians, blood on his hands, the hissed word from his dreams – *Kinslayer!* – and how Trystan had—

'Where's Trystan?' he asked, struggling to rise, but the girl pressed him back. 'I want to see him,' he insisted.

'You will, you will.' The girl spoke as if to a fractious child. 'Now, drink this.' She slid a hand behind his head and raised him up so he could drink from the cup she held to his lips. The liquid smelled of herbs and was bitter, but he drank thirstily, and the darkness closed in again. 'Sleep,' she murmured, her face shimmering and blurring until she was his mother once more, and he was a child. With the last of his strength, he reached out to touch her hand and slide his fingers through hers.

'You've decided to live, have you, you soft bugger.' A man's voice woke him this time, a deep voice barely audible over the rhythmic rasping of stone on metal. 'I suppose I should be glad of it since it'll give me a chance to take your life myself, though I'm wondering now if it's worth the bother.'

Corwynal was still lying on the pallet in the hut, but this time it was the Angle who was with him. He was sitting in the doorway sharpening a sword with long strokes of a stone along the blade.

'That's my sword,' Corwynal muttered.

'I know,' Aelfric replied, continuing to grind away at the edge. 'If it had been sharper, you might have killed more of those painted men.' He set the stone down and gave him a contemptuous look. 'You fought like a fucking woman at the fort. If it hadn't been for me, you'd be a corpse. But your gods must love you.' He laid the sword across his knees and leant back against the doorframe. 'I'm guarding you,' he explained. 'Although I don't know from what. It was the boy's orders, and he has this strange idea I'm his slave . . .' He shrugged, turned to Corwynal and lowered his voice. 'He doesn't trust anyone. Even the girl.'

'The girl? The serving girl?'

Aelfric stared at him, then threw his head back and laughed heartily. 'Serving girl? That's the Princess, daughter of the King. Her name,' he added, 'is Essylt.'

Essylt, Princess of Selgovia, daughter of Hoel, King-Consort of Selgovia, looked different when Corwynal next saw her, shortly after Aelfric had strolled off to find Trystan and tell him he was awake. She'd changed out of her old skirt and tunic and was wearing an embroidered dress in a shade of green that didn't suit her, and she'd brushed her hair and bound it back with a green ribbon, which had the unfortunate effect of making her rather long face look even longer. Perhaps she was aware of all these things, for she seemed self-conscious and awkward, a white flower of a girl, pale and cold.

'My Lord,' she said with a little curtsy.

'Lady Essylt.' He tried to sit up, but the effort made his head swim, so he lay back again. 'I apologise. I didn't know who you were.'

'Why should you? Princesses are supposed to be beautiful, aren't they? To dress as befits their position.' She gestured at her clothes. 'To do nothing.'

Corwynal wasn't sure know how to reply to this but was relieved of the necessity by the door-covering being swept aside.

'Corwynal, I—' Trystan, shaking rain from his hair, stopped abruptly at the sight of the girl.

'Prince Trystan.' Essylt inclined her head with heavy formality, her hands hanging stiffly at her sides. 'Your brother is awake.'

'I can see that,' he said. 'I want to speak with him. Alone.' Then he recalled his manners. 'If you'll forgive us, Lady Essylt.'

Trystan was holding himself very still, his hands curled into claws, and Corwynal knew that, for some reason, he was close to breaking.

'Please,' he asked Essylt. She was still looking up at Trystan but, at Corwynal's plea, she dropped her eyes and ran from the hut.

'What do you think of the Princess of Selgovia?' Trystan asked, stepping over to the doorway to assure himself she'd really gone. 'Quite the little nurse!'

'She seems . . . nice enough,' Corwynal said.

'Not pretty though, is she? Well, I suppose it was too much to hope for. Gaheris is disappointed, of course. Poor Gaheris! He's still feeling guilty about what he did at the fort, even though . . .'

Trystan's voice broke, and he flung his head back and clutched his arms across his chest. Then he whirled around and in two strides was on his knees beside Corwynal. There were tears on his face, but he cuffed them away. 'It was *my* fault! I knew Kaerherdin had gone for help, so we could have waited.

But I wanted to show the Selgovae we could fight. It was pride, Corwynal, not sense. We should have stayed together. Then it wouldn't have happened. You could have *died!*'

'It was an accident, Trys. Gaheris didn't mean to kill me.'

Trystan laughed shakily. 'Just as well he shot wide!' Then he sobered. 'I didn't realise how badly you were hurt!'

'None of it was your fault. We were promised safe conduct. If the Selgovae can't control their allies, then it's they who're to blame. Although it wouldn't be wise to say so.' He smiled reassuringly, but Trystan's eyes slid away. 'I hope you've been diplomatic,' he added, his voice sharpening.

Trystan kept his gaze on the floor. 'I thought you were going to die. I was . . . angry.'

Corwynal closed his eyes, wondering how much had been ruined and what he could do to rectify matters. But little could be done while he lay there, too weak to move.

'Listen, Trys, I'm going to need your help.'

'Anything!' Trystan said, hoping for something difficult and dangerous.

'I want you to make friends with these people. I need to know everything about them – what they want, what they fear, what they value, how to convince them to join us, what to offer them, and why those Caledonians were here. This has begun badly, yet perhaps not so very badly. We were attacked when we had safe conduct, but we saved ourselves. *You* saved us, Trys. They're at fault and know it, and that might give us an advantage. But you must never refer to it again. Do you understand me?' Trystan nodded and got to his feet. 'You weren't very polite to Essylt a moment ago,' Corwynal added.

'I don't like how she spends so much time with you,' Trystan said with a scowl. 'They say she has Caledonian blood, that she favours them.'

Corwynal frowned. He'd suspected the girl's ancestry from the lilt in her voice, but as to her favouring them . . . ?

'What of Hoel?'

'I don't know. He left Meldon yesterday. Went north to meet with his chieftains. No-one knows when he'll be back.'

It wasn't encouraging, but there was little Corwynal could do about it. 'I'll have recovered by the time he gets back, so use the time well, Trys. Try to see something of the country.'

'I don't like leaving you.'

'I have that cursed Angle to guard me, don't I?' He reached out and gripped Trystan's hand. 'I'm relying on you, Trys. Don't let me down.'

Trystan was only the first of his visitors that day, and, like him, the others came to apologise for their part in what had happened at the fort. Gaheris, arriving not long after Trystan had left, was still mortified about injuring Corwynal, but relieved by his recovery, and confessed that he hadn't been looking forward to explaining his death to his father.

'It's g-g-going to be bad enough explaining about Essylt,' he said ruefully.

'Essylt?' Corwynal asked in alarm.

Gaheris glanced at Aelfric, dozing on a stool near the door, and bent closer. 'I'd rather face a h-h-horde of Angles!' he whispered.

Gaheris' fear didn't accord with the sweet-voiced girl who'd cared for him, but when Essylt herself arrived, Corwynal saw her expression chill at the sight of Gaheris. The boy coloured and stammered out a few pleasantries, to which she responded coldly. Then he fled, leaving Corwynal alone with the girl and wondering how to negotiate a marriage between two such reluctant people. He was even more pessimistic when another, rather more surprising, visitor came to see him also.

'I apologise,' Kaerherdin said. He stood by the door, his arms crossed, and gave the impression of a man not accustomed to apologising to anyone. 'I should have taken more men to meet you. The Caledonians were bound to get wind of your visit, but I thought I could outwit them. I was ... arrogant.' A faint rueful smile lifted one corner of his mouth. It was the first time Corwynal had seen Kaerherdin smile.

'I'll recover. I'm being well cared for.'

'Indeed.' Kaerherdin glanced at Essylt, his smile broadening. 'You're in good hands,' he said, putting an arm around her shoulders. Essylt, to Corwynal's surprise and disquiet, returned Kaerherdin's smile and put an arm around his waist. 'But if there's anything I can do ... ?' Kaerherdin added, letting her go.

'There is,' Corwynal said as the tall Selgovian stooped to duck through the door. 'Could you take Trystan hunting? He's fretting here in Meldon.'

Kaerherdin didn't look enthusiastic, and Corwynal guessed he and Trystan had argued, but the Selgovian nodded, and later Corwynal learned he'd done as he'd asked. Gaheris had gone with them, leaving Corwynal alone with Aelfric, who guarded his hut so well that he had no visitors other than Essylt and Ninian.

'You lost a lot of blood,' the Scot told him. 'You need to rest. It will take time to recover, but Essylt says her medicine should help.' He pursed his lips and frowned. 'I thought I knew everything there was to know about healing herbs, but it seems I don't.'

'When will I feel better?'

'Soon,' Ninian said with an irritating lack of precision. 'You just have to be patient.'

Patience had never been one of Corwynal's strengths, but Ninian, as well as being a healer, was an entertaining and amusing companion. He knew a great many stories, and songs too, though he never sang them. 'I used to sing,' he said. 'But that was before . . .' He smiled a little too brightly. 'Before my voice broke.' *Before whatever happened to make him leave Dalriada,* Corwynal concluded. A girl, perhaps? Why else would a young man suddenly decide to become a priest? But if there was a girl back in Dalriada, Ninian never mentioned her, though he talked of everything else, history merging into myth and back again, tales of heroes and warriors, of magic and mystery. He spoke of Dalriada's King, Feargus Mór, known as Feargus the Fox. His sign was the swan, Ninian told him. All the Dalriadan lords had birds as their sign. A black ship? No, he didn't know that one. He was more interested in the sign of the cross, and he talked rather too much about the god the Scots worshipped and even tried to persuade Corwynal that he should turn to Chrystos.

'I already have a god, and he's trouble enough. Why would I need two?'

Ninian insisted that there was only one god, which Corwynal thought ridiculous, and eventually the Scot gave up his attempts to persuade him to his way of thinking, and from then on said little of his god, though he continued to tell stories from his holy book, tales of walls and trumpets, water and wine, and even stranger stories from a land so far away Corwynal could barely imagine it.

Essylt came every day, bringing her bitter medicine, and if Ninian was telling stories, she'd stay to listen. Once the hunting party had left Meldon, taking her prospective husband with them, the frozen little white flower vanished. She changed back into her old clothes and seemed more comfortable with herself.

Oddly, she reminded him of Ealhith, whose qualities he appreciated rather more now he'd given her away. The Princess of Selgovia had the same quiet thoughtful intelligence, and she came to his hut not only to listen to Ninian, but to talk about her land, its history and problems, its blood feuds and old resentments, the winter famines and summer murrains. Selgovia, she said, had isolated itself too long from the world, and its people held too fiercely to their ancient traditions.

'My father has ruled as King since my mother died,' she said. 'But once he dies in his turn, it is I who'll rule Selgovia, and my daughter who'll reign after me, as my mother reigned before me. When I take the throne, my husband will be Consort, if I'm married by then. But I think I will be . . .'

She cast her eyes to the ground as she said this, and Corwynal doubted she was thinking of Gaheris. Perhaps it was Kaerherdin she wanted, or someone else entirely. Lot's proposal was all very well, but, here in Selgovia, faced with the girl whose future might depend on what he negotiated, he regretted having to raise the question of her marriage.

'Essylt, you know what I've come here to ask?' She nodded, the colour coming and going in her face. 'If it was in my power, I'd have you marry whoever your heart desires. Will you remember that?'

She reached out and linked her fingers through his. 'I'll remember,' she said, her fingers tightening on his. 'Oh, I'll remember!'

'I'm back! And so's Hoel. We ran into him just north of Meldon.'

Trystan was wet through and filthy, his tunic stained with blood, his cloak shredded at the hem. He smelled of horses, campfires, pinewoods and leaf-mould. His face was bright with pleasure, but it darkened to concern when he looked down at Corwynal, still lying on his pallet, propped up on a pile of skins. 'Are you no better?'

Corwynal had been in Meldon for more than half a moon by then, but still felt exhausted, and Ninian couldn't explain it. 'I don't think you should take any more of Essylt's medicine,' he'd said that morning. 'It's not doing you any good.' Much to Corwynal's surprise, Essylt hadn't objected.

'It's done its work,' she'd announced, though he could feel no evidence of it.

'The wound's healing,' he assured Trystan. That, at least, was true. 'I'm still a little tired, but it will pass.'

Trystan eyed him doubtfully. 'We can't wait for it to pass,' he said. 'Someone has to speak to the King. If you can't, it'll have to be me, so tell me what to say.'

Corwynal shook his head, not sure Trystan was up to negotiating with Hoel. 'I have to!' Trystan stripped off his gloves and crouched down beside him. 'We've been here too long already. We should be in the north, with Lot.'

'Nothing will happen before Beltein, save for some raiding. Now, tell me what you've been doing. I gave you a task. Did you succeed?'

Trystan smiled, and his eyes sparkled as he perched at the bottom of the pallet and talked about his hunting trip: the forests where they'd cornered a seven-tined stag in a gully, the moors where they'd hunted wolves, how they'd tracked a bear but let it go in the end. The weather had been appalling – rain and gales – but they'd sheltered in settlements when they could, and others had joined them, mostly younger men.

'And they want to go to war,' Trystan said. 'They don't care who with. They just want to fight, and what fighters they'd make! What bowmen they are, what trackers! Kaer says—'

'Kaer?'

'Kaerherdin. He's all right when you get to know him. Anyway, he says there are many who look to the lands beyond Selgovia, and I managed to convince him to think that way himself. Selgovia needs to ally itself with the outside world, and the younger men understand it, especially in the south where they favour the Britons.'

'What of the north?'

Trystan frowned. 'We didn't go north. According to Kaer, the chieftains up there aren't keen on an alliance with Britons, and there are Caledonians guarding their northern border.'

Lot won't like that! Corwynal thought.

'The northern chieftains favour some offer that's been made by the Caledonians, the ones who attacked us. But maybe that's why Hoel went north, to try to persuade his chieftains their interest lies with us. But he's tricky, Corwynal. Like Lot.'

He'd have to be to rule Selgovia. And so would the next King-Consort, but Corwynal doubted if Gaheris was up to the task. Nevertheless, something would have to be negotiated, and he cursed the weakness that slowed not only his body but his mind.

'I assume there's to be a feast tonight? Then do something else for me, Trys. Sing at the feast. You know the sort of thing, songs of battle, love songs, anything to remind them they're Britons. Make them listen and keep them listening.'

'Distract them, you mean?' Trystan said with a grin. 'For how long?'

'Not long,' Corwynal replied, with more confidence than he felt. 'Not long at all.'

Corwynal woke to the sound of someone fumbling at the door curtain. On the far side of the hut Aelfric was snoring, quietly for once, and Corwynal thought it odd he hadn't woken since the Angle usually slept as lightly as any warrior.

'Aelfric?' he hissed, but the Angle snored on, and he decided he'd dreamt the sound. He was still uneasy though, but welcomed the feeling, for this was the first time he'd felt alert since arriving at Meldon, the first time his blood hadn't drummed in his ears at the slightest movement. He reached for his sword – even in the guest hut he kept it within hand's-reach – got carefully to his feet and was ready when the noise came again.

'Steward, I—'

A man was in the doorway, silhouetted against a night sky that was pale with stars, for the rain that had battered the stronghold for the last few days had finally cleared. There was little light in the hut, for the brazier had burned down to ash, but it was sufficient to reveal the empty pallet and the naked blade held unwaveringly at the man's throat. Corwynal was pleased with the steadiness of the blade in his hands, for his legs were trembling as he stood behind the door.

'Step into the light,' he said, reaching for a split log of wood and throwing it into the brazier. The embers sparked into life and light rippled around the hut, setting the carved beasts twisting and turning in the glow from the fire. Flames licked around the wood and revealed Corwynal's mysterious assailant to be an enormously fat man, his long reddish hair threaded with wooden discs and feathers, his neck ringed with chains that glittered in the firelight, as did the rings on the hand that reached into his capacious tunic.

'Whatever weapon you have there, I'd advise you to drop it,' Corwynal said. His own sword was still levelled at the man's throat, but it was beginning to shake.

'It's not much of a weapon,' the man said, pulling out a greasy rib of boar. 'Thought you might be hungry,' he added. 'Heard they'd been feeding you gruel. Care to put that sword down before it falls out of your hand?'

Corwynal lowered his blade, feeling both foolish and relieved, then astonished as the man reached into his tunic once more and brought out a loaf of bread, a skin of ale and two enamelled cups.

'Do you have an entire feast in there?' he asked, lowering himself to the pallet. The man heaved himself down beside him and patted the swell of his belly.

'In here, certainly. I've eaten quite a few feasts in my time.' He smelled of greasy meat, of dogs and smoke and ale – a great deal of ale. This was no assassin but a benignly drunk Selgovian chieftain who'd wandered over to Corwynal's hut from the feast in Meldon's hall.

'He looks like a big eater,' the man said, nodding at the snoring Angle. 'So let's not wake him, eh?' He pulled the bread into pieces, poured a cup of ale, and handed it to Corwynal. 'Go on – eat and drink. Then we'll talk.'

The meat was sweet and tender, the bread fresh and soft, the ale dark and so strong it went straight to Corwynal's head. The man settled himself comfortably with his back against the willow hurdle of the wall and poured himself a generous measure of ale. 'So, what do you think of Selgovia?' he asked.

'I've seen less of it than I'd have liked. I've been ill.'

'So I'd heard. I'd also heard you were Lothian's Steward. Ours is useless, except when it comes to feasting. But you, according to rumour, do rather more than arrange feasts. Sheep now. What's your opinion of sheep?'

Corwynal took another swallow of ale and told the man

what he thought about sheep. And then of pigs and cattle and goats. They spoke of grazing problems, diseases and how best to avoid them, and of Lothian breeds Corwynal thought might do well on the Selgovian moors. They spoke of land, of clearing forests, of drainage, crops and yields, of the few traders who came to Selgovia, of harbours and cargoes, of prices and barter. All of these were things he hadn't realised he'd missed, the everyday tasks of being a Steward. The man listened with interest, made shrewd observations, and was so unlike the Selgovian chieftains with whom Corwynal had negotiated the previous year that he began to feel more optimistic about persuading these supposedly proud and prickly people to join them – if he was ever well enough to do so.

'You'll recover soon enough,' the man said confidently. 'And then you'll sit down in Meldon's hall with the chieftains and persuade them Selgovia's future lies with Lot and not with their allies in the north.'

'How am I to do that?'

The man leant towards him, tapped his nose, and lowered his voice to a whisper. 'By telling them what I'm going to tell you tonight.'

Corwynal laughed. The man must be drunker than he appeared. 'You make it sound very easy! But your King might take a different view of the matter. I hear Hoel's a man of great shrewdness of mind.'

'Great shrewdness of mind! I like that!' The man chuckled. 'Perhaps you've also heard he's a man beset by advisors. But occasionally he makes his escape.' He sighed and shook his head. 'Shouldn't be necessary, but there we are. Give me that ale. I find it aids negotiation.' He poured himself another generous measure and raised his cup, a delighted grin spreading over his face at Corwynal's dawning comprehension. 'So, since I'm Hoel himself, shall we begin . . . ?'

※

By dawn Corwynal was exhausted, and his head had begun to drum once more, not only because of the ale but because, in the course of that night-long discussion, he'd been hard-pressed. Hoel was everything rumour made of him, a clever and cunning man. Nevertheless, they managed to thrash out the basis of an agreement. Corwynal would still have to persuade the Selgovian chieftains of its merits, but he knew now what might be accepted and how certain unpalatable conditions might be made easier to swallow. Nothing, however, was said of a possible marriage until close to dawn.

'What do you think of my daughter?'

'She's . . . I like her,' Corwynal said. It was hardly fulsome praise, but Hoel seemed pleased enough.

'She's not pretty,' he admitted. 'Neither was her mother. Lovely hands, though. Have you noticed? Essylt of the White Hands, they call her. Not that her looks matter, because she's clever like her mother, but few men realise that, and fewer still would like it if they did. They think she comes to speak to you because you're half Caledonian and she favours them. But she doesn't. The Caledonians made an offer you know, a young man of good breeding, and some of my chieftains would be pleased with the match. But others think that boy of Lot's – a pleasant lad by all accounts – might be the better choice.'

'Essylt seems . . . fond of Kaerherdin. And he of her.'

'Oh, they like each other well enough,' Hoel said with a dismissive gesture. 'Why not when they're brother and sister?' Then he barked with laughter. 'You didn't know Kaer was my son? No, I suppose not. He never mentions me. His mother was slave born, so he's no claim on me, and it's turned him bitter. I was surprised to learn he'd made friends with that brother of yours, and that Scots healer. Kaerherdin doesn't make friends easily.'

'Then, forgive me, but Essylt isn't . . . promised?'

'Not by me, and won't be by me. Whoever she marries, be he Caledonian or Briton, it's Essylt who'll do the choosing. But she's a sensible girl.'

Hoel lifted his head at the sound of raucous laughter from close by the hut. Light was seeping past the skin hangings on the door. 'I'd better go before someone sees me and thinks I'm plotting with you.' He grinned and winked at Corwynal. 'Which, of course, I am.'

8

THE NIGHT OF CHANGES

'And another thing...'

Corwynal sighed. The Selgovian chieftains had been talking since before sunset, and now, close to midnight, they were no nearer agreement. Beside him, Trystan shifted restlessly, impatience in every line of his body. On his other side, Gaheris tried to smother a yawn, no doubt wishing he'd been allowed to remain with Aelfric and Ninian in the guest hut. Even Corwynal found his attention wandering, and he gazed around Meldon's great hall, making comparisons with Dunpeldyr's.

It was smaller, older, darker, and, unnervingly – given the Selgovian enthusiasm for suspending the skulls of their enemies from the roof-beams – lower. Indeed, nothing in Meldon, from the muddy courtyard to the badly built shacks outside the walls, compared favourably with Dunpeldyr. Meldon, like Selgovia itself, was locked in the past, a place where things were repaired rather than replaced, and all that was beautiful was old and fragile. Selgovia desperately needed an alliance with a stronger neighbour, but convincing its chieftains of this was like wading through a bog.

He'd begun by telling them of the growing threat of the Angles, grateful Aelfric wasn't in the hall to hear what he was saying. Lot's lands of Gododdin, he told them, would be a buffer between the Angles and the Selgovae, though if Lot was to hold them back, he'd need a border at his back he didn't have to guard, and help in the form of men and mounts, help he was willing to pay a subsidy for.

He'd let this suggestion lie and allowed the chieftains to argue among themselves. But the talk had wound like the carvings that adorned the hall's pillars, disappearing and twisting back on its course until it seemed to be going in circles. Then one of them wanted to know exactly how much subsidy Lot was willing to offer, a question interesting enough to silence the others, and Corwynal was forced to concentrate once more.

'That depends on what assurances you can give him.'

'What assurances can *you* give that the subsidies will be paid?' asked another.

'My word as Steward of Lothian.' They could trust Lothian, he said. Hadn't the treaty he'd negotiated the previous year been honoured? Hadn't Trystan, Heir to Lothian, accompanied him to Selgovia to honour them also? They could trust Gododdin too, he went on, with less personal certainty. Some nodded, but the northern chieftains weren't convinced, and one of them, a tall man with dark hair striped with white like a badger, got to his feet.

'You've spoken of west, east and south, but not of the north. We've friends there, not enemies, and we've kinsmen, as do you, man of Atholl. We're not fooled by all this talk of war against the Angles because we know why Lot musters in Manau, and who he plans to fight. You may choose to be a traitor to your kinfolk, but why should we betray our friends?'

Trystan jumped to his feet. 'Friends who attack guests within your own borders! Guests who were promised safe conduct, guests who were forced to defend themselves, unaided! My brother, to whom you already owe a great deal, almost died because of your *friends!*'

That did it. The hall erupted in dissention. The northern chieftains shouted their denials, and the others yelled back at them.

'Wonderful, Trystan!' Corwynal whispered bitterly. 'Just wonderful!'

Hoel waited until the shouting began to ease before heaving himself to his feet. He didn't say anything, but the noise dwindled to a dull muttering.

'Unfortunately, Prince Trystan speaks nothing but the truth. We offered safe-conduct, and I sent Kaerherdin, foremost of Selgovia's guides, to guard the Lothian party on the way to Meldon. Perhaps I should have sent more men, but why should I have to send even one man to protect guests in our own kingdom? As you all know, we've been made an offer by the Caledonians, and they too have been persuasive, but when I make my decision, it will be based on force of argument, not arms. Let no-one here forget that.' He let his gaze fall on Corwynal, Trystan and Gaheris, making it clear this was a warning to them as well as to his northern chieftains. But the badger-haired man wasn't satisfied.

'The mouthpiece of Lot speaks of subsidies,' he sneered. 'This is a word we've heard before, but in Selgovia we call them bribes. So, tell me, man of Lothian, or Atholl, or wherever your allegiance lies, are such 'subsidies' available also to our allies in the north?'

'They're available to subjects of Selgovia,' Corwynal replied. 'If your 'allies', choose to become subject to your King Consort, they'd have the same privileges. Otherwise, they would not.'

'You want us to drive them out, don't you?'

Corwynal shrugged. 'You pay them to guard your northern frontier. You pay them subsidies or bribes – I leave the choice of word to you – but if you no longer require them to guard you, why should you continue to pay them? And if you don't, wouldn't they choose to go back to their own lands? There's no call to speak of driving anyone anywhere.'

'Can Lot guarantee our northern border?' one of the others asked.

'He seeks to strengthen Manau, which is a client kingdom of Gododdin. In Manau's strength lies your safety. Once Western Manau is regained, it will stand not only between Selgovia and the Caledonian lands in the north, but between you and the Scots in the West.'

'Hah! Does Lot think he can fight the Scots as well as the Caledonians?'

'He's not at war with the Scots. He just wants to re-establish the old frontiers and recover the lost lands of Manau. Lot will fight if he has to, but when he does, he won't be fighting alone. Galloway and Strathclyde have pledged men, and Lot also has a troop of mercenaries who've been fighting the Angles in the south.'

The badger-haired chieftain laughed. 'He must be a rich man, this Lot of Gododdin, if he can buy all these men and still pay us not to raid him while he's from home!'

They still don't understand! Corwynal thought and wondered if they ever would.

'That's not what my brother, or Lot, is suggesting,' Trystan replied, seeking to make amends for his earlier outburst. 'For that would indeed be an insult. Lot wants your allegiance on the same basis as the agreements he has with Galloway and

Strathclyde. He wants men to fight, not men who'll sit behind their frontiers and do nothing. He's heard of the war-skills of the Selgovae. Who in the Lands between the Walls has not? He knows you hold to the old traditions, and perhaps we of the east have forgotten such things, but with your help we can remember them once more. We were enemies once, generations ago, but we're still one people and should be friends. We speak the same language and worship the same gods. We sing the same songs.'

Corwynal sat back. Trystan had them now. He'd sung those very songs here in this hall. The Selgovae might have forgotten the words, but they remembered the sentiments, and now Trystan played them like the strings of a harp, weaving a tapestry of images that reminded them of the old days of pride and victory. This golden age had never truly existed, but Trystan made them believe it had. He told them that the lands of the Britons had once stretched from the mountains to a southern sea so far away a man could journey for a moon's turning and still not reach it. He spoke of wars and heroes and great deeds, and promised those days would come again. It wasn't long before he had the chieftains smiling reminiscently into their beards, and the younger men dreaming of glory to come, and in less than an hour when, in a night, Corwynal had achieved nothing, Trystan won them over.

'We want Selgovia as our ally,' Trystan concluded. 'We want your men, mounted, armed and provisioned for war, to fight by our side under your own banner, against the Angles and the Scots.'

'What about the Caledonians?' someone called out.

'Even them,' Trystan replied. 'Although a leader who sends a troop of men against their former allies would be little more than a fool, and Lot is certainly not that.'

Trystan's words had calmed some of the muttering, and many looked to Hoel for his reaction. But the King gave no hint of his thoughts, and when he nodded, it was not in agreement, but merely to indicate that the discussions were approaching the next phase.

'Fetch ale,' he said, turning to the slave who stood behind his chair. 'I find it aids negotiation.' He glanced at Corwynal, one eye half-closing in a wink. 'Well, Steward of Lothian, what do you have to offer us . . . ?'

In the end, with occasional interjections from his chieftains, Hoel and Corwynal hammered out the treaty they'd already agreed between them. It wasn't overgenerous, for the chieftains would have been suspicious if it had been, but it gave them much of what they wanted: certain trading rights, access to the horse and cattle markets of Gododdin, and a number of 'subsidies' to take the form of iron ore, copper ingots and silver. In all, it was a fair enough exchange for a troop of a hundred men to be hand-picked by the man who was to lead them.

'But who's that to be?' Hoel wondered aloud. 'It's a chancy thing for a company of the Selgovae to ride with their former enemies. They would, in effect, be hostages in your camp, so it seems to me we require our own hostage – a man of your own among ours, someone you value, someone who can speak with Lot. Someone to whom he'll listen.' Gaheris swallowed hard as Hoel steered the discussion in the direction he wanted it to take. 'But why should we trust Lot beyond the term of his own requirements?' Hoel went on. 'What's to stop him, with the might of the armies of Gododdin and Lothian and Manau and Galloway and Strathclyde behind him, from turning on

Selgovia and taking it for his own?' His chieftains growled in agreement. 'We need more,' Hoel said. 'And it's in my mind only an alliance of blood will do. We need a link with the east, a link to the man who's to lead the Selgovae in Lot's army. And that man must prove his faith with us by marrying the future queen of Selgovia, the Princess Essylt.'

The hall erupted at that, for none of the chieftains liked the idea. Perhaps some of them had hoped to marry her themselves. Hoel waited for the shouting to die down, then rose to his feet once more to make one final pronouncement on the matter.

'The alternative would be for Essylt to accept the Caledonians' offer. They're her kinfolk, after all. And that would mean Selgovia standing with the Caledonians, as we do at the moment, surrounded by Britons, but Britons strengthened by Lot's ambition. Not a comfortable position perhaps, but that would be the alternative.'

That quietened them. Hoel sat down again and turned to Corwynal. 'Well?'

Corwynal curbed a smile of satisfaction, for with this agreement he would have achieved all Lot had asked of him.

'On Lot's behalf, I agree to an alliance,' he said, glancing at Gaheris, who'd turned as pale as whey. 'Lot's fond of all his sons,' Corwynal said, putting a reassuring hand on Gaheris' shoulder. 'They're all fine young men, and Gaheris will make Essylt a good husband.'

Hoel smiled. 'I'm sure Gaheris is all you say he is, but he isn't going to marry Essylt.' He paused and looked Corwynal in the eye, a mischievous little grin playing around his lips. 'You are, Steward. It's you she wants.'

A Steward has to be ready for anything – threats and bribes, false promises and downright lies – and Corwynal had dealt calmly and confidently with all of these in the past. But this was different. This wasn't something he could deal with in any way, let alone calmly or with grace.

Marriage!? He'd contemplated marriage only once, eighteen years before, one Beltein morning by a stream in the dappled shade of a willow. *We'll run away together, and then we'll marry.* That offer had been so comprehensively rejected he'd never made another. Offers had been made to him, however, for a Steward has the power to make himself rich, and more than one woman had wanted to show him how. But he'd turned down those offers with laughter and not a single regret. In Meldon, however, laughter wasn't an option. Indeed, he could think of no way out of this because he couldn't think at all. He turned cold, then hot, then cold once more as he looked around the room and realised everyone was waiting for him to speak.

Marriage? He tried to think beyond that single word. *Marriage to Essylt?* She was just a girl! Corwynal knew little about women, less about girls, and nothing at all about virgins. The idea was so ridiculous his first reaction had been to laugh. But laughter wouldn't be appreciated, so he forced himself to address the possibility. If he married Essylt, he'd be King Consort and thus Steward of Selgovia.

With that thought, his breathing began to ease. He'd be able to do the work he knew, work he wanted to do. Selgovia needed the Britons. That was clear enough. But what Selgovia really needed was him. Lot wouldn't like it, of course, but once he thought it through, he'd see that this was a better solution than an alliance through Gaheris. Lot would still get the men he wanted, a troop Corwynal could give to Trystan to command in his name. Much would be gained if he could bring himself to agree, much lost if he couldn't, because then favour would fall on the Caledonian offer. Indeed, when he thought about it as calmly as he could, he had no choice in the matter whatsoever.

'I'd be honoured,' he said, after what must have seemed too long a hesitation. But Hoel nodded in satisfaction, and, though there was still muttering, a buzz of speculation and interest began to run around the hall. Beside him, Gaheris was grinning broadly in rather too evident relief, but it was to Trystan that Corwynal looked. His face, however, was still and expressionless and there was a question in his eyes Corwynal didn't know how to answer. Then, without saying anything, Trystan got to his feet, left the hall, and strode off into the night.

※

'You're surprised.' Essylt was a little pale, but determined.

Corwynal had insisted on speaking to her privately, and Hoel had summoned her to his own chamber the following morning where, after a meaningful look at him, he'd left them alone.

'I'm more than surprised.' What had he said or done to make her think he'd welcome this?

'Are you angry then?'

He ran a hand distractedly through his hair. 'No, I'm not angry. But Essylt, I've seen thirty-seven winters. And you're only—'

'Sixteen. Old enough to marry.' She was older than he'd thought, but it made no difference, and his doubts must have shown on his face, for she stepped closer to him, put a hand on his arm and looked up at him. 'This marriage will be good for both Selgovia and Lothian. We've watched Lothian, my father and I. Oh, yes – we have our spies! We've seen Lothian grow rich and powerful while you've been its Steward. My father wants that for Selgovia, and so do I. We heard a rumour you'd left Lothian for good, and thought to persuade you to become Selgovia's Steward. But my father and I came to... to see another way.'

It made sense, and so it shouldn't have surprised him. She was small and pale and quiet and made him think of the little white windflowers that carpet the woods in early spring. Essylt might be small, however, but, like the windflower, she was able to survive the harshest of conditions. She was clever too, a girl who cared about her country enough to make a sensible choice of consort. Yet there ought to be more to marriage than sense, particularly for a girl with her whole life ahead of her.

'Wouldn't you rather marry someone of your own age, someone you...' *Someone you might come to love.* 'Someone like Gaheris.'

She shook her head. 'I don't want to marry Gaheris. I want to marry you. It has to be you, you see, because—' To his astonishment, she threw her arms around his neck. '—because otherwise I don't think I can bear it!'

She kissed him fiercely, pressing her lips against his, a girl who hadn't been kissed before and wasn't sure how it was done. He began to wonder if she truly wanted him, not as a Steward but as a man, and he felt a strange tender impulse that might have been the beginnings of desire. He bent to return her kiss, intending it to be a kiss of friendship only, but her lips were soft, her body warm against his, and he found himself kissing her properly and wondering if he really might come to want her. Although, right at that moment, he felt little more than curiosity at his own response.

'I see,' said a voice from behind them. Essylt gasped and

pulled herself away, colour flaming into her cheeks. Trystan stood in the doorway watching them, his face closed and distant.

'So, you're to be my sister?' He strolled over to Essylt and looked down at her for a moment before bending to kiss her, first on one cheek, then on the other. She stiffened and closed her eyes, the colour flaring and fading in her skin. Then she tore herself away and flew out of her father's chamber back to the hall. Trystan ignored her flight and turned to Corwynal.

'Don't do this! It's a terrible mistake!'

'I don't have a choice! We want that treaty. We need those men. I can't refuse. Hoel won't accept Gaheris now.'

'Do you *want* to marry her?'

'It makes sense,' Corwynal replied, knowing that if he could convince Trystan he might be able to convince himself. 'The alliance will be good for Lothian.'

'That isn't what I asked. Do you *want* to marry her?'

'I can't go back to Dunpeldyr. I swore I wouldn't go back until the King begged me, and we both know that won't happen. So why shouldn't I be Steward of Selgovia?'

'You can be Steward without marrying the girl!'

'Someone has to marry her. It might as well be me.'

Trystan took him by the arm and shook him. 'Do you *want* to marry her?'

'Curse it, Trys!' Corwynal jerked his arm away. 'If you must have an answer, then, yes, I *do* want to marry her!'

Beltein is the Night of Changes for, with the passing of spring, summer begins and lives change, usually for the better. Beltein had always been marked by three days of truce between enemies, and thus it was a night of celebration in the Lands between the Walls. Selgovia was no exception in that regard, and so, on the Night of Changes, in the fields below the fort, the fires leapt high into the night sky. Cattle, maddened by the flames, bellowed and bucked as they were driven between the purifying fires. Some of the women, garlanded with primroses, were leading a docile old bull between the bonfires. He, like them, was wreathed in flowers, unaware that in the morning his throat would be cut in the Beltein grove, and that one of his sons would become lord of the herd. Corwynal felt sorry for the bull. Indeed, he felt quite out of tune with the night. Beltein was for the young, a night of thoughtless joys he couldn't share. Even the ale he'd drunk failed to induce the usual dull euphoria, and his mind was as cold and clear as the moon-washed sky that hung above the loom of Meldon's hill.

He ought to be looking for Essylt. He'd seen her once in the distance, a pale little figure wearing a wreath of wilting bluebells. She'd been smiling at some jest Ninian had made, but, as Corwynal watched, the smile slipped, leaving a troubled frown. It wasn't the face of a girl who looked forward to being married the following morning, or to anticipating that marriage in the groves of Meldon's woodlands later that night, as so many other couples were already doing. It was expected of them both, and not to do so might be taken as reluctance on his part and therefore an insult, but he didn't go to find her. *Later*, he thought, as he walked beyond the reach of the firelight.

'There you are!'

Trystan was drunk enough to sing himself hoarse or pick a fight with someone twice his size. Corwynal hoped it would be the former.

'I want to talk to you,' Trystan announced.

'Shouldn't you be making love to some impressionable young woman?'

'Yes, I suppose so, but I can't decide which of them's to be the lucky girl.'

'Vain creature!'

Trystan grinned. 'Looking like I do, and being who I am, has its uses. Where's Essylt?'

'I was just looking for her.'

'Out here?' Trystan glanced back at the fires, then gripped Corwynal's arm. 'She doesn't want to marry you, not really,' he said. 'She knows it's the right thing, but she doesn't truly want it. Not in her heart. And nor do you, in your heart.'

Corwynal sighed. 'I suppose not.'

'That's all right then!' Trystan said with a laugh. Corwynal couldn't follow his logic but put it down to the ale they'd both drunk.

There was a burst of laughter from near the biggest bonfire where Aelfric had his arms around two giggling women. Trystan looked back at them, and the light gilded his face into a mask Corwynal didn't recognise. Then he smiled, and the mask vanished.

'I'm going back now. You stay here. You'll probably be angry with me in the morning. But I'm doing it for you! Will you remember that?'

Corwynal laughed at him. 'You're drunk, Trys. Go and sleep it off.'

Trystan shook his head. 'Not yet. I have to find Essylt first . . .'

But if he found her, if he told her where Corwynal was, she didn't come to find him, and so he spent the night alone, watching the fires die down and the stars wheel in the sky, cold and clear and careless of the realms of men. And he thought back to another Beltein night in another forest, eighteen years before . . .

※

The Galloway party should have been in Dunpeldyr days before, but the weather had delayed them, and so Beltein Eve found them in the forest somewhere near Gododdin's border with Lothian. They camped in a clearing beside a pool fringed by a grove of alders. A solitary willow overhung the water and there were late primroses on the banks, the scent of woodruff and mayweed on the air. Corwynal, supposedly in charge, told everyone to stay in camp that night, but with little hope they'd obey him for the Galloway men followed his orders only when it suited them, and it didn't suit them to stay in the camp on Beltein Eve, not when there were so many willing women among the Princess' attendants. So he stood guard himself over the Princess' tent, listening to the sounds of men and women coupling in the woods around him and trying not to think of the woman who lay so close to him, only the thickness of a sheet of leather away. But he couldn't drive from his mind the image of his father's dry hands on her body, his sour breath in her throat, and how he'd . . .

'So, my grim Caledonian warrior guards me still?' *Her voice was amused as, close to dawn, she emerged from her tent.* 'Will you guard me if I go to the river? I'm overcome by . . . by a call of nature.' *She laughed softly, and Corwynal's heart rocked in his chest.*

'But surely your women—'

'—are heeding their own calls of nature,' *she murmured.* 'Come.'

So he went and stood with his back to her after she'd disappeared beneath the overhanging willow. Then she called to him and he turned to see her rising naked from the water like a spirit, holding out her arms to him. The sun rose, sparkling on the dew. 'Come . . .'

By the morning, after an unseasonably chilly night on the slopes of Meldon's hill, Corwynal was cold and aching but resigned. During the night, he'd taken out all his memories and turned them over and over, as if they were scraps of parchment on which a story had been written. But the scraps were crumbling, the lines illegible, the past something that had happened to someone other than the man he was now. He headed back to Meldon, and as he did so the sun rose through the mist, luminous and clear, burning away the haze and, with it, the last of his reservations. So it seemed fitting that Essylt came running down the hill to meet him.

'I'm so happy! I've never been so happy!' she said, taking his hands and dancing before him, all her gravity gone. 'He said you'd be angry with us, but how could you be? You see, I understand why you agreed, since I agreed for the same reasons and . . . and for other reasons that don't matter now. They don't matter at all! And to think . . .'

The words babbled over her tongue like a brook over pebbles, and though Corwynal didn't understand what she was saying, he was enchanted by the thought that the prospect of marrying him could make any woman so happy.

'I was so foolish!' she went on, as they walked up the hill and through the gates. 'I just thought that . . . well, I just thought it would be for the best. I thought you'd be kind, at least. And you would have been, just as you'll be kind now, won't you? You'll forgive us. He said it might be better if he told you, but I said no, it should be me.'

She looked up at him, serious now. 'You had no choice. I see that now. You just wanted the treaty, didn't you? Not me.'

'Essylt!'

Trystan strode over to them, his expression mirroring the tone of his voice. He was angrier than Corwynal had ever seen him, and there was a white look about his lips.

'Trystan! There you are!' Essylt's pale blue eyes sparkled at the sight of him.

'Go back to the hall!'

'But Trystan—'

'Go to the hall!'

She bit her lip on some retort, then smiled a knowing little smile and touched the back of his hand with her fingers. He jerked his hand away, but even this didn't banish the smile from her lips and she ran off to the hall, a trip of happiness in her step.

'She isn't going to marry you,' Trystan said harshly, turning to watch her go. Corwynal pulled Trystan around to face him and saw that he wore an expression he knew of old – defiance and guilt combined, and not a little apprehension.

'What have you done, Trystan?'

He flinched. 'I hate it when you call me Trystan in just that way.'

'What have you done!?'

'Saved you, you idiot! You didn't really want to marry her and stay here for the rest of your life. We just wanted the treaty and the men. That's what we agreed.'

'Trystan—'

'There's still an alliance. Hoel would prefer you, but he'll come around, and afterwards we'll ride away with the troop and forget this place.'

Trystan was braced for Corwynal's reaction, so when he hit him hard across the face, drawing blood from his mouth, he barely staggered. Corwynal expected him to retaliate, but though Trystan's hands curled into fists, they remained by his side. Then, slowly and deliberately, he wiped the blood from his lip.

'Everyone is watching,' he muttered. 'You'll ruin everything.'

'*I'll* ruin everything?!'

Quite a few people had paused in what they were doing to watch the confrontation between the brothers of Lothian. 'Follow me.' Without waiting for Trystan to do so, Corwynal walked off between the roundhouses until he reached the privacy of a deserted alley that ran between the wall of the fort and a couple of low buildings. Then he rounded on Trystan.

'Tell me what you've done.' Corwynal crossed his arms, trapping his hands so he wouldn't lash out again, for he badly wanted to. Trystan leant back against a storehouse wall and, avoiding his eyes, told him the whole story.

If he hadn't been ill, Corwynal would have seen it for himself. Trystan had arrived at Hoel's court angry at what had happened at the fort and ardent in his demand for restitution and revenge. Essylt had seen a young warrior from a far land, handsome and passionate, and had fallen under his unintended spell. But, considering her plain, Trystan had thought no more of her than as someone who would do for Gaheris. Essylt, hurt and offended, pretended to dislike him and avoided him for fear he might see her feelings and laugh at her. Then, since she couldn't have him, she'd decided to settle for the next best thing. His brother.

'But it was me she wanted,' Trystan said. 'That's why I didn't want you to marry her. At first, I thought you really wanted her, but you didn't. You said as much to me last night. You were just going through with the marriage for the sake of the treaty. So it didn't have to be you.'

'You wanted the men for yourself,' Corwynal concluded bitterly. 'So you seduced a king's daughter, a girl you don't even care for. Because *you* wanted those men!'

Trystan's lips thinned, but he didn't try to defend himself, and Corwynal knew it was partly his own fault. If he hadn't chosen to spend the night of Beltein with dead and dying memories rather than a living girl, this would never have happened. But there was little point in apportioning blame. What he had to do now was limit the damage.

'You intend to marry Essylt yourself? I do hope that's part of this masterly plan of yours.'

'Of course! I'm not a fool!' Trystan retorted, stung by Corwynal's sarcasm. 'One day I'll have to marry a plain-faced woman for the sake of some alliance or other. So why not now when we stand to gain something? And afterwards we'll leave and head north to join Lot before it's too late. We don't have to come back.'

'And what of Essylt? Doesn't she matter to you at all?'

'Does she matter to you?'

'What if she does? What will you do about it? What *can* you do? Nothing! It's done now and everyone will have to live with the consequences. You, her, me. No, I don't care for her in the way you mean. But – curse it, Trystan! – she's as worthy of love as any girl, yet will she get it from you? Can she, with honour, get it from anyone else now? You've lied to her, and now you'll marry her and go on lying. She isn't some serving girl!'

'I've had more fun with a serving girl.'

Corwynal lashed out at him, but this time Trystan blocked the blow, caught Corwynal's arm and held it in a vice-like grip. 'I'm a grown man,' he said, his voice low and very certain. 'And heir to Lothian. I can make my own decisions. She wanted me, not you. I've given her what she wanted, and now I'll take my payment. It really is that simple.'

Corwynal stared at someone he no longer recognised.

'Come.' Trystan let go of Corwynal's arm. 'You have to help me make this right with Hoel.' It wasn't a request; it was a command. But Corwynal wasn't ready to be commanded.

'Not until you've listened to what I have to say. You've dishonoured Essylt and yourself. You've dishonoured me too, and for what? A few men you would have got anyway if you'd had the patience to wait for them. A few men, when you could have had a lot more by making the right choice of wife. Will this marriage benefit Lothian? I doubt the King will think so. You've risked Lothian's future simply because you didn't have the self-control to wait, or the sense to think it through. I brought you up to behave like a king, not a spoiled boy who takes what he wants with no thought and no consideration for what anyone else might want or deserve. Essylt for one. Me for another.'

'What . . . ?' Trystan cleared his throat. His face was white now, his voice not quite steady. 'What did you want?'

'For myself? I wanted Selgovia. And one day I might have wanted Essylt. But what I wanted most of all was for you to behave like the man I raised you to be. That man wouldn't have done this. Have you no feelings, Trystan? Maybe you don't, and maybe that's for the best. I hope you never meet a woman who'll touch that cold and ruthless heart of yours, because if you ever find the other half of your soul – the woman you'll want to spend your life with, have children with, whose arms you'll want to die in – it will be too late because, by what you've done today, you'll have to stand by and watch that woman marry someone else.'

Corwynal was prey to a foreboding he couldn't identify and,

sickened and defeated, he turned and walked back to the courtyard.

'Did that happen to you?'

Corwynal kept on walking, but Trystan sprinted after him. His face was still white, but his eyes were blazing.

'Tell me! Did that happen to you?!'

'Is it any of your business?'

Trystan's face stiffened, and the light in his eyes dimmed to a dull resentment. 'Not if you tell me it isn't. Is that what you're telling me?'

'Yes,' Corwynal said, his voice rigidly controlled, because he badly wanted to tell him something quite different. That he was angry because he loved him. That he disliked him and was disgusted by what he'd done, but he still loved him.

⁂

'Are you angry with me?'

'No, Essylt, not with you.'

'With Trystan then?'

Corwynal had left the fort and walked down the hill to the stream that ran through the valley below, and Essylt had found him there, leaning against an aspen whose leaves were fluttering in the little wind that had sprung up earlier that morning. He was staring blindly at the water and wondering what he was going to tell Hoel. That instead of finding his daughter on Beltein Eve, he'd spent the night wallowing in the past? That the man Hoel wanted as Steward of Selgovia had been so terrified of a sixteen-year-old girl he'd let her be stolen from under his nose by his own brother?

'No, I'm not angry with Trystan. I'm just . . .' He shook his head. He wasn't angry, not anymore. He was afraid. Once, years before, he'd stolen a bride from under his father's nose, and now Trystan had done the same thing to him. Yet, if Trystan truly was his son, should he be surprised? Maybe a man's weaknesses passed from one generation to the next. Perhaps Trystan had betrayed him because Corwynal had betrayed his own father. And maybe one day Corwynal really would kill his father simply because his father had killed his, and it was in his blood. But these weren't things Essylt could possibly understand. 'I wish you'd told me how you felt about Trystan,' he said.

She dropped her head, her cheeks colouring. 'It would have shamed me, because I didn't think he cared for me, and you—'

'—were second best? You think that wouldn't have shamed *me?*' He tried to make light of it, but succeeded only in sounding resentful, and she kept her eyes on the ground. Poor child! She'd married a man who didn't love her, and the man she should have married felt little more than relief at his escape.

'I knew you didn't care for me,' she said. 'But I thought we could be friends. We still could be, couldn't we?' There was a little catch in her voice that almost broke his heart.

'We can still be friends, Essylt,' he said, thinking she'd need a friend in the days and years to come.

She smiled and tucked her hand through his arm as they walked back to the fort.

'Have you ever been in love?' she asked.

'Once, a long time ago.'

'What happened?'

'She married someone else then died,' he said shortly.

'Oh,' she said, but didn't ask any more questions. Memories, Corwynal discovered, weren't as easy to dismiss as he'd thought earlier that morning, and now Essylt's shining happiness reminded him all too painfully of his own, for it had been as short-lived as hers was likely to be. The sweetness of surrender that Beltein night had faded all too rapidly. The soaring crest of desire had peaked and rushed on to spend itself in the shallows, as he'd realised what he'd done –betrayed his father, his friend, and his own honour. There had been nothing he could do to make any of that right except take Gwenllian back to her tent and pretend he'd been on guard all night. Even his conviction that she couldn't, after their night together, marry his father, had died a swift death.

But I have to marry him. There would be war if I ran away with you. And how would we live? Be farmers? Don't be so foolish! It's better this way. If we're careful, we can still be together . . .

Perhaps if he'd been heir to a kingdom, like Trystan, things would have turned out differently. Or if the girl he'd fallen in love with hadn't been the daughter of one king and sister to another. Perhaps if he hadn't been so weak, he might have come out of the situation with a measure of self-respect. But, prey always to a touch or a look, he'd given in time after time, even though the whole sordid nature of betrayal had revolted him. And it was already too late. She was carrying a child, she told him a few months later, leaving him to wonder if it was his father's, or if it had been conceived on that Beltein night by the pool beneath the willow . . .

He shook away the memories and forced himself back to the present. *History doesn't repeat itself,* he told himself firmly. Trystan would marry Essylt and grow fond of her in time. She'd bear his children, and no-one would doubt their parentage. They would be happy. Of that Corwynal was determined. Not for Trystan or Essylt but for himself, because he had to prove a man's fate doesn't run in his blood.

But first he had to explain to Hoel that there had been a slight change of plan . . .

To say Hoel wasn't pleased would be an understatement. He ranted at great length about headstrong young women and reckless young men, but, once he understood that as soon as the war was over Corwynal would return and be Selgovia's Steward as originally planned, he came around to the idea. Others, however, weren't so understanding. Gaheris was bewildered by the turn of events, Kaerherdin suspicious, Ninian disapproving. Only Aelfric seemed pleased, though Corwynal couldn't imagine why.

The marriage ceremony, presided over by a couple of Selgovian priests, took place on a hilltop beneath the spreading branches of Meldon's sacred oak. The tree was walked around sunwise for luck, and a goat was slaughtered. The priests conferred over its entrails and looked grave but declared the omens to be propitious. Essylt was still shining with happiness, but Trystan was uncharacteristically sombre. Perhaps he'd already begun to regret his intemperate marriage, and Corwynal wasn't surprised when he raised the question of the bride-price almost as soon as the ceremony was over. Hoel was taken aback by this unnecessary haste but could hardly refuse, and Trystan spent the rest of the morning, not with his new bride but down by the horse pens, picking his hundred men.

Corwynal watched but said nothing. Trystan hadn't asked for his advice and, after their argument earlier that morning, Corwynal didn't think he'd welcome it. In the event, however, Trystan chose his men well, picking those he could train, avoiding the boasters and any whose gear was uncared for, or whose horses were flashy or ill-equipped. He spoke to each man at length, judging their temperament and their reasons for wanting to ride with him. More men had come forward than

Corwynal had expected, so it didn't take Trystan long to choose his hundred, then ask Gaheris to take command of half of them.

Well done! Corwynal thought with reluctant approval. With Gaheris as Trystan's second-in-command, Lot could claim the men were riding under Gododdin's banner. Then Trystan called to someone who hadn't been picked and who was already strolling away from the paddock, his face stony.

'Kaer!'

'I've already given you a hundred men,' Hoel objected.

'I don't want a man gifted by treaty. I want a man who comes of his own free will. Well?' Kaerherdin turned back, a strange expression on his face. 'Will you come?'

Kaerherdin looked at Hoel, at Essylt, at the men, and then at Trystan. 'I'll come,' he said, his face breaking into an uncharacteristic smile. Trystan grinned back at him, but when he turned to Corwynal, his smile had stiffened.

'You'll come too, of course,' he said carefully.

'I don't recall being invited,' Corwynal said with equal care.

'Do you need an invitation?'

'I think, after today, perhaps I do.'

'Corwynal, I—'

Whatever Trystan was going to say was drowned out by the blast of an auroch horn from the gate-tower as, from the north, a party of riders rode into Meldon. They glittered with weapons and were dressed for a feast in bright colours and fine embroidered deerskins. The riders were bare-chested, but their necks and arms were ringed with silver, and more silver was braided into their long dark hair. They were alien and magnificent and, had it not been for the Beltein truce, utterly terrifying.

The Caledonians had come.

9

ATHOLL WILL NEVER LET YOU GO

Eight Caledonians rode into Meldon with a blustery north wind at their backs. They were led by a tall druid who bore a staff topped with the polished skull of a pine-marten. He had the face of a hawk, the druid mark of the serpent on his forehead, and a hooked narrow beak of a nose. His dark hooded eyes gleamed as fiercely as those of Ase, the raven-headed god to whom the druids sacrificed. It was a face from Corwynal's past, from Atholl, and he shuddered with foreboding and the first icings of fear. The man, noting his reaction, smiled thinly, his eyes glinting with satisfaction as Corwynal struggled to free himself from that cold, clever gaze and turn his attention to the others.

All but one were older warriors. Their weapons glittered with silver and were inlaid with polished cornelian and the facetted brown quartz found only in the mountains, but they rode with those weapons strapped to their saddles, and their spears pointed downwards. This was an embassy, not a war-party. Hadn't they heard of Hoel's decision? Or were they here to reverse it? Perhaps the younger one was the match they'd had in mind for Essylt. He was a good-looking young man, only a little older than Trystan. Corwynal noted the tribe and clan marks pricked out on the boy's chest, marks he bore himself, then looked at him more closely.

'Ciniod?'

The name burst out before it occurred to him that the Ciniod he remembered would be twenty years older than this boy.

'This is Broichan, son of Ciniod, King-regent in Atholl,' the druid said smoothly, dismounting and gesturing for the others to do so too.

Corwynal, seeing the boy's resemblance to Ciniod in his sulky mouth and pugnacious jaw, felt the past reach out to take him by the throat.

'I let you go at the fort!' Trystan had also been staring at the young Caledonian. 'I let you *go!*'

'And now I've come back,' Broichan said. Unusually, he spoke Briton, but with the lilting accent of the north. 'I've come to claim the life of one who forsook his people, one who is outcast, his name stripped from the stones and buried in a pit, his soul given to the raven to wander the winds for all of time. I've come for the life of a man who—'

'Enough!' snapped the druid, and Broichan scowled but fell silent, allowing the druid to turn to Hoel, a suave smile softening his hawk-like features. 'Broichan has his own reasons for being here, but for myself I have come for information only, to learn the truth about a rumour that came running through the heather, a rumour that spoke of a marriage.' He nodded politely at Essylt, who shrank against her father. 'I see that rumour spoke truly.'

'My daughter—' Hoel began.

'My wife.' Trystan held out an imperious hand to Essylt, claiming her as a prize he'd no intention of giving up. 'You've come to wish her well?'

'But of course!' the druid said with an expansive gesture. 'Although, in my opinion, she would have done better to bind herself to one of her own, as we proposed, rather than a stranger from the east.' He shook his head in sorrow. 'This distresses me, my Lord King, for by this marriage you appear to have turned against old friends. It's your decision, of course, but I'm curious as to your reasons.'

Hoel, unsettled by the druid's smooth courtesy, shifted uncomfortably. 'As to my reasons, this I will say; my answer might have been otherwise had your kinfolk not attacked guests of mine.'

'Guests who were once your enemies? Enemies who are now your closest friends? One wonders, therefore, if old friends are now regarded as new enemies.'

'That's their choice. But friends don't break agreements.'

The druid's calm faltered. 'Not lightly,' he agreed with an irritated glance at Ciniod's son. 'Nor without good reason. But one life only was sought, and no harm intended to others. Indeed, it was our people who perished, not yours. The attack was . . . ill-conceived. Sometimes a man's judgement is swayed by matters that lie in the past, but there are proper ways to deal with such things, and Broichan now concedes this.'

He let the words lie, and, in the silence that followed, Broichan, in one swift move, took a silver-hafted knife from his belt and flung it towards Corwynal. It thudded into the ground midway between them and quivered balefully.

'A challenge!' Broichan called out. 'I challenge the godless murderer, the man with no name in my tribe! I challenge him to a fight to the death!'

Corwynal stared at the knife, his body refusing to move, his mind refusing to function. *Now? After all this time?*

All around him the Selgovae were muttering, the northern

chieftains the loudest. They'd backed the Britons, against their better judgement, and now they wanted their doubts resolved. This challenge would resolve them.

Arddu? There was no reply. The God had abandoned him the last time he'd tried to fight his kinfolk and did so once more, so Corwynal was left with no choice but to crouch down to take the knife. But, as he did so, the wound in his side tugged painfully, making him gasp, and in that moment of hesitation Trystan dived forward, slithered across the ground in front of him and snatched the knife before he could reach it.

'Don't be a fool, Trys!'

Trystan ignored him and rose to his feet with the knife held high in the air so everyone could see it. 'I accept the challenge!' he said, turning to Broichan. 'It was I who killed your men, I who worship no gods of yours, I who am nameless among your people. But today you'll learn and remember my name! I'm Trystan of Lothian and Galloway and Selgovia – a Briton among Britons! If there's to be a challenge, let a Caledonian fight a Briton!'

The murmurs of speculation and interest swelled to a shout of approval from the Selgovae, especially the northern chieftains.

'This isn't your affair!' Corwynal snapped, furious with Trystan for stealing this challenge as he'd stolen Essylt, furious with himself for the relief he felt despite his fear of what might happen.

'I'm making it my affair. You're hurt. You can't fight. And it was I who let him go.' He jerked his head at Broichan. 'It's my fight now.'

'No!' Essylt ran over and reached up to Trystan, her hands shaking. 'You mustn't fight. Not today.' He ignored her, and she turned instead to Corwynal. 'Tell him not to. It's you they want to fight, so—'

'It's too late, Essylt. He's accepted the challenge,' he said bitterly, knowing Trystan hadn't accepted for his sake, but because he wanted to prove himself to the Selgovae.

'There will be no challenges offered or accepted on the day my daughter marries!' Hoel thundered.

'That day ends at sunset,' the druid pointed out.

'Then let it lie until then. Come, we feast to celebrate my daughter's marriage. Join us. Our people are still allies. Nothing has changed between us.'

The druid looked sceptical. 'I will not insult your intelligence by pretending you believe that. We won't feast with you, but your wishes will be respected. Until sunset then.' Then he walked off with the others.

'Young fool,' Hoel muttered at Trystan, then scowled at Corwynal. 'He can't back down now, but you're the man they want, so you're the man who'll sort this. I won't have my daughter becoming a widow on the day she becomes a bride. If that happens, all agreements between us are cancelled. You hear me? *Cancelled!*'

⁂

Druids are feared through all the lands of the Britons, even though men had begun to turn from the old ways and, increasingly, looked to the priests of Chrystos for guidance. In Caledonia, however, druids still wielded power, and though Corwynal had no desire to face up to what had happened in Atholl all those years before, the druid was the only one with the authority to prevent the challenge.

'Lord, I beg you to intervene.' He knelt before the man in the otherwise empty guest hut that had been given to the Caledonian party. The druid was seated in a high-backed chair, his fingers tapping irritably on the carved wooden arm-rests, as his eyes raked Corwynal from head to foot.

'And why should I do that, Talorc of Atholl?' he asked, calling him by the name Corwynal hadn't answered to in over twenty years. 'Given that someone else has accepted the challenge on your behalf?'

'My brother's a skilled fighter ...' But, under the druid's hooded gaze, Corwynal's confidence faltered. Trystan had sparred with only one man who'd fought in the Caledonian warrior camps – himself – while Broichan would have trained for years. 'I don't want another kinsman's blood on my hands, even indirectly. I'm already a Kinslayer.'

'I know that. You will have noticed, however, that I prevented young Broichan from proclaiming it to the entire Selgovian nation.'

'Why?'

The druid shrugged and gestured for Corwynal to get up from his knees and take the stool opposite him. 'Regard it as a gift.'

'I thank you for that, but now I must ask for another. You could order Broichan not to fight if you chose.'

'Then you're not as confident of your brother's abilities as you pretend. But you must understand the gravity of this challenge, as you must have understood the gravity of what you did in Atholl twenty years ago.'

'I regret what happened,' Corwynal replied, taking care with his words.

The druid leant back in his chair and steepled his fingers together, touching them to his lips.

'Broichan's attack on your party was ill-advised, and he has been made to understand it. His failure has damaged his somewhat fragile pride, a pride wounded further by that plain little girl choosing someone other than himself as Consort. He wants blood. Preferably yours but, failing that, anyone's will do. He's a rash young man and difficult to stop. I chose to allow the challenge against you, although I didn't agree it should be to the death. You're no good to me dead, so I would have prevented him from killing you, had that seemed likely. Now, however, he won't be fighting you, so I see no reason to intervene. But I will – for a price. And you know what that price will be.'

'To return to Atholl and face the judgement of the Druid Council? We both know what the judgement would be and how I would be punished.'

The druid raised his eyebrows. 'Certainly, your crimes must be addressed and, if you were found guilty, those crimes would have to be paid for. But the punishment need not be the death you fear. Times have changed since you were last in Atholl, and now there's to be war they've changed once more.' He leant forward. 'If you remember Ciniod, you won't be surprised to learn that there are those in his court who might welcome you back. Come back and fight for your people and you would be judged less harshly. Come back with me to Atholl...' The druid's voice dropped, became low and sonorous, and for a moment Corwynal wanted quite badly to go, to be cleansed of the past, and it took an effort of will to pull himself free of the man's entangling spell.

'I made a choice, and I chose to be a Briton. I fight for my father's people, not my mother's.'

The druid had been sitting with his hands clasped loosely together, but now he reached out as a snake might strike and grasped Corwynal by the right arm.

'Take it off!' He jerked his head at the bronze armband Corwynal wore on his upper arm. 'Take off that abomination!'

There's a power in a druid's commands that brook no refusal, so he prised apart the armband and let it slide to his elbow, revealing the design pricked into his arm, the serpent and the broken spear.

'You can't *choose* to be a Briton.' The druid traced the design with a fingernail. His breath stank of dust and old sacrifices. 'This marks you for all time as chosen by the gods and the tribe. You're Caledonian, Talorc, son of Gaelen, no matter what name you call yourself by now. You're bound to Atholl, and Atholl will never let you go. Don't think you can fight it. So leave the Britons, Talorc. The war Lot of Gododdin intends to wage cannot be won.'

'It *will* be won.' Corwynal pulled his arm away. 'And I'll play my part, as a man of Lothian. The Confederacy will be defeated because it's not just Lot and his client-kings who ride against you. Strathclyde and Galloway have joined us too, and any Caledonians remaining in Selgovia will be isolated, surrounded and destroyed. Return to Atholl while there's still time; you can't defeat us.'

'No?' The druid laughed. 'You think you have the advantage of us, with all your allies? You think we don't know what happens in the south? Oh yes, we'd heard Strathclyde and Galloway had risen to Lot's call. Yet other calls have gone out and have been answered. Look to the west, for it's from the west that your destruction will come. It's too late for the Britons, but it's not too late for you. Cast off your false allegiance and come north. Submit yourself to the judgement of your people as befits your birth. You ask me to intervene in this challenge? Then pay the price.'

Corwynal knew what the price would be, but it wasn't

something he could contemplate paying so, in the end, he'd achieved nothing. The fight would go ahead as arranged, but Trystan would win because Trystan wasn't going to die here, in land-locked Selgovia, but rather on a stony beach with the sea at his back. Corwynal had been a fool to have sought the druid's help, so he got up to leave.

A fool indeed! The voice rocked through him, the God's laugher burning like acid down the length of his nerves. *You think it's that easy?* The God, who'd deserted him so many times in the past, was back. Blaize had been right all those years before. *What is life if not struggling against a half-imagined fate?* Nothing was simple and nothing was certain, not when a god wanted to see him struggle. So when he reached the door, he turned back to the druid.

'If I promised to come back to Atholl, would you order Broichan not to fight?'

The druid's eyes widened in surprise at Corwynal's capitulation. 'The fight must go ahead, for the honour of all concerned. But it need not be to the death – if I have your word you'll return to Atholl.'

Corwynal was still standing in the doorway, light at his back, so the man couldn't see his relief, for the druid's wording allowed him to use the trick he'd learned from Trystan's fooling of a certain Angle.

'You have my word as Talorc of Atholl. If you will give me yours.'

'You have it, as Domech, Archdruid of Atholl.'

Archdruid?!

The man smiled at Corwynal's start of surprise and consternation. 'Oh, yes, I'm Archdruid now, as was the man you killed. I was fond of him, in as much as I've ever been fond of anyone. Nevertheless, I give you my word. The fight between

Broichan and your half-brother will take place tonight, and tomorrow you and I will return to Atholl.'

Corwynal shook his head. 'Not tomorrow.'

Domech jumped to his feet, his hooded eyes blazing in the firelight. 'You gave me your word!'

'And I'll keep it. But I didn't say when. I've a matter to attend to before I can come to Atholl.'

The matter of a man bearing the symbol of a black ship, a man he intended to fight in place of Trystan, an encounter he might not survive. And if he didn't, the promise he'd just made would be meaningless.

'The gods are not mocked!' Domech snarled, knowing he'd been tricked, for a druid, especially an archdruid, may not go back on a word given.

'I'm not mocking them. I've given my word.'

Arddu was oddly silent. Perhaps he too had been tricked, for if the God wanted Corwynal to keep his promise to return to Atholl, he'd have to keep him alive to do so.

'You'll regret this! In more ways than you can imagine!'

One day, almost certainly, Corwynal thought, with a shiver of foreknowledge. *But not tonight.*

※

'He'll come at you on the left, so you'll have to keep your guard high and . . .'

Aelfric was looking forward to the fight. It would make a change from all that fucking singing. It had been a bad moment, though, when the Caledonian boy had thrown the knife at Corwynal, and Aelfric had understood that this was some sort of challenge. *Bring him back to me.* The promise he'd made to Ealhith was proving more difficult to fulfil than he'd expected because he wasn't the only man who wanted to kill the Caledonian. First the fight in the Inn, then at the fort, now this challenge from a boy who looked like he meant business to a man not long out of his sickbed. Which could result in someone other than Aelfric killing the cursed man. So he'd thanked Thunor when Trystan claimed the challenge for himself. Now, *that* would be a fight worth watching! The Caledonian lad looked mean enough, but Trystan was good, as Aelfric had reason to know, which was why it was odd that now, listening to Corwynal's unnecessary advice, the boy seemed half asleep.

'Trys, are you listening?'

Trystan blinked and came back to himself. 'Yes, of course.' But his voice was slurred and his skin had turned an odd greenish colour. *Is he drunk?* That little girl Essylt, the boy's wife now, had served him mead at the feast, but Trystan had downed only one cup and waved the others away. So he couldn't be drunk. What then? Even Essylt seemed to know something was wrong, for she was staring at him, her face rigid with nerves.

'Don't worry. He'll be fine,' Corwynal said, moving to sit beside her. 'The druid's agreed it's not to be a fight to the death after all.'

The girl turned and stared at the Caledonian. 'Not to the death!?' She looked over at Trystan once more and bit her lip. 'Then I needn't have done it!' she whispered.

Just then the western doors of the hall were flung open, and the Caledonians were silhouetted against the light, the setting sun glittering on weapons and silver torques and arm-rings. Against his will, Aelfric was rather impressed. But the Caledonians hadn't arrived at that precise moment just to intimidate the Selgovae. It was because, with the ending of the day, the fighting could begin.

'A challenge was offered and accepted.' The Caledonian priest's voice reached into every corner of the hall. 'Broichan, son of Ciniod, King-regent of Atholl, challenges the man known to you as Corwynal of Lothian, or whoever will fight in his place.' The boy Broichan grinned and threw his knife down in challenge once more, and it thudded into the beaten earth beneath the rushes that covered the floor. Aelfric glanced at Trystan, expecting him to step forward to formally accept the challenge, but he was ashen now, as if about to faint. Nevertheless, he got unsteadily to his feet.

'It hasn't worked!' Essylt whispered. 'I should have made it stronger!'

What?!

Trystan stepped away from the bench but only managed a couple of steps before falling to his knees and vomiting the contents of his stomach into the rushes. *That looks bad!* Aelfric knew what everyone would be thinking – that this soft young man from the east was sick with terror. The hall erupted with angry shouts and derisive laughter, and not just from the Caledonians. Trystan wiped the back of his hand across his mouth and tried to get up, pushing Corwynal and Essylt away when they tried to help. Ninian ran over, but Aelfric shouldered everyone aside and pulled the boy to his feet. It was then that he smelled the vomit.

Aelfric had smelled vomit before, of course, mostly his own, but this was different. This vomit didn't stink of mead but rather of herbs. It was the same heady aroma he'd noticed in the oddly bitter mead he'd drunk the night Hoel had visited Corwynal, a visit he'd slept right through. It smelled the same as Essylt's medicine, the one that was supposed to strengthen Corwynal's blood but had, in Aelfric's view, had the opposite effect. He glanced at Ninian, who was nodding to himself as if he'd just understood something he'd been puzzling over.

'Essylt's drugged you, Trys,' Corwynal said, having come to the same conclusion. 'Come on, sit down. You can't fight now.'

'You drugged me?' Trystan turned to Essylt, whose eyes were wide with fright. 'Say it,' he demanded. 'Say it so everyone hears.'

'I . . . I drugged you.' She glanced at Corwynal for support, but he just shook his head.

'Louder. Say it louder.' Trystan grabbed Essylt by the hair, making her shriek. 'Louder!'

'I drugged him!'

Silence fell. Then the Selgovae began to mutter, one to another. Hoel looked embarrassed, and Kaerherdin was white-lipped with fury. The Caledonians, on the other hand, were grinning broadly, and the boy Broichan was laughing as he stood beside the knife, his arms spread wide in appeal. Who, he was asking, was going to fight him now?

Corwynal walked over to the knife and bent to pick it up, but faltered once more. Which gave Aelfric his opportunity.

'Too slow. That's the trouble with you old men.' Aelfric plucked the knife out of the floor and twirled it between his fingers, then pushed Corwynal away when he made a grab for it. 'Oh, no you don't! Trystan made me your bodyguard, and it's been dull work until now.' He turned to the young Caledonian and grinned at him. 'Well, boy, ever fight an Angle?'

☙

Men with Aelfric's build usually relied on weight rather than speed, and so, to begin with, Corwynal feared it would be his undoing. Broichan was fast and light on his feet, his weapons perfectly balanced and wielded with the confidence of someone trained for years in the Caledonian warrior-camps. But his whirling spiral of steel couldn't break Aelfric's defence, for the Angle's saex was thick-ribbed and broad and, like his axe, as much of a shield as a weapon. The bigger man didn't need to be fast because he was accurate and moved only as much as necessary. He wasn't showy like the younger man, and Broichan had yet another disadvantage. He'd fought against his peers, against men armed with sword and shield, spear or knife, but he'd never fought anyone like Aelfric. Gradually, as he failed to find the opening he needed, his confidence faltered and the Angle's increased. A feral grin split Aelfric's face, and the men in the hall, crushed up against the walls to give the fighters space, began to favour him in the betting. Even Trystan was watching avidly.

'That should be me,' he muttered as he sipped from a beaker of milk Ninian had given him. A little colour had come back into his face, but his forehead was still beaded with sweat. 'She made me look a fool!' He scowled across the room at Essylt.

'Then you know now how it feels.' Now that Trystan was safe, it could be said.

'What do you mean?'

'You stole something from me last night, something you didn't really want. And today, in front of everyone, you stole my chance to defend my own honour. You made *me* look a fool. And a coward.'

'You'd been ill. *You* were a fool if you thought you could fight.'

'Was that truly the reason? Wasn't it rather that you wanted to show everyone what Trystan of Lothian could do?'

Trystan coloured faintly and didn't answer immediately. He was watching the fight and grunted in approval as Aelfric lunged at Broichan, forcing him to dance out of range.

'I wanted to show *you*, Corwynal,' he said eventually. 'What I did last night was for you, though I know you don't believe me. Today I tried to make amends, and you still don't believe me. You don't even trust me enough to tell me what this challenge is really about. What was Broichan about to say when the druid stopped him?'

Corwynal regretted starting this conversation. 'Not now, Trys,' he said, as he always did whenever Trystan asked about his past. But this time, he wasn't to be put off.

'I would have risked my life for you if Essylt hadn't spoiled everything. You owe me an explanation.'

The muttering of the crowd died away to a low rumble. Or maybe it was just the sound of thunder in the distance. It had begun to rain, a sudden spring downpour that hammered on the thatch of the hall, the run-off churning in the gutter, the downpour sounding like drums beating out of his past.

'Broichan was about to give me the name I earned in Atholl because of something that happened there. I killed an archdruid and... someone else. The archdruid was my grandfather. It was an accident, but they call me Kinslayer now.'

Trystan's eyes widened with shock and disbelief. 'Kinslayer!? But you could only have been a boy when you were in Atholl!'

'Old enough to know better. Old enough to suffer the consequences. Blaize helped me escape, but it's not been forgotten.' He nodded at Broichan as he blocked yet another of Aelfric's crushing blows. 'He's a kinsman also, a second-cousin.'

Trystan looked at Broichan with renewed interest. 'And heir to the King of Atholl. So that makes you—'

'Broichan's not the heir,' Corwynal cut in. 'Kingship follows the female line in Caledonia. However, as my kinsman, he has the right to claim the blood price for what I did.'

'I should have killed him at the fort.'

'Why didn't you?'

Trystan shrugged. 'He looked like you in a way, which makes sense if you're kin. He bore the same markings.'

Not quite the same, Corwynal thought, still feeling the druid's fingernail trace the coils of the serpent, now safely hidden once more beneath his bronze arm-band. But he said nothing of that, and Trystan turned his attention back to the fight, for at that moment Broichan lunged forward in a darting blow that Aelfric parried awkwardly, and Broichan's blade slid through the fleshy part of the Angle's shoulder.

A ripple of surprise ran around the hall, and men craned forward, curious to see how the Angle would react, expecting him to lose his temper. Perhaps Broichan expected it too, had even planned for it, but Aelfric held back, blood running down his arm and dripping from his elbow, and he met Broichan's next onslaught of blows quite calmly, blocking and parrying but not attacking. He seemed to be waiting for Broichan to make some miscalculation. And then, between one heartbeat and the next, Broichan did just that. His right-handed low thrust to the groin was parried by the heavy saex, but Aelfric, instead of bringing up his axe to meet the backhand sweep of Broichan's other blade, ducked beneath it and brought his own weapon down hard on the sword in Broichan's right hand, smashing it to the ground and shattering it at the guard. Broichan, unbalanced, missed his next stroke, giving Aelfric the opening he'd wanted, and his saex thrust upwards to drive deep into the other man's thigh.

'Enough!' Domech jumped to his feet as Broichan went down and couldn't get up. Aelfric raised his axe above his head, but it was only to acknowledge the cheers of the men in the hall.

The other Caledonians helped Broichan limp from the hall, but the Archdruid remained.

'The challenge is answered,' he said grimly. 'Broichan, son of Ciniod, concedes defeat.'

Broichan, his arm around the shoulders of one of his companions, stopped in the doorway and turned to look back at Corwynal. His eyes were glittering with hatred, and Corwynal knew that one day matters would have to be settled between them, one day when he returned to Atholl, as he'd promised both an archdruid and a god. *But not yet*, he thought. *Not for a very long time.*

⛬

A watery sun rose through the thin grey cloud that had hung about Meldon's valley after the rain, and, with the new day, the stronghold came to life. Smoke plumed from the huts as the fires, damped down for the night, were stirred into life. But no smoke emerged from the hut where the Caledonians were lodged. There was no smoke because there was no fire, and no fire because there were no men. The Caledonians had slipped away in the night.

Corwynal kicked Aelfric awake, then prodded Gaheris into consciousness and sent him to fetch Trystan and to tell Kaerherdin to wake Hoel.

'What is it?' Trystan emerged into the hall from a private chamber, rubbing sleep from his eyes and pulling on his jerkin.

'The Caledonians have gone.'

'How? They were supposed to be kept in Meldon until we'd left! Who let them out?'

No-one had, the guards insisted. The gate had remained shut, and they'd seen nothing all night. They hadn't left their posts or fallen asleep.

'Well, how do you explain it then?!' Hoel demanded, irritated at being disturbed before he'd broken his fast 'Did eight Caledonians and their horses fly over the ramparts? Or did the wood-sprites steal them away? Answer me that! And wipe that muck off your faces. This isn't some pigsty!'

Puzzled, the guards rubbed their faces, brushing away a pale fine dust.

'The druid.' Corwynal hadn't forgotten how, seventeen years before, men had knuckled their eyes free of ash and believed they'd forgotten everything.

'Curse it!' Trystan smashed his fist down on a table. 'The route north will be held against us now. We'll have to go east, back to Trimontium. It will be days before we can join Lot, and we're already late.'

'It's worse than that,' Corwynal said. 'Ninian went with the Caledonians.'

※

Corwynal had left the feast early the previous night and returned to the guest hut he now shared with Gaheris, Aelfric and Ninian. Gaheris and Aelfric were still at the feast, and Ninian had offered to treat Broichan's wound. So Corwynal had the place to himself and was glad of it because he needed to think. Why had Domech given him that warning, and what did it mean? *To the west,* he'd said, and a druid could dissemble but wasn't permitted to lie directly, so there had to be some truth in it. Did he mean that the Caledonian tribes of the western seaboard, the Creonn and Carnonacs, had joined the Confederacy? Yet their lands lay more to the north, and they rarely concerned themselves with the ambitions of those further east. So what *had* Domech meant?

Corwynal was still puzzling it through when Ninian came in. The Scot didn't immediately see him sitting against the wall, for the fire in the centre of the room had died down. The Scot bent over the ashes to stir it into life and the flames lit up a face ravaged by indecision. Corwynal cleared his throat and Ninian looked up in alarm.

'I thought you were still in the hall!'

'If Trystan has his way, we'll be leaving early tomorrow, so I thought I'd get some sleep. You should do likewise.'

Ninian nodded and looked down into the fire, his expression uncharacteristically serious.

'I'm not going with you,' he said eventually. 'I don't want to go to war, but it isn't because I'm a coward, though I know that's what everyone will think.' He gave a hard, self-mocking laugh. 'I've never been any good at fighting, but I hope I have a different sort of courage.' He placed his palms together as if in prayer, then opened them out above the fire. 'I really did want to be a priest, you know. But they told me, in the seminary, that I wasn't ready, that I might never be ready. That's why I left, to prove them wrong, but all I proved was how right they were. I'm not ready. I've spent my life waiting for something, and I don't even know what it is.' He rubbed a hand down his face. 'Not that it matters now, because I don't have a choice anymore. My place is with my own people, and maybe I just needed to be reminded of that . . .'

Ninian had clearly drunk too much at the feast, and, when he'd gone to treat Broichan's wound, the Archdruid had touched some raw place in his spirit, much as he'd touched the raw place in Corwynal's.

'Get some sleep, Ninian.'

The Scot nodded wearily, rolled himself in his blanket, and

was silent. Corwynal listened to the logs crackling in the fire, the wind howling in the thatch and the faint trickle of rain in the stone gutter below the eaves, gentle sounds that blurred and thickened into dreams of the past, of a life that might have been, and perhaps those dreams were succeeded by others, for when he woke it was with Domech's words ringing in his head. *Look to the west!* And he understood what the Archdruid had meant, and what Ninian had been trying so very hard not to tell him.

The Dalriads had allied themselves with the Caledonians.

'That's just a guess,' Hoel pointed out the following morning. 'Why should the Scots get involved? What would be in it for them?'

They'd gathered in Meldon's hall, and Hoel had brought out a map. It couldn't compare with Lot's but was sufficiently detailed to show the difficulties they faced.

'That's why.' Corwynal pointed, not at Dalriada to the west, but to the inlets and mountains to the north of the Scots' territories, the lands of the Caledonian Creonn tribe. 'They've been raiding Dalriada for years. I'm guessing the deal will be that they'll be reined in if Dalriada allies itself with the Caledonians against Lot. And then . . .'

He moved his finger to the long peninsula of Ceann Tìre, the Dalriad lands that lay across the Sound of Arainn, to the west of the coasts of Strathclyde and Galloway, coasts that, in the absence of the war-bands and their levy of men, would be unprotected. 'The Scots will strike east,' he said. *Look to the west.* That's what the druid must have meant.'

'S-s-someone should warn my father,' Gaheris said, but even he knew Lot wouldn't welcome this news. If Marc of

Galloway and Dumnagual of Strathclyde learned of this new threat, both would return to protect their coasts, leaving Lot with insufficient men to fight the Caledonians in Manau.

'Why should the druid tell you anything?' Kaerherdin asked.

'He wanted me to join them. I refused,' Corwynal said shortly, sensing his allegiance was once more in question.

'He knew you'd refuse,' Trystan said, frowning down at the map. 'He knows we'd warn Lot.' He looked around at them all. 'So it has to be a trick.'

Was Trystan right? Had both he and Ninian been used? Had the druid come to Meldon not for Hoel's answer, or to persuade Corwynal to return to Atholl, but simply to spread misinformation? *Look to the west!* He glanced down at the map once more and wondered where Lot and his army were. After mustering at the eastern end of the Wall, they would have headed for Iuddeu, the old Briton stronghold that lay to the east of the Great Moss, not far from the main crossing of the River Gwerid, the site of many battles. That's where they'd make their stand.

So, what was west of Iuddeu? The Gwerid twisted and turned through the marshy land of the Moss, hemmed in by an escarpment to the south and the Caledonian hills and forests to the north. But beyond the river, at the end of an old supply route, was a ruined Roman fort on a ridge that overlooked the southern end of Llyn Llumonwy, the Loch of the Beacon – on whose western shore lay lands once held by Caledonians but now in the hands of the Scots of Dalriada.

So that was where they'd come from. Not from the west by sea to land on the unprotected coasts of Galloway and Strathclyde, but overland and then across the loch to fall on Lot's left flank. That's what the druid meant, and what he'd intended to be misunderstood. It was still a guess, though, and

Corwynal needed to be certain.

'I'm going after Ninian.'

He'd intended going alone, but Trystan announced he was going too and insisted on Aelfric going with them.

'He has a bandaged shoulder,' Corwynal pointed out.

'You have a bandaged side.'

'It's almost healed. At least I can ride, which is more than can be said for him.'

'I'm going.' Aelfric scowled at him.

'Why?'

'Why the fuck do you think? Ninian's our friend.'

Corwynal blinked in surprise. It was the first time he'd heard Aelfric use the word 'our'. He was also the first person to say out loud what everyone was thinking – that, ally of the Caledonians or not, Ninian was in danger.

And so, in the end, they were a party of four. Gaheris was left behind in Meldon to get Trystan's hundred men ready to leave, but Kaerherdin, who should have shared that task, announced that, as Selgovia's best tracker, he was going too. It turned out, however, that Selgovia's best tracker wasn't needed since the trail could have been followed by a half-blind child.

The Caledonians had ridden north and into woodland, following a deer trail that climbed up through birch-wood to higher ground where they could follow the ridgeway that led north to the lowlands of Manau and thence across the river valleys to Atholl. It began to rain, and the wood was loud with purling streams and raindrops pattering through the trees. But the rain couldn't obscure the passage of nine horses, and the trail was clear enough. 'Too clear,' Kaerherdin muttered.

The grove, when they came to it, was less than an hour's ride from Meldon, one of the sacred groves of the Selgovae – a ring of oaks, open ground between them, a great patriarch standing sentinel over the others like a stag protecting his herd of hinds. Its trunk was so wide the tree must have stood there even in the time of the Romans, and Corwynal wondered if the bodies of captured legionaries had ever hung from its branches. Then he saw, with a shudder of horror, that a man hung there still.

He was hanging from the lower branches of the sentinel oak. His head was still attached to his body, and he was suspended by his arms, his back against the trunk, his chest a mass of blood, hacked across again and again. He'd been pinned to the tree like the crucified god he'd worshiped, and though it took Corwynal a moment to recognise him, he knew who it had to be.

'Ninian?!'

Aelfric didn't know who said the name first, or who growled in anger and outrage. Perhaps it was himself, perhaps all of them.

Fucking Caledonians! Aelfric thought as he stared at the ruin of the man hanging from the tree, rain dripping from his hair. Then he turned furiously on Corwynal because, no matter what he claimed, he was a Caledonian too. But far from being ashamed, the man was equally furious, and Aelfric recoiled from the expression in his eyes. Kaerherdin was just as outraged, though Aelfric, whose people also revered trees, thought his anger due more to the desecration of the grove than the man.

'I'm going to kill that druid,' Corwynal swore, and Kaerherdin grunted in agreement. The two men kicked their horses, all set to go after the Caledonians. But Trystan, who was between them and the track, yanked on the reins of his stallion and threw the beast in front of them, making Corwynal's mare rear and Kaerherdin's gelding skid to a halt.

'Are you trying to kill us!?' Corwynal yelled at him. Aelfric, reckoning they were going to be there for some time, flung a leg over his horse's shoulders and dropped to the ground, thanking Thunor one of the Britons was showing some sense.

'It's a trap,' Trystan said. 'The trail's too clear. They wanted us to follow. They wanted us to see this.' He waved a hand at Ninian. 'Why else would they do this to someone who was supposed to be their ally?'

'The druid warned me,' Corwynal said, breathing hard through clenched teeth. 'He said I'd regret refusing him. This is what he meant. But I'm going to make *him* regret it!'

'Don't be more of a fool than you can help,' Aelfric said scornfully.

'This has nothing to do with you! I owe my life to Ninian. I don't know how it is with you Angles, but we Britons avenge our dead!'

'You think Ninian wants revenge? You can't have been paying attention to all his blather if you believe that!'

'Aelfric's right,' Trystan said. 'Ninian followed Chrystos. We have to bury him properly.'

Aelfric shook his head in exasperation. What did the Britons keep between their ears? Moss? 'You're wrong, you fucking Caledonian bastard. We Angles *do* avenge our dead – but we make sure they're dead first.'

The resulting silence was deeply gratifying.

'Ninian's still alive,' he said with grim satisfaction as he made for the tree. 'So which of you heroes is going to help me get him down?'

It wasn't until that day that Corwynal realised just how strong Aelfric was. Ninian had been tied to the oak and pinned there by wooden stakes driven through his wrists and ankles, but the Angle pulled them out with his bare hands, his neck barely cording with the effort, and they were able to lower Ninian to the ground and see how badly he was hurt. He'd groaned once when Aelfric pulled out the stakes but, other than this, there were few signs of life. The wounds bled only sluggishly and his heartbeat was faint. It didn't look hopeful.

'Kaer – ride back to Meldon and make sure the men are ready to leave,' Trystan said.

They did what they could for Ninian, wrapping him in a cloak and binding the wounds in his ankles and wrists with strips of cloth torn from Aelfric's shirt. Trystan fetched water from a stream and began to clean the slashes on Ninian's chest. They weren't deep, but as the blood was washed away Corwynal saw a pattern in the cuts and he sat back on his heels in horror. Ninian's chest had been carved with a symbol, the sign of Ase, the dark god of the stones, Ase of the crescent and the snake. The Scot had been sacrificed, and this was more than a message or the fulfilment of a threat. This was a spell, a death intended to force Corwynal back to Atholl. But Ninian hadn't died, at least not yet. The Scot's eyes fluttered open on a groan, and he looked up, his wavering gaze settling on Corwynal.

'My people,' he breathed. 'Stop them. In the name of God . . .'

His shirt and tunic had been cut away, but the Caledonians had left the cross he wore about his neck, and he reached for it to press it into Corwynal's hand. 'Stop them . . .'

'Is it true? Has Dalriada allied with the Caledonians?'

Ninian nodded faintly and closed his eyes once more.

'Where will they land?'

'Laomuinn,' he whispered.

'Llyn Llumonwy,' Corwynal translated. It was as he'd suspected. 'The Loch of the Beacon. West of Iuddeu.'

'How many are there?' Trys asked.

'Stop them...' Ninian muttered then lapsed back into unconsciousness once more.

'Curse it! We need to know more!' Trystan jumped to his feet and began to pace about. 'We have to warn Lot and get him to send men west to block their advance. And we need to do it now!'

Corwynal stared down at the bloodied cross in his hand, but he didn't see it. What he was seeing was a battlefield close to Iuddeu, the Caledonians sweeping down from the north, the Scots from the west, the Britons crushed between them like a nut. He was seeing a defeat that wouldn't end there. For if the Caledonians won they'd overrun Manau and head east for Lothian. The Caledonians of Fife would turn on the Britons and, from all the harbours of the north, black-sailed ships would slip their moorings and head south for the open beaches of Lothian and Gododdin. And through it all he saw the hooded eyes of the druid and his cold smile of satisfaction. *You'll regret this, in more ways than you can imagine.* Then he heard laughter, but it wasn't the druid's.

He looked up; there in the shadow of the oak, lounging against the trunk, was Arddu, his hawk's eyes cruel with anticipation, rain dripping from his antlers and gleaming on his naked body.

You think this the druid's doing alone? You tried to trick a god!

Arddu had come as he'd come before in another clearing in another forest to force him to make a choice.

Stop my people, Ninian had said, and if they were to be stopped, there was no time for delay. Corwynal looked down at Ninian once more and saw a ruin, a man close to death. If he was a dog or a horse, he wouldn't hesitate.

So choose, Arddu crooned in his ear, his breath on Corwynal's cheek smelling of leaf-mould and old blood. *Life or death. You chose before. Choose again. One death, many lives. One life, many deaths. Choose, Talorc of Atholl. Choose, Corwynal of Lothian . . .*

Corwynal felt the forest close in, saw the oak bend its branches to the ground, heard the dark spirits of the trees murmur in anticipation of a death in an oak grove, and then the rustle of their hunger as he drew his knife.

Trystan cried out in protest, but it was Aelfric who moved, lunging towards him to twist the knife out of his grip.

'I'm not letting you kill him!'

'I wasn't going to!' But he knew that ending Ninian's life was what he ought to do. He snatched his knife back, got to his feet, went over to Janthe to find his spare harness, and began cutting it into pieces. 'We have to make a litter to carry him back to Meldon. Trys – I'll need your spare harness too. As for you—' He glared over his shoulder at the Angle. 'Fetch your axe and make yourself useful.'

For once Aelfric didn't reply. He gave Corwynal a long steady look then pulled his axe from his saddle-pack and began to lop branches from the trees.

'Then what?' Trystan asked.

'Then we're going to do what Ninian asked us to do,' Corwynal said. 'We're going to stop the Scots.'

PART III

LOCH OF THE BEACON

SPRING 485 AD

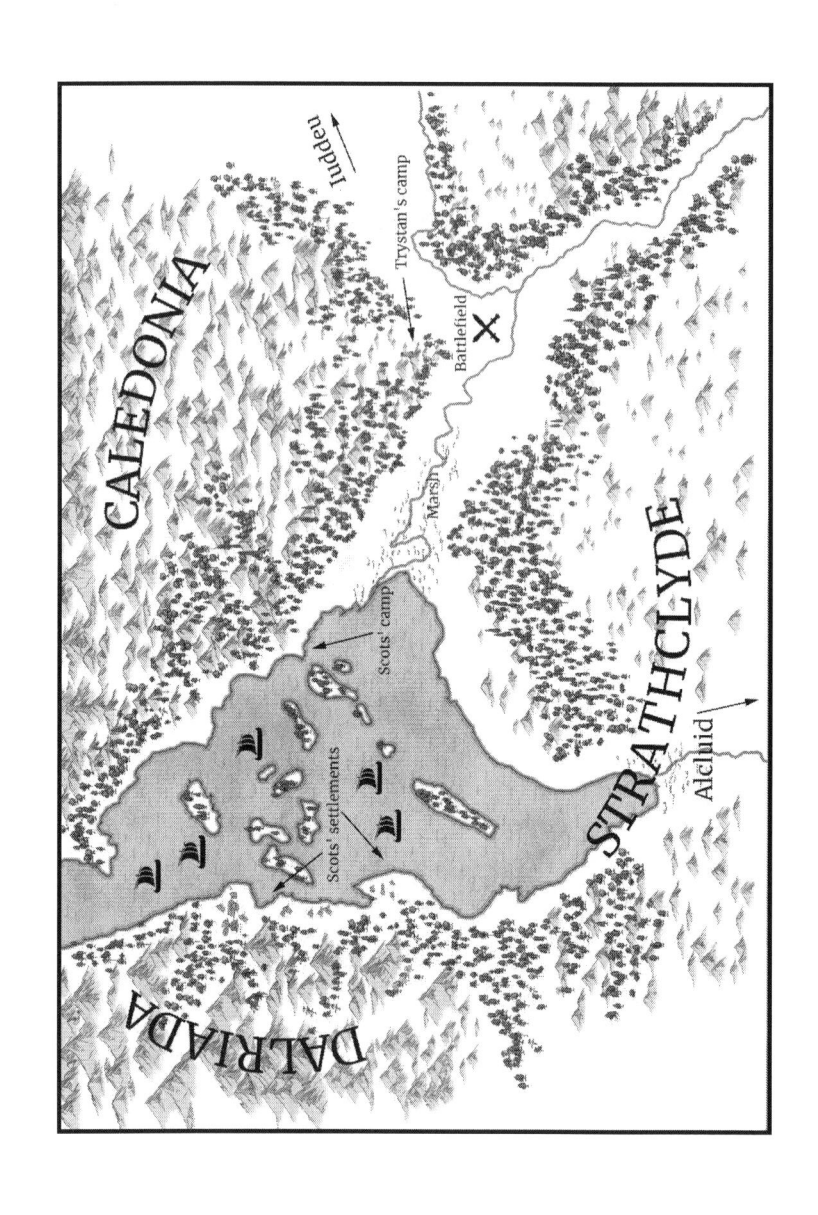

THE BATTLE OF BEACON LOCH

10

THE RAVEN OF GALLOWAY

Hoel tried to talk them out of it, but Trystan was determined, and one might as well have tried to stop a charging boar or hold a salmon in your grasp. Trystan and his Selgovian troop were going to fight the Scots by the Loch of the Beacon as part of Lot's war. 'Scots,' Trystan pointed out to Hoel. 'Not Caledonians.' Since that might have led to a certain ... awkwardness. So it made sense. At least, that was how he persuaded Hoel in the end. Although, in truth, sense didn't come into it, because all Trystan was interested in was the glory, and Corwynal, watched, half-amused, half-exasperated, as Trystan convinced himself that fighting the Scots had been his idea all along.

But, whatever Trystan's motivation, to Corwynal the plan had merit, not just for the Selgovae, whose loyalty might otherwise be in question, but for himself, since fighting the Caledonians hadn't turned out to be as easy as he'd imagined back in Lothian. The Scots, on the other hand, were a different matter. He'd fought them before, and he could fight them again – if it came to a fight. Although maybe it wouldn't, because there might be another way to stop them.

That was for the future, however, as were so many things, including a looming confrontation with Trystan over command and strategy. Then there was revenge for a mutilation, an enemy made, and a promise he'd have to fulfil one day. For the moment, however, he had no misgivings. He was fulfilling the promise he'd made to Trystan in Lothian. He was taking him to war, to a battle Corwynal could give his whole heart to, and, as they rode west down the remains of an old Roman road, he and Trystan were of one mind and one purpose.

The sun burst through the rainclouds and burnished Trystan's hair to gold. The weapons of the Selgovian bowmen glittered in the light as they cantered, clear-eyed and hard-faced, behind them. Banners fluttered in the wind of their passage: the Wolf of Lothian, the Boar of Gododdin, and, green on white, Selgovia's Tree. Trystan, riding beside him, grinned across at him, and a lump formed in Corwynal's throat. In that moment, Trystan was the man he'd always intended him to be, a bright warrior and a leader of men, even if he'd already forgotten the price of everything he'd gained. Corwynal, on the other hand, hadn't been allowed to forget so easily.

'So, you're leaving,' Essylt said coldly when he went to say goodbye to her, something Trystan had failed to do. He'd found her in the guest hut where she'd tended him, and where she now had another patient to care for. The place still smelled of the bitter herb with which she'd drugged both him and Trystan, and which was now keeping Ninian quiet. 'You'll follow Trystan, as I'm not permitted to do.' All trace of the laughing girl of the morning before had vanished.

'We're going to war, Essylt. It's no place for a woman.'

'Why not? I can ride as well as Kaerherdin. I'm as good an archer. Why shouldn't I ride with my husband?' She held up a hand to prevent Corwynal from replying. 'I'll tell you why not.

Because he doesn't want me. He wanted the men. Not me.' Corwynal could think of nothing to say that wouldn't be a lie, but his silence was answer enough. 'And now he hates me for drugging him,' she said bitterly. 'Yet all I did was try to save his life. I suppose you hate me for drugging you too. I kept you weak when you were ill, but I did it for Selgovia. We needed time, my father and I. Time to talk to you, time to make deals. You would have done the same for Lothian.' Once more, he didn't know what to say, and she turned away from him. 'How long does love last?' she asked eventually. 'Does it wither with the years? Does the taste of it grow bitter?'

'It fades if you allow it,' he said without conviction.

'And meanwhile? What am I to do while I wait for it to fade?'

'You're a Princess, Essylt. One day you'll be Queen. You have your duties here in Selgovia and your skills, skills that will be needed if Ninian's to live.

She nodded and squared her shoulders: a young girl taking up a burden no-one her age should have to bear. His heart went out to her, and he felt guilty about leaving. But he couldn't stay. *Stop my people*, Ninian had begged.

'Can you keep him alive?' He looked down at the Scot, who was muttering under his breath. *Feargus*, he said distinctly at one point. *They'll betray him. The Caledonians. They'll let him fight alone. Tell him, persuade him, warn him* ... And then there was a woman's name, repeated over and over, Branwen, or something like it. *She'll know*, Ninian said. *She knows everything*. Was Branwen the girl he'd left behind? Then he began to say another name. 'Essylt ... Essylt ...'

'I'm here, Ninian.' Essylt's voice, so cold and distant a moment before, had become soft and almost womanly. Ninian opened his eyes and looked up at her, but a frown of puzzlement furrowed his brow, and he turned his head away and closed his eyes once more. 'Essylt... Essylt?'

She laughed bitterly. 'You see? Even a dying man rejects me. I'm the wrong Essylt, it seems, so there's no comfort to be found here.' She looked up at Corwynal, her eyes narrowed. 'That's what Trystan wants, isn't it? For me to find comfort elsewhere, since that's what he'll be doing?'

'Of course not!' His denial failed to convince even himself.

'Remind him he's married,' she said fiercely. 'He bought a war-band with his freedom, and I'll keep my side of the bargain if he keeps his. But I won't give him up. Tell him that.'

Corwynal had thought of her as a windflower, but not anymore. She was a rose, a cold white rose with a flush of anger at its throat, a rose that climbed and twisted and drove its thorns deep into the flesh.

⁂

'Are we going to ride all fucking night?' Aelfric demanded when it began to look as if they'd be doing just that. 'Fucking horses!' he growled, shifting in the saddle to ease the chafing in his thighs. 'Where are we going, anyway?'

To fight the Scots. That was as much as anyone had told him, which didn't tell him much, and, when he asked the Selgovae where the Scots were, they just waved vaguely at the sun setting like a great bonfire all along the horizon ahead of them. *In the west*, they said with a shrug, as if they didn't much care. Well, maybe they didn't, but Aelfric liked to know who he'd be fighting. Everything he knew about the Scots came from the stories Ninian had told, but most of those tales had been about that god of his. He'd got more out of Trystan, though that had been little enough. *Fierce creatures, always quarrelling, always singing. You'd like them.*

Not if they sing. Aelfric had had enough singing to last a fucking lifetime.

'If you can't keep up, we'll leave you behind,' Corwynal told him.

You do that! Aelfric thought. He didn't say it, though. For one thing, there was no way he was riding back through those forests on his own, not with all those ghosts and wights waiting to get him. And, for another thing, he didn't know where the fuck he was. All he knew was he was going further and further from the lands he knew.

'I can keep up. I just want to know where we're going.'

'North-west from here,' Trystan said. They'd come down from the Selgovian hills into a broad valley which ran roughly north and had one of those roads the Romans had built running along the bottom. The Romans were giants, apparently, who built stuff out of stone: roads, forts, even the great Wall that lay north of Aelfric's own lands in Bernicia. But when they'd reached the Roman road only Gaheris had taken it, galloping north to take Lot word of the Scots. The rest of them carried on into the west and headed up into hills on the far side of the valley, following a drovers' trail that became increasingly difficult to follow, especially once the sun set. The night was clear, however, and eventually the moon rose behind them, full enough to let them go on riding, though it still wasn't easy.

'We'll pick up another Roman road when we drop down to the Cluta,' Trystan said. 'It'll take us all the way to the Wall.'

'The Wall?' Surely the Wall lay several day's journey behind them?

'The northern Wall. It runs across the country from the River Cluta to the River Gwerid. We'll cross it, then take to the hills to the north and strike west for the loch. That's right, isn't it, Corwynal?'

'You're very confident for someone who's never been there.'

Trystan just laughed. 'It was you who made me study all those old maps! So I know there's an old fort where the road crosses the river. It can't be far now. We'll rest there and press on in the morning.'

True to Trystan's word, it wasn't long before the drovers' trail dropped down into trees and pasture. There was farmland ahead, and a river that twisted in lazy coils through the river valley and glinted in the moonlight. In the distance, crowning a low rise in a coil of the river, Aelfric thought he could make out a fort and the pale thread of a road running up the east bank. A bridge took the road to the far side, where it continued, heading north on the opposite bank. All about the bridge and the road, and surrounding the fort, was a flicker of lights.

'What's that?' Trystan asked. Kaerherdin shaded his eyes against the glare of moonlight to better make it out. He had good eyes, did the Selgovian, but even an old man like the Caledonian could see what was waiting for them down by the bridge.

'That, my dear Trystan—' he said dryly. '—is an army.'

An hour later, kneeling in the mud of the road with his hands tied behind his back, Corwynal wished he'd accepted Trystan's offer.

'Take Aelfric with you.'

Corwynal had shaken his head. 'I'm going to talk, not start a war. I don't need a bodyguard. It's perfectly safe.'

Kaerherdin and a couple of Selgovian scouts had melted into the landscape as only Selgovians could, and when they'd returned, it was to confirm what Corwynal had suspected.

'Galloway,' Kaerherdin said, spitting in disgust. 'I saw the sign of the raven.'

'Any other banners?'

'A ship. Black, I think.'

And so Corwynal had insisted on going alone. 'They know me in Galloway, Trys. They don't know you, and, in case you'd forgotten, you're in command of the Selgovae. You have to stay with them.'

But Trystan didn't like it. 'Can't we go around them? And what are they doing here in the first place? If they're joining Lot, they should have been in Manau by now.'

'We can't go around because we need to be on the other side of the river, and that's the only bridge. If there's a ford further north, I don't know about it. Nor do I know what they're doing there; that's what I'm going to find out.'

Trystan argued, of course. He wanted to press on and swim the horses across the river if they couldn't find a ford. But that would delay them, and anyway both horses and men needed rest.

'Give me until dawn, Trys. I just need to persuade them we're on the same side and they'll let us ride through.'

But Corwynal's first attempt at persuasion failed in the face of Galloway's suspicion of anyone who wasn't from Galloway.

'Lothian?' exclaimed the leader of the picket he'd approached. The man had thrust a torch at Corwynal and, seeing the wolf on his tunic, spat with as much disgust as Kaerherdin. They'd forced him to dismount and hand his weapons over, so he was glad he hadn't brought Aelfric, who would have refused to do either. 'A message from Lot? Do you think I'm an idiot?! Lot's to the north of us, not the south.'

'I know. He's in Manau, which is where Galloway should be right now.'

One of them kicked him from behind, and he fell to his knees. 'Is that any of your sodding business, you Lothian bastard?'

'I'm Corwynal of Lothian, Marc's friend, and—'

They kicked him again and sent him sprawling. 'That's crap! Corwynal of Lothian's in Lothian, with our Prince. Has him chained hand and foot. You, a wizard? Don't make me laugh! Tie him up, Vran. He's a spy, so we'd better take him to The Old Man . . .'

Wizard? Corwynal wondered as they pulled his arms behind him and tied them tightly. *Chained hand and foot?* Was that really what they thought in Galloway? And who was The Old Man?

They dragged him to his feet and marched him up the road towards the main part of the camp. The raven of Galloway was flying from the standards. As was the ship. But it was a different ship from the one in his dreams, and it wasn't black, though in the moonlight it might have seemed so. A torch flared in the wind, close to a large command tent, and Corwynal could see, with a shudder of relief, that the ship on the standard was red.

'So Andrydd commands?' he concluded without surprise, remembering belatedly that a red ship was the sign of the Lord of Loch Ryan. 'He knows me.' *And hates me.* Andrydd had been one of Gwenllian's many admirers and had resented anyone she'd paid any attention to, including the young captain from Lothian. Andrydd was only a little older than Corwynal, but must be the one they called The Old Man. 'He'll be able to confirm who I am.'

'We'll see,' the troop captain replied. 'If you're who you say you are, this will really make his day, and he's in a bleeding bad mood already.' He jerked his head at the large tent, from which could be heard the sound of an argument.

'You want Galloway to be the last to arrive?' a voice demanded. 'You want us to be a laughing stock? We should be moving while there's sufficient light to ride by, not stopping every time you feel like a drink—'

'Who, in the name of all the gods, do you think you are? I'll drink when I like and stop when I like—'

There was a muttered curse, and a figure thrust his way out of the tent, just as the guard pushed Corwynal ahead of him.

'Get out of my way, peasant!' Then, at the sight of the wolf on Corwynal's tunic, the man stopped in his tracks. His eyes flew to Corwynal's face, and his jaw fell.

'You? Here?'

The years, Corwynal concluded, must have changed him as little as they'd changed Andrydd. The other man was older, of course, heavier and greyer, but, apart from that, he looked the same, and he clearly saw no reason to like Corwynal any more than he had eighteen years before. Nevertheless, he nodded at the guard, who hurriedly stripped off Corwynal's bonds. Then Andrydd took his arm to lead him away from the tent, but Corwynal shook him off and moved towards the opening, his heart beating hard in his chest because he'd recognised that other voice.

'No, wait! He's . . . not as you remember. Best leave him.'

Corwynal hesitated, for something in Andrydd's voice spoke of truth and not stratagem, but it was already too late. The flap of the tent swept open and a big man stood in the entrance clutching at one of the guy-ropes with a beefy hand. He was swaying slightly, his eyes wild, his hair disordered, his richly embroidered tunic stained with a dark liquid. Corwynal knew who this had to be, but, to his sorrow, barely recognised him. The other man, however, knew exactly who Corwynal was.

'You?' The man closed his eyes and shook his head as if to

clear away some vision and seemed disconcerted when he opened his eyes and found that Corwynal was still there. 'Corwynal?'

There was something in his voice, if not his person, that Corwynal remembered, something in the way he said his name. 'Marc? Sire?'

The King of Galloway stared at him as if he was looking at a ghost. Then he stumbled and fell to his knees, dropped his head into his hands and began to weep great tearing sobs.

With Andrydd's help, Corwynal got Marc to lie down on the camp bed in his tent and sleep off whatever he'd been drinking. Only when Andrydd had left and Marc was snoring drunkenly did Corwynal allow himself to grieve for the man he'd known. Marc's once-golden hair was streaked with grey, and his broad shoulders were soft with flesh. Marc's eyes had been a clear and vivid blue, but now, when he woke up with the suddenness of the habitual drunk, those eyes were netted with red veins, the whites yellow with dissipation, and he blinked in the lamplight as if he had difficulty focusing.

'Corwynal? I'm not dreaming?' He wiped a hand across his sweating face and heaved himself up. 'I see things sometimes, you know. You . . . Her . . .' He shuddered, then shouted for a servant. 'You there! Bring wine.'

'No, Marc. No wine.'

The servant hesitated, and the King's face turned an unhealthy purple.

'Bring wine, you cretin! Corwynal's my friend. You have to drink with old friends!'

Corwynal nodded at the man but conveyed with a gesture

the request that he take his time. He wanted Marc sober enough to be persuadable.

'I missed you,' Marc said. 'Why didn't you come back with... with Her?'

'You know why I didn't.'

'The boy. Her son.' He smacked a fist on his knee. 'In all these years, I had no word of him!'

'Nonsense! You had spies in Lothian, so you knew he wasn't chained hand and foot by a wizard, as your men seem to believe.'

'I can't help what they believe. But he's in Lothian, isn't he? Cooped up with that sour old man?'

'Lothian's under arms. Where do you think he is?'

'Manau?' Corwynal didn't correct him. Best Marc think Trystan far from there, rather than barely a mile south of the Galloway camp. Corwynal's fear of the black ship was gone, but there were other things to be afraid of, Andrydd's ambitions for one, Marc himself for another. Marc mustn't find Trystan, and Trystan mustn't see his mother's brother looking like this.

'Why aren't you with him?' Marc asked. 'It's said you never leave his side. That much I've learned, if nothing else.'

'I had business in Selgovia, Lot's business. Listen, Marc, Hoel has come to terms with Lot, and he's sent a troop of Selgovae to fight for him. I'm with them. We don't want any trouble, so pass word they're to be allowed to ride through, then press on yourself to join the army in Manau. If you're late, you endanger Lot's strategy and the safety of all Lot's men – and that includes Trystan.'

That persuaded him, and Marc shouted at the servant, who'd returned with the wine, to take that cursed stuff away, bring bread and meat, and send for Andrydd.

'Sire?' Galloway's war-band leader, arriving shortly afterwards, was clearly taken aback to find the King eating, but not drinking.

'We have to press on,' Marc said and, when Andrydd stared at him, 'Well? What are you waiting for? Oh, and a bunch of Selgovae are heading north. They've joined Lot, so let them through.'

'Selgovae?' Andrydd shot Corwynal a suspicious look, not much liking this new decisive Marc. 'If they've joined Lot, let them join us. We can ride to Manau together. Except I'm wondering what, if these Selgovians are so set on joining Lot, they're doing this far to the west?'

Marc frowned at that, suspicious himself now, and Corwynal was forced to tell the truth.

'We're not going to Manau. Dalriada's allied itself with the Caledonians, and we—'

'What?!' Andrydd and Marc exchanged a glance, and Marc heaved himself to his feet. 'Back,' he said with decision. 'Send the word. We're going back to Galloway.'

'No! That's what the Caledonians want!'

'You think I'm going to mess about in Manau for Lot when my coasts are being raided?'

'But they're not . . .'

It took a map to convince them. Marc's map wasn't as detailed as Lot's, but good enough for Corwynal to make his point, and in the end Marc and Andrydd exchanged a nod of agreement.

'It makes sense, I suppose,' Marc said. 'Because we'd heard rumours . . .'

'You have spies in Dalriada?'

'What do you take me for? Of course I have spies in Dalriada!'

'We'd heard the war-branch had gone out,' Andrydd said. 'But there was no sign of fleets gathering, so we assumed they intended moving north against the Creonn.' He frowned. 'Although, according to our . . . sources, the Creonn have been quiet of late.'

So Corwynal had been right about why Dalriada had joined the Caledonians.

'Here,' he said, indicating a place just south of the Beacon Loch. 'That's where they'll land, and that's where we have to stop them. Let me and the Selgovae go, Marc. We need to be on the road by dawn if we're to get there in time.'

'Fine,' Marc said eventually, exchanging a conspiratorial look with Andrydd, though Marc's orders to his war-band leader seemed clear enough. 'Send word to the pickets. There's to be no trouble. These Selgovae can ride through our lines at dawn, and then we'll be on our way ourselves.'

Relieved, but trying not to show it, Corwynal got to his feet.

'Stay, Corwynal.' Marc reached out and gripped his arm.

'But Sire—'

'It's been eighteen years, man. Stay. Talk to me. You can join your men in the morning.'

There was no moving him, so in the end Corwynal had to give in, but he'd succeeded, at least. He'd persuaded Marc to leave the Selgovae alone and hadn't had to tell him Trystan was with them. He'd even convinced Marc to get his army moving to join Lot. A night of reminiscences seemed a small price to pay, but the price was greater than he'd expected, for Marc insisted on wine being served, and Corwynal had to watch the man he'd loved turn into a travesty of what he'd once been.

'Did you teach him that trick with the back-hand feint? Remember, Corwynal?'

Marc was sprawled on his camp-bed, a cup of wine in his hand, an oil-lamp set on a folding table that stood beside the bed. Corwynal sat opposite him on a stool, nursing his own cup and trying to keep the King of Galloway from refilling it as he told him everything Marc wanted to know about Trystan – what he was like, how he fought, what he'd taught him. Was he as good a rider as Marc? He'd be a heartbreaker, no doubt, as Marc himself had been!

'Not any longer though,' the King of Galloway added morosely, succumbing to the swift self-pity of the drunk. 'I should have married, shouldn't I? All my chieftains were on at me to marry, but I didn't want a wife. All I wanted was a son.'

'You can't have one without the other.'

'But I can. I can have Her son. Better Her son than some other woman's. She was... perfect. Do you remember how beautiful She was? How She sang? Does Trystan sing?' Marc swallowed yet another cup of wine and poured more into Corwynal's goblet until it overflowed. 'Drink, Corwynal.'

'It's late, Marc. I have to ride at dawn.'

'Dawn's a long way off. Drink with me. Remember how we used to drink?'

'I've had enough.'

'You've had enough when I say you've had enough! You forget yourself! You forget who I am! People have to do what I say around here! And I say you'll drink with me, you Caledonian bastard! You there, where's that wine?' He turned and gestured to the servant who'd just come in, a man wearing the raven tunic of Galloway. But he wasn't bringing wine; all the man was holding in his hands was a naked sword.

'My brother said he's had enough.'

Trystan stepped into the lamp-light and it ran like water along his blade as he raised it until the point was pricking Marc's throat. 'So let him go.'

Marc stared at him, his eyes going in and out of focus, as he saw, standing before him, spear-straight and golden, a woman seventeen years dead. And he fainted clean away.

⁂

'Come on. Let's go,' Trystan said, lowering his sword and looking scornfully down at Marc.

'What are you doing here?' Corwynal's voice was not quite steady.

'Rescuing you. What are *you* doing here?'

'Achieving what I set out to achieve,' he snapped, his temper only barely held in check, for Trystan had just ruined everything. 'I said dawn. Couldn't you have been patient for once?'

'Anyone would think you didn't want to be rescued!'

'I didn't *need* to be rescued!'

'I saw you. You were on your knees in the road. Your hands were tied behind your back!'

'It was . . . a misunderstanding.'

'A misunderstanding!? So what happened to your tunic?' Trystan gestured to the Lothian tunic, torn in the scuffle in the road. His scolding sounded so like one Corwynal might have given Trystan himself that, in spite of the circumstances, he had a strong desire to laugh. But he managed to suppress it.

'What happened to yours? I see you're wearing the raven of Galloway now.'

'Am I not entitled to? But I don't wear it from choice. We ran into a Galloway picket. They're tied up in a copse down the road. We took their tunics and rode in. It was easy. Now, come on.'

Corwynal sat down and dropped his head into his hands.

'You rode into the camp of Galloway's war-host wearing their raven and you thought it was easy? Have you no idea why, Trys? Did you put it down to the quality of your disguise? Do you imagine no-one noticed?'

'Well...' Trystan began.

'Trys!' Kaerherdin's urgent whisper came from just outside the tent. 'I think we should leave!'

Trystan made for the opening. 'Are you coming or not?' he asked, turning back to Corwynal.

'No. I'm staying here, and so are you,' he said, for escape was no longer an option. 'Help me get him up.' Marc was groaning now, the colour coming back into his face, and together they heaved him onto the bed, where he slouched with his eyes shut, breathing heavily.

'Who is he?' Trystan asked.

'Look closely, Trys. Doesn't he remind you of anyone?'

It wasn't a fair question for Marc no longer looked like his younger self, and even the younger Marc had only vaguely resembled Trystan. Yet there were men in Marc's camp who remembered his sister, Gwenllian, the Fair Flower of Galloway, and those men would have seen the ghost of their Princess riding into the camp. No wonder no-one had tried to stop him. But the men who'd seen that ghost had told others, and now, judging from the murmuring outside, they'd all come to see for themselves.

'He's your uncle, Trys. Your mother's brother. That's Marc, King of Galloway.'

'Very pretty!'

The girl's voice, low and amused, came at Corwynal out of the sun. He was standing in the practice ring, breathing heavily, sweat stinging his eyes, squinting into the light to see who'd spoken. Behind him, flat on his back, lay Daere, his latest opponent, complaining that Corwynal had used a Caledonian trick to beat him.

'Very pretty indeed!' agreed another voice, one he knew. 'Nice backhand,' Marc continued. 'I liked the way you switched hands before the feint to the right. You'll have to teach me that. Teach us all, eh, Daere?'

But Daere just grunted. Corwynal could have beaten him without using that Caledonian move, but he was a stranger in Galloway, with something to prove, and he was glad he'd won in front of Marc and the girl who'd come with him, and who must be the sister he'd heard so much about. She looked a little like Marc, with his fair skin, blonde hair and blue eyes, but where Marc's face was strong and good-natured, Gwenllian's was wilful and beautiful. Corwynal lost his heart to her in that instant.

'. . . do you remember, Corwynal?' Marc's voice, deeper and rougher than it had been eighteen years before, brought him back to the present. They were sitting by a campfire in the midst of the Galloway army, and Marc was regaling Trystan with stories of his mother, reminiscences that had sent Corwynal winging back to his youth.

'Of course he remembers!' Andrydd snapped. He kept looking at Trystan with an expression of both disbelief and frustration, but Trystan returned his gaze blandly and mostly ignored him. His whole attention was on Marc who, having recovered from his drunken faint and realised Trystan wasn't a ghost, but the living breathing image of his much-loved sister, and the boy he'd wanted as a son, had no intention of letting him go.

'I didn't mean the fight!' The girl laughed. 'I meant his markings.'

From the first, the designs on his body had fascinated her. 'Are you a Pict?' she asked, reaching out to draw a finger down the outline of the stag pricked out on his shoulder. His skin took fire from her touch.

'I'm from Lothian, Lady, but I spent some years in Caledonia,' he said woodenly, feeling the blood steal into his face.

'Don't torment the man, Gwen,' Marc said. 'Corwynal's one of my discoveries.' He flung an arm around his shoulders. 'I'm going to make him a troop commander.'

'Perhaps he could command my bodyguard,' Gwenllian suggested, but Marc shook his head.

'Llwyd leads your guard, and I've no intention of replacing him.'

'Llwyd's an old woman,' she said with a pout that Corwynal found utterly charming. 'And the rest of them are old men.'

Marc just smiled. 'With good reason. Can't have some young warrior falling in love with you, eh, my sweet?' He pinched her chin, then cocked his head at Corwynal. 'Not that this one would. These Caledonians are cold fish, you know.'

She smiled a dazzling smile. 'Oh, I'll have this cold fish to lead my guard, just see if I don't!'

And she'd got him in the end. But even as they'd made love by the willow-pool, he'd known he hadn't been the first.

'Of course, I remember,' Corwynal said hurriedly, aware his attention had wandered, and that everyone was looking at him oddly. Trystan frowned across the fire, but Corwynal shook his head at Trystan's concern and thereafter managed to stay in the present as, powerless, he watched Trystan fall under Marc's spell, as once he himself had fallen.

'These Selgovae now... What do you want with them?' Marc asked Trystan. 'If old Rifallyn refused you Lothian's warband, why didn't you come to me, eh? I would have given you as many men as you wanted. Could have given you my whole war-band *and* the levy!'

Trystan's eyes gleamed at that, and he glanced at Andrydd, whose expression had darkened with fury, but made a tactful reply.

'I thank you for the offer, Sire, but I'll continue with my Selgovae, at least for the moment.'

Trystan threw Corwynal a sparkling look. *See, I can be diplomatic when I choose!* 'And with your leave, Sire – uncle – I think we ought to be going...'

The moon had long since set, but there was light in the sky behind the hills to the east.

'No, wait,' Marc said as Trystan got to his feet. 'I've a suggestion before you go...' He rose and led Trystan to his tent, gesturing for Andrydd and Corwynal to follow and, once there, unrolled his map once more. 'These Scots, now. The bastards have to be stopped, like Corwynal said. And it's just the sort of thing I'd have done when I was your age. So you'll head north, cross the Wall and make straight for the Loch?' He traced the route out with his finger. 'Well, suppose another troop came in from the west, like this...' He indicated a body of men moving up towards the south shore of the loch. 'You could crush them between you.'

As the Scots and Caledonians had planned to crush the Britons.

'Yes, but I've only got a hundred men,' Trystan pointed out. 'I don't want to split my forces, especially when we don't know how many Scots there are . . .'

'I'll send some of my men,' Marc said. 'Galloway should play its part in this. See to it, Andrydd.'

'But Sire—' Trystan and Andrydd both protested, but Marc, stubborn as ever, refused to listen to reason. 'It's decided,' Marc declared, rolling up the map. 'You'll cross the Wall and head for the Loch, Trystan. You'll be coming in from the east, so Andrydd'll send a troop further west up past Alcluid. That means they'll be approaching the loch from the south. They can take a look at Alcluid's defences while they're about it, eh?' He exchanged a look with Andrydd Corwynal didn't understand but which silenced any further protests from the Galloway war-band leader. 'Two dawns from now, you both attack. *That* will stop those sodding Scots!'

***

'Did you have to tell him about the Scots?'

It was shortly after dawn, and they were riding north with a showery south-easterly at their backs, having crossed the bridge and left the Galloway camp behind them.

'Did you have to come and rescue me?' Corwynal was irritable with lack of sleep and too much wine. 'But it's done now.'

'I suppose so,' Trystan said, yawning hugely. 'Gods! What a night! I think I'm still drunk.'

Marc had insisted on filling Trystan's cup whenever he'd drained it, but Trystan was drunk more with adulation than wine. Marc had taken him around the camp to show him off to his men, and it had been close to dawn by the time they'd got away, for there were many in the Galloway war-host who remembered Trystan's mother with affection, an affection they clearly felt for Marc himself. His chieftains might hate and mistrust him, and with good reason, but the common people of Galloway loved their once-golden king and, walking around the camp in Trystan's shadow, Corwynal could see why. Marc knew his men, remembered the names of their wives and children, asked after their health, and joked with them around their fires. He was one of them, and now he'd presented them with a young prince, the son of the Fair Flower of Galloway, a boy he treated as if he was his own son. But Trystan didn't realise it since no-one had treated him like a son before – not Corwynal's father, and not Corwynal either, for he'd never allowed himself to. He'd been too concerned with keeping up the pretence of being Trystan's older brother to show him the love he felt.

'I like Marc,' Trys said, still yawning. 'I don't know what I expected – some monster, given how they speak of him in Lothian – but he's not like that, is he? Oh, I know he drinks too much, but we all do that!' he added magnanimously. 'You liked him once, and you still do, don't you?'

Right then, however, Corwynal was all too conscious of Marc's failings: his hedonism and self-indulgence, his determination to get his own way no matter what the cost, his unwillingness to listen to reason, and his delight in playing one man off against another. Yet, Marc wasn't as subtle and devious as the other kings of the Lands between the Walls, nor as self-seeking as his own chieftains. He might behave dishonourably when it suited him – which was often – but at heart he was a simple man trying to make sense of the world, trying to do his best even if his best never seemed to do much good. He'd been a friend when Corwynal had needed a friend, and his affection, once won, was constant and without judgement.

'I suppose so,' he said, but so reluctantly that Trystan snorted.

'That's high praise from you! By all the gods, you're sour this morning! If anyone should be bad-tempered, it's me. We had a perfectly good plan and now it's ruined.'

'Not necessarily. We'll still get there a day before the Galloway men, and there are other things we might try . . .'

Trystan's eyes gleamed in the near-dark. 'You have another plan? What is it?'

'I'll tell you when we get there. It depends on what we find.'

Which wasn't the reason at all. It was because Trystan would object, because it meant breaking one promise in order to keep another. *Stop my people*, Ninian had said. And because it almost certainly wouldn't work.

In normal circumstances Trystan would have badgered him for the details, but he just yawned once more, and when he spoke again, it was to change the subject.

'I hadn't expected the Galloway men to treat me like a god.'

'Don't let it go to your head,' Corwynal advised him dryly, but Trystan just grunted in amusement.

'How can I when I have you to remind me I'm mortal?' He seemed half-asleep in the saddle. 'I can do that, can't I? Rely on you to be there to remind me? Or just to be there . . .'

'I'll be there,' Corwynal said. *I'll be there, at your side, at your back. I'll be there when the man who wears the black ship tries to strike you down. I'll be there to stop him.*

※

'So much for our plan!' Trystan complained when, a day after they'd left the Galloway camp, he, Kaerherdin, Corwynal and Aelfric lay in a dripping thicket of bracken on the edge of a hill that overlooked the Scots' camp on the south-eastern shore of the Beacon Loch.

'Look! More of them!' he said, jerking his chin at the islands that scattered the southern end of the loch beyond which five more of the Scots' fifteen-man coracles were heading for the shore, their sails filled with a fluky westerly breeze.

It was early still, not long after dawn, and the Selgovian troop had camped on the far side of a low ridge a couple of miles to the east, a ridge crowned by the tumbled-down walls of an old Roman fort. As soon as there was enough light the four of them had worked their way north then west, Aelfric grumbling all the way, to climb a steep-sided hill that overlooked a little harbour just north of the marshy shallows of a river that ran into the loch. The Scots occupied a good defensive position, with the hill at their backs, marsh to the south and their boats to hand, should they wish to retreat. But none of that explained why the plan wasn't going to work. It was simply that there were too many of them, three war-bands at least, with more on their way.

As yet, there was little movement in the camp below. It had rained in the night and was still drizzling. Some of the Scots had tents and stayed within them; those without tents huddled in groups of two or three beneath sheets of oiled canvas lashed to spears. A number of standards hung sullenly from poles, but the fickle breeze lifted them for a moment, and Corwynal could make out a sea-eagle on one standard, a grey gull on another, and something black on a third.

'What's that?' he asked. 'A ship?' It certainly looked like the hull of a ship and a mast, a pennant flying from the top. 'A black ship?'

The wind picked up a little and tugged the standard free. Beside him, Kaerherdin, with better eyes than any of them, shook his head. 'It's a black swan. Ninian spoke of it as one of Dalriada's signs.'

Corwynal felt the tension seep out of his body, but he couldn't relax completely, for there were other matters to worry about. Such as what they were going to do now.

'We need another plan,' Trystan said.

Corwynal knew what Trystan wanted, of course – to fight the Scots here and now, to make of the fight a desperate battle the bards would sing about through all the kingdoms of the north. Trystan wasn't a fool, however. They only had a hundred men, and the Scots had three hundred at least. Even with the Galloway troop they were supposed to meet up with – an arrangement none of them liked – they wouldn't have enough. Yet the alternative was to make a shameful retreat, to live and fight another day, to slip south and join the Galloway troop, then ride east to link up with the rest of the army, with the Scots marching in their rear. For surely the Scots were only waiting for the remaining ships to arrive before doing just that.

'We came to stop them.' Trystan turned to Corwynal. 'You had some other plan, didn't you?'

'You won't like it.'

'Maybe not, but I'll listen.'

Corwynal laughed. 'That will be a first! But the plan's simple,' he said. 'We go down there, the four of us – you, me, Kaerherdin and Aelfric. We ride, unarmed, into that camp. And talk them into going home.'

II

THE MUSIC AND THE DANCE

'They could just kill us,' Trystan pointed out as the four of them picked their way along the marshy bank of the river that flowed into the loch just south of the Scots' camp. Corwynal was carrying the green branch of parley. Trystan, still wearing his stolen Galloway tunic, had Lothian's Wolf standard, Kaerherdin the Selgovian Tree, and, since Gaheris had left it behind, Aelfric carried a pennant bearing the Boar of Gododdin.

'They won't. Not today.' Corwynal hadn't truly expected to find the sign of the black ship in the Scots' camp, not here, so far from the sea, but it had been a bad moment when he'd mistaken the swan for a ship. He was still dizzy with relief at being wrong, and annoyed with himself for not remembering Ninian telling him that the lords of Dalriada all took birds as their signs, and a swan was the sign of their king, Feargus. The black ship wasn't there, and that meant Trystan was safe, at least for today.

'They won't listen, you know,' Trystan had said when Corwynal had told him of his plan, but then, amused by the sheer effrontery of it, agreed it was worth a try. 'It might delay them until the Galloway men get here...'

Because, if they were to fight the Scots at all, they'd have to wait for the Galloway troop to join them, and even then it would be close. So Trystan had sent a scout to make contact with Andrydd's men who'd be approaching the loch from the south along the river that ran out of the loch further west and joined the Cluta by Alcluid, Strathclyde's stronghold.

'And they'd better be here before nightfall if they're to find their way across this river,' Trystan said, looking at the marshy ground that lay between them and the southern shore of the loch, something that hadn't been detailed on Marc's map.

Neither Corwynal nor Trystan had liked Marc's plan and liked it even less now they'd seen the terrain. They'd have to hope that Gaheris had reached the army in Manau and persuaded his father to send a troop west to support them. If he did, they might just have the numbers to fight the Scots, even without the Galloway men – as long as no more of the Scots arrived.

'There are too many ifs,' Corwynal said. 'Which is why we have to try persuading them not to fight. Anyway, Ninian wants us to stop them, not kill them.'

'Why should they listen?'

'Because they're being used.'

He'd been thinking it through it all the way from Meldon. Why had the Caledonian Confederacy allied themselves with the Scots of Dalriada? On the face of it, it seemed simple – a Scots army to fight the Britons in exchange for a cessation of hostilities in the north of Dalriada. But Ninian's near-death had told a different tale.

They'll betray him, he'd said, speaking of his king, Feargus. *They'll let him fight alone.* Had Domech, believing Ninian would die in the oak grove, boasted of a planned treachery?

Were the Caledonians going to use the Scots to defeat the Britons then turn on them? It would certainly suit the Confederacy to have the power of Dalriada broken, a power that threatened their own ambitions in the west. But a weakened Dalriada wouldn't be in the Britons' interests. Better the Scots in the west – Scots who could be negotiated with – than the Caledonians, who could not. So Corwynal had to persuade Feargus to give up the fight and go home.

But none of the men who received them beneath a leather awning stretched between some spears planted close to the Scots' standards looked in the least persuadable.

The rain was easing by then, and the camp was fully awake. Fires were burning, and men were fishing from the edge of the loch or sharpening spears. Once the Britons reached the Scots' camp, however, everyone stopped what they were doing to watch them, and three men, clearly leaders, emerged from the tents set closest to the standards. Two were big bulky men with sufficient similarity of feature and build to suggest they were kin, brothers perhaps. But the third man was quite different.

He was a little younger than the others, a tall man, and spare, his face grim of feature. It was a hard face, what could be seen of it, for he wore the robes of a priest of Chrystos, the hood drawn up against the rain and fastened close about his neck. The rain clouds had edged away by then, and a wan sun was shining on Corwynal's back, but he felt the chill of the man's shadow reach out and touch him, not on his body but, somehow, on his future. This man was dangerous, and, when he threw back his hood and loosened the ties at his neck, Corwynal understood why.

Beneath his habit, gleaming in the sunlight, was a great golden torque. But the sparkle of gold couldn't outdo the glitter of the man's sea-green eyes, nor the gleam of his hair, which was as red as a fox's pelt. This was Feargus himself, the man they called The Fox, and not, Corwynal suspected, because of the colour of his hair.

'We'd begun, my brothers and I, to believe this land was empty,' he said. He spoke in the Gael tongue and gestured to one of his attendants to translate, but Corwynal forestalled him.

'It isn't. This land's more densely populated than you might consider . . . comfortable.'

'Indeed?' Feargus blinked at Corwynal's facility with his language. 'You are, perhaps, the vanguard?' He looked pointedly behind the Britons as if expecting to see a host appear over the hill, then raised an eyebrow in mock surprise when he saw nothing. One of the older men snorted in amusement.

'Others will come,' Corwynal said. 'These lands belong to Caw, King of Eastern Manau.' In truth, if anyone had a claim to the land on the east shore of the Loch, it was Strathclyde, but he doubted the Scots would know that. 'Caw has many allies, Lot of Gododdin, for one. Caw and his allies won't stand by and allow anyone to invade even a small part of his lands.'

'Really? I'd heard that Western Manau had already been taken by the Caledonians, and that they hold them still. Don't you Britons call them The Lost Lands?'

Corwynal shrugged. 'Lost lands can be found once more. They can be re-taken, and those who took them driven back into the hills. And perhaps those who hold Caledonian lands by tribute or conquest will have to look to their own frontiers.'

The older men muttered at that, but Feargus silenced them with a gesture. 'We pay tribute to no-one.'

'Then take care you're not defeated,' Corwynal replied, with a smile to soften the threat.

Feargus laughed. 'You're here to give us advice on warfare? We don't need any. Come, tell us who stands against us.' He gestured at the symbols on their tunics. 'I don't know these tribe-marks, though I've seen the wolf sign among the Caledonians.'

Corwynal stiffened at this confirmation that the Scots had dealings with Atholl, though it shouldn't have surprised him.

'The wolf is Lothian's sign,' Trystan said. 'My brother's from Lothian, as am I.'

'You carry Lothian's sign, yet you wear the Raven.' Feargus pointed out.

'I wear it to honour my kinsman, Marc of Galloway.'

Feargus narrowed his eyes at that. No Dalriad had any love for Galloway, and the feeling was mutual, but he said nothing and nodded for Trystan to continue.

'I'm Trystan, heir to Lothian, and this is my brother Corwynal. The man who bears the sign of the tree is Kaerherdin, son of Hoel of Selgovia, whose troops march with ours.'

Kaerherdin, hearing his name, nodded gravely, and the two older Scots exchanged a glance. Clearly, they'd heard of Selgovia.

'What of him?' Feargus jerked his head at Aelfric, who grinned with a feral glint of teeth.

'He's Aelfric, son of Herewulf of Bernicia, and is of the Angle nation. He bears the standard of Gododdin, Lot's kingdom, to whom his people pay tribute,' Corwynal said, grateful Aelfric couldn't understand what he was saying because he'd be bound to deny it.

The two older leaders looked concerned at that, but Feargus just smiled and invited the Britons to sit. Then he introduced the other men as his foster-brothers, Loarn, Lord of Dunollie, and Oengus, Lord of The Isle. Leather cups of ale were brought, and Aelfric sniffed at his suspiciously before drinking it down in one swallow. Corwynal, sipping his, tasted honey and some sort of herb, but it wasn't unpleasant.

'And I, though you've probably guessed, am the Lord of Dunadd and King of Dalriada,' the red-headed man said. 'They call me Feargus Mór, which means Feargus the Great in your tongue. Now, tell us why you're here, other than to make empty threats.'

'We're not here to make threats. Rather, we bring a message from one of your countrymen. I'm here to warn you that you stand against the allied strength of the Britons, united for the first time in generations. You think to fall on Lot's flank. You think to march east and find his attention turned to the north. You believe Dalriada and the Caledonians will be fighting the Britons together, but you won't be. Your so-called allies will betray you. They'll let you bear the brunt of the Britons' attack, and only then will they fall on Lot's forces. And whatever remains of your army will return to lands burned and ravaged by the Creonn nation, who are under no-one's control but their own, no matter what you've been promised.'

Feargus frowned, for these were serious allegations, but, after a moment's consideration, he just shrugged.

'Why should I listen to one who bears the marks of the Caledonians yet rides beneath the Britons' banner? A man who shows so little loyalty to his own lands?'

Trystan's hand came down on Corwynal's wrist and gripped it like an iron slave-band. The pain drove the intemperate response from his throat.

'You speak of what you can't know,' Trystan said evenly. 'My brother bears the blood of two nations, yet his allegiance is given only to one, to Lothian, which he's served all of his adult life, as warrior and councillor to the King. Let no man accuse him of disloyalty to lands or king, or even his own gods. My brother doesn't follow Chrystos, but many of my countrymen do, and so does a friend of ours, a priest from Dalriada. It's his tale we bring across three frontiers . . .'

Trystan began simply. There was a man, he said. He didn't use the old bardic formulas, the druid tricks of voice and cadence, but the rhythms were there, and, within moments, the chieftains of Dalriada were sitting back and listening, enthralled, to the tale Trystan began to spin. He changed things, of course, and spoke of Trimontium as if it was a great fortress built by giants, rather than tumbled-down ruins ringed by broken walls. The Mansio was mentioned, but not that Ninian had been gambling there. He elaborated on the fight at the inn and somehow implied that they'd saved Ninian from a horde of barbarians whose nationality was not made quite clear. Then he spoke of the dark woods of Selgovia and the attack by the Caledonians, but omitted Ninian's refusal to fight, choosing rather to expand on his healing skills. Ninian, he told them, had been a valued companion who'd trusted them to bring his people a warning.

'A good story, well told,' Feargus said, nodding at Trystan when he'd finished. 'Worthy of one of our own bards. But still a story.'

'A true story,' Corwynal insisted, 'told to us by a real man.'

'Who could, I imagine, have come himself to tell us of these things?'

'Indeed. And he would have done so had he been able to. But he could neither walk nor ride. He could barely talk. But when he could speak, it was to ask us to bring you a warning. And to prove it he sent this token.' Corwynal brought out from beneath his tunic Ninian's cross, still encrusted with his blood, and held it out to Feargus. 'The Caledonians, your so-called allies, crucified him.'

Feargus sprang to his feet, snatched the cross from Corwynal's outstretched hand and examined it carefully.

'I gave Ninian this cross,' he said, looking up at Corwynal with narrowed, suspicious eyes. 'You two, come with me.' He jerked his head at him and Trystan. 'I would know more of Ninian's warning.'

Feargus ignored his foster-brothers' protests and walked down to the shore and out along a little pier that jutted into the loch. Corwynal and Trystan had no choice but to follow him, leaving Aelfric and Kaerherdin to guard their horses.

'My brothers are fools,' Feargus said, half to himself, his attention on a boat approaching the pier from the western shore of the Loch where Dalriadan lands bordered Strathclyde's. 'Ninian was a fool too, but in a different way. So tell me what he said.'

'That I should stop you,' Corwynal said. 'That the Caledonians aren't to be trusted. That they're using you. Go home, Feargus Mór. Defend your lands. This isn't your war.'

'My foster-brothers have made it my war,' Feargus said bitterly. 'They allowed themselves to believe the promises. But I have never trusted Caledonians, so perhaps you're right. We will return to Dalriada to protect our lands against the ravages of the Creonn—'

Feargus stiffened, his gaze sharpening as the faint haze of smoke over one of the Scots' settlements on the far shore thickened to a dirty yellow cloud of burning thatch.

'Which seems already to have begun . . . Dhearghal!' Feargus beckoned one of his spearmen over. 'Tell my brothers to get their ships ready to leave. We return to Dalriada. No, wait—'

The boat he'd been watching reached the pier and slewed into the pilings. An old man, his head bound in a bloodied rag, scrambled onto the pier and fell to his knees at Feargus' feet. Others lay in the boat, more than one of them hurt.

'They came at dawn, my Lord! Those who were left tried to fight them, but with the war-bands from home . . .'

'The Creonn!' Feargus' brows snapped together, and he glanced at Corwynal. 'So you spoke the truth.'

Maybe he had, but Corwynal could make no sense of what was happening. *Now? Before the fighting's begun? And why this far south when the Scots army is so close to home?*

But the old man shook his head. 'No, Lord. It was Britons from Strathclyde. They wore the sign of the salmon, and they came from the south at dawn, burning as they rode.'

'But, Sire, this can't be!' Corwynal protested. 'The Strathclyde war-band is in the east, with Lot.'

A young boy eased himself painfully to the edge of the boat. One arm dangled limply, and his face was white beneath a mask of bruising and smoke-blackened skin.

'Not all of them, clearly!' Feargus' green eyes glittered with rage. 'So this was your plan – to persuade us to leave and let our allies fight alone, to have us head north to fight the non-existent Creonn while Strathclyde attacked our lands in the South? But they couldn't wait, could they? The temptation was too great.' His lip curled in disgust as he turned on Corwynal. 'Their lack of patience has just ruined your schemes, however. I'll return to deal with Strathclyde, but my brothers will remain to fight as we promised – to fight and defeat you.' He turned to his spearman. 'Get rid of these liars.' The man drew back his spear, but Feargus stopped him with a gesture. 'Not like that! They've guest rights, and we're not barbarians. Let them take their horses and go.' He glared at Corwynal. 'You spoke the truth in one thing only. Caledonians aren't to be trusted, and you're a Caledonian. There was no message from Ninian. But this is his cross, so you must have killed him and taken it.'

'That's not true!'

'Corwynal!' Trystan hissed and tried to pull him away, but his honour had been called into question. His warning had been genuine, his motive to save the lives of both Britons and Scots. Something was wrong. Dumnagual of Strathclyde was too cautious a man to risk outright war with the Scots.

'What are you waiting for?' Feargus demanded when he didn't move. 'Dhearghal, see they leave the camp, then rouse the men. We've work to do. Hot and bloody work!'

As if already feeling the heat, Feargus tore off the priest's robes. Beneath, he wore the light leggings and tunic of the Scots, but the golden torque showed his kingship, as did the richly embroidered symbol on his white tunic. Silver thread edged the design, but it wasn't the black swan borne by his men. It was a ship. A great black ship.

'We were lucky to get out of there alive,' Trystan said after they'd picked their way along the river and headed for their camp.

They'd been showered with insults and clods of mud as they'd left the Scots' camp, but nothing worse. Now, safely out of spear range, they reined in to look back. At least half of the ships that had been drawn up on the shore were rowing furiously back across the loch, heading for the burning settlements on the far side. The leading ship flew the swan standard, which meant Feargus was leaving. The black ship had gone.

'What's wrong?' Trystan asked, peering at him. 'We succeeded, didn't we? Half the Scots have gone, and once the Galloway troop arrives, or Lot's men – or both – we'll have enough men to fight the rest of them.'

'They left for the wrong reason. I don't believe Strathclyde is raiding their villages.'

'Then it must be the Creonn. Does it matter? Come on, let's get back to our camp and see if there's word of the Galloway troop. And then . . .'

Corwynal stopped listening to Trystan's plans. There was treachery here, but not Strathclyde's. Caledonian, more likely, even if it seemed mis-timed. But Trystan was right. It didn't matter that his own honour had been questioned because he now understood the shadow that had fallen over his future, like the black sail of a ship sweeping across the sun. He knew now who his enemy was – Feargus of Dalriada – and so his path was clear. The death he'd dreamt *could* be averted. All he had to do was keep Trystan away from the King of Dalriada until he could kill the man himself.

'Aren't you listening?' Corwynal forced himself to concentrate and let Trystan's enthusiasm sweep him away. And why shouldn't he? Between them, he and Trystan had persuaded Feargus and his war-band to leave. Which just left Loarn and Oengus' war-bands to fight. And so he could fulfil his promise to a god too. Trystan and he were going to fight the Scots, and the man bearing the black ship wouldn't be part of that battle.

But the gods favour a man who struggles against his fate, not one who avoids it, and Corwynal didn't remember that until dawn silvered the east and brought with it the first notes of war.

They shivered in the bleak cold that comes before dawn, having snatched only a few hours' sleep since nightfall. Beacons had been seen during the night, fires running from hilltop to hilltop, so Lot's war must have begun further east. The Scots would have seen the beacons too, but had not yet struck camp. There was, however, still no sign of the Galloway men, and the scout who'd been sent to find them had returned, having failed to make contact.

'Let's go up the ridge,' Trystan suggested. 'We might be able to see something from there.'

They climbed through birch scrub to the open summit of the hill on which stood the remains of the old Roman fort. To the north, a fire burned on a shoulder of Beacon Hill, and, on the high ground further east, more fires pulsed in the night – Caledonian fires summoning the gods of battle. Corwynal's blood leapt in response, and Trystan's cry of anger and frustration was yet another answer.

'Where are they?' Trystan squinted south-westward, the direction from which they expected the Galloway troop to come, but there was no movement on the moonlit open countryside. Nor, when they looked east, could they see any sign of men having been sent by Lot in response to Gaheris' warning.

'No-one's coming,' Corwynal said. 'So we'd better—'

'No! Don't tell me.' Trystan thumped his hand against the remains of the fort's outer wall, sending a shower of rubble scattering into the heather, then took a breath, as if he was about to plunge into deep water. 'Listen to me. There's a thing that has to be said.' He spoke with quiet but cold assurance. 'There can be only one leader here, and it will be me. No, wait.

I know what you're going to say. That I'm too young, too inexperienced. But this is what I was born for. This is what you made me, so let me be what I'm meant to be. Of course I'll still listen to you – I'd be a fool to do otherwise – but when the time comes to make decisions, I'll make them, and I don't want to have to argue or justify myself. You know it makes sense because that's something you taught me too. So, trust me. Trust my judgement. Trust your training. Trust yourself.'

Trust your own blood. Trust it in me. Was that what Trystan was asking him to do? To trust in a connection between them more powerful than that shared by brothers?

Corwynal swallowed painfully, for this wasn't the time or place to talk of such things. And because the answer he was going to give him wasn't the one Trystan wanted. Right then, he *was* too young and inexperienced, but one day he wouldn't be, and that was why Corwynal had to refuse now – so Trystan could survive this battle and gain that experience. But before he could speak, Trystan's head lifted.

'Listen!'

Corwynal held his breath and heard it too, the sound of men moving along the track from the loch. 'Galloway?' Trystan breathed. 'About time . . .' Faintly, borne on the wind, they heard the knock of weapons, stifled curses that hissed together into a dull mutter, and the soft quiver of footfalls. Infantry, then, not horsemen. It wasn't the Galloway troops who were on the march but Loarn and Oengus' war-bands. Corwynal's heart thudded into a new rhythm. *Trust me.* He still hadn't given Trystan an answer. Then his heart began to beat faster and louder. Except it wasn't his heart at all, for the sound came from the east. A horseman was on the track, an outrider, surely, of the men Lot must have sent.

They sprinted down through the trees. Their camp was

already stirring into life; horses were whinnying with excitement, and men were shouting to one another. Then, through the tumult, Corwynal heard Gaheris' voice.

'T-T-Trystan? Thank the g-g-gods I've found you!'

'Where are your men?' The road behind Gaheris was empty. 'The Scots are almost upon us!'

'Men? There's only me. Where's the G-G-Galloway warband? K-K-King Marc said there was a plan . . .'

'They haven't arrived,' Trystan said bitterly. 'They're probably lost. I sent a scout to find them, but . . .' He shook his head. 'There are two war-bands of Scots heading our way. Too many for us, Gaheris. Curse it to the five hells! We'll have to fall back and join up with your father's men.' He glanced at Corwynal and smiled wryly. 'You thought I'd fight them here, without waiting for Galloway, didn't you?'.

'Perhaps,' he said, trying to conceal his relief that Trystan had decided otherwise. *Trust me.* Maybe he could.

'But you have to!' Gaheris exclaimed, his voice cracking. 'That's why my father s-s-sent me. They're hard pressed by the Rock. The C-C-Caledonians crossed the Moss under cover of night, and we're s-s-surrounded. You must have s-s-seen the beacons! He s-s-sent me to tell you the S-S-Scots can't be allowed to join up with the C-C-Caledonians because if they do, we're lost! You – we – have to hold them, d-d-delay them. We have to fight them h-h-here!'

And with Gaheris' words, Corwynal knew he'd been betrayed by everything he'd believed in. His dream, the God, even fate itself.

'Then that's what we'll do,' Trystan said, speaking not to Gaheris but to Corwynal, who nodded grimly. *Trust your training.* So even that betrayed him, because the boy he'd trained, the leader he'd turned him into, the king he wanted him to become, could never have considered an alternative.

Yet, strangely, Corwynal felt almost happy. The future fell away, leaving only the present, only the next few hours. His spirit was no longer shackled by his fear of the black ship, of that unknown shore where Trystan's blood would soak into the grass. He was no longer constrained by his father's belief that one day his son would take his life. None of these futures existed anymore because, unless the gods intervened, on this day they would die. Not immediately perhaps, and not without cost, but, in the face of the sheer number of Scots, defeat was inevitable and so therefore was death. All that was left was to make of their deaths a song that would be sung in all the courts of the West: in Dunpeldyr, in Meldon, even in far-off Dunadd. They'd hold the Scots here and, though they'd lose the fight, they might, by their deaths, win the battle.

Corwynal could hear Arddu laughing. He was in his head, his blood, his bones, his nerves. It was the laughter of a god who liked to watch men struggle, who'd let him bring Trystan to the Loch, believing he was saving him from another place in which he would die. The God must have been laughing all the way from Lothian.

But the struggle wasn't over. Perhaps death awaited them, but that didn't mean Corwynal wasn't going to fight. First, however, he had to give Trystan an answer, but not the one he'd intended to give. That belonged to the past, and the future no longer mattered.

'What do you want me to do?' he asked, giving Trystan the trust he wanted and, as he did so, all his doubts fled. In that moment, they were one person, one blood, one warrior, and both of them would find music that day.

'Do you remember how we fought Aelfric?' Trystan asked. 'It was a good fight, wasn't it? That's where I want you. Not at my back, but at my side.'

Corwynal nodded, and Trystan erupted into action, into command. Kaerherdin was to spread the best of their archers out along the road, spearmen to flank them. Gaheris was to fetch their horses. And as for Aelfric...

'You're released,' Trystan said. 'I no longer hold you to your oath. Go while you still can.'

'Other oaths keep me here.'

'If Galloway doesn't come, the death you've promised my brother will be stolen from you.' But the Angle just grinned, a flash of teeth in the growing light.

'Not if I can help it!'

'Then mount up, man,' Trystan said, as Gaheris brought their horses, Aelfric's roan among them.

'I'm not fighting on a fucking horse. I'll fight on my feet,' Aelfric said, grinning and hefting his axe. 'As you will before the end.'

'I'll fight on my knees if I have to!' Trystan laughed. 'Come on then! For Lothian! Lothian! Lothian!'

And screaming out their challenge, they rode into battle and the dawning of a red, red day.

Afterwards, Corwynal remembered each thrust, each slash of the sword. He heard the wind on the blade's edge, his own voice screaming. Afterwards, he could see the shape of the battle, the way the centre crumbled, and how the edges of the line fell away under the rain of arrows from Kaerherdin's men. He heard the thunk of an arrow piercing leather, the thud of a spear penetrating flesh, the scream a heartbeat later. He heard the roar and smelled the blood and the fear, his own rank in his nostrils. He felt the dry-mouthed terror, the tearing rasp in his chest, the burning of his muscles, his stomach rising up to meet his raw and aching throat. But that was later. That was afterwards.

At the time, in the blood-washed beating heart of the battle, there was only the music and the dance. The world slowed and crystallised around him into fragments of movement, and, afterwards, he could recall each flash of sunlight on the blade, the gleam of bone in a ruin of blood, the glints of silver and mail and snarling teeth. He heard no sounds, not at the time, no screams, no grunts of pain, not even his own breath. All he could hear was the music. But this was no instrument he'd ever heard, no voice he recognised, and if there were words they were in a tongue unfamiliar to him. And yet he knew their meaning, for this was the music of the gods of War. Camulos and Taranis walked with him that day, and it seemed to Corwynal that, beside him, Trystan was their bright spirit of death, the flame to Corwynal's shadow, and they fought side by side, each shielding the other. He was aware of crossing threshold after threshold, of doorways looming, of death a heartbeat away, of life thrilling through his veins.

Later he understood they'd broken the Scots' shield-wall with their first screaming charge into a mass of men confused by the Britons' flanking attack and who weren't expecting opposition. Feargus' foster brothers had sent out scouts, but they'd fallen to the silent hunters of Selgovia, though he didn't know that until later. At the time, all he knew was his arm, rising and falling, Janthe rearing and screaming her own challenge, her hooves and teeth weapons as vicious as those Corwynal himself wielded. He sawed at the reins, jerked her around, slashed down at an upraised face, hacked away a shield or a spear-thrust.

'Back!' Trystan shouted, but Corwynal was already turning, surging free of the mass of men before they engulfed them. They reformed, turned once more, the weight of their mounted assault breaking the Scots' line for a second time and forcing them back against their companions who, trapped in the narrow place between hill and wood, fell and died.

Hold them there! Lot had demanded and hold them they did. One hundred men against three times that number. They held the Scots back, but at no small cost. They broke their shield wall again and again, but each time their impetus carried them a little less far. Each time there were fewer of them as men and horses fell. Out on the flanks, the Selgovians' arrows ran out, and they drew their swords and mounted their little ponies. The Scots found ways through the woods and burst through a thin line of horsemen on the flank of the hill. Gradually, the line against which the Britons fought broadened, and the arrowhead of their attack blunted. Gradually, knee to knee, shield to shield, and then, as horses fell or were wounded, shoulder to shoulder, the Britons were forced back. Aelfric's prediction was right; Janthe and Rhydian were winded and labouring, and Gaheris' mount had been killed beneath him, so they ended up fighting on their feet. But Corwynal knew it was the beginning of the end. The music began to fade, and the world returned, full of sound and fear, a world in which his body was aching and hurt and he was profoundly weary.

Beside him, Trystan still fought like a flame, but no longer with the incandescent fire of his first attack. Now he burned firm and steady. On his far side, Gaheris still swung his broad sword with grim precision, but he was tiring too and falling back, each time taking longer and longer to recover. On Corwynal's left, Aelfric still fought like the barbarian he was, crooning something in his own tongue, a hymn of death that was likely to be his own. Corwynal caught his eye once, and the Angle grinned fiercely, a white flash in a face bloodied by the spray from his own axe. Suddenly, right there in the heart of the battle, Corwynal wondered why they were there. Why were an Angle and a Caledonian fighting for the Britons against an army of Scots? He wanted to stop, to lay down his weapons and reach out to his opponent and ask why he was fighting. But the thought died as swiftly as it had arisen, as the man's head was severed from his neck in one great sweep of Aelfric's blade, even as the Angle cursed Corwynal for his stupidity.

It was then that something changed. There was little to tell him at the time. No sound, for he was deafened. No sight, for he was blinded by his own sweat. But he knew all the same. Something had changed. Someone had come. They all felt it, Scots and Britons alike. There was a tremor in the line, a pressure at the rear of the Scots that transmitted itself to the front. They'd come. For a moment a veil was drawn aside and Corwynal could see black birds flying on standards. *The ravens of Galloway!* But then he saw them more clearly. They were birds, but not ravens, though they were black. These were the black swans of Feargus of Dalriada, and, at their head, the King himself, wearing what must be the personal standard of his house – the black ship. Feargus had returned.

The world stopped. Sound fell away. All around him, men fought and died, and Corwynal was barely aware of it. He was in the dream and understood at last how the meaning of the dream was twisted, just as Blaize had warned him. Yes, there had been gulls in his dream, and here they were, far from the sea, Loarn's men with their grey gull standards screaming all around him. And here was the mossy grass on which Trystan would fall to the giant, who was no giant at all, but a man. Yet didn't they call him Feargus Mór? All that was missing was the sound of the sea. But then he heard that too – great waves of battle crashing all around him like surf on a shingle beach. It was the sound men make when they know they've won, the roar of relief and triumph and the battle fury that would sweep them all away. The Scots, reinforced by Feargus' men, roared and crashed like breakers. Corwynal was in the dream and the dream was now, the dream in which he'd watched and watched and done nothing.

With the pressure of the new arrivals, the Briton line began to edge backwards, and Trystan was screaming orders to everyone to retreat and reform. Corwynal ignored him, and, screaming his own challenge in the tongue of his mother's people, he surged forward. All his aches were forgotten. All his weariness burned away in a great swell of music. He'd never felt so powerful, so invincible and, for a time he hoped would be enough, so immortal. The world shrank down to one inevitable act. He was going to kill Feargus Mór before he could fight Trystan, and what happened afterwards no longer mattered.

⸎

'What the fuck's he doing?'

Aelfric paused to wipe blood out of his eyes as Corwynal surged past him. A wounded Scot rose from the ground at his feet, and Aelfric swung his axe without thought, hammering it through the man's breastbone.

'Back!' Trystan yelled, and everyone retreated. All but one.

Has he gone mad? Aelfric wondered, as he tugged his axe free. He was no berserker himself, but he knew one when he saw one, and the Caledonian was fighting like someone consumed by the fire of Thunor's furnace. Until then, the cursed man had seemed unassailable. He'd only made one mistake when, for some stupid reason, he'd stopped right in the middle of the fight and just stood there with his mouth open, staring at his opponent. Aelfric had taken the Scot's head off. *That was for you, Ealhith*, he'd told himself at the time, but he wasn't so sure that had been his reason. Aelfric had been at the Caledonian's side throughout the battle, had watched him fight, seen how he shielded Trystan, how the two of them had fought as if they were one man, like that time by the river in Lothian, and Aelfric was conscious of a grudging respect.

'Back!' Trystan yelled once more. 'Aelfric! Corwynal... Corwynal!'

But the Caledonian had gone mad and was carving his way through the mass of Scots who were pouring onto the battlefield, scything them down as if they were no more than harmless stalks of grain, heading for... What *was* he heading for? The place was confused, as all battlefields were, a narrow field between two rivers, bounded by the ridge with the ruined fort to the north, slightly higher land to the east, boggy ground to the south. Fresh Scots forces had poured in from the direction of the Loch around the base of that low ridge, and the Caledonian was making for a forest of standards that stood on an outlying rise, and from where this new attack was being directed.

'Oh, shit!' Trystan was peering north. 'That's Feargus...'

'I'll fetch Corwynal,' Aelfric said. 'I'll drag him back by the throat if it kills me.'

Which, he thought with grim resignation, it very likely would.

Corwynal didn't take his eyes from Feargus as he cut his way towards him, his battle-trance so powerful he could kill with no more thought than he might give to the swatting of a fly. Men who stood between him and Feargus had to die. It was as simple as that.

The King of the Dalriads watched him from his vantage point on the shoulder of the ridge, from where he was directing the attack, dispatching men to that wing or another and receiving messages of reverses or triumphs with no more than a nod of the head and a calm measured response. His household warriors ringed him, a shield wall on rising ground that no-one but a madman would attack. But Corwynal was no longer sane, and perhaps Feargus understood that.

'Let him through!'

The line of shields broke apart, and Corwynal rushed forward, knowing it had to be a trap, but that he'd get no second chance. He lifted his sword in a great arc as he ran, but then he saw them. The swan-standards planted on the hill were stained with blood, for on each pole was speared the severed head of a man, and Corwynal recognised those heads because he'd seen them only days before. They were from Galloway.

Corwynal knew then he was defeated. The return of Feargus' war-band had trumpeted the Britons' defeat, but this was personal. This had turned him into the liar Feargus already believed him to be.

'These are no Creonn! Nor men of Strathclyde!' Feargus gestured at the heads. 'They're from *Galloway!*'

So, the opportunity had been too irresistible to the Galloway troops, the fertile lands stripped of fighting men, the chance to blame Strathclyde for the incursion. They wouldn't have expected Feargus to return across the Loch to defend his people and would have assumed they'd still have time to join Trystan as Marc had planned.

'I believed I spoke the truth.'

'You lied then, and you're lying now,' Feargus snarled. 'That's why I'm here, why I came back to a war I didn't want to fight. To claim an answer for your lies!'

His contempt stung Corwynal to a prideful, guilty anger.

'I didn't lie! But if it's an answer you want, Feargus Mór of Dalriada, then I'm here to let you have it.'

'And I.' The voice came from further down the hill, a clear voice that carried over the grim sound of battle and froze Corwynal's blood. Then a muttered curse in the Angle tongue told him Trystan hadn't come alone.

※

Laughter rocked all around him, through him, mocking and derisive. *You think you command your own fate? You think by acting you can change anything? You acted. But see where that has led you...*

Feargus gave a faint mocking smile, but to Corwynal he was no longer Feargus. He was no longer a man wearing the symbol of the black ship. He was naked and antlered, the God himself, laughing as he watched Corwynal struggle as if he was a fly caught in a spider's web, taunting him, tempting him, testing him, then betraying him.

But not defeating him.

He launched himself forward, snarling his fury and defiance. There was still time to kill Feargus before Trystan could reach them. But two of Feargus' household warriors stood in his way, men who were fresh and had the advantage of higher ground. Corwynal was weary enough to make mistakes, and he made one now. He twisted away from a low spear thrust, missed his step on the rising terrain, slipped and fell heavily. His sword arm slammed into the ground, and one of the warriors stepped forward and stamped on his fore-arm. He heard the bone snap, his own scream.

'Corwynal!' Trystan shrieked a warning, and he rolled to one side. The spear aimed at his chest struck his shoulder instead and tore through his mail to bite deep into muscle. The man's body followed, a flung axe in his throat. Blood sprayed his face, and the man's weight pinned him to the ground. Trystan screamed his name once more, but he couldn't move, could do nothing but watch the sun glitter on a blade held high above him. The second of Feargus' men grinned down at him, and he knew that grin would be the last thing he saw in this life. But the grin filled with blood and the blade fell harmlessly away as a blossom of black bloomed in the man's throat. It was the bolt of a Caledonian crossbow.

'Corwynal, they've come!' Trystan knelt by his side and helped Aelfric roll the dead Scot away. 'They've come!'

'I know, Trys,' he said weakly. He hadn't defeated the God after all, for now Arddu had sent the Caledonians to finish what Feargus had begun. Corwynal tried to get to his feet, but his right arm flared into agony when he put his weight on it, and he rolled back onto a shoulder that screamed with a different pain. Yet this was nothing compared to the agonies his kinfolk would inflict on him when they captured him.

'Don't let them take me,' he whispered.

'Who?' Trystan slid an arm under his good shoulder and helped him sit up. They were alone on the ridge. Feargus and his warriors had fled, Aelfric in pursuit, and the sound of battle was different. It was no longer a roar of triumph but a wail of defeat and flight.

'The Caledonians,' he said, but Trystan looked at him as if he was mad, then laughed in delight.

'They're not Caledonians, you fool! Look up there!'

All along a ridge to the east was a line of cavalry and at its centre a tall figure on a great white horse. His mail was gilded and glittered as if he was the rising sun, and above him flew a great green banner with a rearing black bear. It wasn't the Caledonians who'd arrived, but Lot's mercenary from Gwynedd.

Arthyr had come.

The horsemen poured down the hillside and thundered into the Scots' flank. They turned and fought, but their line soon crumpled, and they began to flee. The golden warrior reined in his horse and kicked it up the slope to join them on the ridge.

'Well met, brother!' Arthyr reached down a hand to grasp Trystan's as his men pursued the fleeing Scots. 'I'm sorry we were delayed. We had the Caledonians to deal with first, but I see you've saved us a few Scots!'

He grinned infectiously, and Corwynal began to understand why men followed this mercenary, this myth. He was beautiful in the way Trystan was beautiful, regular of feature, raven-haired and blue-eyed. But it wasn't his beauty that drew men to his side. It was his bright delight in a life lived on the edge of death. Trystan looked up at him with silent uncritical adoration, and Corwynal couldn't find it in himself to be jealous.

'And those few Scots are getting away!' an amused voice pointed out as another rider joined them, an older grey-haired man who dismounted and handed his mount's reins to Trystan. 'Take my horse, lad, and round up your men. There's still work to be done.'

Trystan looked at the older man in some surprise, for the mount was a fine one, but Arthyr nodded encouragingly.

'Come on, boy. Let's drive them out of Strathclyde, or wherever in the five hells this place is!' He raised a hand in farewell, and then he was gone, Trystan following, with Aelfric, who'd returned from his pursuit of the Scots, loping along behind the riders.

'An Angle, eh?' the grey-haired man mused, following Aelfric's progress down the valley. 'And you, by the look of you, a Pict. What strange times we live in!'

'A Caledonian,' Corwynal corrected him. 'And only half a Caledonian at that.'

'Ah, like Blaize!'

'You know Blaize?'

The man glanced down at the body of the Scot who'd almost killed Corwynal and the black bolt that protruded obscenely from the man's throat. 'It's a weapon of the devil, but it can be accurate – fortunately for you, since it must have been a difficult shot.' Another horseman rode up the hillside, a man wearing his long dark hair pinned back in a silver ring and the usual expression of long-suffering exasperation on his face.

'Why is it, Corwynal, that whenever you and Trystan are out of my sight for more than a day you get into some sort of scrape from which I invariably have to rescue you?' Blaize slid down from his horse with a gesture of impatience that didn't fool Corwynal for a moment. 'Look at you! Broken your arm, I reckon, and that shoulder looks nasty.' He stripped away Corwynal's mailed tunic and undershirt with little regard for his gasps of pain, then bound his shoulder roughly, splinted his arm with a broken length of spear and announced crossly that it would have to do because he had other wounded men to deal with. Then he disappeared back down the hill. The grey-haired man helped Corwynal to his feet, and together, in that oddly peaceful place, they watched the Scots being slaughtered.

They fought back of course. They lacked neither courage nor leadership. Corwynal saw Feargus in the distance, his household warriors fighting a rear-guard action. His war-band retreated steadily and held the Briton troops back for long enough that those reaching the shore had time to launch their boats and escape. Feargus had been defeated in a war that wasn't his own, betrayed by his allies as Corwynal had warned him would happen, for the Caledonians had fled rather than support the Dalriad troops. Perhaps Feargus would believe him now, and that mattered to him because things like that had begun to matter once more.

The struggle hadn't been in vain after all; he'd amused Arddu sufficiently for the God to let him win, and now it was over. He'd lived through the dream, but instead of watching and watching and doing nothing, he'd acted. He had a wounded shoulder, and a broken arm to show for it, but he also had Trystan's life, Trystan's future, and his own. The Scots' ships escaped across the Loch, but many of the Scots fled north along the eastern side of the loch pursued by the Galloway troops, who'd finally turned up. Trystan was returning from the pursuit, riding back to him, light gleaming on his hair, Arthyr glittering at his side, the two of them a glow in a world that blurred and bloomed like the sun rising on a new morning.

'He fought well,' Corwynal said, nodding at Trystan, his voice thick with unshed tears of relief and love.

'Yes,' the man sighed. 'He did indeed.' The same suppressed emotion was in the older man's voice, and Corwynal glanced sharply at him, but he wasn't looking at Trystan. He was looking at Arthyr.

'He's not as I imagined him,' Corwynal confessed, following the man's gaze. 'I'd heard the stories and thought them exaggerated. I knew he was a mercenary, yet all I heard was talk of the myth. But now I see he's everything they said of him and more. Except—'

He stopped. What was he doing, talking about Arthyr to one of Arthyr's own men? But the man raised an encouraging eyebrow. 'Except...?'

'Except the Arthyr I'd heard about would have known the name of the place for which he fought.'

The man laughed. 'He does. It's Western Manau.'

'But he thought it was Strathclyde.'

'Oh, Bedwyr never bothers with details like that!' the man said affectionately, still looking down at the golden-armoured man, still with that burning love in his eyes.

'That's Bedwyr? Then where's Arthyr?'

'Here,' the grey-haired man said with a rueful smile. 'I'm Arthyr. The Mercenary and not the Myth. At least not yet.'

PART IV

IUDDEU

MID-SUMMER TO SAMHAIN 485 AD

12

A GIRL AS LEGGY AS A COLT

Corwynal's arm knitted cleanly, but his shoulder festered and he was laid up for the best part of a moon's waning. The camp where the wounded had been taken, a fog and fly infested swamp down near the Gwerid in the shadow of the Rock of Iuddeu, was the usual chaos that follows a battle. There weren't enough healers or bandages, the water was foul, and the tents leaked. Supplies went missing and what food there was spoiled quickly in an unseasonal heatwave, but Corwynal, gripped by wound fever, didn't know about these things at the time. All he was aware of was the voices, Arddu laughing at him, and the druid warning him that Atholl would never let him go. But neither were really there, and later other voices dragged him out of those dreams.

'Do something!' Trystan's face, coming and going in Corwynal's vision, was shadowed with the aftermath of battle, and his voice was sharp and angry, though not with him.

'What do you want me to do?' Blaize sounded irritable and frustrated.

'I don't know! Just make him better.'

If Blaize did anything, Corwynal couldn't tell, but when the fever slackened its grip on him at last, he found he was no longer in the camp. Instead, he was lying in a cold and spartan little chamber in Iuddue's fort. Perhaps the cleaner air up on the Rock helped, for his fever burned itself out and, with it, his longing for war and battle. He'd defeated the black ship and proved to himself that he could still fight. It was enough, and now it was over.

Or so he thought.

The battle had been won, but the war was still being waged. Most of the Scots had fled back across the loch, but the rest escaped north on foot, pursued by the Galloway troops who'd come late to the battle. They'd caught up with the Scots, captured one of Feargus' foster-brothers and his household, and exacted a pledge of tribute from Feargus of Dalriada in exchange for their release.

As for the Caledonians, they'd been defeated, but not decisively. Lot claimed it as a victory, naturally, but most of them had escaped back to their glens, and there weren't enough Britons to do anything about it, given that Marc and his war-band had returned to Galloway, Dumnagual and his war-band to Strathclyde, both to protect their lands against the other. The King of Strathclyde had taken offence at Marc's men having raided the Scots' territories through his own lands, then extracting tribute from the defeated Scots. Corwynal suspected Dumnagual had secret arrangements with Feargus, arrangements that were now in question, and that might destabilise the west.

Lot wasn't pleased Marc and Dumnagual had left, but Corwynal thought it a good thing, even if it meant the burden of fighting being borne by the war-bands of Lot's more immediate supporters, Gododdin, Lothian and Manau, together with Arthyr's men and Trystan's Selgovae. Two fewer kings to deal with would make life simpler, because once the fighting was over the peace would have to be managed. And that, in Corwynal's opinion, would be more of a battle than the one they'd just won, but that fight, thank the gods, had nothing to do with him.

Lot, however, thought otherwise.

⸙

'Bastard!' Lot muttered into his beard.

Corwynal dragged his attention from the dance of dust-motes in the shaft of sunlight that was flooding through the open door of Iuddeu's smaller council chamber and regarded his overlord with some apprehension. They were waiting for Blaize to join them to discuss something or other, but Corwynal was struggling to concentrate. The headache that had never truly left him since he'd been wounded at the battle of Beacon Loch was pulsing behind his eyes. He'd been sleeping badly, still plagued by dreams of the black ship, even though he knew what it meant now since he'd questioned the Scots prisoners himself. The sign had belonged to Feargus' wife, a woman seventeen years dead, and the King of Dalriada hadn't worn it to war until now. He'd thought it would bring him luck, apparently. Instead, it had brought the opposite, and Corwynal doubted if the man would ever wear the black ship symbol again.

'Devious bastard!' Lot repeated, forcing him to pay attention. The King of Gododdin was pacing back and forth and scowling at Corwynal, who was sitting as close as he could to the fire-pit, despite the heat of the day. He couldn't get warm anymore.

Lot wasn't referring to Fearghus however and, though he might, with some justice, have meant Blaize, he was actually talking about Arthyr. Lot had enlivened Corwynal's recovery with a series of complaints about this, that and the other, and he'd gathered that certain of Lot's plans were now in ruins, and all because of Arthyr. Lot had expected to take over Western Manau once it was won, but the lands owed tribute not to Lot, or even to his client king, Caw of Eastern Manau, but to Caw's niece, Gwenhwyvar, daughter of Caw's late brother Ogryfan, a girl no-one had taken account of since, at sixteen, she was little more than a child. But a sixteen-year-old girl was old enough to marry – and she'd decided to marry Arthyr.

'Thing is, Corwynal, I had plans for that girl.' Lot threw himself down in a chair that stood next to a table covered with maps and scraps of parchment. 'I wanted her for Gawain. Even before all this, when she didn't have any lands to speak of, I thought it best to have her in the family, just in case. Caw had the same idea, of course, wanted her for his eldest, Heuil, even though they're full cousins. If only Gawain had stirred himself, I might have had my way, but the silly ass didn't get around to it. Trouble with Gawain – and all my lads, come to that – is that they're good in a fight, but none of them can handle women. I blame it on their mother.' Lot shook himself as if a chill had crept into his bones. 'But let's not speak about her,' he went on quickly. 'Point is that Arthyr beat him to it, a man more than twice the girl's age! But the chit was adamant she was going to have him. Let me give you some advice, Corwynal. Never plan anything that involves a woman. They always come along and ruin everything.'

Lot scowled down at the table. Those maps and scraps of parchment, on which notes and lists had been scribbled in execrable Latin, detailed Lot's thwarted schemes, and now he swept them aside, reached for a flagon, poured two cups of ale and handed one to Corwynal.

'At least my plan for Selgovia worked out,' Lot said, brightening a little.

Corwynal had, until now, managed to avoid the subject of Selgovia, since Lot was a man who liked to dwell on other men's failures rather than their successes, but he seemed suspiciously sanguine about the matter.

'I'm sorry I couldn't persuade Essylt to marry Gaheris.'

'Oh, *that*!' Lot said airily. 'To be honest, I didn't really hold out much hope, Gaheris being as useless as Gawain with women. But I'd heard the girl was plain and thought she might be grateful. I never imagined you'd get Trystan to marry the chit. Didn't think you'd let him even if he wanted to, which is why I didn't raise the possibility.'

'You *wanted* Trystan to marry Essylt?'

'The girl's neither here nor there,' Lot said, dismissing her with a wave of his hand. 'I wanted Selgovia's backing, and now we have it, thanks to Trystan's pretty face. Hoel must have taken a fancy to him too.'

'Actually, Hoel wanted Essylt to marry me,' Corwynal said sourly, still feeling an unsettling sense of both loss and relief.

'You?' Lot stared at him for a moment, then chuckled. 'So the boy snapped her up from under your nose? Like Arthyr stole Gwenhwyvar from Gawain! Now that's rich!'

'It wasn't like that.' But Lot wasn't interested in any disappointment Corwynal might have felt.

'Bastard!' he repeated bitterly, still referring, Corwynal assumed, to Arthyr. 'Wouldn't have expected a man like him to fall for a girl as young as Gwenhwyvar. Although I doubt it had anything to do with the girl herself. That devious bastard knew exactly what he was doing – making himself another contender.'

'Contender for what?'

'Dux bellorum, of course! War-leader, battle-chieftain, call it what you will. This war isn't over, you know. There are the Caledonians to deal with, then the Scots and, after that, the Angles. We can't fight them with just one war-band. We need the war-bands of all the Lands between the Walls, and we need them to be well led – by someone who has the support of all the others. There's been talk, mutterings. The men want a war-leader, and the name that keeps coming up is Arthyr's.'

'And why not? He'd make a good war-leader.'

When Corwynal had met Arthyr on the battlefield, he'd liked him immediately. Now, having got to know him rather better, his first impression hadn't changed, and he'd come to admire the older, quiet man with the dry sense of humour. One couldn't help liking Bedwyr either, even though he was Arthyr's complete opposite: a man who laughed often but didn't think too frequently, who loved fighting, drinking and women, but whose affection for Arthyr was deep and enduring, an affection Arthyr more than returned. But it wasn't Arthyr's friendship with Bedwyr that caused Lot to scowl as he leant towards Corwynal and lowered his voice to a mutter.

'Why not? Because it wouldn't stop there. Arthyr's ambitious. But for what and how much, that's what I don't know. That's what no-one knows. Not even that cursed uncle of yours.'

Lot, Corwynal understood, wanted Arthyr to remain a mercenary, someone bound to him by silver and provisions. But now Arthyr had his own source of these things. He had indeed made himself another contender, and not just for the position of war-leader. If he was as ambitious as Lot believed, perhaps he could even make himself High King, the role Lot wanted for himself.

'So that's why I need a man in Arthyr's camp, so to speak,'

Lot went on. 'That's why I need you.'

'You want me to join Arthyr's war-band?' Corwynal asked in surprise.

'Of course not! He wouldn't have you, not in the state you're in right now. And anyway—' Lot paused, his eyes sliding away, and cleared his throat. 'No, that's not it at all. What I need, Corwynal is—'

'Have you told him yet?' The room darkened for a moment as Blaize stepped through the shaft of sunlight at the doorway. 'Has he agreed?'

'Curse you, Blaize!' Lot exclaimed. 'Give me a sodding chance!'

'Told me what? Agreed to what?'

Blaize sighed, poured himself a cup of ale, threw it back in one long swallow, and wiped his mouth on his filthy sleeve. 'I told you to let me handle it,' he said, scowling at Lot.

'Handle what? Handle *me?*' Corwynal began to have a bad feeling about this. 'What in the five hells is this about?'

'Look about you, man.' Lot waved a beefy hand to indicate the dusty council chamber. A rat was nosing along the wall near the door, and the rushes were stale and lumpy with bones and dog shit. 'Listen!' Corwynal could hear men arguing, horses whinnying, thirsty cattle lowing in distress. 'And you can't pretend you don't smell it,' Lot went on. That too couldn't be avoided. Iuddeu reeked of too many men and not enough water. It was the stench of blocked drains, of a fort that until recently had been little more than an outpost, occupied in the summer by lookouts and hunting parties who'd never attempted to repair the years of neglect. Now it was the command centre for Lot and Arthyr's army, and, though most of the troops were in the field, a fair number remained in the fort, inadequately housed and fed. The barracks' roofs leaked, the stables were partly ruined, and the roads that ran to and from the fort were fetlock-deep in mud. No-one seemed to be in charge, but both Lot and Blaize were looking at Corwynal with identical expressions of exasperation and impatience as he groped his way towards the reason he was there.

'No,' he said flatly. 'I'm not going to be Iuddeu's Chamberlain. I'm joining Trystan as soon as my shoulder's healed.'

Trystan and his Selgovians were stationed in an old Roman fortlet that stood on a ridge to the north of Iuddeu. They were clearing the remaining Caledonians from the river valleys and driving them back into the hills of Atholl. Corwynal worried about him, of course, but less sharply now the black ship had been defeated. Nevertheless, he'd every intention of joining the Selgovian troop at the first opportunity.

'We need you in Iuddeu more than Trystan needs you in the north,' Blaize said. 'This is what you're good at, Corwynal.'

'Leave the fighting to younger men,' Lot advised him.

'Too old, am I?' A pulse of anger flared behind Corwynal's eyes and set his head throbbing. 'Do I need to remind you of what this old man achieved? Maybe I do, given the tales I hear around Iuddeu: stories of the battle, of the defeat of the Scots, of Trystan the hero, tales in which I play no part.' He eyed Blaize sharply, prey to a sudden suspicion. 'Why is that?'

'Because Trystan's young and handsome, and you're not,' Blaize said shamelessly. 'I'm not responsible for what men choose to believe, and it isn't Trystan who's been telling these tales. Ask him if you like.'

'He's here? In Iuddeu?'

'Just arrived. He's up on the rampart, waiting for you.'

'Gods, Trys, have you grown?'

It was less than a month since the battle, but Trystan looked decidedly broader across the chest, and might even be taller. His grin was a white blaze in his sun-browned face, his grip, as he threw his arms about Corwynal's shoulders, fierce enough to make him yelp with pain since his wound was still tender.

Trystan began to tell him about his adventures in the hills. 'No serious fighting, just skirmishing,' he said with a dismissive gesture. 'But I can't wait to get back.' He leant over Iuddeu's rampart as he talked, watching the cloud shadows sweep over the Heights, the hills that swelled out of the plain a little way north of the fort. But Corwynal had seen that view too often to find it interesting, so instead he looked at Trystan and saw other more subtle changes: a new confidence and the separateness that comes with leadership and responsibility. There was a reserve in him too, and, with his next words, Corwynal began to understand the reason for that.

'What are you going to do once your shoulder's healed?' Trystan turned his back on the hills and leant against the rampart wall, his ankles crossed in front of him, his hands thrust into the opening of the sheepskin jerkin he was wearing. As a posture of relaxation, however, it was entirely false, for Corwynal had heard the quick intake of breath before he spoke and noticed the faint tremble in his hands as he pushed them into his jerkin. 'Will you go back to Lothian?'

'You know I can't do that.'

'Selgovia then. You told Hoel you'd return once the war was over.'

'It isn't over, and I thought we had other plans.' *Come adventuring with me.* 'But it seems I no longer have a part in *your* plans.'

How close they'd been at the battle, facing death together.

Now that closeness was gone, leaving Trystan a stranger.

'I need to go alone.' Trystan let his eyes slide away, then leant over the rampart and pretended an interest in an argument going on down by the main gate.

'Why? To prove yourself? You already have. Everyone is talking about how you were the hero of the battle by the Beacon Loch.'

'They talk about what you did as well.'

'No, they don't,' Corwynal said curtly, wondering if success and adulation had turned Trystan's head.

'Gods, Corwynal!' Trystan smashed his palm down on the rampart edge and spun to face him. 'Do you think I want all the glory for myself? That I want to fight alone because I don't want you to share it? Is that what you truly think of me? Because that isn't the reason. It's because you broke your promise to fight by my side, as we agreed before the battle. That was what I was *relying* on.'

'But I did—'

'Yes, to begin with. And while you did, we were invincible. You and I together, one man . . . But then you went off on your own. It was as if you'd gone mad.'

'Maybe that's what it was,' Corwynal said, unable to explain why he'd gone after Feargus. 'A sort of battle-madness.'

Trystan shook his head. 'No. I know what battle-madness is. It's music and joy and . . . You know what I mean because you feel it too. But what you did that day was different.'

'Whatever it was, you shouldn't have followed me. *That* was madness.'

'I kept my side of our bargain, and Aelfric kept his oaths. It was you who broke your promise, so how can I trust you again? How can I take the risk?'

'It isn't your risk to take.'

'But it is! Don't you see? If you put yourself in danger, how can I not come to your aid? Even when I know I shouldn't. We should have pulled back when the Scots were reinforced. If Arthyr's men hadn't come, we would have died there. All for the sake of your . . . madness.'

Trystan was right, and Corwynal knew it, but he still resented being talked to as if he was a badly behaved recruit. Part of him wanted to put Trystan over his knee and thrash the certainty out of him, but he forced himself to swallow his resentment.

'I'm aware of that,' he said stiffly. 'It won't happen again, I promise you.'

Trystan looked at him narrowly, wanting to believe him, but after a moment he shook his head, leant on the rampart once more and scowled into the north.

'It's not just that,' he said. 'It's the Caledonians. Aelfric told me what happened in Selgovia at the fort. You couldn't kill any of them, not your own tribe. That's why you're not coming with me. I don't know where we're going or which tribe of Caledonians we'll have to fight. Maybe it will be warriors from Atholl and, if it is, I can't have someone in my troop who might hold back or, if the mood takes him, go off on a pointless suicidal attack that I'd couldn't stop myself from supporting. You see that, don't you?'

Trystan's colour was heightened, and his lips were pressed firmly together. He was unhappy, but determined. Corwynal turned away and stared at the hills that soared out of the plains, but he wasn't seeing them. Instead he was remembering the deep glens, the high hidden passes, the straths and settlements and fortresses where the Caledonians would regroup, the wolf-tribe of Atholl among them. He wanted to fight them – to be able to fight them – but, after Selgovia, he wasn't sure he could.

So why should Trystan trust him when he didn't trust himself?

Trystan's decision was the right one, a decision made by a man rather than a boy, a man who wasn't going to let affection cloud his judgement. Corwynal knew he should applaud this, but all he felt was the chilling sense of separation that had begun in Selgovia when Trystan had started to become the man he'd taught him to be, a leader of men. One who didn't need him anymore. That hurt, but he'd promised a god he'd let Trystan live, and that meant letting him go, letting him make his own mistakes, letting him learn from them, and trusting him to survive without Corwynal's protection. He'd saved Trystan from the black ship, so his role as protector was over. Except it could never truly be over.

He looked down at the fort, at the bustle of men and mounts, of carts and wagons. He listened to the rumble of discontent and smelled the stench of human and animal waste. Down by the gate the argument had come to blows, and a man from Arthyr's troop was fighting a Gododdin man over the rights to a cartload of fodder. Someone should do something about it, he thought, and so he nodded, accepting both Trystan's arguments and what seemed to be his own personal doom.

He returned to the council chamber to find Arthyr had joined Lot and Blaize. The three of them were deep in discussion, but when he stepped through the door, they all looked up expectedly.

'All right,' he said. 'I'll do it. But there will be conditions . . .'

And so he became not only Chamberlain of Iuddeu but Steward of Western Manau, the man responsible for supplying Arthyr's army, for finding horses and weapons and supplies, for re-building forts and roads, supply depots, signal towers and harbours. He'd be in charge of making sure things were where they ought to be when they ought to be there and that no-one stole them on the way. He'd have to extract tribute from people who wouldn't want to give it, make unpopular laws and see they were enforced. In Arthyr's absence he'd have powers he insisted on being given, powers that made Lot blanch and Blaize frown, for they'd make him as powerful as any of the kings.

But Arthyr accepted his conditions with no more than a wry smile, knowing Corwynal hadn't made them because he wanted power. It was warriors who won the battles and took back the lands, warriors who were praised in the songs the bards made to celebrate their deeds. It was the thinkers and planners, however, who'd hold the lands after they'd been won, and who'd have to fight just as hard to turn war into a lasting peace. And he became Steward for this reason also; to make sure that when Trystan was fighting in the north, he wouldn't run out of food or mounts or weapons. If Corwynal couldn't be at his side, he'd be at his back, protecting him as he always had, in the only way Trystan was willing to allow him.

'Good,' Arthyr said, getting to his feet with the air of a man who'd just dealt with a minor piece of unpleasantness and was now free to get on with what really mattered. 'But you'll need help. From someone who knows these lands and their people.' His bright purpose shadowed for a moment. 'My wife,' he explained. 'Gwenhwyvar.'

...arrowheads... charcoal... timber... oatmeal... four draught horses... trenching tools... an engineer—

'An engineer?!' Corwynal looked up from Arthyr's extensive list of requirements to find the older man watching him, half amused, half sympathetic. 'Where am I supposed to find an engineer?'

Arthyr shrugged. 'I've no idea, but I need one, so you'll try, won't you?' Laid out on the table between them in the storeroom next to the stables, once Arthyr's room and now Corwynal's, was Lot's map, obscured by a jumble of letters and lists.

'Lothian's war-band's requirements seem somewhat easier to deal with,' Arthyr said, picking up and squinting through one of the lists. He tossed the scrap to Corwynal who snorted with exasperation, for it was virtually illegible, and must therefore be from Madawg, who apparently wanted several barrels of bear. It would serve him right if Corwynal sent him exactly that, except finding a bear would be almost as difficult as finding an engineer.

He sighed. Being Steward of Western Manau was proving to be more difficult than even he'd expected.

'You mentioned help,' he reminded Arthyr, willing now, as he hadn't been a few days before, to accept the assistance of a sixteen-year-old girl about whom he'd heard conflicting rumours. Blaize had warned him against accepting Arthyr's offer, but had left Iuddeu without saying why. Lot had gone too, having returned to his Gododdin stronghold of Ad Gefryn, and wouldn't be back until the Summer Fair at Lughnasadh. 'You'll keep me informed, of course . . .' he'd said, giving Corwynal a significant look.

About Arthyr, he understood. Arthyr and his ambitions, whatever they might be. Corwynal was to be Lot's spy, but he wasn't happy about it, for he'd grown fond of Arthyr, a man who appeared to have no weaknesses. Even his oddly intense friendship with Bedwyr seemed more of a strength than a weakness, and he wondered afresh why Arthyr had married a girl he'd never met before.

'They say she's beautiful,' Trystan said with a shrug. He was still in Iuddeu, waiting impatiently for a draft of remounts from Meldon. 'But they would say that, wouldn't they, her being a Princess. They said it about Essylt.' He flinched, as if this reminder of his wife was a horsefly landing on his skin. 'This will be the same – a political marriage,' he went on, unwilling to believe the man who'd become his hero could think about love when there was war to be waged. Right then, Trystan had no interest in women, only in fighting. 'If she's so beautiful, why did Arthyr leave her in Dun Eidyn?'

But now the girl had arrived in Iuddeu, just as Arthyr was about to leave once more.

'Time to head north,' Arthyr said. 'I'll base myself at the old fort by the ford on the River Tava for the summer and leave you in charge in Iuddeu.' He paused, ran a hand through his greying hair, but wouldn't meet Corwynal's eyes. 'Keep Gwenhwyvar busy, won't you? I don't want her anywhere near the front line. It's too dangerous.'

That was undoubtedly true, but Corwynal suspected Arthyr really meant for him to keep her away from him and Bedwyr.

'Arthyr, listen—' he began, uneasy about the prospect of dealing with any girl, far less one rumoured to be wilful.

'Just keep an eye on her.' Arthyr smiled that rare disarming smile that bound men to his purpose. 'And I'll keep an eye on Trystan for you.'

'You're taking him with you?' Corwynal asked, half afraid, half relieved, since Trystan, kicking his heels in Iuddeu, was bored enough to get into trouble unless he was given something to do.

'I'm taking everyone I can. You can send on the remounts he's waiting for, along with anything else. Do we have a deal?'

It was a fair bargain, so he nodded and they turned to the rest of their business: the forts that had to be rebuilt, the roads that should be repaired, grain to be harvested and cattle to be slaughtered, all the details, small or large, that might win or lose the campaign. And information about the enemy was part of it.

'... so this is the Caledonians' main stronghold in Circind?' Arthyr asked, indicating a position on Lot's map. Before Corwynal could answer, the door burst open. It was as if one of those little twisting winds that whirl about the moors on hot days in summer had blown into the room, and the draught from the open door sent parchments swirling to the floor.

'Arthyr! There you are!'

'Gwenhwyvar!' Arthyr jumped to his feet, his face darkening. 'I said I'd send for you.'

'Pooh!' she said, stripping off her gloves and favouring him with a blinding smile.

So this was Gwenhwyvar, Queen of Western Manau, Chatelaine of Iuddeu, and Arthyr's wife, the girl who was here to help him but who Corwynal thought was more likely to cause trouble.

They all said she was wilful. That, Corwynal could believe. Some had said she was beautiful, others that she was no more than passable. Too tall, too thin, too clever for her own good. Manipulative, innocent, charming, sullen. No-one was able to agree, but, now she was here, Corwynal understood why, for she seemed to be all of these things. Sixteen and just coming into a beauty that lay more in the shape of her bones than in skin or hair. Sixteen, with the knowingness of an older woman, but ignorant, as yet, of the world. Not a girl, but not yet a woman, a creature on the cusp, so vibrant she blinded everyone to her true nature, including herself. Beautiful, charming, innocent, deadly.

Corwynal's breathing stopped. He felt as if he stood on the

edge of a cliff, rocks far beneath him. Then he was in that training ring in Galloway with the sun in his eyes. Eighteen years before, he'd fallen, devastatingly, for a face as striking as this one. The light from the door quivered as the years swam dizzily in the suddenly muggy air of the room, and he felt sweat break out all down his spine. Then the air cleared, and he stepped back from the edge, for he was no longer nineteen. He was thirty-seven, and this girl was young enough to be his own daughter. With that thought, he could see Gwenhwyvar for what she really was: a girl, as leggy as a colt, a girl who was no more than passably good-looking. Her mouth was too wide, her hair fair rather than gold, her eyes hazel instead of being a dizzying blue, her nose too long, her chin too determined. He also saw that she wasn't quite as sure of herself as she pretended, and that Arthyr's reaction to her arrival had hurt her.

'Sent for or not, I'm here now,' she said briskly, bending to pick up the parchments that had swirled to the floor. 'What's this?' she asked, glancing at the list Corwynal had been discussing with Arthyr. 'You want an engineer?' She tilted her head to one side and smiled. 'I think I know where to find one . . .'

It's going to be all right. Gwenhwyvar was close to Trystan's age and, like him, ready to take the world in her hands. No doubt she'd make mistakes but might be willing to learn from them. If she was prepared to work with him, then Corwynal could teach her, as once he'd taught Trystan. He glanced at Arthyr, who'd stepped back into the shadows, distancing himself from the girl he'd married to gain a kingdom, and understood that this was his unspoken role. Gwenhwyvar was Queen of Western Manau, and Corwynal was to turn her into its Steward. Only when he'd done so would he be free to leave.

But it might be ... interesting.

Until that moment, he hadn't realised how much he missed his role of tutor, of shaping a young and intelligent mind. Oddly, he'd never once considered what his life might have been like if the child his father had forced on him all those years before had been a girl rather than a boy. A daughter. He would like to have a daughter. Perhaps one day he would, a child he could acknowledge as his own, a toddler reaching up to him, laughing and calling him father. Although of the child's mother, the one in this dream, he could make out no detail.

He was still staring at Gwenhwyvar, smiling at these rather strange thoughts. Arthyr was watching him, his face a mask, and the girl, her head tilted to one side, was regarding him curiously.

'You're a Pict?'

'A Caledonian,' he corrected her. The tuition had begun. 'Half-Caledonian.' She was looking at the patterns on his arms and chest, for the day was hot and he'd half-unlaced his tunic and rolled up his sleeves.

'Was it—?' She stopped, biting her lip. But he knew what she wanted to know.

'Painful? Yes. It was excruciating.'

She laughed, throwing her head back to reveal the long, lovely line of her throat. *She is beautiful!* Gwenhwyvar was a creature of movement, of muscle, with a grace she hadn't yet mastered. She was like sunlight on water, and those who thought her no more than passable had seen her at rest, not like this, laughing as she bent to pick up the remaining pieces of parchment, then rising and turning as the room darkened. Someone was standing in the doorway, blinded by the light outside, peering into the storeroom.

'Corwynal?' Trystan asked. 'Have you heard—?'

Trystan saw Gwenhwyvar and stopped. The years swum dizzily once more, and Corwynal was nineteen again, in a training ring in Galloway, seeing a woman coming out of the sun. Now it was Trystan emerging from the light, Trystan with the same grace as his mother, the same hard beauty. Gwenhwyvar stared at Trystan, and he at her, both curious, both intelligent, each of them knowing who the other must be and what rumour said of them. Trystan smiled a little smile of devilry and challenge Corwynal knew was likely to lead to trouble. Gwenhwyvar's lips twitched, and her chin rose a little as she accepted that challenge, ready for trouble herself, perhaps even welcoming it.

Arthyr cleared his throat and broke the spell. 'Corwynal *has* heard. We leave tonight, so I hope your men are ready, Trys.'

'Oh... I...' Trystan hadn't seen Arthyr standing in the shadows. 'So soon?' he asked, and Corwynal felt a tremor of disquiet for, until this moment, he'd been desperate to leave. 'I'm still waiting for remounts.'

'They'll be sent on. Corwynal will arrange it – with Gwenhwyvar's help.'

Trystan's eyes flew to Corwynal's, but his face was unreadable. When had he learned to control his expression like that? Yet there was no mistaking the coolness of his gaze.

'Very well,' Trystan said, accepting but, for some reason, not liking the situation. Then he flashed a grin at Gwenhwyvar. 'But it won't be long before I'm back.'

Corwynal expected Arthyr to correct Trystan's expectation, but the older man just shrugged. 'No, probably not,' he said, before turning to Corwynal. 'So, I think we're finished here...?' They weren't, but he nodded and Arthyr left. Moments later, Trystan followed him but turned in the doorway.

'I'll leave Aelfric with you,' he said.

'No, you won't,' Corwynal said, for Aelfric was as keen as Trystan to get back to the fighting. He didn't want a bad-tempered Angle moping about Iuddeu. In any case, Trystan would need all the men he could get. So why was he offering to leave the best of them behind? Did he want Aelfric to spy on him? Didn't he trust Corwynal with Gwenhwyvar? Perhaps Corwynal's first reaction to the girl had been correct. She was to be feared, but not for himself. The black ship had tried to come between him and Trystan and had failed. But the black ship wasn't the only danger in the world. There was one right here, but it wasn't one he could fight. It wasn't one he had any hope of defeating.

Women! Aelfric thought sourly. *Why do they have to spoil everything?*

He and Trystan were riding back to Iuddeu, and Aelfric was now depressingly familiar with the route, though it had changed over the course of the last couple of months and was no longer a muddy track through scrubby woodland, but a broad road, paved and ditched in places, with grassy rides on either side. That was Corwynal's doing, Trystan told him, as were the posting stations along the way, the messenger service and, more importantly, the regular supplies that reached their camp in the foothills of the ridge that overlooked the Tava. The man made a fair enough Steward, Aelfric concluded grudgingly, though in his opinion none of that stuff was necessary.

'Why can't we just live off the land?' he'd asked. The country into which the Britons were advancing was good farming country, and there were plenty of settlements.

'Because we're here to govern, not raid,' Trystan told him loftily. It was exactly the sort of thing the Caledonian would have said. Aelfric shook his head in disgust. Fighting was all very well, but when you'd won a man should profit by it. So where were all the cattle and slaves? Where were all the women?

'No women,' Trystan announced after flogging one of his men for raping a peasant. 'Not unless they're willing. We're here to stay, and once the harvest's in we want these people to pay their tribute to us, not the Caledonians. We need them on our side, not at our backs with knives in their fists. So no stealing, no rustling, and if you want a woman, try using your best smile.'

There was an ironic cheer at that, even from the man who'd been flogged. Trystan was only seventeen, but already he had a loyal following, and not just among the Selgovae. Others had come to join him, attracted by the belief that he was lucky, that he had Arthyr's favour and, importantly, the Steward of Iuddeu's support. Trystan didn't need to use his best smile to have women falling at his feet. Which, Aelfric assumed, was why they were riding back to Iuddeu yet again, though this time, according to Trystan, it was for the Summer Fair. Lughnasadh, they called it.

'There will be a huge feast on the last night, The Night of Gifts,' Trystan told him. 'And a market for the three days of the Fair, with contests of skill. Horse-racing, archery, wrestling, that sort of thing.'

Aelfric liked the sound of a huge feast, and some of those contests. Not horse-racing, of course, and he was no more than a passable archer. Wrestling, however, was something he excelled at.

'What are you entering?'

'Everything, probably,' Trystan replied distractedly. Iuddeu was in sight by then, looming through the summer haze of dust and insects, the fort crowning the rock, the sprawling settlement at its foot, the lookout tower on the adjoining hill. But Aelfric suspected Trystan wasn't thinking about the fort or the Fair or the contests. He was thinking about Gwenhwyvar, Queen of Iuddeu, Arthyr's wife. And Trystan with a wife of his own, that little girl in Selgovia.

Idiot! Aelfric thought with a certain amount of sympathy. It was all too easy to forget your responsibilities, and Aelfric was uncomfortably conscious that, once again, he'd forgotten his promise to Ealhith. *Protect him*, she'd said, meaning the Caledonian. But, with the man stuck in Iuddeu, as far from the fighting as it was possible to get, Aelfric didn't think he needed protection anymore, even if Trystan disagreed.

Two months before, Trystan had asked Aelfric to stay in Iuddeu with Corwynal and 'keep an eye on him' but hadn't explained why. In any case, Corwynal had told him to go with Trystan and keep an eye on *him*, and that had been more to Aelfric's taste because it meant the possibility of fighting. Sure enough, there had been a few sticky moments up on the border, and if Aelfric hadn't been there, the outcome might have been different, so he'd earned his place in Trystan's troop. As if that had ever been in doubt. Surely Ealhith would have wanted him to protect Trystan as well? Not that Aelfric had seriously given any thought to Ealhith's possible views on the matter. He'd gone with Trystan because he wanted to, but now, approaching Iuddeu, and with time to think, he wondered afresh why Trystan had asked him to stay and what he'd been so afraid of.

'There!' Trystan pointed up at the battlements. They were close enough now to make out not only the lookouts on the ramparts but others who'd gone up to watch the road north. One of them, a dark-haired man, waved a hand in greeting. 'It's Corwynal!' Trystan raised his own hand in response and then let it fall as someone else joined him, her long, fair hair lifting in the breeze. 'Gwenhwyvar,' Trystan muttered. 'I might have known...'

Aelfric stared at him. Was *this* what Trystan had been afraid of? Was *this* what he'd wanted Aelfric to 'keep an eye on'? He started to laugh. 'You're jealous!'

'Me? Jealous? Don't be ridiculous!'

'Ridiculous? Me? Do you seriously think that girl would look twice at Corwynal? A man old enough to be her father? And him useless with women into the bargain? Anyway, she's married to Arthyr. And you're married too, in case you've forgotten.'

'That has nothing to do with it,' Trystan said, colouring a little. 'I think of Gwenhwyvar as my sister.'

So they'd been doing all that to-ing and fro-ing to Iuddeu on account of a *sister?* Aelfric didn't think so.

'You don't have a sister,' he pointed out. 'Woden's balls, Trys, your brother may be a fool with women, but I never thought you were! If you've fallen for that skinny chit, you're an idiot, and an even bigger one if you think Corwynal's your rival.'

'You didn't see how he looked at her,' Trystan complained, then shook his head. 'You wouldn't understand.' He kicked his horse into a canter and disappeared down the road.

'No, and I don't want to,' Aelfric told the disappearing figure. Nevertheless, he found himself uncharacteristically thoughtful. Trystan had wanted him to stay in Iuddeu to stop Corwynal making a fool of himself over another man's wife. Ealhith would have wanted Aelfric to stop him too. 'How?' he asked the horse, who just flicked his ears and said nothing, so he kicked the beast into a trot and set off after the boy.

Corwynal and Gwenhwyvar had vanished from the ramparts, but someone else had appeared, someone who was standing on tiptoe to look over the rampart and wave a greeting.

'That's Essylt.' Trystan reined in his mount and waited for Aelfric to catch him up. 'What's *she* doing here?'

Things were about to get interesting, Aelfric thought. But not in a good way.

13

YOU MIGHT TRY TRUSTING ME

'Can anyone enter?' Essylt asked.

It was the second day of the contests, a hot and muggy afternoon, with the smell of mown hay in the fields and thunder in the air. There would be rain come the evening, Corwynal thought, less concerned about the tented village that had sprung up at the base of Iuddeu's rock than the grain ripening in the fields – their badly needed harvest – which would be flattened if there was a downpour.

'Sorry,' he said, dragging his attention back to the present and to the targets that had been set up for the archery contest, just about to begin. 'What did you say?'

'You look tired,' Essylt said, looking up at him.

Corwynal laughed ruefully, for it was the truth. Supplying Arthyr's army was difficult enough, and he would have preferred to cancel the Fair on the grounds of it being an unnecessary distraction and expense, but Gwenhwyvar had insisted it go ahead. She was Queen of Western Manau, something she reminded him every time they argued about anything. She'd organise everything, she'd declared, so he'd backed down but had sworn to himself that if she ran into difficulties he wouldn't get her out of them. But she hadn't needed his help, and because, until now, the weather had held up, the Fair was accounted a success – apart from the one thing over which Gwenhwyvar had no control; Arthyr, the man everyone wanted to see, hadn't turned up.

Lot, who'd arrived a couple of days earlier, had insisted all the troop commanders return to Iuddeu for the Fair for 'discussions', so was annoyed his most senior commander had yet to put in an appearance. Arthyr might be Gwenhwyvar's husband, but he seemed to avoid that role entirely. Poor Gwenhwyvar.

'So, can anyone enter?' Essylt asked once more.

Corwynal looked down at the girl by his side and wished she hadn't come. He didn't want to be reminded of everything that had happened in Selgovia: his own personal failure, seeing a side of Trystan he hadn't much cared for, then Ninian's mutilation. The young Scot, thanks no doubt to his god Chrystos, was recovering, but was not yet well enough to travel. So Essylt had come alone, trusting to her new husband's welcome. Trystan, however, on learning of his wife's unexpected arrival in Iuddeu, had been less than gracious.

'I wish you'd told me you were coming.'

'Do I have to inform you whenever I leave Meldon?' Her smile of welcome had faltered.

'I might not have been here.'

'What makes you think I've come to Iuddeu to see you? Maybe I came to see your brother.'

Trystan, surprised, had laughed, and was still laughing when Gwenhwyvar ran up and, ignoring the badly dressed girl beside him, threw her arms around his neck. 'Trys! It's been so long!'

By Corwynal's reckoning, it had been barely half a moon since Trystan had last been in Iuddeu on some pretext or other, and, sooner or later, Essylt would learn that for herself. She'd also hear the rumours that were being whispered about Iuddeu – that her husband and Gwenhwyvar were over-friendly. Gwenhwyvar's greeting suggested the rumours might be true, even though Trystan unwound her arms from his neck and threw Corwynal a look of appeal as he did so. He just shrugged. *You got yourself into this. Get yourself out.* But Trystan didn't know how.

'Essylt, this is Gwenhwyvar, Queen of Western Manau and Arthyr's wife. Gwenhwyvar, this is Essylt, Princess of Selgovia and ... *my* wife.'

The two women assessed one another, and Essylt, noticing Gwenhwyvar's openly critical appraisal, responded with a flash of dislike. It was hardly surprising. Gwenhwyvar was taller, fairer, and dressed in a green dress that suited her. Her arms were bare and brown with summer, and there was a slim gold torque about her neck, gold bracelets set with pearls around her wrists. Essylt, on the other hand, was wearing a beige dress embroidered in the Selgovian style. Clumpy wooden jewellery hung around her neck, and she'd dressed her hair in two thin plaits that didn't suit her. Painfully aware of the disparity in their appearance, Essylt's bearing was stiff, and she just nodded curtly at Gwenhwyvar. Corwynal thought it likely that, hurt and angry, she was simply unable to speak, but doubted if Gwenhwyvar would understand that. Nevertheless, having been raised in her uncle Caw's court of Dun Eidyn, she knew how to be gracious.

'Essylt. I'm so pleased to meet you at last! I've heard so much about you from Trystan.'

'Have you?' Trystan asked in surprise, thus ruining Gwenhwyvar's effort. She threw him a sparkling look of both reproach and mischief, and, unable to stop himself, he laughed once more. Essylt hadn't been amused, however, and now, two days after that uncomfortable arrival, she still wasn't amused, for Trystan had paid her scant attention since then, being intent not so much on spending time with Gwenhwyvar but on entering every contest there was to enter and winning most of them. And it looked as if he was going to win the archery contest too.

'Kaer would beat him if he was here,' Essylt said waspishly. Kaerherdin had been left in charge of the Selgovians in the north. Perhaps if he'd been in Iuddeu, Trystan might not have behaved quite so badly, though, in truth, there was little he could be accused of other than a lack of consideration of his own wife. All the young men of Iuddeu clustered around Gwenhwyvar like moths about a flame, but Trystan stood apart from them, and seemed amused rather than jealous of the attention she gave them. To Corwynal, that distance spoke of a private understanding between them that went beyond friendship. *Are they lovers?* he wondered uneasily, but tried to banish the thought for fear Essylt would see it in his face, and perhaps she did.

'They all admire her, don't they?' She nodded at the archery ground where Gwenhwyvar was standing with the contestants, laughing as they vied for her attention. Trystan, however, was concentrating on stringing his bow and choosing the straightest of his shafts. He was to shoot against Heuil, Caw's eldest son, his chief rival in the contests, and it wasn't going to be easy for rainclouds were piling up in the west, and the light was flat and misleading.

'Are you in love with her too?' Essylt asked when Corwynal didn't answer.

'Me?' He looked at her in surprise. Was that what she thought? What everyone thought, Trystan included? Even

Aelfric had been giving him some strange looks recently. But maybe it wasn't so surprising, given how much time he had to spend with her. She might be imperious and wilful, demanding and unreasonable, yet there was no denying how charming she could be when she tried. And so he'd been careful, not quite trusting himself. He avoided her when he could, argued with her when he had to, and frequently lost his temper. Eventually, however, they'd reached a wary understanding, as Gwenhwyvar had come to see that, occasionally, he might be right, and, for his part, he'd come to understand how similar she was, in so many ways, to Trystan. She had the same wild courageous spirit, but hers was trapped in a girl's body, and she was married to a man who didn't care for her. So, no, Corwynal didn't love her. Rather, he pitied her, just as he pitied Essylt, who was in much the same position.

'I'm fond of her, as I'm fond of you.'

'Do you ever regret it? Not finding me at Beltein?' She turned away, a faint blush staining her cheeks.

He didn't know what she wanted him to say, so he said nothing, and perhaps she didn't really expect an answer. 'Why did the gods send me Trystan, whom I longed for more than anything, and then betray me?'

'Trystan hasn't betrayed you, Essylt.' He hoped he was right.

'He will.' She glanced over at her husband. 'Sooner or later. With Gwenhwyvar or someone else. He never pretended to love me, so I suppose I shouldn't complain. You would have pretended, and maybe that would have been worse.'

'I would have pretended until it was no longer necessary,' he said staunchly, looking about for a way to escape this conversation, and Essylt, seeing his barely concealed desire to flee, smiled a sad little smile.

'At Beltein, when you walked off into the darkness, I

thought you wanted to be alone with your ghosts. Then, when you told me you'd loved someone who'd died, I wondered if that was one of your ghosts and if she was still alive for you.'

'Not anymore,' he said because, finally, it was true. 'Love never lasts forever, Essylt. It dies in its time.'

'I won't let it die!' She ran off across the field towards the archery butts and the group around Trystan. He'd just loosed his third shot, which struck the target close to the centre. His three shots were grouped closely together, beating Heuil's placement. Corwynal, going after Essylt, heard Heuil curse at Trystan's retreating back as he strolled over to the target to retrieve his shafts.

'Didn't Trystan shoot well?' Gwenhwyvar declared, slightly flustered, since the two women had been avoiding one another. 'You must be so proud.'

'My brother could have beaten him!' Essylt snatched up Trystan's bow, plucked three arrows from his quiver, nocked the first to the bow and let it fly even as was retrieving the last of his shafts. Her arrow thudded into the centre of the target, only a hand-span from his head.

'Essylt!' Corwynal cried out in alarm as she nocked the second arrow to the bow. Trystan whirled around, searching for the archer who'd made that shot, and when he saw it was Essylt, he went very still, his eyes widening as she let the second arrow fly and then the third. Both slammed into the target next to the first, her grouping closer than his. There was a moment's silence, then someone began to clap. Gradually, others joined in.

'Good for you, girl!' Aelfric called out from somewhere near the back of the crowd.

Then a flash of lightening ripped the clouds apart, and thunder rolled all around them. A drop of water struck

Corwynal's arm and then another, pattering into the silence left by the thunder. In a moment, it was raining in earnest, water drumming on the ground and sending everyone scurrying for the shelter of the fort.

'I do believe I've won,' Essylt said to no-one in particular, throwing back her head, closing her eyes, and letting the rain pour down over her face. But she hadn't won at anything that mattered, and everyone knew it.

⸙

'She tried to kill me! It was poison in Meldon. Now this!'

It was much later that day, and Trystan, still angered by what had happened, was pacing back and forth in Corwynal's chamber. Rain dripped from his hair and the hem of his cloak, since the thunderstorm that had ended the contests that afternoon was still battering Iuddeu. But Corwynal, concerned about damage to the crops and the prospect of flooding along the river plain, had little patience for Trystan's complaints.

'Don't be stupid! She drugged you in Meldon to save your life. She wasn't trying to kill you today either, and you know it! She just wanted to show that she was as good an archer as you. You might respect her for that if you can't respect her for anything else.'

Trystan stopped pacing. 'What's that supposed to mean?'

'What do you think it means? Why can't you be kinder to her? It wouldn't take much.'

Trystan shrugged off his cloak, tossed it onto a chest, and threw himself into the chair that stood on the other side of the table where Corwynal had been trying to work. 'You wouldn't understand.' He thrust his feet out to the smoking brazier and shoved his hands into the pockets of his jerkin.

'Try me,' Corwynal said, not bothering to conceal his irritation. In truth, Trystan's behaviour and the turn in the weather weren't the only reasons he was in a foul mood. The crack of thunder that had heralded the storm had also signalled Arthyr's arrival and the arguments that had followed.

'About sodding time,' Lot had muttered, and, sure enough, before Arthyr could change out of his wet clothes, he'd been summoned to a meeting of the troop commanders which Corwynal, as the troops' quartermaster, was expected to attend.

'It's not good enough!' Lot declared. 'We need to take the whole of the plain to the north of the Tava, not just the west. We have to push on through to the coast, to the harbours. We haven't the ships to stop those Caledonian bastards at sea, so we need to burn them out on land.'

Arthyr just shrugged. 'We can do all that by the end of the season, if that's what you want. But whatever gains we make, we won't be able to hold them through the winter without more men. The Caledonians are just biding their time, waiting until we're too thinly spread, which we will be if we occupy all the positions you expect us to.'

'He's right,' Corwynal said, an opinion Lot had neither asked for nor wanted, as he'd made clear to him after the meeting had broken up.

'You're supposed to be on my side. Not questioning my strategy.'

'I thought we were all on the same side. And the strategy isn't at issue here. It makes sense to hold the whole of the plain south of the high ground, if we can find the men to do it, but we'll need supplies as well as men, supplies we don't have.'

'We've just taken Fife! We'll have all their tribute.'

'Persuading them to pay it won't be easy.'

'Force them. Go yourself. You can leave that girl, Gwenhwyvar, in charge in Iuddeu, can't you?'

But Corwynal wasn't sure if he could. Gwenhwyvar had proved herself more capable than he'd expected, but hadn't had to deal with a crisis. One was bound to arise, and he wanted to be in Iuddeu when it did, but Lot misunderstood the reason for his hesitation.

'So it's true,' he said irritably. 'That girl! Half the army sniffing around her like dogs after a bitch in heat, your boy Trystan among them. That's why you don't want to leave. God's blood, man! I left you in charge of her!'

'She's Arthyr's responsibility, not mine.'

'Maybe so, but Arthyr's a fool. What's he doing stationing a good-looking boy like Trystan so close to Iuddeu if he's going to leave his wife to entertain herself? What's Trystan playing at? And, more to the point, what are you doing letting him?'

It took Corwynal some time to persuade Lot there was nothing behind the rumours, which wasn't easy when he wasn't convinced himself, and he resented the position Trystan had put him in. So, later that day, when Trystan came to complain, he wasn't sympathetic.

'Make me understand, Trys. Because, right now, I don't.'

'Yes, you do. You're itching to say "I told you so", and you'd be right. I should never have married Essylt. You should have married her.'

'My dear Trystan, that was what I intended,' Corwynal reminded him dryly.

'You could still, in all the ways that matter.' Trystan looked down at the floor and moved the rushes about with the heel of his boot. 'Hoel wanted you for Selgovia, and you wanted it too. Not for the men, or for Lot, but for yourself. Well, you can have Selgovia because I don't want it. You said you're not going back to Lothian, and I don't blame you. So why not go to Meldon? Take Essylt back, Corwynal. Keep her there. Do what you like with Selgovia, and when Hoel dies – and he's not a young man – then it's yours.'

It was a generous offer, but all Corwynal could think about was the pale little girl waiting for a man who not only didn't want her, but was willing to give her away. And of a second, languishing in Iuddeu, unloved by her husband and bored enough to turn to someone else. Then he thought of the girl who'd looked so like Trystan, the girl who'd played one man off against another, who'd wanted someone she shouldn't have and refused to be denied. Was Trystan like her in more than looks? He was her son after all, beyond any doubt, and, with that thought, Corwynal felt the past reach out to shadow the present as, outside, thunder rumbled.

'I see,' he said coldly.

Trystan looked up at the tone in Corwynal's voice. 'No, you don't. I do *try* to be kind to Essylt, but when I am, she just wants more. She wants everything, more than I have to give. She winds herself about me so tightly I feel as if I'm suffocating.' He eased a finger about the neck of his shirt, as if even the thought of Essylt robbed him of breath.

'And Gwenhwyvar doesn't suffocate you?'

Trystan stiffened. 'I'm not talking about Gwenhwyvar.'

'Shouldn't you be? How do you think Essylt feels when she sees you flirting with her?'

Trystan gave a bark of laughter. 'You think I'm *flirting* with Gwen? You really don't understand, do you?'

I do, Trystan. I've stood where you stand now, loving a girl I couldn't have, risking my country and my honour and ruining two lives in the process. Don't do what I did. But how could he tell Trystan about his own mistakes without revealing who he'd made them with? How could he give Trystan the advice he so badly needed?

'I understand you regret marrying Essylt, but it's too late now, and, yes, I did warn you.' *One day you'll meet the woman who's the other half of your soul.* Was Gwenhwyvar that woman? She was Trystan's own age, a good-looking girl of royal blood who might have been a match for him if circumstances had been different. Now he was trapped, and Essylt, who held the key to his prison, had no intention of letting him go. 'The best thing for you to do, the best thing for everyone, is to keep away from Iuddeu.'

'I see,' Trystan replied in the same tone Corwynal had used earlier, and Corwynal wondered if he really imagined him to be a rival for Gwenhwyvar's affection. If so, the boy was more besotted than he'd thought.

'Come with me,' Trystan said after a moment. 'Back to the front line. I was wrong after the battle. I shouldn't have refused you. So come with me now.'

Corwynal shook his head. Whatever Trystan's reasons for asking him – whether he genuinely believed he'd been wrong or simply wanted to get a supposed rival away from Gwenhwyvar – it was now too late.

'I have responsibilities now, responsibilities you forced me to take up. I can't just drop them when it suits you. And some of those responsibilities are yours. I'll have to escort Essylt back to Meldon, since you clearly don't intend to. But it won't be because I want her or Selgovia. It'll be because someone has to be kind to her since you can't seem to be. Then I have to go to Fife for Lot to gather in the tribute, which will be unpleasant to say the least. But I'll do that because it's my responsibility. It's time you faced up to your own. Forget Gwenhwyvar, Trystan.'

'You really believe there's something between us?'

'I don't know what to believe.'

Trystan got to his feet, snatched up his still dripping cloak and made for the door, but turned in the doorway. His eyes were cold and very blue. 'You might try trusting me,' he said softly, then turned on his heel, swept aside the hanging and stepped out into the rain.

⟁

Corwynal was used to being hated. For the whole of his life he'd been different, a Caledonian among Britons, a Briton among Caledonians, the enemy of two peoples, neither of whom had allowed him to forget it. Small wonder, he sometimes thought, that he'd ended up as a Steward, for Stewards were men who were needed but rarely loved. Yet, as a Steward, Corwynal had found his place among the Britons, and for a time he'd been able to forget he was neither one thing nor another.

But in Fife he wasn't allowed to ignore what he was. The tribes of Fife might go their own way when it suited them, but at heart they were as Caledonian as their cousins north of the Tava and, as such, had no intention of making his life easy.

'I don't know why you put up with it,' Aelfric complained when they arrived at yet another settlement with a gale at their backs, only to be greeted with the usual sullen stares. Nothing was said in Corwynal's hearing, of course. There were no curses, no gestures of disgust, no failure of hospitality, but there was no mistaking their antipathy and resentment. On top of that, he had to put up with Aelfric's bitterness at having been sent to act as his bodyguard when it turned out his person was in no danger whatsoever. His mind, however, was a different matter.

'What do you expect me to do?' Corwynal threw himself down on a pallet in the guest hut they'd been given, exhausted by more than the journey. 'Force them to smile as I take half their harvest? Would you smile? As long as they give me what I want I'm content.'

'Are you?'

Of course he wasn't, but it was almost over, this months-long journey in which he, Aelfric and the small party of men Arthyr had been able to spare, had criss-crossed Fife, travelling from one settlement to the next as Corwynal assessed the harvest, the herds and the flocks, and extracted the share due to Iuddeu. Another man would have returned long ago, but Corwynal had spent time in each settlement, trying to be fair, trying to make the landholders see reason. Now, in the middle of October, they'd reached a settlement on the north-eastern coast, where a sandy bay bounded by long ribs of rocks gave shelter to a fleet of black-hulled Caledonian ships. The fleet had interested Aelfric, but only briefly, and it wasn't long before he was moaning again.

'We should have been back in Iuddeu ages ago.' The Angle propped his shoulders against the door frame and folded his arms across his chest. 'It's been months since a woman smiled at me, far less let me fuck her, and that, let me tell you, is a long time for a man like me, if not for a cold fish like you.'

'Then you'll be relieved to hear we're starting back tomorrow.' But Aelfric didn't greet the news with the joy Corwynal expected.

'Why?' he asked, narrowing his eyes suspiciously. 'Why now?'

'Curse you! Are you never content? Because I want to be back in Iuddeu well before Samhain.'

It was the truth, but not the whole truth. Why now? Because an autumn of frustration and moaning and bad weather and worse dreams was surely enough time. *You might try trusting me*. So he'd tried. For all the time he'd been away, when he'd heard little from Iuddeu, he'd trusted Trystan, hoping for the best and fearing the worst. But now it was time to go back and find out if that trust, however reluctantly given, had been earned.

※

Lot wasn't pleased, a state of mind which had become depressingly familiar. Why was it all so difficult? Surely everyone could see that their advantage lay in Lot's own ambitions. Yet it seemed they couldn't.

'Fools!' Lot chewed at his beard as he contemplated, yet again, his wine-stained map of the Lands between the Walls and tried to assess his odds of success. Slim. That's what they were. And it was all Corwynal's fault.

'Any word?' he demanded of one of his attendants, not for the first time. He'd sent out scouts to find the bloody man, but so far not one of them had come back. Did that mean trouble in Fife? Worse, did it mean the Caledonian bastard had gone native on him? It was, he supposed sourly, always a risk, so maybe he shouldn't have sent him to Fife to collect the tribute. Yet the tribute had arrived, which surely it wouldn't have done if Corwynal had chosen to side with his mother's people. So, where in the five hells was the man? He should have been back a month ago. He should have been in Iuddeu, preventing what had happened.

Lot wondered if he should have predicted it, but, after thinking about it for a moment, he shook his head. Lot wasn't in the habit of blaming himself for anything, especially when there were others worthier of blame.

'Bloody Marc!' It was Marc who'd caused Lot's current

problem by sending a raiding party into Strathclyde. Which would have been fine if Dumnagual had reacted as he'd done on every other occasion by mounting a retaliatory raid into Galloway. But, no, the cursed man had broken with tradition and had come whining to Lot instead. Which might have been a gratifying acknowledgement of Lot's pre-eminence had he not gone on to make a quite unacceptable suggestion.

'You need to do something about that pirate of Galloway,' he'd complained. 'We need a war-leader. Arthyr. It ought to be Arthyr.'

'Bastard!' Lot slammed his fist down on the map. All about him in Iuddeu's draughty hall, servants jumped, and warriors edged away nervously, for Lot's temper had been far from certain since Dumnagual had forced his hand. 'Bastard!' The Strathclyde king must have known Lot was thinking about a war-leader. But not Arthyr. No, Lot had someone else in mind – until that had been ruined by what had just happened.

'Curse this!' He glared about the hall and wrinkled his nose. The place stank of too many men and far too many dogs. Couldn't that girl Gwenhwyvar organise something as simple as clean rushes? But she'd given him a pert answer when he'd complained and asked why Lot couldn't persuade his men not to throw bones on the floor, which just encouraged the dogs.

Gwenhwyvar! The thought of her made his stomach turn to acid because he blamed her too. And Arthyr, of course.

'Send out another scout,' he ordered. 'In fact, send several. I want to know where everyone is and when in the five hells they're going to get here. Any news, I'll be up on the rampart. At least it doesn't stink up there.'

True enough, but it was cold, bloody cold. It wasn't Samhain yet, but already there was snow on the hills to the north-west, and a bitter wind blowing from that direction had set the standards that flew from Iuddeu's ramparts snapping like the beasts they portrayed. His own boar was there, and Gwenhwyvar's hind. Not that Gwenhwyvar counted, but Arthyr would, though Arthyr's bear was missing since he hadn't, as yet, responded to Lot's summons. Marc's raven was absent too, but a scout on a lathered horse had reported that his party would arrive later that day, thanks be to the gods. Marc might inadvertently have started this issue of the war-leader, but at least his choice of who that ought to be wasn't in question. Which was more than could be said for the rest of them.

Dumnagual, whose salmon standard fluttered above him, had already made his choice clear, slippery old fish that he was, but Caw, whose stag standard flew next to Lot's boar, was less dependable, even though Lot was supposed to be his sodding overlord. Caw had his own choice for war-leader, and if he didn't get the man he wanted, Lot didn't know which way he'd jump. But surely Lothian could be relied on? If the Old Wolf turned up, of course, which he might not. And nor might Hoel of Selgovia, whose vote Lot had counted on too – until that business with Trystan. If only Corwynal had been here, curse him!

'He's just arrived, Sire.' One of his servants had come running up to the rampart to disturb him.

Lot's unfocussed gaze sharpened. 'Who, man? Marc? Rifallyn? Arthyr? You think I can read your mind, you cretin?'

'The Steward, Sire, Sorry, Sire. Shall I—?'

'Send him up, idiot! Right away. No, I don't care how long he's been in the saddle. Right away, you hear me! And clear everyone else off the ramparts . . .'

For there were things to be said, things to be made clear and, above all, things to be sorted.

'Corwynal! Where in the five hells have you been?!'

Lot's voice boomed across Iuddeu's ramparts, cutting through the wind, but his face betrayed no pleasure at Corwynal's return, which, given that he'd ridden through half a night and most of a day in answer to his overlord's summons, brought by a short-tempered scout, was aggravating, if not entirely unexpected.

'In Fife,' he reminded him, holding hard to his own temper. 'Where you sent me.'

'Where I sent you *months* ago! What have you been doing there? Enjoying yourself among your kinfolk so much you decided not to come back to where you might actually be useful?'

Corwynal's teeth ground together as he stifled a retort. It was best to say nothing, for if he started, there was no telling where it might end. He was tired, saddle-sore, resentful, and not a little afraid. Why the summons? The scout couldn't, or wouldn't, say. And why was Iuddeu so crowded? Why, judging from the standards, was Dumnagual here? Or Caw?

'No, sorry, that was unfair,' Lot said after a moment, peering at him. 'You don't look as if you've been enjoying yourself.'

If Corwynal hadn't already decided to say nothing, this uncharacteristic apology from Lot would have stunned him into silence. But his overlord's sympathy, if that was what it was, didn't last long. It never did.

'Which makes me wonder why you stayed away,' Lot went on irritably. 'And just when I need you. I've summoned the kings to the Samhain gathering. We're to choose a war-leader. A Dux Bellorum.'

Suddenly, it all made sense: Dumnagual, Caw, the crowded stables and courtyards. It made even more sense once Lot told him about Marc's raids, which didn't surprise him, and Dumnagual's reaction, which did.

'...and the sodding man wants it to be Arthyr,' Lot concluded.

Corwynal nodded. Arthyr was the obvious choice, but he could understand why he wasn't Lot's. The next High King – who Lot fully intended to be himself – would need a war-leader whose personal loyalty to him was unquestioned. And Lot wasn't the only king who'd object to Arthyr as war-leader. 'Marc won't like that,' he observed. Marc would oppose anyone Dumnagual supported.

'Caw suggested Heuil,' Lot said, rolling his eyes.

'Naturally.' Corwynal shrugged. No-one apart from Caw would support his occasionally brilliant but largely erratic eldest son. So that would mean the war-leadership falling to Lot's eldest son, Gawain. Stolid, reliable, unimaginative Gawain.

'It's too soon, curse it! He's young still, needs to prove himself.'

Corwynal looked at Lot in surprise, for Gawain had been leading Gododdin's war-band for years. 'I wouldn't have thought him too young.'

'Really?' Lot brightened. 'Well, if you think so, then that's all right. Except—' He scowled. 'He's just gone and bloody spoiled it! That sodding escapade! If you'd have been here, you could have stopped it. Or Arthyr could, but he's never here. Women! Why do they have to ruin everything? I blame Gwenhwyvar, of course, not the boy. And Arthyr. And you.'

'Gwenhwyvar?' Corwynal was confused now. Clearly, things had changed a great deal since he'd left. 'And Gawain?'

'Gawain?' Lot stared at him. 'What in the five hells are you talking about? Gwenhwyvar and Gawain? Are you mad? No, it's Trystan. Gwenhwyvar and *Trystan!*'

A cold hand clutched at Corwynal's innards. So all those

months of trusting him had been for nothing.

'Thing is—' Lot went on, '—it was all going so well! But Blaize was right. I should have moved after the battle. He was popular. He was lucky! And he's from the Lands between the Walls, not like Arthyr. But I thought it would be better if he had a few more successes under his belt. And let Arthyr have a few defeats – minor ones, of course. That was the plan. Plans!' he muttered sourly. 'Why do I bother?'

'You want Trystan as war-leader?' Corwynal felt the world shift beneath him.

'Who else? Oh, you thought I meant Gawain! God's blood, no! I'm fond of the boy, of course, but he isn't war-leader material. No, it has to be Trystan, and it would have been if it hadn't been for this latest piece of nonsense. And you—' He poked Corwynal in the chest with an accusatory finger. '—you assured me it was just a rumour. Well, let me tell you . . .'

He did, at great length and with a lot of bluster and complaint, though the story itself was a simple one. One of the outpost forts in Trystan's area had been fired in his absence. Trystan had been at Iuddeu at the time and naturally had ridden north to join his men. Gwenhwyvar, leaving some story that she was going to visit her uncle, Caw, at Dun Eidyn, had gone with him. Perhaps they would have got away with it if Dumnagual hadn't forced Lot to call the gathering of kings and send messages to the war-bands summoning their leaders back to Iuddeu, and if the man he'd sent to Trystan hadn't been one of Arthyr's kinsmen, and if, when he'd found Gwenhwyvar in Trystan's camp, he hadn't made rather too public a fuss about it.

'Not exactly caught in the act, but a bad business, Corwynal, a very bad business. Why weren't you here to stop the pair of them?'

Because Trystan had asked him to trust him. So he had. But Trystan had let him down.

⁂

'He told you then.'

Trystan was waiting for him in the Steward's room and, in marked contrast to Lot, seemed not only pleased but relieved to see him, then, after a moment's frowning contemplation, concerned.

'You look done in. Lot might have given you the chance to rest first.'

'He didn't. And nor, it seems, are you.' Corwynal sat down in the chair behind the littered table. The room, after his months of absence, was cold and musty, and the newly lit brazier was having little effect on the temperature, which didn't help his mood. 'Well . . . ?'

'Well, you'll have heard. Lot wants me for war-leader,' Trystan said blithely, rejecting the bench on the other side of the table in favour of pacing back and forth, too full of excitement to sit down. 'I thought he was joking at first, but Blaize explained how it made sense politically, and I can see that now. Oh, I know what you're going to say – that I'm too young. But I'll learn as I go along, and I'll have you to help me, won't I? In fact, I need you to help me now, because not everyone will see things as Lot does. Marc will be on my side, of course, and Rifallyn, I assume. Caw, I think I can handle, though he wants it for Heuil. But no-one else does, and Caw knows it, so if I offer Heuil a decent command, Caw will come around. Then there's Dumnagual, but I doubt it's even worth talking to him, because if everyone else supports me, it doesn't matter what he thinks.'

'There's Hoel,' Corwynal reminded him. 'How will he choose, do you think?'

Trystan's bright flame faltered for a moment and he stopped pacing to throw himself down on the bench, then pulled out a dagger from his belt and twirled it between his fingers.

'He might not come,' he said in the end, his attention on the light flashing from the spinning blade.

'And why might that be?'

Trystan looked up, the knife stilling between his fingers. 'You know,' he said dismissively. 'The rumours.'

'More than rumours, if Lot's to be believed.'

'Lot? You believe Lot? Without waiting to hear my side of things?'

'Tell me then,' Corwynal suggested, leaning back so his face was in shadow, but Trystan leant forward into the light, his face open and guileless. The story, as he told it, was short and to the point, without any excuses or regrets, and much as Lot had described. Trystan had gone back to his men, as he'd promised, and stayed on the frontier. He'd come back briefly to Iuddeu but hadn't even seen Gwenhwyvar before he'd heard about the fort being fired. Then, just as he was leaving, she'd asked him to take her to the frontier. She'd been bored in Iuddeu and angry at Arthyr's continued absence. Trystan had refused, of course, then left, but she hadn't taken no for an answer. Two of her attendants had been going to visit their families in Dun Eidyn, and everyone assumed she'd gone with them. Instead, she'd followed Trystan's troop. Alone.

'Which can't have been easy, for we were riding hard,' he said with grudging admiration. He agreed he should have sent her back with a guard, but he couldn't spare anyone, and anyway there had been a whole camp of men to vouch for the innocence of her presence, including Gaheris who couldn't lie to save himself. Then one of their scouts reported a gathering of Caledonians in the hills. Trystan had wanted to see for himself. So had Gwenhwyvar. There had been an argument, insults exchanged, boasts made that couldn't be retracted. They'd both gone with the scout to spy on the Caledonian camp.

'You fool! What if you'd been captured?'

'Kaerherdin's men were close by, and we were careful. We got close enough to count them, to see what sort of arms they had, how many horses. And we were just about to leave – give me credit for some judgement! – when there was a disturbance among the Caledonians. A messenger from the north, I think. I thought we'd been seen, because they all mounted up and set off. They hadn't seen us, as it turned out, but, even so, they got between us and Kaerherdin's men. We tried to cut around them but got separated from the scout, then lost our way. That was all. We rode back together, hours after everyone else, and found one of Arthyr's men, waiting with a message from Lot. It didn't look good, I agree, but what they're saying isn't true. I swear it.'

Corwynal looked at him long and hard, remembering a time in Dunpeldyr about six months before Trystan was born, a hunting trip in the forest. He and Gwenllian had become separated from the others, and they too had ridden back hours after everyone else. At least they'd had the sense to arrive separately.

'I trusted you,' Corwynal said bleakly, knowing he shouldn't have done. He and Gwenllian had lied to everyone and expected to be believed. As Trystan did now.

'You don't believe me?' he asked in astonishment, and it was his surprise that made Corwynal flare into anger.

'No, I don't believe you. You've behaved like a selfish and spoilt young man ever since we left Dunpeldyr, particularly in Selgovia, and now you expect me to believe this ridiculous story? I'm sorry for you, believe me in that, but you've brought it on yourself. You were so determined to make a name for yourself, to have a troop of your own, you went behind my back and seduced a girl who would have forgotten you if you'd left her alone. But you couldn't, could you? You married Essylt and now you don't want her anymore. So why don't you ask Hoel to take her back? I'll tell you why; because you know how much you'd lose: Hoel's support, his men, Kaerherdin and the others. You can't afford that, especially now you've an even bigger name to make for yourself. You want that name, but you want Gwenhwyvar too, even though she's married to the next war-leader. Oh, yes, Trystan. Arthyr will be the next war-leader, because it won't be you. Not now. No matter how clever you might be at fighting, there's a great deal more to life than what you want or think you want, a great deal more to being war-leader than beating Arthyr. Because that's all it comes down to, isn't it? You can't bear for him to be chosen, because then he'll stay in the north. You think he'll go back to Gwynedd if you win and leave Gwenhwyvar behind. For you.'

Trystan had risen to stand on the other side of the table. His hands were clenched behind his back, and the blood had drained from his face.

'You're wrong!'

'Grow up, Trys! You want to be Dux Bellorum? Then prove to everyone you're old enough, responsible enough, and that you're prepared to make a sacrifice. Prove it to *me!* Give up the woman you want and settle for the one you have.'

A muscle flickered in Trystan's jaw. 'I see,' he said, in tones icy enough to match Corwynal's own. 'You think I'm in love with Gwenhwyvar. You wouldn't believe me even if I told you what I thought or felt, but I shouldn't have to do that. I shouldn't have to ask you to believe me. But maybe you don't believe me or understand me because you've never cared for anyone! As for being war-leader, yes, I do want it, but it has nothing to do with Arthyr or Gwenhwyvar, or you. I came to ask for your help, Corwynal, but I don't need it, and I won't ask for it ever again. So don't ever ask me for *my* help!'

Then he was gone, leaving Corwynal angry, hurt and confused. All he wanted to do was drag Trystan back and thrash him soundly, then ask his forgiveness. He knew he'd gone too far, that their argument hadn't really been about Gwenhwyvar, or the leadership, but about something more profound. But he didn't know what it was.

14

DUX BELLORUM

Until the party from Lothian arrived, Aelfric was glad to be back in Iuddeu – in civilisation as, oddly, he'd come to think of it. In Iuddeu the women smiled, and the ale was decent enough once you got used to it; even an Angle slave had no difficulty in getting his hands on either. So, as soon as he got back, after that bloody hard ride all the way from Fife, the first thing he did was find himself a woman. The second was to down a drink or two – or three – so he wasn't entirely sober when he wandered down to the main gate to see what was going on, and, as a consequence, his reactions were slower than they ought to have been.

What he should have done was make himself scarce, but all he did was stand there gawping when the Lothian party trotted through the gate in a smirr of drizzle just as the sun was setting. By the time someone had dropped from his horse, flung an arm around Aelfric's shoulders and pounded him on the back in a comradely way, it was already too late.

'Well met, you bloody Angle bastard!'

'Madawg!?' He'd got to know Lothian's war-band leader after the battle with the Scots. Indeed, he'd got to know most of Lothian's war-band – decent lads once you'd drunk and whored with them often enough. Which he had. 'What the fuck brings you to Iuddeu?'

It was a stupid question, since they'd all been on about it in the tavern. The Briton kings had come to Iuddeu to choose a Dux Bellorum, whatever the fuck that was. Aelfric had been too interested in the bottom of his tankard to ask, and that turned out to be an oversight.

'Not what.' Madawg glanced behind him and lowered his voice. 'Who.'

That was when Aelfric should have run, but a shadow swept over him, and he froze like a hare caught in the sights of an eagle.

'Ah, the Angle,' said a deep soft voice with a core of steel. A dark man, shadowy against the last light of the day, was looking down at him with thinly veiled amusement. 'Bring him,' the King of Lothian said, snapping his fingers and kicking his horse in the flanks to trot into the lower courtyard.

'Just say "Yes, Sire", or "No, Sire". Other than that, keep your trap shut,' Madawg advised, taking hold of Aelfric's upper arm so he couldn't get away.

Saying nothing, however, was easier said than done. Impossible actually when he was alone with Rifallyn of Lothian, in a private chamber that, somehow, in an already packed stronghold, the old man had appropriated, and where he revealed just how much he knew about Aelfric of Gyrwum.

'Ealhith!' Aelfric concluded, his fists balling. 'You forced her to tell you!'

'Not at all! She seemed eager to unburden herself. I don't know what it is about me, but men – and women – seem incapable of lying to me, so I wouldn't bother trying if I were you. What I want, Aelfric of Gyrwum, is for you to tell me everything that's happened since you left Lothian. Tell me about my son.'

'Trystan? Well, he's—'

'Not Trystan.'

It took some telling, and by the end of it Aelfric felt squeezed dry and badly in need of a drink – several drinks, But the old man wasn't finished with him yet.

'You seem to have made quite a place for yourself among your enemies.' The King cast a lazy glance over Aelfric's person, his gaze lingering on the gold embroidery on his tunic and the knife at his belt. Aelfric felt the blood rise into his face. He might be a slave, but he wasn't treated like one. He had his freedom, his weapons, and there had been plenty of opportunities to have gone back to Dunpeldyr, dragging the Caledonian with him. But he'd taken none of them. Worse, he'd left Ealhith to the mercy of this cold old man who was far worse than the painted Caledonian devil he'd gone to Dunpeldyr to rescue her from in the first place.

'She's mine now,' Rifallyn informed him. 'Ealhith was my son's, but he gave her to me, for which I'm grateful. She's been a great comfort to a lonely old man. I'm sure you take my meaning. No – I don't advise it.' Aelfric's hand had moved to the hilt of his knife. 'My men are within call. And, in any case, you know who's to blame for her fate. You could have returned to Lothian at any time. If you had, I might have given her back to you, valuable though she is to me for so many reasons.' He leant forward, his voice dropping to a whisper. 'But you didn't come.'

Aelfric's hand slipped from the hilt of his knife, and he couldn't meet the old man's eyes. He felt sick and guilty, and furious and impotent, because everything Rifallyn of Lothian had said was the truth.

'I'd thought of bringing her with me to Iuddeu,' the King

went on, leaning back. 'It might have amused her to see how well you're doing. Or maybe not. But it would have amused me. Sadly, she's suffering from a woman's complaint. It isn't something that's likely to kill her, so you needn't concern yourself, but perhaps you don't. Concern yourself, that is.'

At which point, Aelfric finally took Madawg's advice, bit his tongue and kept his trap firmly shut.

⁂

'Bastard!' Aelfric muttered once he was released in what felt like the middle of the night. 'Bastard!' He wasn't sure if he meant the old man, the Caledonian, or himself. All he knew was that he badly needed several drinks, and so he made for the nearest tavern.

It was even later by the time he staggered out, feeling little better but not, absolutely not, drunk. Aelfric of Gyrwum was never drunk. Nevertheless, it was some time before he found the person he was looking for, and even then it was only by chance that he came across the man as he hurried down an alleyway between two stables, trying to keep out of the rain.

'So, Steward, have you heard the news from Lothian?' Aelfric enunciated the words clearly as he stepped into the Caledonian's path.

'What news would that be?' the man asked, sounding amused.

'You've forgotten,' Aelfric concluded. 'Old men like you forget. But I didn't. I never forgot, not in all the years. I swore an *oath*, Steward.' He reached out and grasped the man's tunic.

'You're drunk.' The Caledonian tried to prise Aelfric's fingers apart. 'Come on, Aelfric. We're both getting soaked . . .'

'I swore an oath!'

'We all do that, man.'

'A man, am I? I thought I was less than a man, less than an animal. I thought I was a slave. Like her.'

'Her?'

'You *have* forgotten, haven't you? You gave her away and thought no more about her. You cold-hearted bastard!' The world tilted beneath Aelfric's feet, but he righted himself by grabbing the doorframe of the entrance to one of the stables.

'You're talking about Ealhith?'

'You gave her to that sour old man! And now she's his whore!'

'No, she's not.' The Caledonian no longer looked amused. 'My father promised—'

'And you believed him? You think she wanted this? How would you know what she wanted? Did you ask her? No, you just took her, then threw her away!'

'I didn't – take her, that is.'

'I don't believe you!'

'Believe what you like. It's the truth. But why should you care? Unless you wanted her for yourself—'

Aelfric hit him. The Caledonian wasn't expecting it, but, for some reason, Aelfric's blow went awry and slid harmlessly along the man's jaw, and he backed away from him. But Aelfric was far from finished. He roared and charged, head-butted the other man in the stomach, and brought them both down into the churned mud and horseshit of the alley. 'I'm going to kill you, you bastard!' It was what he'd sworn, after all.

The Caledonian managed to wriggle out from underneath him and backed away once more as Aelfric lurched to his feet.

'I'm not fighting you, you stupid Angle! Not when you're drunk.'

'I'm not drunk, you worm!'

The Caledonian hit him then, a carefully placed blow to the stomach, pivoting on the balls of his feet so his whole weight was behind it.

Pathetic! Aelfric grunted as he absorbed the punch, rocked back on his heels and answered with a blow of his left fist. The Caledonian ducked and rolled out of reach, but at least the bloody man was taking him seriously now.

'Aelfric, for the gods' sake . . . !' The Caledonian looked about anxiously, but the place was deserted, the lookouts sheltering from the rain, so all the man could do was duck and weave, thinking, fool that he was, that he'd tire Aelfric out.

'I'm going to kill you!' How had he forgotten his oath? He hit the Caledonian hard, a crashing blow to the ribs that made him cry out. Then the man came back at Aelfric, fighting dirty now, kicking him in the shins, then following it up with a knee in the groin that was bloody painful. Even drunk – which he definitely wasn't – Aelfric should have been able to block these blows, but somehow he couldn't – or didn't want to. Dimly, through the fog of ale, he began to understand he wasn't fighting the Caledonian to punish him for the crime of abandoning and forgetting a woman. Aelfric was allowing the bloody man to punish him for the same crime.

By this time, they were doing each other serious damage. The Caledonian had a badly bruised hand and was half blind from a cut above his eye. Aelfric's mouth had filled with blood and he thought one of his teeth might be loose. If the sodding man had ruined his best smile . . .

'C-C-Corwynal? Aelfric! What are you d-d-doing?'

Only Gaheris could ask such a stupid question.

'Do something!' the Caledonian gasped as Aelfric lunged at him. 'Find Trystan!'

What the man thought Trystan could do escaped Aelfric, but

Gaheris ran off, saying he'd be back in a moment. He wasn't though, and so their fight went on, but Aelfric began to remember something important – the cold killing rage the Caledonian had called on in battle. In this fight – so far – he hadn't done so, but if he did, this could turn out to be a fucking big mistake. So Aelfric was half relieved when, out of the corner of one eye, he saw someone come down the alley. It would be Trystan, come to reason with him, and by then Aelfric was willing to be reasoned with.

But it wasn't Trystan, and whoever it was hadn't come to talk. Aelfric felt something crash into the back of his skull, heard himself grunt as the world blazed into excruciating light, a light that faded from the edges of his vision as he toppled, slow as a feather, heavy as a great oak, down and down and down into the dark.

⁂

'Brawling? At your age?' Blaize scowled down at the Angle, sprawled in the dirt of the alleyway 'And he'll take some shifting,' he added, but didn't attempt to move him. Instead, Blaize favoured Corwynal with a pungent criticism of his behaviour, maturity and intelligence, but Corwynal ignored him – he'd heard most of it before – and by the time Blaize reached the end of his diatribe, a solution to the problem of moving the Angle had turned up.

'Couldn't you find Trys?' Corwynal asked Gaheris once they'd managed, between them, to drag Aelfric into the stable and prop him up against an upright.

'No,' he said woodenly. Unlike his father, Gaheris was a terrible liar. *Don't ever ask me for my help.* It seemed as if Trystan had really meant it.

'Tell him I didn't need his help after all.' Gaheris looked troubled, but nodded and left. Blaize threw Corwynal an enquiring look, but didn't ask anything and instead turned his attention to Aelfric.

'He'll live,' he announced after feeling the back of the man's head. 'Angles have thick skulls. But he won't be pretty in the morning. And nor—' Blaize cocked an eye at Corwynal. '—will you. Come on, let's leave him to sleep it off, and I'll take a look at that cut in better light.'

Later, in Corwynal's room, Blaize probed his face in the light of an oil-lamp and manipulated his hand while Corwynal swore under his breath.

'Oh, don't make such a fuss!' Blaize rubbed the usual stinging salve into the cut above his eye and bound his hand. 'Nothing's broken, but keep your hand moving or it'll stiffen up.' Then he sat back. 'What was the fight about?'

'He was drunk, but I think it was about Ealhith.'

'The mousy little thing who shared your bed?'

'She wasn't mousy and—'

'—didn't share your bed,' Blaize cut in with a snort of derision. 'I believe you because I know what a fool you are, but no-one else would. I don't suppose Aelfric did, and I guess he's heard she's with child.'

'With child?' How could Ealhith be with child? She was just a child herself. Then, with a tremor of guilt, Corwynal remembered he'd given her away. 'To my father?'

'So they say.' Blaize shrugged. 'I doubt he'll acknowledge it, but who's ever been able to predict what my brother will do? If he does, you'll have another half-brother, and I another nephew. As if the ones I already have don't cause me enough trouble. So, what exactly has Trystan been up to, and why weren't you here to stop it?'

'I was in Fife. Anyway, Trystan's a man now. He doesn't listen to me anymore.' He tried, but failed, to keep the bitterness from his voice.

Blaize regarded him narrowly. 'Does that mean you're not going to support him for the war-leadership tomorrow?'

'How can I support him? He's far too young. Surely you don't approve of this plan of Lot's?'

'It wasn't Lot's plan.'

'It was yours?' Corwynal wondered why he was so surprised by that.

'Why not? Trystan may be young, but youth is something we all recover from, unfortunately. All he needs is luck and the right advice from people he listens to. Me. You.'

'Not me, and he won't listen to you either. No, Blaize. He's too young.'

'He isn't Arthyr, and that's all that matters.'

'Arthyr would make a good war-leader.'

'I agree, but would it stop there? And would it stop here in the north? Arthyr's from Gwynedd. He's fought the Saex in the south for years, and it's given him a vision of one land for the Britons, a land free of invaders. But it's too big a vision. If we're careful, if we're lucky, if we choose the right war-leader and the right High-King, something, here in the north, might survive the tides that threaten to overwhelm us. We've survived this far, and more by luck than judgement because we're surrounded: Caledonians to the north, Scots to the west, Angles to the east. But it's the Saex to the south who're the real threat. They've already destroyed the old Roman heartlands in the south and east. Now they're sweeping northwards and westwards like a spring tide with the wind behind it, and it won't be long before our fathers' people are driven back to the mountains to dwindle and vanish and become nothing more than the sound of a harp wailing on the wind.' Blaize's eyes darkened with foreknowledge, and his voice fell away to a whisper. But after a moment he shook himself free of the vision and when he spoke once more, it was with grim determination. 'We have to hold, not in the south – the south's doomed – but here between the Walls. We don't need a visionary who wants to hold everything. Grasp for too much and nothing will survive. Arthyr isn't the right man.'

'What about Gawain—?'

'An idiot.'

'—or Heuil?'

'Unreliable. Anyone else you can think of? No? It's too soon, I agree, but right now Trystan is the only realistic alternative, and tomorrow it will be decided. Marc, Rifallyn and Hoel will support Trystan. Dumnagual and Gwenhwyvar will back Arthyr, and I suppose Caw really ought to support Lot's candidate but even if he doesn't Lot will choose Trystan, though he'd prefer to appear neutral.'

This sounded like a plan long in the making, and Corwynal began to understand a few things that had puzzled him: why Trystan had been manipulated into going to Selgovia, and why Lot had seemed pleased rather than the reverse when Corwynal had failed to ally Selgovia with Gododdin.

'How long have you been planning this?'

But Blaize met his unspoken accusations unflinchingly. 'Years, actually. I've been watching Trystan grow up with this in mind. And Lot's been watching Arthyr.'

What else was his uncle planning? Blaize hadn't brought Atholl up recently, and Corwynal hadn't told him about his promise to Domech. Nor was he going to. 'Arthyr's a serious candidate, and not just for war-leader. Men trust him.'

'Perhaps. But he's no longer young.'

'Trystan's too reckless, too thoughtless, too selfish, maybe. Yes, he'll grow out of these things, I hope, but we're not talking about the future. We're talking about now. I don't want him chosen as war-leader.'

'It doesn't matter what you want. You don't have a say in the choice.'

'Maybe not,' Corwynal replied, wincing as he got to his feet. 'But others do.'

'Where are you going?'

Corwynal didn't reply, but squared his shoulders in the hope it would help him face someone he didn't want to see.

He was going to talk to his father.

***

It was late by then, but a single lamp was still burning on the altar of the little wattle-walled hut squeezed against Iuddeu's lower wall, which served as a church for those who followed Chrystos. The light flickered in a draught, throwing back shivering reflections from tarnished silver vessels on the altar and the gold embroidery in the hangings on the walls, but served only to deepen the shadows in the rest of the building. And there, in the shadows, was where Corwynal found his father, a little after dawn on this, the last day of autumn.

'You may come in,' said the dry, familiar voice as Corwynal hesitated on the threshold. 'My god won't eat you.'

Corwynal wasn't so sure. He'd never been comfortable with his father's god. How could a dying and mutilated man have any power at all? Yet power he clearly had, and Corwynal, crossing the threshold, felt a hiss of rejection as Arddu stirred uneasily at the base of his nerves. *Beware...*

Right then, however, it wasn't Chrystos Corwynal was

afraid of. His heart began to thud sickeningly in his chest as his father turned towards him, took in his muddied and torn tunic, the cut over his eye, and sighed with his usual embittered disappointment.

'Couldn't you even beat a drunk slave?'

'That drunk slave is out cold in a stable. Did you send him to find me?'

'Why should I? Ah . . . you're talking of Ealhith, the Angle girl who used to warm your bed. Do you know, Corwynal, I rarely have reason to thank you, but this is one such occasion. She's proved very useful to Lothian's present Steward.' He paused, his golden eyes glinting in satisfaction at Corwynal's puzzlement. 'Myself.'

'You?!'

'Why not? It amused me to discover what you were making such a fuss about, but it isn't difficult being a Steward.'

'Perhaps if you had someone constantly trying to undermine your decisions, as I had, you'd find it harder. And as for Ealhith—' He gestured to his damaged face. '—she was the cause of this.'

His father just shrugged. 'You gave her away.'

'I gave her to a man who promised to be kind to her!'

His father raised an eyebrow. 'In what way have I not been kind?'

'You said . . .' But Corwynal could no longer remember what his father had promised, or if he'd promised anything at all. Maybe he'd been naïve to imagine his father would treat Ealhith as he'd treated her. 'I wanted her to have a choice.'

'She's a slave. Slaves don't get choices. She was mine to use as I pleased. It's hardly my fault if that Angle of yours takes exception to that fact. It was you who chose to indulge him in a brawl. As for Ealhith, I believe she's content. She's to have a child, you know. My only hope is that if it's a son, he'll turn out to be less of a disappointment than the rest of my family. My brother, for example. My son.' He paused, leaning forward. 'And my heir, about whom I hear such tales. Who left Lothian a boy and who, by all accounts, now considers himself a man. Old enough and experienced enough to choose himself a wife, I hear.'

Corwynal might have known his father would attack him at a point of weakness.

'It's a good alliance.' He couldn't bring himself to call it a marriage.

'Alliance? You pledge Lothian to an alliance with Selgovia, which has always been our enemy, and don't even consult me?!'

'I went to Selgovia at Lot's behest, not yours. He's Lothian's overlord, and he wanted Selgovia. I gave it to him.'

'Don't try to tell me he didn't intend Selgovia for that son of his!'

'He made no conditions.'

'So you made your own. You sold Lothian's inheritance for a rabble of bowmen and a plain-faced girl.'

'She's not plain and—'

'Ah! Not plain? Not to you, eh, Corwynal?'

Corwynal's blood quickened, but he held hard to his temper. 'The terms of the alliance are advantageous to Lothian.'

'That's for me to say, not you.' His father paused, leaning back into the shadows once more. 'So Trystan has discovered ambition, has he? Runs in the family, being ambitious . . .'

'Why shouldn't he be ambitious? He's heir to Lothian and Galloway—'

'We will not speak of Galloway!'

'Why not? Trystan's Marc's nephew, and Marc has no heir. He offered Trys Galloway's war-band. Did they tell you that?

The King of Galloway offered his nephew leadership of Galloway's war-band because the King of Lothian failed to offer his heir what was rightfully his. If Trystan's ambitious, Sire, it's because you've forced him to be so.'

'So, when I die, when Marc dies, and Hoel dies – none of us young men – he'll rule three lands. Do you imagine that's what he wants? You might want it – no, don't deny it – but Trystan doesn't.'

'Yet you call him ambitious?'

'He's ambitious for something more, something greater, something dangerous. Once you realise what that is, it will be too late for anyone to stop him.'

'I . . . I don't know what you're talking about.'

'No? Then you've been away too long, attending to Trystan's business with that girl from Selgovia, and Lot's business in Fife, when you should have been here in Iuddeu.'

I will be calm, Corwynal decided. He hadn't come to speak to his father to defend himself, but to protect Trystan.

'Are you here in Iuddeu to support him?' he asked.

'I'm here because I was commanded to be here.'

'You wouldn't come just because Lot commanded it.'

Rifallyn gave a bark of laughter. 'True. I didn't intend to answer Lot's summons. I'm an old man. To travel such a distance . . .' He let his voice waver into the fading whine Corwynal knew to be pure affectation, for his next words were crisp and clear. 'Then I heard certain rumours. About Ogryfan's girl, Gwenhwyvar, who's married to this Arthyr of whom we all expect so much. I hear he's away a great deal and that he too made a marriage in exchange for a rabble of men. Safe enough, I suppose, when the woman's plain, but this Gwenhwyvar's a pretty thing, I believe. Pretty enough for a man to lose his head over, eh? Or so I hear.'

Corwynal said nothing, and his father smiled his wolf-smile once more, but after a moment it faded, and when he spoke his voice was low and icy. 'What I do not want to hear is that a son of mine is making a fool of himself over another man's wife. Because I might think history was repeating itself, and I don't want to think that. Do you understand me, Corwynal?'

'I'm not sure I do.' This wasn't a conversation he wanted to have with his father. 'I'm not here to talk about the past. It's the future that concerns me. Lot wants Trystan for war-leader and he'll expect your support.'

'Of course. Trystan means Lothian, and Lothian means Gododdin. In Lot's view at least.'

'Have you promised him your support?'

'I haven't promised anyone anything. Lot will just have to wait to find out my opinion.'

'Which is?'

His father smiled. 'If I can make Lot wait, why not you?'

'Trystan's too young!'

'War is a young man's business, and this will be no war of one season or even a few. Do you think that mercenary from the south has the stomach for even one of our northern winters?'

'I don't know, but if he does, if he's chosen, then perhaps in a few years, when Trystan's ready—'

'He's ready now. He's made for war because you turned him into something you never were – a battle chief.'

'I could have been, if only—' Corwynal stopped himself just in time.

'No, Corwynal. You wanted other things and you still want them, things in which Trystan has no interest. He wants to fight the world, but you want to shape it, to leave something behind. He wants change, but you want permanence, and I rather think this Arthyr shares your . . . failings.'

'Sire, Father, I beg you—'

Rifallyn lifted a hand. 'Please don't beg. It would be uncomfortable for us both. Lot will have to endure not knowing my mind, and, anyway, my decision may prove irrelevant. But if it isn't, well . . . It promises to be an interesting evening, don't you think?' He rose to his feet, and the shadows swirled about him like a cloak. 'You may accompany me if you wish,' he said. 'All the kings will have their advisors, and I omitted to bring any with me. Not that I'd listen to them, but we could pretend, couldn't we, Corwynal? We've always been good at that, you and I. Pretending.'

Samhain. The Night of Endings. All men fear it. They bar their doors and keep the fires burning and the lamps lit until the sun rises on a new day. Few sleep on the night of Samhain for fear of what dreams might bring. Fewer still brave the darkness itself, for the doorways that open on each night of the seasons' turnings yawn even wider at Samhain, and the spirits of the dead can pass through the shield-wall of memory and time and into the world of the living.

In the old days, the dead were honoured. Places were set for them at the Samhain feast, and in some of the Lands between the Walls that was still done. But in Gododdin and Lothian, and Manau also, the dead were driven away with fire and torches and candlelight and the deep roar of the fire-pits. Samhain, in those lands, had become a night of defiance and denial. Autumn was guttering to a close as the nights lengthened, and it wouldn't be long before winter leached all colour from the world, but, for one night, men chose to forget these things. In the face of death, they celebrated life, and so they donned their finest jewellery and richest garments, dyed in reds or greens, or the deep blue that comes from the southern lands. And that Samhain eve, in Iuddeu on the night of the choosing, was no exception.

Lot, alone among the kings, wore a red dyed so dark it was almost purple, as befitted an aspirant to the High Kingship. Even those unaware of Lot's ambition were conscious of the importance of that particular Samhain and had also dressed for the occasion. Marc, who'd arrived only that afternoon, was resplendent in crimson and gold, and Dumnagual, vying with him in this as in everything else, was wearing green and silver and looked a little more regal. Even Hoel, who'd turned up after all, was wearing a tunic that, if in no way magnificent, was at least free of grease-stains. Rifallyn too had abandoned his usual plain woollen robe for one richly embroidered with silver. And Trystan looked like the king he'd be one day, the glitter of gold about his person failing to compete with the fine-spun gleam of his hair. Corwynal's weren't the only eyes drawn to him that night, some in approval, like Marc. Others, Dumnagual and Caw among them, were harder to read as they glanced from Trystan to Arthyr and made the inevitable comparisons.

For Arthyr, alone among the leaders, had made no effort to impress. He looked as if he'd just dismounted after a long ride and wandered into a gathering whose purpose he didn't fully understand. He wore his usual brown hunting leathers, and nothing about him glittered that night. His face was pale beneath his summer campaigning tan, and he looked cold and ill, his grey hair dull in the torchlight, his expression remote. He'd been the last to arrive and had taken his place quietly, as if what was to happen that night had nothing to do with him. He nodded to acknowledge the greetings he received, but singled no-one out for special attention, and Corwynal noticed that Blaize, on the far side of the hall, was smiling in satisfaction as he looked around the hall and took note of the disposition of the kings and their supporters.

Lot's faction, naturally, was the largest, surrounded as he was by his sons Gawain, Agrafayne, Garwth and Gaheris, and his chieftains and client kings, Rifallyn and Caw among them. Trystan had taken a place of his own between Hoel and Marc and his chieftains, a position Corwynal imagined to have been Lot's idea rather than his own. Trystan looked across the hall, perhaps searching for him, but Corwynal had edged into the shadows, not wanting Trystan to see the effects of his fight with Aelfric, and it was there, at the margin of the hall where the lesser men stood, that he found someone he hadn't expected to see again.

'Ninian?! By all that's wonderful! What brings you to Iuddeu?'

The young Scot was thinner and paler than when they'd first met in Trimontium, but he looked considerably better than the last time Corwynal had seen him in Meldon, when he'd taken Essylt back after that disastrous Summer Fair. 'How are you? Have you fully recovered?'

'Oh, I'm well enough.' Ninian tilted his head, peering at Corwynal's bruised and battered face. 'Better than you, at any rate! I can walk again, if only with a limp.' He shrugged. 'It doesn't matter.'

But it seemed to Corwynal that the Scot, who'd lost part of himself in that forest glade, had found something to take its place, something that burned behind his eyes, consumed him and turned him silent.

'As to being in Iuddeu, I had a fancy to see it, and as it was practically on my way . . .'

'You're going home?'

'Ultimately,' Ninian said vaguely. Then he grinned and for a moment was his old, carefree self. 'I'm glad I came. I wouldn't have missed this for anything!' he said, gesturing to the crowded hall.

'Wouldn't have missed what, you Scots bastard?'

Ninian was enveloped in the embrace of a large man who stank of blood and vomit, hay and horse-piss.

'Aelfric!' Ninian disengaged himself with some difficulty, then stepped back and noticed Aelfric's face. 'What happened to you?'

'Oh, this?' The Angle shrugged and gestured with a split-knuckled hand to a swollen jaw and a purpling eye. 'Got into some sort of fight. You should see the other man!'

'I just have.' Ninian tilted his head at Corwynal.

'You?!' Aelfric gaped at him. 'I was fighting with *you?*'

'And lost,' Corwynal said.

'Don't make me laugh!' Aelfric shook his head in disbelief, then winced and felt the back of his skull.

'Someone hit you over the head,' Ninian told him, after probing through Aelfric's tangled thatch of hair.

'Bastard!' he said without heat. 'That would account for it. You couldn't have beat me on your own, you Caledonian weakling. Anyway, judging by the taste in my mouth, I'd been drinking. You wouldn't have been able to touch me else. But I'm glad to see I managed to land a few punches of my own.' He grinned at Corwynal's battered face. 'Is that why you're here cowering in the shadows, and not over there with that brother of yours?'

'I'm not cowering! And Trystan doesn't need me.' It was no more than the truth. What was to be decided would be decided by the kings. Corwynal's approval, or lack of it, would mean nothing. Perhaps that was why Trystan hadn't thought it worth his while to come to his aid. 'He doesn't need you either. So, why are you both here? This has nothing to do with either of you.'

'Yes it does,' Ninian said. 'Whoever your war leader is, he'll take the fight to both the Scots and the Angles.'

Would he? It was something Corwynal hadn't considered until now, but Ninian was right, as was Corwynal's father. Whoever was chosen on this Night of Endings would begin a war that would be years in the fighting. But, when Lot stood up to speak, Corwynal had the strangest feeling this wasn't a beginning at all. Rather, something was just about to end.

15

THE NIGHT OF ENDINGS

Corwynal had many reasons to mistrust the King of Gododdin, not least his willingness to sacrifice anything and anyone to his own ends. Lot had forged a Kingdom from the old tribal lands of the Votadinae, but that hadn't been enough for him. Patiently, step by step, he'd worked his way towards this night, making and breaking alliances, grasping at any opportunity that presented itself, and turning setbacks into triumphs. Nevertheless, Corwynal couldn't help but feel a grudging respect for the man nor fail to be impressed by the subtlety of his mind and the breadth of his vision for the future.

Yet when Lot got up to speak, he began not with the future but the past. He talked of the coming of the Romans and what they'd left behind. The Britons had fought the Romans, he reminded everyone. Then they'd fought one another, but now there were other enemies to fight. One day, however, there would be an end to the fighting, and a new power would arise out of the ruins of war. He didn't talk of a kingdom, the old Roman province of Valentia that had lain between the Walls, but everyone understood that was what he meant. Nor did he speak of a High King, though they all knew who'd be the first. The Britons had to stand together, Lot told them. They had to put aside the rivalries of the present for, in the future, when tales were told of their day, these rivalries wouldn't be remembered. They had to fight together and make a strong base within the Walls. And after that . . . ? Lot shrugged. Who could say? Skilfully, he promised each king what he secretly hoped for: Dumnagual the opportunity to take the land north of Strathclyde, Marc the old Carveti holdings around Caer Lual, his own sons the territories south of Gododdin, sufficient to give each of them a kingdom of his own.

'But none can act alone,' he warned. 'None of us is strong enough. We need to fight together under one leader so that, instead of holding our frontiers, we can take the fight to our enemies and drive them back into the mountains!'

Not into the sea, Corwynal noticed, with a shiver of disquiet, and glanced at Ninian and Aelfric to see if they too understood Lot was speaking of the Britons' enemies as the Caledonians rather than the Scots or Angles. But neither Aelfric nor Ninian gave any hint of their thoughts and they just watched and listened as the words Battle-chief and Dux Bellorum began to be whispered around the hall. Lot let the whispers grow before raising his hand for silence.

'You're right, my friends and kinsmen. The time has come to choose a war-leader.'

'King Lot for Dux Bellorum!' cried one of his own chieftains, a cry taken up by some of the others. Corwynal expected Lot to be displeased, but he just smiled and shook his head, and Corwynal understood he'd arranged for that shout of acclamation.

'Were I a younger man . . .' Lot said regretfully. 'Were I not ruler of Gododdin . . . It's a heavy charge, my friends, one I don't take lightly. No, the role of Dux Bellorum is best suited to a young man with no other responsibilities.'

'Or allegiances?' asked Caw, the blunt-spoken King of Eastern Manau.

Lot frowned, irritated by this unplanned interjection. 'Such a man must have allegiance to us all.'

'Precisely,' Dumnagual said, looking pointedly at Trystan before letting his gaze drift visibly to Marc and Hoel at his side.

So it began, the debate that was to decide which man would lead the war-bands of the Lands between the Walls north into the plains, and thence to Atholl and beyond.

'They'll choose Trystan, won't they?' Aelfric murmured.

But no name was voiced, and, for the moment, the discussion centred around the support each king would pledge: a carefully judged assessment on the part of each, ranging from Marc – who'd offer his entire war-band to Trystan but not to Arthyr – to Dumnagual, who took the opposite position.

Eventually, with Lot goading, encouraging or mocking as required, all of them made pledges of men, mounts and supplies until the as-yet-unnamed war-leader would have a standing army of five hundred and the right to call on ten times that number in the campaigning season.

'Formidable.' Corwynal's father gestured him over to crouch at his side. 'Is it enough, do you think, to make Lot High King?'

'Only if he gets who he wants for war-leader.'

'Oh, I think Lot will manage to make himself High King no matter who's chosen.' Corwynal wondered why this hadn't occurred to him before. Was Lot's support for Trystan no more than a ruse to ensure Arthyr was chosen? But, if it was, it didn't seem to be working.

'Gawain for war-leader!' Lot's son, Garwth, called out impetuously.

'Don't be an idiot!' his father snapped.

'Why not?' Gawain demanded. 'Why in the five hells not?'

'Because I'm an old man,' Lot said with exaggerated patience. 'And one day the rule of Gododdin will pass to you, my son. I'll not last much longer.'

'Really?' Gawain looked surprised, but interested.

'Really,' Lot confirmed with heavy irony, for it was well known he intended to live forever.

'Let it be one of my brothers then.'

'Which brother did you have in mind?' Gawain failed to notice his father's sarcasm, and everyone watched in amusement as he mentally considered each of his brothers in turn.

'Not me,' declared Gaheris. 'If it was my choice, I'd choose T-T-Trystan.'

'Fortunately, it's not your choice,' Caw retorted. 'And as for Lot passing Gododdin on to Gawain, let me say here and now that I'm very far from being on my deathbed, and my son Heuil won't take the throne of Eastern Manau for many years to come.'

And so the debate moved on. Arguments broke out all around the hall as this man or that was supported or rejected, but none of it mattered. The kings might pretend to listen to their chieftains and advisors, but it was they who'd decide, and eventually the list of possibilities shrank to the two everyone expected – Trystan and Arthyr. Now each of the kings was required to declare his support for one or the other.

'Trystan!' Marc shouted out before anyone asked him. 'As bonny a fighter as I've seen. Just like me when I was his age, eh, Dumnagual?'

'You were young indeed when you first led your father's war-band,' Dumnagual agreed. 'As is Trystan, and, though I don't doubt either his abilities or his ... potential, I think we should choose a man of longer experience. A young man's task,

I think you said, Lot. But not a boy's.'

There was uproar at that, Trystan's supporters shouting Dumnagual down, Arthyr's supporters agreeing. But Trystan took no part and just smiled a little at Gaheris' incoherent indignation.

'I still say my son, Heuil, is the best choice,' Caw insisted.

'No-one else agrees with you, so make up your mind,' Lot snapped. 'Trystan or Arthyr?'

The two kings looked at one another. In principle, Caw, as a client king, was Lot's man, but since Arthyr rather than Gawain had married Gwenhwyvar, relieving Caw of the fear of Lot's influence in Western Manau, he was no longer to be relied upon.

'Arthyr's my neighbour now,' he reminded Lot. And with Arthyr absent, as inevitably a war-leader would be, Caw might reasonably hope for his own influence to grow, so no-one was surprised when he announced his decision. 'Arthyr then. I choose Arthyr,' he said with a smirk.

Lot couldn't have been surprised either, but he looked less than pleased, for now he'd have to cast the final vote. But the choosing was far from over, and everyone turned to Arthyr. As King-consort of Western Manau, he was entitled to have his choice taken into account. Nevertheless, he hesitated.

'I don't rule Western Manau. Gwenhwyvar does, so she should speak for herself.' He turned to her for the first time that evening. 'Do you want me to be Dux Bellorum? With all it will mean?'

She looked at him uncertainly, not understanding what he wanted her to say, and glanced across the room at Trystan as if he might have the answer. But he just smiled ruefully, and so she turned back to Arthyr and let her glance travel thence to Bedwyr, standing behind him, his hand on his shoulder. Something elemental passed between Arthyr's wife and his best friend, a meeting of wills that was like lightening striking a tree on moorland. Bedwyr tensed and Gwenhwyvar, seeing his reaction, allowed herself a small secret smile.

'Yes,' she said.

Bedwyr sagged in relief, but Arthyr just nodded and turned to Hoel.

Now it was Corwynal who tensed. What had Hoel heard, and what did he believe? Was he here to support Trystan or punish him? Hoel caught Corwynal's eye and smiled grimly, but gave no hint of what he was going to say. For the first time in generations, the ruler of Selgovia had power among the men who'd been his enemies, and who still didn't trust him, and he savoured the moment by letting the silence draw out. Breaths were taken and held, Corwynal's among them, but Hoel had to speak in the end.

'I support Trystan,' the old pragmatist said. 'He's won the loyalty of my men, and that matters more than the promises of kings.'

Lot nodded briskly. 'So, it comes down to me,' he concluded. 'I hadn't intended to get involved, but, in the circumstances, I'm forced to give my opinion. As you all know, it was I who persuaded Arthyr to come north, and I haven't regretted it. However, I feel that, in the matter of a war-leader, we'd do better with one of our own, one with links of blood and marriage to half the kingdoms, a true man of the north.' He looked over at Trystan, who lifted his chin in anticipation. 'Trystan, son of Rifallyn of Lothian, nephew of Marc of Galloway, son-in-marriage to Hoel of Selgovia, I ask you to accept the honour we bestow on you and become our war-leader, our Chief of Battles. Trystan for Dux Bellorum!'

So, it was done. Corwynal watched Lot sit back in his chair with the air of a man who'd achieved everything he'd set out to achieve. Gaheris whooped and slapped Trystan on the back, and men began to call out his name. 'Trystan, Trystan, Trystan!' Corwynal was barely aware that his father had got to his feet and crossed the room to where Trystan had risen to acknowledge the cheers of his supporters. Curious to hear what Rifallyn had to say to Trystan, everyone fell silent.

'Well, Trystan, you are to be congratulated.'

'Thank you, Sire.'

'Oh, don't thank me. I didn't have the training of you. It's your brother you must thank.'

'And I do.' Trystan looked over at him, his eyes shining, their bitter words of the previous day quite forgotten. 'I owe him everything. Everything.'

His father turned to Lot. 'You hear that? Everything.'

There was something in his voice that made the hair on the back of Corwynal's neck rise. Blaize looked up in alarm, and Lot frowned, trying to anticipate what Rifallyn might say. But no-one had ever been able to do that.

'I hear, Rifallyn. What of it?'

'It occurs to me, my dear Lot, that no-one has asked my opinion on the matter of our new war-leader.'

'But I assumed . . . Surely you support your own son!'

'You didn't support yours,' Rifallyn pointed out. Trystan paled and sat down, and Corwynal would have been relieved if some horrible premonition hadn't settled coldly on his heart.

'Sire—' He stepped forward, but his father held up a hand to silence him.

'I have two sons, of course,' he said to Lot. 'I must think of them both. Trystan has said he owes everything to Corwynal who, as many know, is half-Caledonian.'

'But—' Corwynal started to protest, but Lot beat him to it.

'What are you suggesting? No-one questions Corwynal's loyalty.'

'Indeed, no,' Rifallyn agreed, but Corwynal could see doubt creep around the hall. 'Yet Trystan depends heavily on his brother's advice in all things. My concern is the nature of that advice in the event of the war-leader facing some of Corwynal's own kinsmen.'

'But, Sire—' Trystan began before Lot cut him off.

'What nonsense! Corwynal supports Trystan and always will.'

'Has anyone asked him?'

'My opinion doesn't matter,' Corwynal said desperately, seeing the chasm open before him.

'Your father has called your support for your brother into question, for reasons I don't understand,' Lot growled. 'Say what you think, man! You trained Trystan. You, of all people, must know what he's capable of. Do you support him?'

He hesitated. That's all he did. He paused for a heartbeat while he tried to see if there was a way out of this situation. He still thought Trystan too young and knew what the war-leadership would turn him into. Corwynal wasn't ready for that change, yet he knew Trystan deserved this. He only hesitated because he loved him and was afraid for him, because this was Samhain and not only the living but the dead were watching. It was only for a heartbeat, but Trystan, pale enough to begin with, lost all remaining colour in that moment of hesitation.

'Of course,' Corwynal said. It sounded hollow, even in his own ears.

'There you are, Rifallyn,' declared Lot, accepting Corwynal's words and not the manner in which he'd delivered them.

'Not quite,' his father said. 'We're here to choose a war-leader, and it seems to me that such a role is more of a doom than an honour. The war of which we speak will be years in the waging, and the man who leads the war-bands will grow weary of the saddle, the ache in his sword-arm, and the cold of rough camps and hollows in the heather. I wouldn't wish such a life on any man, but if a man must be chosen, let it be Arthyr of Gwynedd.'

He gathered his robes around him, nodded briefly to Lot, acknowledged neither Trystan nor Arthyr, and walked slowly out of the hall.

Corwynal saw Blaize, white-faced with anger, stride from the hall. Lot looked as if he'd laboriously climbed a mountain, only to fall off at the very top, and was contemplating making the climb all over again. But no-one was interested in Blaize or Lot. Everyone was looking at Arthyr, this middle-aged, unprepossessing man who stood in the middle of the hall, his hands gripping the hilt of his sword which he'd placed point down, like the cross of the god he worshipped. And yet he didn't give the appearance of someone who'd just achieved a long-held desire. Rather, he looked like a man already weary of the saddle, whose sword arm ached on cold nights, but who'd just accepted his own personal doom.

Yet if Arthyr doubted himself, he was the only one who did so, and, one by one, men started to yell out his name, his own supporters to begin with, then everyone else. It was only then, with a twist of fear in his guts, that Corwynal allowed himself to look at Trystan, bracing himself for his hurt and accusation. He would have guessed Corwynal had gone to see his father, would have assumed it was him who'd persuaded the old man to support Arthyr, and he would have misunderstood Corwynal's hesitation. But Trystan wasn't looking at him. He was watching Arthyr as he accepted the oaths of fealty from the men who'd become the new war-leader's captains. Bedwyr, naturally, was the first. He knelt at Arthyr's feet and swore his fealty in a voice shaking with emotion.

Trystan pushed his way towards Arthyr and came to stand before the man he admired, the man who'd just dashed his hopes. Everyone, aware of this, stopped shouting, curious to see what he'd do. Might he offer a challenge? Arthyr, perhaps expecting it too, tightened the grip on his sword, but Trystan just dropped to his knees.

'I'm yours to command,' he said, loudly and clearly.

Arthyr smiled for the first time that day, then bent to raise Trystan up, and they exchanged the kiss of fealty, as others pressed forward to take their oaths: Gawain and his brothers, Kaerherdin, Caw's sons, Dumnagual's men, Marc's commanders, and Madawg from Lothian. One by one, the war-band leaders of the north swore fealty to their new battle chief. Not the kings, of course. They'd swear only to the High King, whoever that proved to be. And Lot was still determined it would be him. He'd clearly convinced himself this was no more than a setback, and he smiled as he came forward, took Arthyr's hand and exchanged a few words with him before slapping him on the back in a comradely way. It wouldn't be long, Corwynal thought, before the wily old boar persuaded everyone this had all been his doing and that he was more than a magnanimous loser. He was a winner.

Trystan, however, wasn't as experienced at hiding his disappointment, and, as he stepped away from the crowd about Arthyr, Corwynal saw his defiant pleasure in Arthyr's victory fall away. But when Trystan noticed Corwynal watching him, his expression hardened, and he turned his back on him to shoulder his way through the crowd as he headed for the door.

Corwynal went to follow him, but had to pass Arthyr to do so, and the new war-leader caught him by the arm.

'No, don't kneel,' Arthyr said when he started to do so. 'I don't need your fealty.'

'You don't trust me? You believe what my father said?'

'You and I aren't enemies, and nor is Blaize. Indeed, I need you both, but you know where I'll be campaigning, and I don't believe in putting a man in a position where he'll be foresworn.'

Why not? Corwynal wondered bitterly, as Arthyr passed on to talk to someone else. *Haven't I broken every vow I've ever made?*

'I notice he didn't ask me to swear an oath,' Aelfric said, having strolled over from his place of concealment.

'Would you have given it?'

The Angle pursed his lips. 'There was a moment, back there, when I wanted to, but it passed, like wind in the belly. So, you have your Bretwalda, and I think we Angles will regret this day in years to come.' He nodded thoughtfully and stretched his arms above his head, making his muscles crack. 'I think I'll get drunk again. Would the Steward of Iuddeu like to get drunk with me?'

Corwynal shook his head.

'Even if I promise not to fight him?'

Corwynal smiled at the Angle's persistence. 'Later, perhaps. I have to find Trystan first.'

'He's angry. Let him cool down before you speak to him.'

It was good advice. He should have taken it.

The drinking dens in the lower town were full that night. It was Samhain, after all, and no-one would sleep until the morning. But the mood this Samhain, after what had happened in the hall, was more frenetic than usual, and men were still arguing, loudly voicing their support for this one or that. Corwynal was sure Trystan would be in one of the dens, drinking to Arthyr's triumph and explaining why he was glad he hadn't been chosen himself. He searched them all but couldn't find Trystan and suspected he didn't want to be found. So he went back to the Fort and headed for his room in the barracks, passing Trystan's quarters on the way. The door was ajar; Trystan wasn't in the drinking dens after all. And he wasn't alone.

They were silhouetted against the lamplight, their arms around one another, Gwenhwyvar's cheek pressed hard against Trystan's. The sight robbed Corwynal of breath as he realised that what he'd accused him of, and what Trystan had denied, was true after all. Trystan and Gwenhwyvar were lovers.

It was only then Corwynal understood that, in his heart, he'd believed Trystan to be innocent, and the realisation of how wrong he was felt like a mortal wound. For the whole of his life, he'd tried to protect Trystan, to turn him into a man unlike himself, a man who'd deal with the world openly and truthfully. Now, when Trystan looked up and saw him standing there, he knew how badly he'd failed.

'Not here,' Trystan murmured to Gwenhwyvar, letting her go. 'Later. I'll come to you. But go now.'

She caught the direction of his glance, heard the warning in his voice, then turned and gave a startled exclamation, one hand going to her throat. She might have spoken then, perhaps to offer some explanation, but Trystan forestalled her.

'Later, Gwen.'

Then she was gone, brushing past Corwynal to run back to the hall, leaving him standing there, uncertain if he could move but knowing he had to.

'I apologise for interrupting you.' His tongue was stiff, his words too precise.

'It would have been better if you hadn't.' With an ironic gesture, Trystan invited him to enter, then sprawled on a bench by the shuttered window and gestured to a stool next to the brazier. Corwynal ignored the stool, closed the door and leant his shoulders against it, his arms crossed to hide the shaking of his hands.

'Do you have anything to say to me?' he asked.

'Many things, but now you're here, they seem . . . irrelevant.' Trystan's voice was as tightly controlled as Corwynal's. 'All I'll say is that I'm leaving. Oh, and you might tell the man who calls himself my father he'll not see me in Lothian for many months, or possibly years. If, indeed, I ever go back.'

'Where are you going?'

'Why should you care? I swore fealty to Arthyr as one of his captains, so I must go where I'm bid.' For all Trystan's control, bitterness crept into his voice.

'It's not a dishonourable position.'

'Did I say it was? He's promised me fighting, come the campaigning season. That's what matters, so perhaps, one day, I can prove my worth to you.'

Too late, Trystan. All you've done is prove yourself to be a liar and an adulterer, as I was. I tried to make you better than me, and I've failed. But Corwynal couldn't tell him that. So he said nothing and let Trystan be the one to break the silence.

'You made your opinion of me clear enough in the hall. You and the King. Of all the people in the world . . .' Trystan's voice shook a little, and he stopped, then recovered himself and went on quite calmly. 'But it shouldn't have surprised me. He's always hated me, and you've always resented me.'

Once Corwynal might have denied it, would have cursed him and lashed him with a tongue known to be sharp. He would have been angry, and made Trystan angry too, and they would have shouted themselves into an understanding. This time, however, he was beyond anger, and all he felt was how cold it was in that room.

'If you say so,' he said.

'I didn't ask to be born! I didn't ask to be given into your care! Surely you had another choice?'

Yes, he'd had another choice – freedom through the death of a new-born child. But even at Samhain, in the presence of the ghost of a woman seventeen years dead, Corwynal couldn't tell Trystan that either, so he just shrugged.

'It wasn't for my sake, was it? It was for hers. Your father's wife. Your stepmother!'

Did Trystan understand now? Loving another man's wife, had Trystan begun to suspect the truth of his own birth? But the distance that had grown between them was now too great for Corwynal to reach out and tell him that truth. It was as if they stood on two ice-floes on a widening river, with nothing but freezing water between them.

'It was for no-one's sake.'

'Is that all you have to say about it?'

'Yes, that's all I have to say.'

Trystan leapt up, flung open the shutter and leant out. It was raining heavily now, and, when he turned back to the room, his face and hair were wet.

'All my life, I've tried to win your approval. Today I understood how far short I've fallen in your eyes. Very well. So be it. It will be a relief not to have to try anymore.'

He turned his back on Corwynal to stare out into the Samhain night, moonless and starless, and it seemed there was nothing more to say.

Corwynal closed the door behind him as he left, but hadn't gone far before it was flung open once more.

'Wait!'

Corwynal spun around. Only half an apology from Trystan and he would have swallowed his pride and tried to make things better between them. Only a word.

'From this day forth, I have no brother! I have no father! I don't want to see you ever again. Do you hear me? *Ever again!*'

⸙

Aelfric was well on the way to being pleasantly drunk when the Caledonian turned up.

'Find Trystan, did you?' he asked, peering blearily at the other man. He didn't look well. Beneath the purpling bruises on his face Corwynal was as pale as one of those Samhain ghosts the Britons talked about, and, in spite of the heat in the inn, he was shivering. *It went badly then*, Aelfric concluded, without surprise. The bloody man should have taken his advice and left the boy to stew.

'I saw him,' the Caledonian said shortly. 'And he's leaving, so you'll be on the road in the morning.'

Aelfric groaned. He'd thought he'd seen the last of a horse for a while. In the morning, and with a hangover...? He peered bleakly into his empty flagon and wondered if he should call it a night. 'Maybe I'd better get some sleep,' he said. *Woden's balls, I must be getting old!*

'Trystan won't,' Corwynal said. 'So I wouldn't bother if I were you. Anyway, you offered... earlier...'

Aelfric stared at him. It must have been really bad! 'Well, if you're paying...'

He was. Aelfric was a slave, after all, as the cursed man pointed out. His only friend, he said several flagons later. 'My only friend, an Angle who wants to kill me...' Which was either deeply tragic or excruciatingly funny, a question they debated at great length, eventually losing themselves in a morass of argument until Aelfric suggested they settle the matter with a fight. At which point, the Caledonian passed out.

PART V

GALLOWAY

SAMHAIN 485 TO BELTEIN 486 AD

16

THE NIGHT OF THRESHOLDS

Corwynal was ill the next day, retching dryly, his head pounding and his throat burning. So he stayed in his room, to which someone must have carried him since he couldn't remember getting there himself, where he lay, staring at the roof beams and waiting for the pain to go. But it didn't. By nightfall, his body ached all over, and it hurt to breathe. He'd stopped retching by then but felt sick and feverish, and by the time someone finally came to see what had become of him, Corwynal was convinced he was dying.

'Woden's balls! You're a sensitive creature!' Aelfric, leaning against the doorframe, looked none the worse for a night's debauch. 'A few jugs of ale, and you're fit for nothing.'

Certainly not for arguing. 'I'm ill,' Corwynal croaked. 'Fetch Blaize.'

But Blaize had left Iuddeu, so it was Ninian who came. He was kind, even sympathetic, but Corwynal would have preferred Blaize's sarcasm, and Ninian's evil-tasting draught didn't make him feel any better. Nor did his diagnosis.

'You have the lung-fever,' Ninian said, his expression grave, for people died of the lung fever. But Corwynal no longer cared, and he let the fever swallow him up and welcomed the darkness that flooded into his head then ebbed away to leave an echoing space in which there were only the voices – Ninian's, Gwenhwyvar's, Aelfric's deep rumble, even his father's dry sardonic voice. But never Trystan's, except in echo. *I have no brother. I have no father.*

Eventually, however, he could tell dream from reality and knew the voices to be in his head since he was alone. The fever had gone, and he managed to get himself to his feet and, with a little more effort, pull on some clothes. He made his way unsteadily out of his room but had barely made it to the courtyard before a surge of breathlessness forced him to sit down on a bench by the wall, where he peered blearily at the too-bright day and wondered where everyone had gone.

The fort was quiet. The banners of the kings no longer flew from the ramparts, and the air had the wet, penetrating cold that comes with snow. Indeed, over by the south wall, in the shadow of a little wan sunlight, lay the remains of a drift, and the practice ground was muddier than usual. It must have snowed and thawed while he'd been ill, but, beyond that observation, he'd no way of telling how much time had passed. Not that it mattered, because everything seemed very far away and long ago, and so he went on sitting on the bench and watched the small comings and goings of the fort as if they'd nothing to do with him. Then he saw a big man come up from the gate, carrying a load of firewood.

'Aelfric?' Even his own voice sounded muffled and far away. 'What are you doing?'

'What does it look like?' The Angle dropped the roped bundle to the ground, then stretched and strolled over to join Corwynal on the bench, shaking his head disapprovingly. 'I don't know another man whose hangover lasts for a moon.'

That long? Thoughts came to him sluggishly, only to slip

away once more, like fish. 'Shouldn't you be... somewhere else? With... with...' To his horror, he couldn't even say the name.

'Trystan?' Aelfric's voice hardened. 'Not in his opinion. He said something about not being able to share anything, or anyone, with you. Which was fine with me, except he told me he was leaving me behind.' The Angle shifted on the bench, his weight making it tilt alarmingly. 'I warned you not to talk to him that night! Whatever you said, he was still angry in the morning. He gave me a choice – stay in Iuddeu with you, or go back to Lothian with the King.'

Back to Ealhith and the chance of freedom. And yet, Aelfric was still in Iuddeu. Corwynal was strangely moved, and, oddly, since most of that night was a blur, he remembered they'd pledged undying friendship until one of them managed to kill the other.

'Thank you,' he said.

Aelfric's lip curled with the usual scorn. 'Don't thank me! I didn't choose to stay with you, if that's what you're thinking. I decided to back to Lothian.'

'Then why are you still here?'

'Because he's still here. The King. Your father.'

⁂

'Well, Corwynal, they tell me you've been ill.'

His father looked at him critically, measuring the truth or otherwise of this rumour. 'I had a touch of fever myself,' he added. But if he had, there was no sign of it and his father looked as indestructible as ever, like an old oak, knotted and dark at the heart, but still vigorous.

They were on Iuddeu's rampart, to which Corwynal had

forced himself to climb, mounting each step with increasing breathlessness. His head pounded and his ribs protested, but he refused to give up – only to find that the man he'd been avoiding was standing in an angle of the wall looking eastward over the flooded and frozen water meadows and the flat silver sheet of the widening river. Corwynal would have retreated then, despite the effort it had taken him to get there, but his father saw him and beckoned him over to join him.

It was the first time they'd seen one another since Samhain. Even after Corwynal had begun to recover, he hadn't felt strong enough to face the old man, and his father couldn't have been very interested in his son's welfare since he hadn't sought him out. The other kings and their war-bands were long gone, most back to their own lands, some to cold quarters in the roughly re-built forts on the frontier. Most of Lothian's war-band had returned to Lothian under Madawg's command, and the rest had gone north with Arthyr and, Corwynal assumed, Trystan, since Kaerherdin and his men had returned to Selgovia.

'No doubt you'll be returning to Lothian now you've recovered, Sire.'

'No doubt.'

Corwynal waited, but Rifallyn said nothing more. Had he really thought his father would beg him to return to Lothian with him?

'You're taking Aelfric, I hear,' he said, to break the silence.

'The Angle slave? Is that his name? Yes, it might be amusing to have a pair, but I'm forced to remind myself that, unlike Ealhith, I wouldn't possess him entirely. And half a man is of little use to me. You may keep him.'

'He wants to go back to Lothian.'

'His wishes are of no interest to me. He has a certain affection for Ealhith, which I might find inconvenient. I never believe in deliberately exposing a man to temptation, a piece of advice I assume you gave Trystan, but who, regrettably, showed no sign of heeding it.'

'We let him down at Samhain, you and I,' Corwynal said, recalling, with a spasm of pain, the Night of Endings. *Well-named*, he thought.

'Of course we did, but he won't understand why until he's quite a bit older. Young men are notoriously blind and unforgiving.' Rifallyn turned away and looked across the low lands towards Lothian, and Corwynal wondered if he was talking about Trystan or himself. 'You'll be going after him, I suppose,' his father added.

'Go after him? How can I? He made it clear he didn't want me, and, after the doubt you cast so very publicly on my loyalty, how can I go anywhere near the Caledonian frontier?'

'I didn't question your loyalty. I questioned your feelings.'

'Since when have my feelings mattered to you?'

'Since when has it mattered to you what I thought your feelings might be?'

One didn't play games of words with his father, for one rarely won, so Corwynal abandoned the attempt and lapsed into what his father would no doubt interpret as sullen stubbornness. 'I'm not going after him,' he said. 'He wouldn't come back even if I did. He asked me to tell you that you shouldn't look to see him again in Lothian for months, or a year, or possibly ever.'

'Dear me! How dramatic! Now both of you have sworn never to return. Well, you can tell Trystan, should you happen to see him, that if he doesn't return to Lothian, he might find he's no longer the heir. There are others who'll have a claim to the kingdom on my death, Ealhith's son, should she bear one, for example . . .'

Corwynal closed his eyes. After everything he'd sacrificed! But he wasn't going to beg.

'If you want him back, I suggest you fetch him yourself,' he said stiffly.

His father smiled faintly, as if he'd been waiting for this suggestion. 'Didn't the Angle tell you then? No, I suppose not. Trystan didn't go north, you see. He went south, with Marc, to Galloway. And I think you know as well as I what that will mean.'

※

'Why didn't you tell me he'd gone to Galloway?' Corwynal demanded of Aelfric.

'Why didn't you ask me where he'd gone?'

'Because I assumed he'd gone north.' Then he understood. 'You thought if I didn't know, I'd go back to Lothian. *That's* why you didn't tell me.'

'No,' Aelfric said stubbornly. 'You silly bastard.'

Corwynal lashed out at him, an ineffective blow that grazed the Angle's cheek and did little damage other than to Corwynal's own dignity.

'You're a slave,' he reminded Aelfric. 'Trystan gave you to me. You go where I say you go and do what I tell you to do. And you tell me what I want to hear!'

'He went to Galloway to get away from you. Is that what you want me to tell you? Marc persuaded Arthyr to let him go south. Trystan went angry and restless and ripe to get himself into any sort of trouble you care to name. Is *that* what you want to hear?'

It wasn't, but Corwynal knew it would be true. *All my life I've tried to win your approval. It will be a relief not to have to try any more.* So he'd gone with Marc, who'd spoil him and give him anything he wanted. He'd gone to Galloway's dissolute court where any number of men would be glad to see him lose his honour. Or his life.

'But you'll go after him,' Aelfric concluded, much as Corwynal's father had done. They all expected him to ride to the rescue of Trystan's virtue and bring him back to fight Corwynal's kinsmen, then to take the crown of a kingdom he'd always – he admitted it now – wanted for himself. But Corwynal remembered all too clearly Trystan's final words. *I don't want to see you ever again.*

'No. I'm not going after him.'

⸙

'I still think you should wait until the Spring,' Corwynal said, clasping Ninian's hands in farewell. The young Scot's bones felt as if they were held together more by will than muscle and tendon, and Corwynal wondered if he really would make it back to Dalriada. But Ninian was determined to set off that day, even though it was late in the year for any sort of journey. He was heading north, he'd said. He'd pick up the old road that linked the Glen Forts and which would take him west to Beacon Loch and his people's lands on the far side.

'I've delayed long enough already,' he said. 'But we'll meet again one day, I hope.'

Corwynal doubted they ever would. The events of the summer meant he'd never be welcome in the Scots' lands. Even if Ninian managed to persuade the King of Dalriada that Corwynal hadn't intended to trick him, it remained a fact that he'd tried to kill Fearghus, and kings didn't forget or forgive that sort of thing. No, he couldn't ever go to Dalriada now, so he'd never see Ninian again, and he felt oddly bereft as he watched the young Scot's frail but determined figure ride out of Iuddeu's north gate and disappear behind a fold in the hills.

His father left for Lothian the same day, without Aelfric and without saying goodbye. Corwynal watched from Iuddeu's rampart as the small party of horsemen headed down the old road that would take them first to Dun Eidyn and thence to Lothian and Dunpeldyr. He waited to see if his father would raise a hand in farewell before he vanished, but he didn't, and the riders eventually disappeared into a grey landscape that lay beneath a sky heavy with the promise of snow.

It was a promise that was soon fulfilled. Only a couple of days later it snowed so heavily the roads became blocked. Then, before the snow could thaw, the skies cleared, and the temperature plummeted. Iuddeu's black rock was isolated in a glinting frozen plain surrounded by white clad hills that stood out sharply against the frigid blue of the winter sky. And when the weather finally changed, it was only to bring more snow that, driven by gales, deepened the drifts and Iuddeu's isolation.

The mid-winter feast was a cheerless and meagre affair as everyone tightened their belts and hoped the stores would last. Corwynal's mood, in particular, was as grey as the weather as he waited for a message that never arrived. His gloom seemed to be shared by everyone who remained in Iuddeu. Aelfric was morose, and Gwenhwyvar had been tight-lipped ever since the night of Samhain when Corwynal had found her in Trystan's arms. Nothing had been said about that by either of them. Corwynal blamed her just as much as Trystan and didn't trust himself to speak. Gwenhwyvar, however, didn't appear to be ashamed. Rather, she simmered with anger, almost as if she thought Corwynal was the one at fault. And so they didn't speak to one another more than was necessary for the running of the fort and the supply, when possible, of the outposts.

So life went on, cold and hungry and anxious, as life often was in winter in the Lands between the Walls. The first moon of the year, the wolf-moon, waxed and waned unseen behind clouds heavy with snow. Everyone said that was a bad omen, and the mood in Iuddeu wasn't helped by the sound of wolves howling all around the fort.

At least there was no raiding, for Caledonia was as gripped by the winter as the lands further south. The Caledonian war-parties would be keeping to their fires, sharpening their weapons and planning the spring campaign, all the while laughing at Arthyr and his troops as they shivered in their makeshift quarters. At least Trystan wasn't among them, Corwynal reminded himself, though he couldn't decide if that was a good thing or a bad. Had Trystan forgiven him by now? He doubted it. Had he forgiven Trystan? Corwynal wasn't sure about that either, though he hadn't stopped loving him. How could he? But he refused to ask himself if Trystan still loved him. Until the message arrived from the south.

Come to Meldon. I need you . . .

Corwynal's heart lifted when the note arrived, because he thought it must be from Trystan. But a closer examination of the water-stained scrap of parchment, brought by an exhausted Selgovian messenger who'd battled through a blizzard, showed the hand to be unfamiliar, a rounded childish hand with mistakes in the Latin Trystan wouldn't have made. Anyway, Trystan was in Galloway, not Meldon. This note was from Essylt, a private message for Corwynal to accompany the verbal one her messenger had brought; Hoel, King Consort, the man who'd ruled Selgovia for over ten years, was dead.

I need you . . .

But, however much she might need Corwynal, it was

Trystan Essylt wanted. She would have sent the same message to Galloway, and surely Trystan wouldn't refuse the call. So, if Corwynal went to Meldon, he and Trystan would meet once more, and perhaps there, where everything between them had begun to go wrong, they could start to make things right again.

'I'm leaving for Meldon,' he announced, having taken Gwenhwyvar the news of Hoel's death.

'Good,' she said, not even looking up from the letter she was writing at the table in the Steward's room.

'Do you have a message for Essylt? Or . . . or for Trystan?' It was the first time since Samhain that he'd mentioned him to Gwenhwyvar.

'To Essylt?' She laid her pen down and looked up. 'Tell her I'm sorry for her loss. To Trystan? I've no need to send him any message.'

He could have left it there. It was obviously what she wanted, but he needed to clear the air between them before leaving, to say the things he'd dammed behind his tongue all winter.

'Is it over then?'

'Is what over?'

'Your affair with Trystan. Come, Gwenhwyvar, we both know what I saw, both heard what he said. Everyone knows how it was between you.'

'Everyone knows, do they?' She jumped up, knocking her chair over as she did so. Her eyes were hot and angry. 'How can they? Do you imagine I'd betray the man I love for some sordid little affair with anyone, far less Trystan? You're his brother. You ought to know him better than he knows himself. So why don't you understand us?'

'But you . . . I thought . . . Gwenhwyvar, don't you love him?'

'Love Trystan? Of course I do, but not in the way everyone

with their appetite for scandal seems to think. I thought you were above all that, but at Samhain I realised you were just like everyone else – small-minded, petty little creatures!' She paced back and forth behind the table at which she'd been working, the words spilling from her. She too had been reining in her tongue ever since Samhain. 'Oh, yes, it would have been easy, wouldn't it, to take a whole series of lovers, and Arthyr wouldn't have minded as long as I was discrete. Is that what you thought I was doing?'

'No! I . . .' But of course it had been.

'And yet you thought Trystan and I would . . .' She threw up her hands in disgust, picked up her chair, seated herself once more, and leant forward, her hands clasped tightly together in front of her. 'You don't deserve that I should explain anything to you, but I will, for Trystan's sake, if not for yours. Sit down, please.'

'I prefer to stand.'

She smiled faintly, in control of herself now. 'Well, I would prefer you to sit. I won't have you glowering over me. You seem to have forgotten that I'm Queen of Iuddeu, and you're just a Steward – a role I'm quite capable of fulfilling on my own now. So this message from Selgovia is opportune. Go to that little creature in Meldon who values you more than you deserve. She'll need your help since she won't have Trystan's.'

'Why not? Essylt will have sent for him.'

'And you think he'll go?' She shook her head. 'Trystan did Essylt a great wrong in marrying her, and he won't compound that wrong by pretending to be someone he isn't. I know him, Corwynal. How is it you don't? Now please, for the love of whatever god you believe in, *sit down!*'

Corwynal sank into the chair she pointed to and ran a hand over his face, trying to rearrange his features as he tried to rearrange everything he'd believed. 'You were never lovers?'

'No.'

'But I saw how he looked at you when he first saw you, as if... I'd never seen him look at anyone like that before. I *do* know him, Gwenhwyvar. Afterwards he wanted only to be in your company. And I saw you together. What else was I supposed to think?'

'You were supposed to believe him, to believe *in* him. Why shouldn't he want to be in my company? And as for what you saw at Samhain, what exactly did you see?'

'I saw you holding one another.'

'I was holding *him*. Didn't you see his tears? Did you think them mine? Don't you know how much you hurt him that night? He was with me because of you, Corwynal, and later he did come to my room, but all we did was talk. That's all we've ever done. Don't you realise how it is between us?' She shook her head in exasperation at his baffled expression. 'You really don't understand women, do you? You understand nothing!'

She jumped up and began to pace back and forth once more, her fists clenched, her eyes glittering with angry tears.

'Shall I tell you why Trystan spent so much time in my company? Because, to begin with, he saw me as a danger to you. He decided to throw himself between us like a shield. It took some time before I could convince him you didn't care for me in that way. And as for what Trystan saw when he first looked at me – he saw himself. I'm what he might have been if he'd been born a girl. He sees me as the sister or brother he's never had because you've never really been a brother to him. All you've been is critical and demanding, and at Samhain I think he despaired of you ever loving him in the way he needs you to.'

'But I love him more than my own life!'

She stopped pacing, sat down again, and leant towards him.

'Then perhaps you should go to Galloway and tell him so.'

'He doesn't want to see me again.'

'Don't be so foolish,' she said tiredly, but there was a little softness in her voice now. He dropped his head into his hands and ground his fingertips into his temples to drive away the pain that had begun to lance through his forehead. Gwenhwyvar was right. He hadn't treated Trystan like a brother because he wasn't sure if he *was* his brother, but he hadn't treated him like a father either because he'd doubted that too.

'Does he hate me?'

'He resents you and blames you, and he may never forgive you, but he doesn't hate you. So go to Galloway and tell him you're sorry. But go and see Essylt first. Poor Essylt!' She smiled grimly. 'I ought to like her better, for we're in similar situations, women but not wives, both of us wanting men we can't have. Trystan will never love her, and I pity her for that, but she'll want my pity as little as I want hers. And I don't want yours either.'

He stared at her. He accepted now that she didn't love Trystan, but surely . . .

'I thought you loved Arthyr.'

'Of course I do! As you do. As Trystan does. As everyone who comes to know him does. I admire and respect him and might even lay down my life for him. But that isn't what you mean, is it?'

'Then why did you marry him?' he asked in confusion. Truly, women were beyond his comprehension!

'It was a mistake,' she said flatly. 'I thought I was marrying the man in golden armour, the man they told me was Arthyr.'

'So it's Bedwyr you love?'

'Surprising, isn't it?' she said bitterly. 'And rather sad. A man loved by another man. But we can't help who we love. I expect you know that already. So go to Essylt and tell her Gwenhwyvar salutes her. I hope she'll find happiness with someone else, but don't tell her that. Maybe one day she'll give Trystan the freedom to find the one woman in this world who'll truly be the other half of his soul.'

'Is that what you believe? That there's one person?'

'Yes,' she said firmly. 'Even for you.'

※

'Surely they're not going to leave him up there?' Aelfric asked in disgust, pulling his fur-lined cloak tightly around his shoulders, for the wind was howling through the clearing and setting the tall oak swaying, the one with the high platform on which they'd laid the body of Selgovia's king. Already ravens were gathering, even as the priests danced around the tree to the wailing of a flute that raised the hairs on the back of Aelfric's neck.

Savages! Aelfric thought sourly when Corwynal told him they'd leave the body there until there was nothing left. 'They do the same thing in Caledonia,' he'd added, which didn't surprise Aelfric in the least.

'Promise me one thing,' he said. 'If I die in these lands, don't let the ravens pick out my eyes. I want to be burned.'

'In the unlikely event of you dying before me, I promise,' the Caledonian said with a wry look. In truth, they'd come close to dying together, just getting to Meldon. The blizzard that had delayed the Selgovian messenger had blown up again as soon as they'd reached the hills. But the man had managed to sniff out the route, and, with Aelfric forcing his way through drifts that had come up to his waist, and the Caledonian coaxing the cursed horses along, they'd finally made it. Only to find that the little girl Trystan had married had turned into a queen.

Aelfric didn't approve of queens. Women were tricky enough, in his opinion, without actually giving them power, and the new queen of Selgovia had evidently begun as she meant to go on, for hanging from the wall of the stronghold, close to the gate, was the corpse of a woman, naked and mutilated.

'She was one of the King's slaves,' whispered the Selgovian messenger who'd come to Iuddeu. 'He was with her when he died. His heart failed him . . .'

So little Essylt had taken her revenge. Corwynal looked troubled by the sight of the corpse, but Aelfric wasn't surprised. He'd always thought the girl had a core of iron, and when she emerged from the hall to greet them, Kaerherdin and her chieftains flanking her, Aelfric noticed that her eyes, though red and swollen, were dry, and that she was wearing the old man's heavy torc as if she'd been born to it. Which, of course, she had been.

But when Essylt saw the two travellers, something of the girl Aelfric remembered showed in her face, and a blush of pleasure lit up her pale skin. It didn't last long, however, for when Corwynal pushed back the ice-clogged hood of his cloak, her outstretched hands fell and her body sagged with disappointment.

'So, Trystan hasn't arrived,' Corwynal said flatly. Aelfric shot him a look; the Caledonian was just as disappointed as the girl. He and Trystan had argued on the night of the Choosing, the night Aelfric and the Caledonian had got drunk together. But now the man seemed ready to make it up and tried to make excuses for the boy.

'The snow will have blocked the routes from the south.'

'No,' Kaerherdin said stonily. 'I sent men to check the passes and went myself to look for him. He's not coming.'

That's not good, Aelfric thought. For any number of reasons.

'But you're here, and I haven't welcomed you properly,' Essylt said, mastering her disappointment and stepping towards Corwynal, smiling and holding out her hands. 'You'll stay, won't you?'

'For as long as you need me,' he said.

And that wasn't good either, though Aelfric couldn't have said why, and he didn't understand until much later.

※

'What, exactly, do the women do at Imbolc?' Aelfric asked suspiciously.

Corwynal glanced at Kaerherdin who was sharpening a wolf-spear for the Imbolc wolf-hunt, but the tall Selgovian returned his look with such studied innocence it was evident he'd been spinning the Angle a tale.

'It's some sort of magic, isn't it?' Aelfric went on.

'It's a woman's mystery,' Corwynal replied, for in Selgovia Imbolc, the Night of Thresholds, was a woman's festival and the night belonged to Briga, Goddess of the hearth. 'So you'll have to ask a woman.'

Essylt had been staring into the middle distance, but now she looked up and smiled at him. It was good to see her smile, Corwynal thought, for her spirits had been low since her father's death and Trystan's failure to come to Meldon, but now, half a moon later, she seemed to be recovering.

'They tell each other stories by lamplight.' She smiled at Aelfric's transparent disappointment. Kaerherdin's description must have been more promising. 'Then they light the little lamps and place them at each door to light their men back from the fields. And when they've lit the lamps, they let down their hair, wind strings of dried rowan berries around their necks and dream of their men.' She dropped her voice and leant closer to the Angle. 'And some of the woman, especially those whose men are drunk or lazy, dream of men other than their husbands. So a wise man doesn't drink too much at the feast in case he returns to find another in his wife's bed.' Aelfric looked interested now, and she lowered her voice to a whisper. 'And maybe there *is* a magic on the night of Imbolc, for they say that, on that night alone, a woman has the power to summon the man she truly desires.'

Aelfric's jaw had dropped, but he shut it with a click of his teeth and scowled about to make sure no-one was laughing at him. 'How does a man know if he's been summoned?' he asked, as if he didn't care one way or the other.

'He doesn't,' she replied. 'He has to take his courage in his hands and knock on the right door. Isn't that right, Corwynal?'

But he'd stopped listening. He was remembering other things women did at Imbolc, of how one had screamed and died birthing a child who might, or might not, be the son of her husband. He was thinking that in the morning Trystan would be eighteen years of age and that, for the first time in his life, Trystan would celebrate his birth-day without him.

Corwynal had no intention of going on the Imbolc wolf hunt, for the wolf was the totem animal of his mother's tribe, but on Imbolc Eve he joined the men at the feast down on the river meadows. Behind them, the hill of Meldon loomed against the night sky, and the fort that crowned the hill was alive with lights, for the women had lit the Imbolc lamps and set them before the doors to welcome in the spring. It was a pretty sight, but a wintry one, and there was little, other than the lamps, to signal the beginning of spring, for it was colder than any Imbolc festival Corwynal had known in Lothian. It was different in another regard also; this year, for the first time in seventeen years, he didn't go to the feast with the express purpose of drinking enough to dull the memory of the screaming in Dunpeldyr's empty hall and the room filled with blood. In the last year, his Imbolc ghost had slipped unnoticed into the past where she belonged, and he no longer had to drink to drive her away.

'Are you coming back to the fort?' Aelfric asked, strolling over with Kaerherdin. Both were rather drunk. 'I'm minded to knock on a few doors once I've finished this ale.'

Kaerherdin laughed. 'Half the kitchen maids are expecting him!'

'More than half!' Aelfric grinned. 'It's going to be a long and busy night.'

'Essylt's maid's been giving Corwynal the eye,' Kaerherdin said, nudging Aelfric, who looked sceptical. Corwynal smiled but said nothing. In truth, the girl had given him a very definite invitation, and she hadn't been the only one. He hadn't intended taking any of them up on their offers, but now he began to reconsider. Maybe it was because of the ale he'd drunk, but he found he longed for a woman. Not just for the act itself, but for the warmth of another person beside him and the possibility of laughter. Not love, of course. Even if Gwenhwyvar was right and there really was someone in the world who was the other half of his soul, he thought it too late for him to find her.

Several cups of ale later, the three of them wandered back to the twinkling fort, weaving slightly and arguing about the finer points of wolf-hunting. Aelfric disappeared in the direction of the servants' quarters, leaving Kaerherdin and Corwynal in the royal courtyard.

'Trystan should have come,' Kaerherdin muttered. 'He should be here. With her.' He nodded at the door that led to Essylt's quarters at the back of the hall and prodded him in the chest. 'You tell him, when you see him, he should have come.'

'I'll tell him,' Corwynal said. Kaerherdin nodded solemnly before wandering off to his own assignation, leaving him alone, not sure where he was going. It was then he heard singing, a low humming song such as women sing to children, a simple tune that took him back to his own childhood. Essylt didn't have a strong voice, but it was pure and tuneful and, though there were no words in the song, it made Corwynal think of firelight and warmth, of red berries and waterfalls of hair, and he drew closer to listen. But either the ground was uneven, or he'd drunk more than he'd thought, because he stumbled, fell against the door and sprawled into her chamber.

'Essylt, I—' His apology dried in his throat as she rose from a pile of cushions set beside the brazier. A comb was in her hand, and her long fair hair was loosened from its usual severe plaits and fell over her shoulders almost to her waist. There were dried berries wound about her neck, long strings of them hanging across her breast, as red as blood against her pale gown. There was little light in the room, only a couple of Imbolc lamps twinkling from an alcove and the light of the brazier burning yellow and sweet with the smell of apple-wood. The flames threw shifting shadows across her face, and, for a moment, she was almost beautiful.

'Trystan should be here,' he blurted out.

'I know,' she said quite calmly, still combing out her hair and drawing sparks from it in the darkness. 'But he isn't and you are, so do shut the door.'

He did as she bade, and she reached past him to slide the bar into its sockets and swing the hanging back into place. The faint thud and the slide of fabric had a frightening but exciting sound of finality about it, and he wondered afresh why he was there. Had Essylt really made a woman's magic to bring him to her room? But she just smiled at his puzzlement.

'I'm glad you've come since I have a question to ask, the question I asked you in Iuddeu. Perhaps this time you'll give me an answer.' She took a deep breath, as if to give herself courage. 'Do you regret what happened, and didn't happen, on the night of Beltein?'

'Essylt, I've regretted it so many times.' It was the truth, but somehow it didn't come out as he'd intended, for she smiled tremulously and asked another question.

'Then will you be Selgovia's Steward? Will you be *my* Steward?'

Her two questions were linked in some way, but Corwynal had drunk too much to work out the connection. All he knew was that he'd wanted this once and still wanted it. He was no longer Steward of Lothian or Western Manau, but the work was in his blood, and he liked Selgovia, whose hills reminded him of the north, and whose tough people on their tough little horses made him think of the people of Atholl. And thinking of Atholl made him think of his argument with Blaize the previous year. *Trystan doesn't need you, and you don't need him. It's time you began living for yourself.* Why shouldn't he make a life here, in Selgovia?

'Yes,' he said, forgetting it was Briga's night, Imbolc, the Night of Thresholds. So he didn't see this one looming.

Essylt was trembling as she stepped closer, close enough for him to feel the warmth of her body and smell the scent of her skin, close enough for him to bury his face in that waterfall of hair, to take her face between his hands and lift it up to his, to kiss her as he'd kissed her all those months ago when he'd searched for a response in himself and found nothing. But this time, he did. This time a vague affection swelled into desire and something more, a conviction that this was a woman he might come to love, a woman who could be a partner in life, perhaps even the other half of his soul. His hands were in her hair, hers around his neck, her breasts against his chest, his thigh pressing between her legs. He bent his head to her throat, and she arched her back with a moan as he drew her down to her bed. The strings of berries broke as he pulled off her gown and tore off his own clothes, the berries spilling themselves all around them like droplets of blood.

'Please...' She was whispering over and over, reaching for him. 'Please...' Then they were moving together in the light of the little lamps, their bodies slick with sweat, and she was arching herself up towards him. 'Please, Corwynal... Give me a child...'

Abruptly, all desire left him, and he was suddenly and terrifyingly sober, aware he was passing over a threshold he mustn't cross.

'What's wrong?' she asked as he pulled himself away from her and the cold Imbolc air flooded between them.

'We can't do this.' He reached for his clothes. 'You're my brother's wife.'

'But you came to me! You said you'd be my Steward!'

Only now did he understand what she'd meant by that. 'I can't give you a child. I mustn't. Not—' *Not again.* 'Everyone would know. Trystan would know.'

'You think I care?!' Her face was angry now as she pulled the bed furs over her body to cover her nakedness. 'You think *he'd* care?'

'I'd care.'

'You didn't a moment ago. You didn't until I mentioned a child. I want a child. I want—' Her face crumpled as she began to weep. 'I just want someone to love who might love me back.' She looked up at him, her face blotched and ugly, her eyes cold and accusing. 'You would have loved me as long as it was in secret. Do you know how despicable that is?'

Of course he knew. He'd known when he'd loved his father's wife. How could he have contemplated loving his son's wife? Had he learned *nothing?*

'I should never have come here.'

'Then why did you?'

'I don't know.'

'Get out! Get out and never come back!'

He stumbled from the room, and the door slammed behind him, the bar thudding into its sockets. He leant against it on the other side and heard Essylt weep loud wracking sobs of humiliation, anger and loss. It was the loss that hurt him and kept him there, all night long, listening to her weep until finally, close to dawn, she could weep no longer.

Then he went to find Aelfric to tell him they were leaving.

17

THE MOTE OF MARC

'You're not going to be sick, are you?' Aelfric stared at the Caledonian in surprise. They'd barely left the mouth of the river, and the sea was as flat as a virgin's chest. Nevertheless, the cursed man had turned green as soon as they'd unmoored from the wharf.

'Of course not,' Corwynal croaked, then staggered to the gunwale and was violently ill all down the side of the ship taking them to the Mote.

'Fucking typical!' Aelfric muttered and walked off to speak to the crew, cursing the Caledonian as he'd cursed him all the way from Meldon. Aelfric had been looking forward to that wolf-hunt.

'We're leaving,' the man had said on the morning of Imbolc before the hunt had even begun. He'd refused to explain why, though Aelfric had a pretty good idea. Something had happened during the night of Imbolc, while Aelfric had been busy with all those serving lasses. It would have been some failure on Corwynal's part, he'd concluded. The man was useless with women. But Aelfric didn't understand quite how useless until they took their leave of the little Queen of Selgovia.

'You can tell Trystan, should you happen to see him, that if he wishes to include Selgovian archers in his troops in the spring, he'll have to come to Meldon to discuss it with me in person,' she said coldly and very publicly.

Fair enough, Aelfric thought. The boy should have come for Hoel's wake.

'And tell him this also, that if he wants his freedom, he'll have to come and beg me for that too.'

'I'll tell him,' Corwynal said, not looking at her.

'Then I wish you a safe journey. Kaerherdin will guide you as far as the headwaters of the Tuaidh Water. You can join the old road there.' She nodded to Kaerherdin who left to see to the horses.

'Essylt, I—'

'As for you—' she'd cut in, a steely glint in her eyes. 'Don't bother to come back to Meldon unless Trystan's with you.' It was then that Aelfric understood how badly Corwynal had failed. It hadn't been Essylt's serving woman the Caledonian had made a fool of himself with. It had been Essylt herself.

You fucking idiot! Aelfric was furious, and not just on account of missing the wolf-hunt. It was because, instead of heading back to Lothian as he'd expected, they were going in the opposite direction. To Galloway.

'Is this it then?' Aelfric asked when they finally reached the coast after a long and distinctly unpleasant journey through the hills and river valleys to the south of Meldon.

With the passing of Imbolc, the first day of spring, winter had taken its leave. The wind shifted into the south-west and the temperature rose, but then it started to rain and didn't let up for the whole of their journey south. Frozen tracks turned first to slicks of ice running with water, then to rutted muddy quagmires. Streams the horses should have been able to wade across became impassable torrents, and, time after time, they were forced to retrace their steps and pick their way up sodden heather-clad hillsides to avoid the worse of the spate-swollen streams. Eventually, however, the river they were following emerged from the hills and broadened as it twisted back and forth through a narrow coastal plain, and the going became easier.

By that time, Aelfric had a cold and the Caledonian had slipped into a sullen silence, which suited Aelfric just fine. *Bloody man!* he thought. *Fucking idiot!* And he wasn't too impressed when they finally arrived at what passed for the sea in these parts and found nothing on the edge of a muddy estuary but a huddle of low dwellings and a broken-down wharf where a single vessel, a trader and horse-transport, tugged impatiently at her mooring ropes.

'Is this the Mote I've heard so much about?' he asked sceptically.

'No. That's further west. This is the Annan where, unfortunately, we have to take ship.'

Take ship? Aelfric's sodden spirits rose, but the Caledonian's appeared to sink even lower. It wasn't until they'd reached the mouth of the estuary and the bloody man began to throw up that Aelfric understood why. The Caledonian hadn't the stomach for the sea.

And to think I wanted to kill him! He eyed the retching and wretched man hanging over the gunwale and wondered if it was worth the bother. If Ealhith could see the Caledonian right now, she wouldn't be so smitten. So what was Aelfric doing trailing after him like this when what he should be doing was returning to Lothian and dragging Ealhith back to Bernicia where she belonged? All right, it had been amusing for a while, what with all those battles and fights and stuff, but now . . . ?

Nevertheless, it was good to be at sea again, if only on a trading ship, and, in truth, he was curious to see what would happen when Corwynal and Trystan met once more. It would be interesting, he decided. Very interesting indeed.

'Corwynal!? Is it really you?'

The man who'd come to the lower gate of the Mote held his torch closer to Corwynal's face and stared at him in disbelief. Corwynal didn't recognise him at first, for he was wearing a hooded cloak drawn up against the drizzle, but when he pushed it back the man turned out to be Dynas, Steward of Galloway and Castellan of the Mote.

'It is indeed!' he said. 'By all the gods, Dynas, you haven't changed!'

'Nor you, Corwynal, nor you,' Dynas said. Both were lying. Corwynal's face might be the same, but nothing else was. As for Dynas, he'd grown sleek and fat and had lost most of his hair. All that remained of the fussy young man Corwynal remembered was a faint expression of anxiety that, having been a Steward himself, he understood all too well.

'You're here to see Marc, I suppose.' Dynas glanced up at the hall that stood on the summit of the crag. Even from the lower gate, Corwynal could hear laughter and raucous song, shouting and the banging of tankards on tables, all of which told him a feast was in progress. 'It's not a good time,' Dynas went on. 'Better leave it until tomorrow. But not too early. After midday is the best, before he ... well, that's the best time, I find.'

'Drunk, is he?' Corwynal concluded. 'I've seen Marc drunk before.'

'It's not just him.'

'Gods, man, I've seen whole war-bands drunk!' He pushed

Dynas aside and walked unsteadily up to the hall, for the land was still moving beneath his feet. The door to the hall stood open, and he paused on the threshold, buffeted by the noise. The smell of spilled wine, roast meat and wet dogs hit him in the pit of his still sensitive stomach. Dynas was right. Everyone was indeed drunk, but it wasn't so surprising. Lothian's war-band was capable of drinking itself into a state in which none of them could stand, and Galloway's war-band clearly had the same ability.

Marc, slumped in his chair, was idly fondling the serving girl sitting in his lap, but Corwynal wasn't interested in Marc. He looked about the hall, searching for a younger man, and found him all too easily. Trystan's golden hair was tousled, his face flushed with wine, his voice hoarse with singing. He was leaning, none too steadily, against one of the tables, one hand pouring a flagon of wine over a half-naked woman who was squealing in mock protest as two other men licked the wine from her generously proportioned body. Trystan, however, seemed barely aware of her. All his attention was on the song he was singing and in which he was directing the hall in a yelling, banging chorus. It was one of Madawg's cruder songs, banned by Rifallyn from Dunpeldyr's hall.

Corwynal's heart, which had raced uncomfortably as he'd searched the hall, now slowed to a dull disappointed thud.

'Water,' he said to Dynas, who'd joined him in the doorway. 'Cold, clean water.' Dynas motioned a slave over and murmured to him. A few moments later, the slave returned with a flagon just as a crash from behind Corwynal told him that Aelfric, left to bring their gear from the boat, had arrived.

'Allow me.' Aelfric took the flagon, walked across the hall, and threw its contents in Trystan's face.

There was, amazingly, a long moment of silence while

Trystan, water dripping from his hair, stared at Aelfric and tried to focus. He struck out at him, but the Angle just leant away from the blow and caught Trystan by the elbow when he unbalanced and almost fell.

'You Angle bastard!' Trystan pulled himself free of Aelfric's helping hand. 'What in the five hells are you doing here?'

Aelfric turned and looked pointedly towards the doorway. Trystan followed his gaze, and the colour left his face when he saw Corwynal standing there. Then he straightened and, with exaggerated care, placed the flagon of wine on the table.

'So, my brother has deigned to visit Galloway?' he said, speaking with the same exaggerated care.

'Corwynal? Corwynal!' Marc exclaimed, waking from the stupor into which he'd fallen. Corwynal heard his name being whispered around the hall as the shock of Aelfric's action wore off and men resumed drinking, eating and arguing.

'What're you doing here?' Marc demanded. 'Have a drink, man!' He waved to Dynas, who brought Corwynal a cup with his own hands.

'Hail, Marc, son of Gwrast, King of Galloway!' Corwynal raised the cup to salute Marc.

The King of Galloway heaved himself to his feet, pushed the serving girl away and swayed alarmingly, but righted himself by clinging to the back of his chair. 'You Caledonian Lothian bastard!' he roared. 'Come here and sit beside me!'

Corwynal had little choice but to do as Marc demanded, but as he walked down the hall, Trystan put out a hand to stop him.

'Why are you here? Why now?'

'Go to bed and sleep it off, Trys,' Corwynal said gently. 'I'll talk to you in the morning.'

Trystan smiled without humour. 'Better make that the afternoon. I expect to be busy until then.' He reached down and pulled the woman to her feet. She was a dark-haired, dark-skinned woman with full generous breasts, of which she was clearly very proud. 'Do you have a sister?' he asked, putting an arm around her waist. 'Yes? Then take her to my room and warm up my bed. I'll be there shortly.' He raised an eyebrow. 'Care to join us, brother? No? Don't you like women?'

'Go to bed, Trys,' Corwynal repeated, his voice no longer gentle. Had he battled his way through rain and flood and been sick all the way from the Annan for *this?* Trystan's mocking laughter followed him as he went to take his place beside Marc, but when he turned to look down the hall, Trystan had gone.

Corwynal woke early and in a bad temper. He'd tried to drink as little as possible, but Marc had kept refilling his cup. Now he had a headache that exacerbated the ill-temper caused by what had happened in the hall. Yet what had he expected? That Trystan would be ready to listen to whatever he had to say? He'd come to Galloway to apologise, but now he thought the spoiled, self-indulgent young man he'd discovered would do better with the sort of thrashing he used to give him.

So, despite his headache, Corwynal didn't wait until the afternoon before going to see him, even though he didn't expect him to be alone. He'd be with one, if not two, women, but he knew he could deal with those. What he didn't expect was for him to be with a man.

'You're too late,' Aelfric said. 'I sent the women away.'

The Angle was sitting on a chest, his arms folded, watching Trystan throw up into a basin.

'Wasted on him, they were,' Aelfric continued. 'Nice tits though, all four of them.' He eyed Trystan with good-natured contempt. 'Haven't you Britons got weak stomachs!' He took a pull from a flagon of ale and bit into a hunk of bread, grinning as he chewed.

'Perhaps you could fetch some breakfast for the Heir of Lothian,' Corwynal suggested. Trystan raised his head from the basin, wiped the back of his hand across his mouth, and groaned in protest.

'Breakfast,' Corwynal insisted and took Aelfric's place on the chest once the Angle had gone. Trystan lay back against the pillows on his bed, his eyes closed, his face a distinct shade of green. He looked terribly young, and Corwynal's mood softened.

'Trys—' he began.

'I know what you're going to say,' Trystan cut in, his eyes still shut. 'I know why you're here. You've come to protect me from the consequences of my own folly.'

'Have you been foolish?'

Trystan opened his eyes, groped for a cup beside his bed, sat up cautiously and sipped some water. 'No more than you must have expected. I drink too much, but what else is there to do?'

'You used to find other things to do in Lothian.'

'Oh, *Lothian*,' Trystan said dismissively, with an unwise shake of his head that made him wince. 'It's Marc, I suppose. You think he's a bad influence.'

'And is he?'

'He spoils me.' Trystan set the cup down and leant back against his pillow. 'I rather like it, and do you know why, Corwynal? Because he likes *me*. It's as simple as that. He doesn't criticise or complain. He gives me whatever I ask for, whether I deserve it or not. He doesn't judge me.'

Trystan's eyes were half-closed against the daylight, but he was regarding Corwynal steadily, as if he knew why he was there and what he'd come to say.

'All right,' Corwynal said, taking a breath. 'It's true. I've judged you, and I've not always been right. I'm here to apologise for that, and—'

Trystan gave a bark of laughter. 'By all the gods! An admission! That you've actually made a mistake!'

'Don't be facetious, Trys. I've never pretended to be perfect.'

'Yet you expect me to be?'

'I hoped you might be. I wanted to believe you were.'

'But you didn't believe *me.*'

'No, and I should have done. I was wrong about you and Gwenhwyvar. I'm sorry.'

'It's taken you long enough to come and tell me.'

'I was ill, and then Gwenhwyvar wouldn't speak to me until I was about to leave for Meldon. I expected to find you there and—'

'So you apologise with one breath and criticise with the next? You see? You're still judging me. You think I didn't go to Meldon because I regret marrying Essylt and wanted my freedom. You don't believe I have the courage to face her. Well, yes, in part you're right, but that isn't why I stayed away. It was because, if I'd gone, it would have given Essylt hope that one day I'd come to care for her as she cares for me. But I won't, so don't you think it would have been cruel of me to go back? I stayed away for her sake, not mine, and maybe for yours too.'

'Mine?'

'You should have married her. She's a sweet girl, really. And you wanted Selgovia.'

'Then why, in Arddu's name, did you seduce her that night?'

Trystan shifted irritably. 'Because I could see you were reluctant. Because, at the time, I thought you deserved more. Because I was a little drunk and maybe that's why the solution seemed so terribly simple. A sacrifice of my freedom for yours. But you didn't see it that way. You thought I was ambitious and envious and selfish and . . . and all the things you said the next day. I was stupid – yes, I admit it – but I was stupid for *you*. And now I wonder why I bothered, because I know all about you now.'

A chill struck Corwynal in the pit of his stomach and went running along his veins. What had Trystan heard here in Galloway where so many of Corwynal's youthful follies had taken place?

'What's that supposed to mean?'

'I've haven't spent the winter just drinking and fooling about with women. I've been asking questions and listening to the answers. There are no secrets here, not like there were in Lothian.'

Corwynal's chill deepened. 'What secrets?'

'About my mother. No-one ever mentioned her in Lothian, but in Galloway they talk about her all the time. They tell me how beautiful she was, how clever, how she loved to dance and sing, how she could twist any man about her little finger – her brother, his chieftains, freedmen and servants. All but one man. You, Corwynal, the cold-hearted Caledonian. You didn't like her, did you? You resented any woman who might take your own mother's place in Lothian. And to think I once thought you must have cared for her, and that was why you cared for *me*. But you've never cared for anyone, have you?'

Corwynal swallowed hard. 'Trys, I—'

'Have you?'

Why not tell him? Arddu, who'd been absent for the whole of the winter, drew close as he always did in moments of choice. *Tell him his mother was a whore. Tell him he's a bastard, that he's no heir to Lothian. Tell him you deceived your father and your friend and yourself. Tell him how you've lied to him for eighteen years. Tell him how despicable you are. He won't be the first or last to believe it . . .*

'No, I didn't think so,' Trystan said bitterly when Corwynal failed to say anything. 'You were my guardian and my tutor and you taught me everything – except how to care. Because you don't know how. So maybe I'm not the one to blame for Essylt's unhappiness. Maybe you made me heartless, because you are.'

Corwynal stared at him, the world reeling. Did Trystan really believe that? Was it even true?

'I'm not heartless,' he said with little conviction.

'Then name one person you've loved.'

You. He'd travelled to Galloway to say it, but, now he was here, the old fear of where it would lead clutched at his heart and closed up his throat.

'You can't,' Trystan concluded. 'Even Ealhith. She was in love with you and you didn't even *notice.*'

'That's ridiculous!'

'What is? That she was in love with you or that you didn't notice? Both, I suppose. Poor Ealhith, and poor Essylt. Yet, when you didn't come to Galloway I began to hope, despite everything I've learned about you, that you might have stayed for Essylt's sake.' He gave a twisted little smile. 'I hoped you could make one another happy. So I stayed away for that reason too. Yet here you are, in Galloway.'

And so Corwynal couldn't tell him about Essylt either, couldn't confess to what he'd done and how he'd run from her, coward that he was. How he'd tried to make a life without Trystan and failed. He'd come to Galloway to apologise and then leave, but his need to protect Trystan from anything that might harm him overwhelmed him once more.

'Do you want me to leave Galloway?' he asked stiffly, his

voice hoarse, his body rigid, fear running like melting ice through his veins as Trystan said nothing and just looked at him without emotion.

'Marc wants you to stay,' he said in the end. 'So stay. At least you came to apologise about Gwenhwyvar, if about nothing else.' His expression had softened a little, and Corwynal's heart began to ease. It wasn't over then. They could come back from this and be friends again. Given time, Corwynal could convince Trystan how wrong he was.

But, half a moon later, everything he did just proved to Trystan that he was right.

⸙

'Bastard! Slippery underhand bastard! If I could just get my hands around Dumnagual's scrawny little neck, I'd—'

Marc paused in his diatribe to slam his fist down on the arms of his chair and glowered around at his councillors, gathered together in Galloway's council chamber, a building close to the main hall of the Mote. Everyone was there: the major chieftains of Galloway, a token bishop, Trystan and Corwynal. 'Well, what are we going to do about it?'

'We'll do whatever you wish, Sire,' Andrydd said smoothly. 'If you could just tell us what that is, exactly.'

'You tell me,' Marc grunted. 'You're our war-band leader.'

'Am I?' Andrydd raised an eyebrow. 'Well, I'm glad that's settled, because I've had reason to doubt it of late.'

Trystan's lips thinned, but he said nothing. Corwynal hadn't been at the Mote for long before learning of the rivalries that were rife in Marc's court, principally between Galloway's ambitious war-band leader and Marc's nephew.

'We should carry out a punitive raid up the coast,' Trystan

said. 'Burn any ships we come across.'

'Burn a few ships?' Marc's voice rose. 'What's the good of that if the slimy toad's building a war-fleet?'

This was the news that had just reached Marc from one of his many spies in Strathclyde, but Corwynal didn't believe it. Dumnagual was a devious man and quite capable of turning a spy to his own advantage. He would know how jealous Marc was of his own position as fleet-master and was probably trying to provoke Marc into aggression. If so, Marc was falling into his trap, and no-one seemed to see it except for Corwynal.

'You have no proof,' he said.

'I don't need proof! The man's a slimy underhand bastard.'

'He'd say the same of you.'

It was true, of course, but Marc's colour deepened. 'When I want your opinion, Corwynal, I'll ask for it.'

'Indeed, my Lord King,' Andrydd agreed with a thin smile. 'You should only listen to the views of your Council, which doesn't include Corwynal, so perhaps he should be asked to leave. Unless, of course, you wish to make him a member of the Council? I'm sure we'd all value his experience and... opinions.'

Marc glanced around the room, but none of them wanted Corwynal there, and even Trystan avoided his eyes. When Marc was younger, he wouldn't have cared what anyone thought, but he was more cautious now.

'I'll speak to you later,' he told Corwynal with a nod of dismissal.

So he was forced to leave, but had no intention of letting the matter drop. A punitive raid on Strathclyde could so easily turn into a battle. And a battle could turn into a war that would drag everyone else in. So he made his way down to the harbour where the Goose, the ship in which he and Aelfric had travelled to the Mote, was taking on a cargo of fleeces. Her captain, Maredydd, a Rheged trader out of Glannaventa, was well known not only as a buyer and seller of wine and iron-ore, dogs and slaves, cloth and raw wool, but of information.

'A fleet of ships, eh?' he said when Corwynal tracked him down to a nearby inn. 'Not that I've heard, but I'll tell you who'd know. The Scots of Dalriada. If anyone's building ships for Strathclyde, it's them.'

Corwynal supposed it made sense, given the war and Dalriada's defeat. Galloway had exacted tribute from the Scots for releasing Feargus' foster-brother, but they'd be struggling to find enough trade goods to pay it. Selling their ship-building skills to Strathclyde might be one way of earning the price of the tribute. It was possible, even likely. But that didn't make it true.

'Do you sail into Dunadd?' he asked Maredydd.

'Not exactly, Dunadd being inland. Their main port's to the west, but it's a bloody long way and the currents are something fierce. I usually go to an anchorage in a sea-loch to the east of Dunadd. Awkward approach though, can be nasty at this time of year. But it's not worth going to either these days, because the Scots aren't trading any more – got nothing left to trade on account of the tribute demand. Bad for business, that war was. Very bad. I lost three of my men to the levy and only one came back, so I'm short-handed now, and unless I get another oarsman, I'm going no further than Glannaventa.'

'You *sold* me?'

'Maredydd's short of a crewman and—'

'You fucking *sold* me?' Aelfric stared at Corwynal and wondered why he was so surprised and – yes – hurt. He was a slave, after all, so what did he expect? 'You bastard!' After everything he'd done for the man, the number of times he'd saved his life, that fucking awful journey to Galloway and—

'I thought you'd be pleased,' Corwynal said in an aggrieved tone. 'You've been hanging about the harbour ever since we got here. Anyway, I've not sold you. I just loaned you.'

'You think that's better?'

'Listen, Aelfric, I've paid Maredydd to go to Dunadd to find out if a rumour I heard is true. I need someone I trust to go with him.'

And that was the final straw.

'Woden's Balls, what sort of an idiot are you? I'm your *enemy!* I've sworn to kill you. The last thing you should be doing is *trusting* me!'

The Caledonian looked puzzled. 'You mean you won't go?'

'Of course I'll go! But if you think for one moment I'm coming back, then you're even more of a fool than I'd taken you for!'

Aelfric stormed off, torn between a powerful desire to laugh and an even more compelling desire to take the man by the throat and shake some sense into him. *Trust!?* What had he done to deserve *that?* It wasn't as if he'd ever saved the man's life because he liked him. Or respected him. Or anything. It was humiliating, so it was, and he was cursed if he was going to come back. In fact, he definitely wasn't. Fucking definitely!

Corwynal might have persuaded Maredydd to go to Dunadd, and forced Aelfric to go with him, but he still had to convince Marc to see reason, and making Marc see reason was never an easy task. He'd hoped to find him in the hall later that day but was told he was on the Royal Terrace, a place Corwynal had been avoiding since coming to the Mote. There was a picture there, he'd heard, of the Fair Flower of Galloway, and he didn't want to see it, didn't want to remember. But when he emerged into the sunlight of the terrace, he couldn't avoid it; there it was, on the opposite wall, the image of the woman he'd loved. Or it had been. Now it was a ruin.

'A mistake.' Marc, sitting on a bench in the shade of the other wall, followed Corwynal's appalled gaze. 'Couldn't take the weather...'

Because it wasn't a painting. It was a mosaic, something Corwynal had heard about but never seen, a picture made up of tiny coloured tiles set in some sort of mortar. Or it had been. Most of the tiles lay on the ground, a glitter of colour on the beaten earth of the terrace, and there was nothing to be seen of the woman's features, for the face was gone, victim not so much of the weather but, Corwynal thought, of a hammer. But he didn't say so. He wasn't here to deal with the past. It was the future that concerned him.

'Did you agree to raid Strathclyde?'

'Why shouldn't I?' Marc sounded defensive and belligerent, and Corwynal knew he'd have to tread carefully.

'Because it could be a trap Dumnagual hopes you'll fall into.'

'But the bastard's building a war-fleet!'

'Or a trading fleet.'

'A trading fleet until it attacks my ships, my ports.'

'Until it does, you're in the wrong, Marc. And we have Arthyr now.'

'Arthyr? What's it got to do with Arthyr?'

'He's war-leader, so he's responsible for keeping the peace between the Kingdoms, and Dumnagual will use that. If you raid Strathclyde he'll just throw up his hands in horror and go running to Arthyr, and you'll have to face him as well as Dumnagual.'

'I don't care! I didn't vote for Arthyr. Anyway, I could take them both on!' But Marc was looking less certain now. 'Be reasonable, man! I can't wait for that slippery old fish to attack me first!'

'No, of course not. But if it's a trap and you *don't* fall into it, think how furious Dumnagual will be.'

Marc looked interested now, but after a moment he shook his head. 'I can't do nothing. Not if he's really building a war-fleet.'

'I'm not suggesting you do nothing,' Corwynal said. 'I'm suggesting you get proof and then *you* go running to Arthyr and demand he do something about it. Which will put Dumnagual in a very awkward position . . .'

Marc pursed his lips, rose to his feet, went over to the wall at the edge of the terrace, and looked down at the ships lying along the wharves. 'How do I get proof?'

'The Scots will know, so send someone to Dunadd to ask questions.' Corwynal went to join Marc and followed his gaze. The Goose, Maredydd's ship, was getting ready to leave on the evening tide, and from their vantage point on the terrace, Corwynal could make out Aelfric hauling on one of the hawsers. There was a stiff breeze blowing out of the east that would make for a swift passage down the coast to the Rhinns. 'I know someone who's going that way and it wouldn't cost much . . .'

'All right,' Marc said. 'We'll do it your way. But Trystan won't be pleased.'

'What does it have to do with Trystan?'

'I gave him the command, and he's already left for the

Strathclyde frontier. I'll get him recalled, but I'll leave it to you to tell him why.'

'Was this your doing!?'

Trystan stormed into the hall, stripping off his riding gloves as he did so and tossing them to one of his men. He was mud-spattered, having ridden hard from the frontier in a temper that was evidently still simmering. 'Did you persuade Marc to call off the raid?'

Men had turned at the sound of his raised voice and were drawing closer to listen to what promised to be an interesting argument between the brothers of Lothian. Corwynal frowned a warning at Trystan, and he made an angry gesture of exasperation before striding out of the hall. Eventually, after a carefully judged interval, Corwynal followed him to the stables.

'I didn't persuade him of anything. He thought better of it and decided it was a bad idea,' he said, leaning against the doorframe as Trystan brushed down his sweating mount. Rhydian whinnied in protest at the overly powerful strokes and turned to bite him. Trystan jumped out of the way, flung the brush down and turned to face Corwynal, his hands on his hips.

'A conclusion you helped him reach!'

'Why not?' Corwynal asked, annoyed Trystan didn't have the sense to see beyond his own desires. Since their argument the morning after Corwynal had arrived in Galloway, relations between them had been cool but not unfriendly, and he'd thought they were on their way to being friends again, so he saw no reason to curb his tongue. 'Someone had to. He's ill-advised here. Anyone can see that. *You* should have seen it. You shouldn't encourage him in these pointless raids.'

'Pointless?! Dumnagual's building a war-fleet. Who do you imagine he's planning to attack?'

'It won't be that simple. He's a subtle man, Trys. And Marc isn't.'

'I'm so tired of subtlety!' Trystan complained. There was a sulky note to his voice that turned Corwynal's annoyance into anger.

'So you'd raid Strathclyde villages? You'd kill farmers or fishermen who're just trying to defend their homes and lands? Women and children will be left to starve because they've the misfortune to live in Strathclyde rather than Galloway. And all because you're *tired of subtlety!* You think that's honourable? You think you're going to fight Strathclyde's war-band? You're not because they won't be there. Dumnagual has more sense. More than Marc and more than you. This is a trap, Trystan, but I didn't think you'd fall into it. You're part of Dumnagual's calculations. Don't you see that? A bored young man—'

'Who could have been something else,' Trystan snapped. It was as if he'd raised a weapon to begin the fight they should have had in Iuddeu, the matter for which Corwynal hadn't apologised since he didn't see why he should.

'A bored young man who's shown, so very clearly, he's not ready to be Dux Bellorum.'

Trystan's head snapped back at that. 'Is that truly what you believe? After all you taught me? After all you made me aspire to? Are you angry because you've failed?'

'No.'

'Then because you succeeded too well?' Trystan asked, his voice sharper now. 'Perhaps I was in danger of becoming more than you planned. You want me to be King of Lothian, and that's all.'

'*All?* Is that not enough for any man?'

'For you, perhaps. Well, Lothian doesn't matter to me. You rule it if you like. Because I don't want it!'

Corwynal took a step back, as if he'd been struck. His father had warned him, but he hadn't believed it since everything he'd done, all his sacrifices, had been to one end – that Trystan would one day rule Lothian with him by his side.

'Then what *do* you want?' he asked, his voice heavy with scorn to mask how deeply Trystan had wounded him.

'A name, Corwynal. To be remembered. Can you even begin to understand that?'

I know you now, Trystan had said, and yet, by this question, he showed how little he did know.

'Begin to understand?' Corwynal held hard to a voice that threatened to break. 'Of course I understand. I wanted the same thing once.'

When I was eighteen like you, When I had dreams I could reach out and touch.

But the young never listen to the old, or they misunderstood what's been said, and Trystan, failing to hear the emotion in Corwynal's voice, did so now. His chin came up, and his eyes glittered dangerously.

'It's why you tried to keep me in Lothian, why you never let me out of your sight, why you refused to support me at Samhain. You were afraid I might succeed where you'd failed. You couldn't bear to see me become what you wanted but never could have been.'

Empathy evaporated and was replaced by a wash of white-hot anger. 'Failed? Yes, I failed. Because I had other things to think about. A child who needed my care, a child I gave all that up for!'

'No-one asked you to. Did they? *Did they?!*'

Only a dying woman's scream. Only a name called out. Only

his own conscience. He opened his mouth.

He doesn't want Lothian, Arddu whispered *So tell him he's not the heir. Tell him he's nothing more than your bastard. Take Lothian from him. Then take Selgovia and Galloway too. Take it all from him until he has nothing. Until he is nothing!*

Corwynal shut his mouth with an audible click of teeth, biting back whatever he'd been about to say.

'No, I thought not.' Trystan's eyes narrowed, and his voice was sharp enough to draw blood. 'No-one asked you to look after me. You did that for your own reasons. You knew you wouldn't be allowed to rule Lothian, so you decided to rule it through the child no-one wanted. Everything you've done, everything you've taught me, has been to that end. Well, you can have Lothian! You can have Selgovia and Essylt, but I won't let you take anything else from me, and certainly not my future. So don't interfere in my life ever again. *Ever!*'

Trystan pushed him out of the way and strode across the practice ground, but Corwynal remained in the stable, against the wall where Trystan had thrown him, a hand clutched to his chest. It wasn't painful, but they say that about a mortal wound – that you don't feel the pain.

18

THE FILI OF DALRIADA

'I sent the boy to clear out that old fort on the Fleet,' Marc told him when Corwynal had recovered sufficiently to go and find Trystan, only to learn that he'd left the Mote on Marc's command. 'Thought I'd make it up to him for cancelling the Strathclyde raid. Gave him a troop of my best men.'

Corwynal couldn't decide if this was a good thing or not. Perhaps with time and distance, Trystan would realise he'd not meant any of the things he'd said and would be ready to apologise. But it would be some time before Trystan could return to the Mote, because the task Marc had given him wasn't an easy one.

The River Fleet flowed through a land of twisted hills and narrow inlets that lay to the west of the Mote, a land inhabited by the Cruithin, a people distantly related to the Caledonian tribes of the western seaboard, and who'd long been a thorn in Marc's side, though, on this occasion, the Cruithin weren't the immediate target.

'Outlaws,' Marc said curtly. 'Kinslayers, thieves, and murderers. Landless, lordless men. A bunch of them are holed up in that old fort. Should have razed the place to the ground when I had the chance, but Trys will sort them out.'

Corwynal didn't share Marc's optimism. He remembered the fort, ruined many years before. Marc was right; he should have torn it down rather than leaving it to become a refuge for outlaws. They'd take some shifting now, and Trystan knew nothing about siege warfare, nothing about fighting among a hostile people he didn't understand. *You need me*, Corwynal thought. *But you don't want me. Not anymore.*

Come adventuring with me! How long ago that seemed.

'I'll give him the fort for his own if he can take it,' Marc added.

And that was worrying too, because, until now, Marc hadn't favoured Trystan over his own chieftains. If he rewarded him with the fort, it would put him closer to the throne, closer to being formally named as Marc's heir, closer to the jealousies and resentments of the Galloway chieftains, many of whom had their eye on the throne themselves, Andrydd chief among them.

The relief Corwynal had felt when the black ship had been defeated had evaporated. Now he understood how much he'd relied on the fate he'd dreamt to keep Trystan alive until he could face that fate. Now, anything and anyone could kill him. And so Corwynal fretted about the Mote, waiting for news. The seed moon waxed and waned, and all about the settlements of Galloway men began to sow their grain in the ploughed fields, but no word came from the west. It wasn't until the grain was showing as a faint greening in the fields that a messenger finally arrived to tell Marc that Trystan had brought the outlaws to battle, defeated them and retaken the fort.

The aftermath of a battle isn't a pleasant thing to witness, but Corwynal had seen enough in his time to feel no disquiet when Marc announced he was heading west to congratulate Trystan and insisted Corwynal go with him. Yet, right from the start, this was different.

They were no more than half a day's ride from the Mote when they came across a smouldering settlement, its little fields trampled, its cattle and sheep left to lie where they'd been slaughtered. A horse lay by the roadside, its belly slit open, flies buzzing around the coiled intestines, and a dog, thin and starved looking, nosed at the body of a man. Corwynal dismounted and went over for a closer look. The man, judging by his clothes, had been a farmer, and was armed only with a short hammer. Inside the hut lay the body of a woman, trapped beneath a roof beam that had fallen in when the hut burned down. Beside her lay a child, its head split open. All bore the caste marks of the Cruithin.

He returned to Janthe and rode on in silence, but all around him Marc's men chatted amiably about times when they too had fought the Cruithin and seemed to think little of this savagery. His disquiet deepened as they neared the fort and he saw dead men hanging from trees by the roadside, the butchered carcasses of cattle in the fields and, once, a hunting dog, its throat cut. In the hills, the greasy smoke of burning settlements was rising. Towards noon they passed one of the god places of the Cruithin, a flat plane of rock carved by the ancients into complex rings and patterns whose meanings had long since been forgotten. Blood pooled in the little cups and depressions, and the village that had sacrificed at this stone had also been burned.

'That's the trouble with these people,' Marc complained. 'Their men-folk melt into the hills, so you have to attack their villages to bring them out. You'll remember that, Corwynal.'

'If we burned the villages, Marc, I don't remember it. If we killed women and children, I don't remember that either. But my memory isn't what it was, so maybe we did.'

They hadn't, though, and Marc knew it. The Cruithin of Galloway were Marc's people, but he'd come to regard them as little more than animals, and it was clear his opinion had spread to the war-band. And his nephew. The sickness in Corwynal's stomach became a cold hard stone, and by the time they'd reached the fort he was coldly furious, for by these acts, ordered or allowed, Trystan seemed to have thrown everything Corwynal had taught him right back in his face.

Where did I go wrong? What have I set loose on the world?

The afternoon dissolved into a grey mizzle that came off the sea, a foul drenching rain that smelled of kelp and sourer things – the burning of thatch and animal hides. The Cruithin village by the river below the old fort was occupied by Trystan's men, and most were drunk. A girl ran screaming across the open space between two huts, a man in close pursuit. She disappeared and Corwynal heard a struggle, muffled screams, then silence. Over by a pigsty, a white hound-puppy, newly weaned, whined against the lifeless bodies of its mother and littermates. Marc showed more sympathy for the dog than for the villagers, but did nothing about either.

The fort, when they reached it, was a mess. The breastwork was breached, tents had been thrown up in haphazard fashion, latrine pits were not yet dug, and horses were tethered too close to the only spring. Trystan hadn't arrived yet, and the fort was in the charge of one of Marc's chieftains, a close-eyed, hard-faced man of middle years, who seemed to regard Marc's arrival as a great inconvenience. He muttered about finding another tent somewhere, but Marc waved him away, telling him that if a spare tent could be found, it should be used for the wounded, many of whom were lying out in the open. Instead, Marc, his retainers, and Corwynal, crouched in the shelter of a section of the seaward wall where a willow hurdle covered with oiled hide had been thrown over a pair of planted spears. There Marc held court, the Marc Corwynal had once known, the man who never complained about the cold and wet, and who greeted chieftain and spear-bearer alike by name.

It was fully dark when Trystan arrived, his approach heralded by a clattering of hooves on what remained of the trackway to the old gate. He stopped under the archway and tossed his reins to a companion before sliding to the ground and looking around. His expression, in the flaring torchlight, was forbidding, but it eased a little when Marc made his way over to him, grasped him by the shoulders and kissed him on both cheeks. Only then, as a smile began to light his face, did Trystan notice Corwynal standing behind Marc. His smile froze, and Corwynal could see him gathering himself as tightly as he felt himself to be gathered. Corwynal gripped the pommel of his sword to stop himself from reaching out and striking Trystan, and clamped his teeth firmly together so the accusations wouldn't come bursting out. *Do you know what's been done in your name?* Yet he couldn't say nothing, for silence was its own accusation.

'Congratulations,' he said, but everything he hadn't said was evident in the tone of his voice, and, hearing it, a muscle flickered in Trystan's jaw. Marc, however, was impervious to the tension and flung an arm around Trystan's shoulders and echoed Corwynal's words with much more warmth.

'Congratulations indeed, my boy! You've had a hard fight of it by all accounts, but you'll soon knock this old place into shape. "Trystan's fort" they'll be calling it before long.'

Trystan looked doubtfully around the muddy chaos of the ruins. 'It'll take more than a name to make this place live again.'

'My thinking exactly,' Marc declared. 'And that's why I'm giving you the lands as well.'

Corwynal frowned, for the gift of land would be yet another signal that Marc intended naming Trystan as his heir, but Trystan misinterpreted the frown, and his chin went up. 'Thank you, Sire. I . . . I'm grateful.'

'It's no great favour, lad. No-one's ever got much out of this land, but no doubt you'll find someone to help you, eh Corwynal?'

He knew what Marc meant – that Trystan would find someone to look after the land and fort while he was away adventuring. Someone who'd be left with all the responsibilities and none of the pleasures. Someone like Corwynal. Trystan certainly needed him, and it was work which, in other circumstances, he'd have wanted to do. But how could he work with someone who'd allowed these things to happen?

'I have no doubt of it,' he said coldly.

'But surely you—' Marc began, his face falling, for his gift of land to Trystan was a way of giving it to Corwynal.

'No, uncle,' Trystan cut in. 'Corwynal has long been advised to give up being a Steward. He's clearly decided to take that advice seriously at last.'

'I wouldn't, in any case, want to interfere,' Corwynal added waspishly. Trystan said nothing, but held Corwynal's eyes for a moment, his expression unreadable, before looking away. Marc finally became aware of the tension and glanced uneasily from one to the other, then suggested he and Trystan look around the defences. The two of them walked off, Marc's men following, leaving Corwynal standing alone, shivering in the rain, still sick, still disgusted, but no longer just with Trystan.

Later, he went down to the village. There were wounded there, and, though he had no special healing skills, he knew how to treat battle wounds and, moreover, understood the people better than most. They didn't exactly welcome him, but neither did they turn him away, and there was work enough to keep him from thinking about Trystan. But it was difficult to avoid hearing of the cruelties that had been carried out by Trystan's men, and the people cursed the young Sun-Lord, as they called him for his bright hair.

'They took my daughter,' a woman kept saying. 'They took my daughter for the Sun-Lord.' Corwynal recalled the girl chased in this village, the man pursuing. Trystan might not have asked for her, but he wouldn't have turned her down. So he'd be spending the night in his tent with a girl, while Corwynal bound wounds and listened to talk that revolted him.

He snatched a little sleep in what was left of a stable rather than returning to the fort, since Marc had to pass the village on his return to the Mote, and Corwynal intended joining him when he did so. Marc arrived late the following morning with his companions and some of the less seriously wounded of Trystan's men. And Trystan himself.

The horsemen stopped at the edge of the village, and only Trystan came forward. Corwynal rode to meet him, his heart thudding uncomfortably, but Trystan hadn't come to see him. He stopped near one of the ruined huts, and a girl, mounted behind him, slipped from the saddle. The woman who'd mourned the loss of her daughter came out from the hut, gave a great wail of astonishment, embraced the girl and drew her inside.

'You returned her then,' Corwynal said unnecessarily.

'Not exactly.' Trystan gave a wry smile that wasn't for him. 'Are you going back to the Mote?'

'Yes,' he replied tonelessly.

Trystan nodded, giving no indication if he welcomed this answer or not. 'You should go back to Lothian,' he said.

'So should you.' Neither meant that they should go together.

'I'm afraid I have ... responsibilities here. As you can see.' The girl came out of the hut again, a satchel over her shoulder. Her mother was weeping and gripping her arm, but the girl unwound the woman's fingers, murmured something, then came across to Trystan, held up a hand and allowed herself to be pulled up behind him once more.

Trystan looked at him, a challenge in his eyes as he waited for his response, but Corwynal couldn't trust himself to speak. Was this Trystan's idea of responsibility? Bedding a girl taken by force? In a blinding burst of temper, he jumped down from Janthe, went to the stable and came back with a wriggling hound puppy, one he'd tracked down the previous night.

'Then here's another responsibility,' he said, thrusting the animal at Trystan and forcing him to take it. 'Her mother was killed, and all her litter-mates, so she's no-one to care for her. But you're the lord of this land now, Trystan. So she's in your care, as are all the others whose kinfolk have been slaughtered. I wish you joy of them. I wish you joy of your fort and your land and your people.'

Trystan didn't reply, but his eyes burned into Corwynal's. The puppy, gripped too tightly, whined and pissed over Trystan's leggings, but neither he nor Corwynal found it amusing. Trystan yanked his horse into a snorting rear, pulled it around, and kicked it into a canter, away from the village, away from Marc and his men.

Away from Corwynal.

⟐

'A ship!'

The lookout's cry roused Corwynal from his introspection, and he looked up to find Marc regarding him impatiently.

'Are you going to move or not?'

Between them, on a low table in Marc's private chamber in the Mote, was a game of fidchell. Corwynal was losing badly, and it was his move, but he'd been thinking not about the game he was playing with Marc but another larger game being played out, without him, in the west.

'I concede defeat,' he said, getting to his feet. Marc grunted in annoyance, for the game was far from lost, and Corwynal hadn't been in the habit of letting himself be beaten until recently. 'Aren't you interested in the ship?' he asked.

'This is a port,' Marc pointed out. 'Ships come and go all the time. Anyway, you hate ships.'

Which was true, but Corwynal was waiting for one long-overdue, Maredydd's ship, though the reason he'd sent it was no longer important. Marc was already complaining about the gold he'd paid for the Goose to go to Dunadd, since more recent spies' reports from Strathclyde had shed doubt on the earlier rumours of a war-fleet, and Corwynal suspected those rumours had been started by Maredydd himself.

'If it's that Rheged bastard, I'll flay him alive,' Marc muttered. 'Unless he's got something really interesting to tell me, such as that the Scots' tribute is on its way.'

It was only a few days before Beltein, by which time the promised tribute was supposed to arrive, but there had been no word of it, and no-one really believed it would come. What Marc would do if it wasn't paid was anyone's guess, but Corwynal no longer cared. He was less interested in the tribute than the possibility of Aelfric coming back to Galloway, despite him swearing he wouldn't.

Why he missed the Angle, Corwynal couldn't have said, for the man had been a thorn in his side from the start. The half warrior, half animal, took pleasure in exposing all of Corwynal's weaknesses and follies, and no doubt Aelfric could have told him exactly where he'd gone wrong with Trystan and would have delighted in doing so. But Corwynal didn't think the Angle would return. Why should he? They weren't friends, despite that drunken conversation on the night of Samhain, Aelfric's reluctant care of him when he'd been ill, or their shared near-death in the snows of Selgovia. Yet Corwynal still hoped the ship nosing up the channel would be the Goose and that the big Angle would be wielding an oar as it headed for the wharves. So he went out onto the terrace that overlooked the river, only to find the ship wasn't the one he'd hoped for.

'By all the gods!' Marc exclaimed, having followed him outside. 'Those sodding Scots have come after all!'

But even Corwynal, no expert, could see that the ship rowing up the river towards the wharf wasn't a merchant laden with the grain and leathers, salt and furs of tribute, but a much smaller craft, one build for speed and a swift slipping away from a burning settlement.

This was a warship.

'Lugh's light be upon this place and all who dwell here,' the Scot announced in flawless Briton. The ship had moored in the outer harbour, and its crew had slid a boarding plank onto the wharf, but only a single man had strolled ashore.

'May the peace of Manannán guide you safely in his father's kingdom,' Corwynal replied in Scots, wishing Marc hadn't insisted he be the one to meet the Scots ship.

'I'm not the most popular person in Dalriada,' he'd pointed out. 'I came within a hair's-breadth of killing Feargus. Then there was Galloway's burning of the settlements on the west shore of the Loch. They blame me for that.'

'All to the good,' Marc said blithely. 'Let them remember who won the war and why they're paying the tribute. Which they'd bloody better be,' he added. 'So, it's you I want to go and, anyway, you speak Scots. You don't have to say who you are . . .'

Corwynal did as Marc asked, but, from the first, it felt as if they were losing the opening moves in a game they ought to be winning.

He'd accompanied Dynas, who looked spruce enough, but the rest of the men Marc sent were a sorry collection of the Mote's guards, visibly ill-prepared and badly dressed. Even Corwynal hadn't had time to change his tunic, and the one he was wearing had been washed so often it was an indeterminate shade of grey, in marked contrast to the clothing of the Scot.

Britons were fond enough of display and they loved gold, but those who could afford it preferred to set it off with fabrics dyed in deep expensive colours. Even the Caledonians, with their love of silver and furs, were less striking than the Scots who valued colour above all things, and clashing colours at that. This Scot was no exception. His red tunic was brightened to scarlet by a narrow band of green, and his cloak, the colour of a summer's sky, was lined with buttercup yellow, all colours designed to astonish and disturb. And the man who wore them was no less astonishing and disturbing.

He was a tall man and lean, with a face too angular to be

called handsome. And yet he was striking, for his eyes were the strangest of colours. Many Scots, especially those whose hair, like that of Feargus, was red, had green eyes, as this one did. Yet this man's eyes weren't the warm green of spring leaves. Rather, they were the colour of sea ice and looked just as cold. His hair was striking too, a waterfall of silver that, on first glance, made him appear old. A second glance, however – and this man would always merit a second glance – revealed him to be younger than Corwynal by about five or ten years. But a third glance confounded that impression, for it seemed to him that the Scot had seen too much of the world and had found it so weary he was forced to make a game of it. And it was a game he was playing now.

'As to that—' the Scot said, reverting to his own tongue. 'Manannán gave us little peace on the way here and—' He cocked an eye at the sky, '—is unlikely to give us an easy time of it on the way back.'

'Ask about the tribute,' Dynas whispered in Corwynal's ear.

'Not yet,' he hissed back, but the Scot heard and smiled blandly.

'I am Ferdiad, Fili to Feargus Mór who is King of Dalriada and the Isles, Lord of Dunadd, Son of Eochaid Muinremuir, foster-son of Earc, and descendent of Lugh, Lord of Light.'

He stretched out his arms, his voice growing great, not loud but nonetheless powerful, melodic and ringing, and it didn't surprise Corwynal to see that a harp in an embroidered bag hung from one shoulder. He bore neither sword nor spear, but didn't need to. That voice was weapon enough.

'This is Dynas, son of Gronw, Steward to Galloway,' Corwynal said formally. 'Marc, King of Galloway, Lord of the Mote, son of Gwrast of the line of Coel awaits you. On his behalf, I welcome you to Galloway.'

You don't have to say who you are, Marc had said, so Corwynal didn't name himself. In any case, he had no formal position in Galloway, and his silence should have told the Scot as much. To ask would have been the height of bad manners, but the Scot was staring at him, those strange green eyes asking a question. *Who are you?*

'I hadn't thought to meet a Caledonian so far south,' the man remarked.

How does he know I have Caledonian blood? None of his markings were visible, but perhaps enough of a trace of the north remained in his voice for the sensitive ear of a singer to detect it.

'Do you meet many Caledonians in Dunadd?' he asked.

'No,' the Scot said flatly. 'My . . . experience of Caledonians dates to earlier – much earlier – times.'

Those already cold eyes had chilled still further. Now they were chips of frosted malachite, without life, without warmth, without any trace of amusement. Corwynal shivered as something rippled through him, stirring along his bones and nerves, the God making his presence felt, silent as yet, but watching avidly as if he was waiting for something to happen. It occurred to Corwynal that it might not have been wise for him to have met the Scot, given that Feargus had been betrayed not only by Galloway but by the Caledonians, his so-called allies.

'I'm from Lothian,' he said, but, far from reassuring the man, those ice-green eyes bored into him as if the Scot wanted to tear his face open and flay his mind apart, stripping it bare of all concealments.

Tell him your name! the God hissed, a lash of command that burned through his blood.

'I'm Corwynal of Lothian,' he said before he could stop himself.

It was as if something opened then, a gateway creaking ajar, a door that had barred both the past and the future. He heard a sound he couldn't have described – a sigh or a groan, a denial or a welcoming. All of these things, or none. How long that moment lasted he couldn't, later, have said. All he was left with was a sense that this was a beginning, perhaps the beginning of the end, and that nothing would ever be the same again.

This man is my enemy, he thought. *He knows everything about me.* He stared at the silver-haired, green-eyed Scot with the cold arresting face and braced himself for the man's reaction – a denunciation maybe, a refusal to speak to someone who'd almost robbed Dalriada of its beloved king, or the disgusted rejection of a half-Briton, half-Caledonian liar. But Ferdiad just smiled, and somehow that was worse than anything, and his voice, when he spoke, was a slow slithering of vowels across a tongue Corwynal was certain had the power to poison.

'Of course you are,' the Scot said softly, allowing his eyes to slide away, and, freed from the intensity of that cold green gaze, Corwynal was able to breathe once more and might have thought he'd imagined everything had it not been for the pulse in his blood and nerves and the conviction that this man, this lightly built Fili armed only with a harp, was more dangerous than any warrior he'd ever faced in battle.

'So—' Ferdiad said, raking the assembled men with an amused critical gaze and letting it fall, finally, on Dynas. 'You asked about the tribute . . . ?' He followed Dynas' puzzled glance at the warship, tugging at its mooring ropes as the tide began to ebb. 'Oh, I've not brought it with me!' he went on. 'I am merely its . . . herald. So, take me to your King.' He smiled, at Dynas, at Corwynal, at all those who'd come to greet him. It wasn't the smile of an unarmed man in the land of his enemies, but rather of an entertainer who'd come not only to entertain, but to be amused himself. 'And then . . .' he continued, his voice rich with anticipation. '. . . then we will talk about the tribute.'

⁂

'He sent a harper?' Marc exploded. 'Who does Feargus of Dalriada think I am? Who does he think *he* is? Not a sight of the tribute we're promised, just this single bloody bard. I've a mind to send him back to Dunadd with his head well separated from his body!'

'He's a Fili, Marc, and—'

'I don't care what he is! All I care about is the tribute. What does Feargus think he's playing at?'

'He's paying you a compliment.'

'A compliment?'

Corwynal sighed, wishing Marc would take the trouble to understand his enemies.

'This man's much more than a harper or a bard, though he's both of these things. A Fili is a royal messenger and the reciter of Feargus' ancestry. There's only one Fili in the whole of Dalriada. It's as if Feargus had sent you gold when you would have settled for iron.'

But Marc wasn't convinced.

'He should have had an honour guard at least,' he complained. 'And Dynas told me he spoke of Lugh and Manannán. I thought Feargus followed Chrystos. So what's he doing sending me a pagan to deal with?'

Which was a bit rich, coming from Marc, who only paid lip-service to the priests of the crucified god.

'You follow Chrystos too, yet you listen to those who don't,' Corwynal said diplomatically.

Marc grunted. 'You, you mean, you pagan bastard? Well, maybe I do. So, should I speak to this man?'

'I think you must, but be on your guard, Marc.'

'Why? He's no warrior, according to Dynas.'

'He's still dangerous. So don't—' *Don't drink*, was what he wanted to say, but he knew Marc would take no heed of that. 'Don't underestimate him.'

'So – where's my tribute?'

Corwynal winced at Marc's bald question, though until now the King of Galloway had been more patient than he'd expected. Marc had chosen to meet the Scot in the presence of those of his Council who were in the Mote already, and, though he'd been overly stiff, he'd said nothing tactless, and the formalities had passed without incident. Marc's impressive but largely fictitious ancestry had been recounted, and his chieftains had been introduced by their titles and allegiances. Andrydd, newly arrived from Loch Ryan, was wary, and the other chieftains were suspicious but silent. Dynas was there in his capacity as Steward, but Corwynal was only present as interpreter, should Ferdiad choose to speak in Scots. But when it became clear the Scot was fluent not only in Briton but Latin, Marc dismissed Corwynal and placed Ferdiad between himself and Andrydd, so Corwynal could hear little more than snatches of their conversation. Nevertheless, it was clear from Marc's snorts of laughter that Ferdiad was being amusing. Now, however, in response to Marc's question, the Scot raised his voice, though it was hardly necessary because everyone in the council chamber had fallen silent and craned forward to hear the answer.

'It's not due until Beltein,' he said with a smile.

'Which is only three days hence,' Marc pointed out.

'Which is why it's already been delivered to Galloway.' Ferdiad's smile broadened. 'We didn't want to be late.'

Marc and Andrydd exchanged a glance. 'If it's in that ship of yours, let me tell you here and now that it isn't the amount we agreed,' Marc said pointedly.

'Oh, indeed! However, the ship I came in isn't the tribute ship. That is... elsewhere. But it *is* in Galloway.' He smiled again, his glance shifting between Marc and Andrydd. 'You specified the amount and the time by which it should be delivered. You said it should be sent to Galloway, but you didn't say where exactly. So, tides and winds being what they are – nasty unchancy things – we decided to deliver it to the part of Galloway lying nearest to our coasts.'

'The Rhinns? You delivered the tribute to Loch Ryan?' Marc shot a glance at Andrydd, who shook his head.

'Not by the time I left.'

'Not Loch Ryan,' Ferdiad said, a glint of amusement kindling in his cold eyes. 'Further north. An island. We call it Carraig Ealasaid, but it's claimed by Galloway...'

'The Rock?!' Marc exclaimed. 'You delivered it to that godless lump of stone?'

'Oh, it's far from godless! A small group of priests of Chrystos live there, and I would guess that if their god has a taste for lamentation, he visits quite frequently.'

Having demonstrated the cleverness with which the Scots, very inconveniently, had complied with Galloway's conditions, Ferdiad sat back, ready to be amused. Andrydd, who'd made the arrangements but had failed to specify exactly where the tribute was to be delivered, looked furious, but there was little he could say.

'Better take a ship and get there before those thieves from Strathclyde get word of it,' Marc snapped.

'Oh, it's quite safe,' Ferdiad assured him. 'We have it under guard.'

'Under guard?' Andrydd asked suspiciously.

'By the Morholt, who captains the tribute ship and whose warship lies in your harbour. Have you never heard of the Morholt? No? You surprise me.'

The Scot took his harp, set it on his knee and began touching the strings faintly, as if testing their tone. Then he plucked a single note and let it ring into silence before continuing. 'The Morholt is the Champion of Dalriada. He's a man of long memory and short temper, a man who had business in Ulaid earlier this year and, as a result, was unable to accompany Feargus to the battle by the Loch of the Beacon. Had he done so, things might have gone differently, and I might not have had the pleasure of visiting Galloway and meeting so many ... interesting people.' He threw Corwynal a swift glinting smile that was full of malice, then plucked a few more notes, a sliding scale that rose unexpectedly at the end. 'The Morholt is rather old-fashioned in his views. He took exception to the ... circumstances of Feargus' defeat and therefore questions the legitimacy of the claim for tribute.'

'Your king was beaten,' Andrydd said flatly. 'He offered tribute in return for the lives of his foster-brother and his men. There's no question about the legitimacy of the claim.'

'Oh, quite,' Ferdiad agreed, as another run of notes fell from his hands. 'Feargus doesn't deny it, and he is, above all things, a man of honour ...'

'And we of Galloway are not? Is that what you're saying?' Marc demanded. 'Because if you are, you're walking on very dangerous ground!'

Ferdiad smiled, and the notes began to take form, though he seemed unaware of it. Marc had protested too much, conscious that Galloway's sacking of the western shore of the Loch under Strathclyde's banner had been an underhand trick, and that Feargus' return to defend his lands had been instrumental in his eventual defeat. Ferdiad had a point, and something in the music seemed to confirm it.

'Not at all,' the Scot said easily. 'I'm merely explaining that though Feargus has provided the tribute, the Morholt wishes to . . . discuss the matter further.'

'There will be no discussion,' Marc said. 'This Morholt can back off and let us collect the tribute as promised, or else my war-fleet will be slipping their moorings and heading for Dunadd.'

Ferdiad ignored the threat and continued to draw a tune of increasing complexity from his harp.

'The Morholt proposes a discussion that may be to your advantage, my Lord King. A discussion not of words but weapons, a challenge in the old manner, the gods to determine the rights and wrongs of the matter. Dalriada's Champion challenges the Champion of Galloway.'

Now the notes came together in an old melody that made the heart race. It was a song of pride, a tale told by firelight, of warriors whose names were still remembered, of men who'd become gods. Everyone in the room felt the same stirring, and there was more than one of them, Marc included, who might have stepped forward to accept the challenge. But Corwynal was untouched by Ferdiad's spell.

'This is ridiculous!' he burst out. 'The tribute is owed to Galloway. It was never part of the agreement that anyone had to fight for it.'

'You don't have a Champion?' Ferdiad asked, raising an

eyebrow in mock surprise.

'That isn't the point. The point is that it's unnecessary. Why should Galloway agree to this?'

Marc frowned a warning at Corwynal to be quiet, but repeated his question, putting it more bluntly.

'What would be in it for us?'

Ferdiad shrugged, as if this was a small matter. 'If you win, the tribute will be doubled.'

'What are you playing at?'

Ferdiad, having left Marc and his Council speechless, had smiled and slipped away from his place in the council chamber, saying he would leave Marc to consider the proposal. Corwynal followed the Scot as he headed back to his ship and caught up with him half-way across the lower courtyard.

'Playing? I'm not *playing*. It isn't a *game*, Corwynal of Lothian. Now, if you'll excuse me . . .' He glanced pointedly at the hand on his arm, but Corwynal didn't let him go. He still had questions.

'Do we know each other? Have we met before?'

Ferdiad pursed his lips in a moue of disappointment. 'Few who've met me ever forget,' he said. 'You, on the other hand, are quite unmemorable.' He shrugged, prised Corwynal's hand from his arm with strong harper's fingers and made for the gate.

'This isn't Feargus' idea, is it? You've no authority for this proposal.'

'It's not my proposal. It's the Morholt's,' Ferdiad said, turning back. 'He's easily bored and somewhat impulsive. Usually I can control him. In this case, however . . .' He smiled. 'Maybe I don't want to. But what are you afraid of? Rumour has it there's no Champion in Galloway to accept this challenge.'

But there was someone with the necessary confidence in his own abilities and the skills Corwynal had taught him, with a pride he'd taught him too, someone who'd willingly take up the challenge and might even demand the right to do so. Fortunately, Trystan was safely in the west and wouldn't find out about all this until it was too late.

'Not of Galloway, no,' he said. 'I assume a challenger would have to be from Galloway?'

Ferdiad shrugged. 'I believe honour would demand it. Why? Were you thinking of yourself? Forgive me, but you seem . . . rather too old.'

Corwynal bristled at that but didn't rise to the challenge, and Ferdiad smiled a slow serpent smile. 'You're afraid, aren't you? But not for yourself. Who, then?'

My brother. My son. No matter their disagreement, no matter how disgusted he was with Trystan's behaviour, nothing had changed Corwynal's need to protect him. He said nothing and just turned on his heel and walked back across the courtyard, aware of that cold green gaze following him, as did Ferdiad's soft sibilant laughter.

※

'Tell me you're not seriously considering this,' he demanded of Marc when he finally got him alone.

'I don't see why I shouldn't.' Marc leant back in his chair in his private room, but didn't invite Corwynal to sit.

'Because you stand to lose everything,' Corwynal replied, appealing to Marc's avarice. 'I assume that's part of the deal? That if Galloway loses, it gives up the tribute?'

'I can afford it. The Scots can't.'

'Exactly! So what does that tell you, Marc? This Morholt, whoever he is, is a professional champion. Who do you have to stand against him?'

'I could have done it.'

'Yes, twenty, even ten, years ago. Not now. Galloway doesn't have a champion. Only a few men have the skills to stand against a champion out of Hibernia: Bedwyr, Heuil, Gawain. None of them are from Galloway.'

'You've forgotten Trystan.'

'Trystan's not from Galloway either.'

'He's my nephew.'

'Your sister's son. How will you face Gwenllian in the otherworld if you're the cause of his death?' Marc blinked at that, and Corwynal sensed victory. 'Listen to me, Marc. This proposal doesn't come from Feargus. Ferdiad's playing a game with you, but if you refuse, then not only will you get the tribute, but Trystan will be safe. Don't send for him. Promise me you won't.'

But Marc shifted uncomfortably and wouldn't meet his eyes.

'You haven't, have you?'

'Of course not! But he said he'd be back at the Mote before Beltein, so he's probably on his way.'

In the old days, when he and Trystan had been friends, Corwynal would have known of Trystan's plans.

'Then send someone to stop him. For the sake of our friendship, Marc, for the sake of his mother, your sister. *Promise me!*'

Marc promised, somewhat tearfully, and Corwynal took his leave and made his way back across the courtyard, light-headed with relief. It was evening by then and stars were pricking the darkness. Corwynal looked up, picking out the Gods' creatures that were strewn across the sky – the salmon and the goose, the great stag in the north, the God himself low on the horizon and, in the west, the wolf with his bright all-seeing eye.

It was the last thing he saw before something crashed into the back of his skull, and a blinding light swallowed the night for a moment, before darkness returned, crushing him beneath its weight.

'What are you doing here, Corwynal?'

The darkness cracked open and light flared inside his head before shrinking back to the flame of an oil lamp. He was desperately thirsty, and there was a bitter taste in his mouth. His arms had been dragged behind him and roughly tied with a strip of hide, and liquid had been forced between his lips. Then he'd been thrown into a stable that stank of cattle, and his head had cracked against a beam. It was then that the dreams had come, dreams of horses riding through the night, of a door crashing open, of flames and song and the plucked notes of a harp. He'd dreamt of voices shouting as the horses rode away, their hoof-beats fading into the distance. Then he was standing on a stony beach with the sea booming all about him . . .

'How long?' he croaked, trying to sit up. Although his arms were free now, his shoulders ached abominably and his wrists throbbed, but these pains were as nothing compared to the one in his head. Someone pressed a dish of water to his lips and he drank it down in noisy gulps, scraped the crusted blood from his eye and peered blearily at his rescuer.

'Everyone looked for you,' Dynas said. 'Trystan asked where you were but no-one could find you.'

'Trystan?' He grasped Dynas by the tunic. 'He came?'

'Yes, but he left again. You'll not catch him now,' Dynas insisted, but Corwynal shook his head, wincing. It couldn't be too late. It mustn't be too late. He got to his feet and staggered to the door. It was still dark, but light was rising behind the hills to the east. He'd been unconscious for a whole night, but there might still be time... The pain in his head blossomed as he tried to run. His legs refused to obey his will, and he was sobbing with frustration by the time he made it to the hall.

'Corwynal, it's no use.' Dynas had followed him from the stable and now he stepped in front of him as he made for Marc's chamber. 'Marc's drunker than I've ever seen him. He's raving, speaking to a woman eighteen years dead and begging her to forgive him.'

Corwynal leant against the wall next to the entrance to Marc's quarters then slid to the floor as his legs gave way. 'What happened?'

'Trystan arrived last night and, when he learned of the challenge, he forced Marc to name him heir, to make him a man of Galloway, to name him Champion. It was the Scot, you see, playing that music of his.' Dynas shook his head. 'Somehow, it all seemed such a wonderful idea. A blow for honour and glory, a return to the old days. No-one wanted to see Trystan named heir, but they were all carried away by the music. Marc regrets it now, but it's too late. That's why he started drinking.'

'The Scot?'

'Gone. Left on the tide.'

But tides were strange unaccountable things. Corwynal staggered outside, his heart thumping, his head throbbing. Feeling as if he was wading through a swamp, he made for the rampart that overlooked the river. A ship was easing its way out into the channel, and he knew it to be the Scots ship by its sleek shape and the speed of its departure. It rowed out beyond the channel, and then the sail was hauled up, bellying full as it caught the wind. The rising sun picked out the design on the sail; it was the symbol of a great black ship.

19

TRYSTAN'S FORT

Corwynal watched the Scots ship tilt to the wind and head west, and knew he'd been tricked by everything he'd believed in: by dreams, by fate, by the God himself. Yet in his dream he'd watched Trystan die. In his dream, he hadn't been left behind.

'I have to get to the island before Trystan.' But even as he spoke, he knew it was hopeless.

'There's not a ship in the Mote that could catch up with that warship.' Dynas had followed him to the rampart. 'You'd do better going overland and picking up a ship further west. You might overtake Trystan on the way.'

Corwynal stared at him, confused. 'Didn't he go with the Scot?'

'Marc insisted he take a Galloway ship to bring the tribute back. He's gone to Loch Ryan. He'll be stopping at his fort on the way.'

So it wasn't too late. All he had to do was stop Trystan going to the island, then go in his place. If he took the old trackway across the moors, he'd avoid a long loop in the road and should reach the fort before Trystan left. Stopping only to collect his weapons, he saddled Janthe and headed west.

His head was pounding, and nausea was making him dizzy, but he pushed Janthe hard along the pitted and flooded track, and she didn't let him down, great-hearted beast that she was. Eventually, as the light was fading, they dropped down from the moors to the Fleet and splashed through the ford. Janthe was blowing with weariness by then and, just below the fort, she took exception to a body hanging from a tree and refused to go on. The crows had taken the corpse's eyes, but in life they would have been close together, and Corwynal recognised the man as Trystan's fort commander. *What brought that about?* he wondered, without much caring, as he dismounted to lead the exhausted Janthe up the trackway to the fort where, to his relief, two standards were flying, those of Lothian and Galloway. Trystan hadn't left yet. There was still time to stop him.

⁂

The walls had been repaired and the old ditches re-dug. A gate hung from the entranceway, which was crowned with a new wooden tower. The gate-guard looked closely at Corwynal, but one man leading a weary horse posed little threat, so he let them enter then pointed to where Corwynal might find Trystan, recommending he be quick about it if he had a message, because Trystan was leaving as soon as the moon was up.

Inside the fort, the improvements were even more noticeable. The horse lines had been moved away from the water supply, latrines dug in the down-slope, tents placed in straight lines, stables erected and roofed with bracken. All of this was evidence of an efficient quartermaster. *He doesn't even need me for that*, Corwynal thought bleakly. Not that it mattered.

Nothing mattered except stopping Trystan.

The sun had almost set by then, but the fort was still busy, men tending to their mounts, or carrying water and fodder. Fires had been lit, and barley bannocks were being baked in ovens set against the walls. The smell made Corwynal's stomach crawl with hunger, despite the dry apprehension in his throat as he approached the tent he'd been directed to, one on the end of a row but no bigger than the others.

'If you've a message from the Mote, I'm to tell you he doesn't want to hear it. He's busy, see?' The man who stood on guard jerked his head at the tent. Corwynal could hear Trystan speaking to someone in tones of endearment. The Cruithin girl, no doubt. *He doesn't need me, and he doesn't want me.*

'I'll wait until he's less busy,' he said, preparing himself for a long wait, but Trystan must have heard his voice for the tent flap was thrown back, and Corwynal found himself face to face, not with the boy he'd come to protect, but a man who regarded him with neither surprise nor welcome.

'What happened to your head?' Trystan asked idly, clearly caring about that as little as he cared about Corwynal's arrival.

'I was knocked unconscious last night and tied up.' Corwynal shrugged as if this was an everyday occurrence.

Trystan gestured for the guard to move out of earshot, but didn't invite Corwynal into the tent. 'Why?'

'Someone didn't want me to interfere.'

'You think it was me?' Trystan's voice was sharp now.

'No, Trys. I think someone in Galloway wants you dead.'

Trystan laughed grimly at that. 'That's no surprise! So, you were imprisoned? I thought you were . . .' He made a dismissive gesture with one hand.

'Sulking? I wasn't. I was put out of action by someone who overestimated my powers of interference.'

Trystan narrowed his eyes but said nothing, then stepped aside from the opening to the tent and, with a gesture, invited him to enter. 'Would you like something to eat?'

Corwynal hesitated. 'I'd hoped to speak to you alone.'

Trystan grinned. 'I insist,' he said, then turned to someone inside the tent. 'Get up, you lazy bitch!'

Corwynal stiffened. Nevertheless, he went in, only to see, lying on an old cloak on the bed, not the girl he'd expected but a white hound-puppy wearing a studded leather collar. The dog was bigger than Corwynal remembered and considerably cleaner, but it was the one he'd forced Trystan to take.

'You kept her?' The dog sat up expectantly, wagging its tail.

'Of course! You gave me no choice. But – confess it – you thought I was talking to the girl!'

'Well, yes. I did think that. What did you do with her?'

'Sent her back to her mother. She didn't want to go.' Trystan pushed bread and cheese towards Corwynal and a pitcher of thin ale. His sick apprehension hadn't entirely vanished, but hunger displaced it for a while, though his head still ached.

'You still don't understand, do you?' Trystan asked, sitting down on the pallet. The dog pawed at his hand until he began to fondle its ears. 'You thought it was all my fault, the burning and the raping. Well, I suppose, ultimately, I was responsible. In Selgovia I picked my own men, but I didn't have time for that here. I was in too much of a temper with you, so I took what I was offered and then, once I was here, I couldn't be in two places at once. I chose to clean up the western side of the hills. There were outlaws up on the crags and dislodging them took longer than I'd expected, but I was patient – unlike the man I'd chosen to take command in the east. The Cruithin weren't exactly co-operating, but neither were they harbouring the outlaws. He chose not to believe that, and his justice, as he saw it, was swift. When I returned and found out what he'd done, my justice was equally swift. You probably saw him, down by the river.'

Trystan spoke calmly, coldly even, but his mask of concealment cracked a little and he dropped his eyes. 'I'd like to tell you I found it hard. But it wasn't. I was angry, not so much at what he'd allowed to be done, but because he'd taken my reputation away from me.' He took a deep breath and looked up, under control once more. 'I needed a gesture, you see, something to shock and rein in the men. Something to demonstrate to the Cruithin that rape and burning would be punished and that I'd make restitution. Hanging him was the gesture I needed, but none of that was the real reason. It was simply that I was angry, and not just with him, or even myself. I was angry with you.'

'Trys, I—'

Trystan threw up a hand 'Let me speak, because I need you to understand. I was angry with you because, yet again, you judged me without waiting to hear my side of things. Then I was angry because you stayed away. I know I told you I didn't want to see you again, but surely you didn't believe that? So I came back to the Mote, only to find that no-one knew where you were. I assumed you were avoiding me. At least *that* wasn't true. But I'm still angry, and I've had lots of time to think about my reasons. I'm angry because you've tried to turn me into something I'm not, because there are times when you think you've succeeded, and then I disappoint you. I *have* disappointed you, haven't I? I've disappointed myself, because I'd really like to be the person you imagine. And I've tried, Corwynal. Believe me, I've tried. But I keep falling short of your high standards and haven't been what you wanted me to be. Instead, I've just been myself: wrong-headed and flawed, selfish and ambitious and . . . and human. I'm no hero, though that's what I'd like to be for your sake. I crave glory, but I know I don't deserve it. I didn't accept the challenge because I needed to prove myself to you, though I'd like that to be the reason. I accepted because I wanted to accept, even though I can see what it's doing to you. And because I need to be free.'

'Free? Of me?'

'Of your expectations. I've accepted who I am. Why can't you?'

'Trys, I—'

'No! Let me finish! I accepted the challenge to show you who I am, what I am, what I want. I'm not a child anymore. I can make my own decisions and can't be ruled by concern over what you might think. I can't let your fears for me stop me from living!'

'Or dying?' Corwynal asked. 'Trys, listen to me. Everything you've said is true. There have been times when you've disappointed me, when you've done and said things I didn't understand. I brought you up to be a king, and there were times when I thought I'd failed, and if I've seemed critical and resentful, it's because I blamed myself for that failure, not you. But I didn't bring you up to be everything I failed to become. I just wanted you to be the best so you'd have the best chance of living. You accused me of resenting that I had to give up my ambitions for you, but it's not true. I gave them up willingly and have never begrudged it, never looked for thanks or repayment except in one thing – that you live your life. If I've ever interfered in that life and, yes, I admit I have, it's because I wanted to protect you. You're only seventeen—'

'Eighteen now.'

'Seventeen, eighteen, what does it matter? It's too young to throw your life away on this pointless challenge. I want to see you live, in any way you choose. Be anything you want, even something I don't approve of, and I'll accept it. As long as you *live*. I want to see you grow older and fall in love with some beautiful woman, have children with her—'

'Not with Essylt then,' Trystan said wryly.

'With anyone you want, and I won't try to stop you, as long as you're alive to do it. Give up this challenge, Trys! Because if you go through with it, you'll die.'

'You don't have much confidence in either your training or my abilities.'

'If it was any other fight than this, I'd trust you absolutely, but I've dreamt this, Trys, so many times. There's a man with a black ship on his tunic, a beach, gulls. I've seen you fight him, seen you lose your sword. I've seen the blow that kills you, a backhand from the left, deep beneath the ribs. I've seen his sword shattering on bone, and I've seen the blood, too much to stop.'

Trystan stared at him. 'You've dreamt my death?' he asked. 'You've seen the man who kills me?'

'Not clearly, but it has to be this Morholt. He's huge, Trys, bigger than Aelfric. You can't beat him.'

'How long have you dreamt this?'

'Ever since you joined the war-band. I didn't know what it meant, and I didn't recognise the black ship until last summer. Then I thought it was over, for Feargus bore the sign and he was defeated. I believed that was what the dream meant, and that I'd managed to change your fate. But I haven't, because it's not over after all.'

Trystan took him by the shoulders and shook him angrily. 'Is this why you tried to keep me in Lothian? Why you didn't want me to go to war? Why you threw yourself at Feargus, alone, and almost got yourself killed! You *fool*, Corwynal! Why didn't you *tell* me?'

'It was my burden. I didn't want it to be yours too. And I wasn't sure. But now I am. Don't go, Trys! Let me go in your place.'

Trystan looked at him steadily, his head tilted to one side, and for a moment Corwynal thought he might agree.

'No,' he said quietly.

'But I just told you—'

'That's why. Don't you understand? This is what I've been talking about. My need to be free of your expectations, your fears. I have to change what we are to one another. No – listen to me.' He crouched down at Corwynal's feet as he had when he'd been a boy and put a hand on his knee. 'Blaize told me you saved my life when I was born,' he went on. 'He said you gave up everything for me. You didn't want to burden me with a dream, yet you've burdened me with that sacrifice, no matter how willingly made. And now you want to burden me with another? You seriously expect me to let you fight a man you dreamt defeated me? Why should you succeed when I didn't? Listen, Corwynal – you've been my guardian and tutor, but these roles are over. You've tried to be a brother and failed, but I never minded because I don't want you for my brother. I want you to be something else entirely. I've wanted it for years, but never had the courage to ask. I'm going to ask you now, though I'm still afraid you can't be the man I need you to be.'

Corwynal stared at him. Did he know? Had he always known? And didn't hate him for it? *I'm your father, Trystan.* Finally, the words could be said without the fear of what would follow. And if he claimed Trystan as his son, he could demand a son's obedience and force Trystan to let him go to the island in his place.

'I know what you're going to say.' He gripped Trystan's hand tightly as the last of the sunset blurred his vision. 'And, yes, I can be that man.'

'Can you?' Trystan returned the grip. 'Can you really be my friend?'

His friend. The light sharpened as the tears that had welled spilled down his face, and he fell back into the shadows once more, his relief thinning like candle-smoke until it vanished, and only the fear remained. *Not his father. His friend.*

'Can you be unjudging, uncritical, offering advice but not expecting it to be taken?' Trystan went on. 'Can you trust me? Can I trust you? Because that's what it means. Shall we try? I've decided to accept this challenge. As my friend, you've advised against it, and, after due consideration, I've rejected your advice. You've offered to go in my place, and I've decided to reject that offer. So, assuming you're still my friend, will you come with me and not interfere? As my friend, will you make me that promise? Because, I tell you now, I'm going to the island to fight the Morholt, and either you give me your promise, or I leave you behind.'

'You expect me to stand by and watch you be killed?'

'You don't have to go, but if you do, I'd have you witness the will of the gods – and not interfere. Can you do that?'

And so Corwynal was defeated, not by the Morholt, or fate, or even the gods, but by Trystan himself. He was asking Corwynal to let him live, and so watch him die. Corwynal turned away and looked, for no particular reason, at the puppy. She gazed up at him with the appealing eyes of a dog, but all Corwynal could see were a stag's eyes looking back at him.

You asked for his life and I gave it to you, Arddu reminded him.

A year of life, for which he should be grateful, but for which he was now expected to make this bitter, bitter payment – to give Trystan the promise he demanded or be denied the chance to be with him at the end.

'Yes, Trystan,' he said, humbled by the boy he'd created, the man who'd gone so far beyond his own imaginings. 'I can do that.'

Trystan's fingers tightened on Corwynal's for a moment, and then he let him go.

'I've fought some battles in my time, but none so hard as that one!' he observed lightly. 'Finish your meal. I've some small matters to attend to before we leave.'

'Can't your quartermaster see to everything for you?' Corwynal asked with little interest. How could Trystan expect him to eat? But part of their agreement was that he pretend.

'I don't have one. Where would I find a quartermaster to meet your exacting standards, and therefore my own? I do that work myself.' Trystan smiled ruefully. 'And hard work it is too, but I was trained by a perfectionist. So, if you'll excuse me, I'll just make sure everything is perfect.'

Corwynal, Trystan, and a few of Trystan's men, rode through the remains of a night lit by flaring torches and the sliver of a moon, then a day of short sharp showers blown on a blustery wind that had shifted to the south-east. The tracks west of the River Fleet were even worse than those between the Mote and Trystan's fort, but Rhydian was fresh and Corwynal, who'd left the exhausted Janthe behind, was mounted on a raking sorrel with a high opinion of its abilities but which carried him safely, if not comfortably, over forty miles across country. Even so, it was late afternoon before they rode down to the Loch that sheltered the bigger vessels of Galloway's fleet, and which was overlooked by Andrydd's fort, perched on the side of a hill above the harbour.

'We're not stopping,' Trystan said once they'd reached the scattering of dwellings that lay between the fort and the wharves and sheds of the port. They made their way down a narrow alley to a sailor's tavern close to the inner harbour where they dismounted. 'The Scots' ship had a fair wind, and I don't want to keep them waiting...'

But Corwynal knew that wasn't the reason for the unseemly haste. Trystan had ridden through the night to outrun any possible message from the Mote. He'd know as well as Corwynal that Marc would have sobered up by now and come to his senses. He was bound to have sent someone to Loch Ryan to stop Trystan from leaving, by sea most likely, for the wind had been fair, and a ship could have come as swiftly by sea as they had overland. It wasn't too late for all this to be stopped, if not by Corwynal, then by Marc. Then it occurred to him that Marc would send Andrydd, unaware that, far from stopping Trystan, the war-band leader of Galloway, hoping Trystan might die in this challenge, would do everything in his power to ensure he went to the Rock. Indeed, it had probably been Andrydd who'd arranged for Corwynal to be got out of the way two nights before. If so, he'd overestimated Corwynal's powers of persuasion, since here he was, readying himself to witness a dreamt-of death.

I can't do this! The refrain had drummed through his head all the way from Trystan's fort, a counterpoint to the beating of hooves. *I can't do this!* The rising panic took him by the throat and robbed his legs of their remaining strength, and he sat down heavily on the edge of a horse-trough. Trystan, who'd despatched one of his men to the harbour and another to speak to the tavern keeper, eyed him narrowly.

'You look terrible!'

'I'm fine,' Corwynal said between gritted teeth, though he wasn't. The previous day's ride had been bad enough, but now his head was aching vilely. It was fortunate the sorrel had known what it was about, for he hadn't, and it was a miracle he'd managed to stay in the saddle at all since his vision was blurred, and he'd felt nauseous long before they'd reached the sea. Now, seeing the ships tossing at their moorings, and smelling the indefinable mixture of rotting seaweed and bilge-water that hung about all harbours, he knew he was going to throw up.

Trystan looked at him steadily, then nodded, as if coming to a decision, and rose to his feet. 'If you say so. I've a few things to see to before we leave, so could you take the dog into the barn and tie her up? I don't think I'll take her to the Rock after all.'

Trystan had carried the puppy in a basket strapped to his saddle, and it had whined all the way and been sick more than once. Corwynal knew how it felt.

'I don't know why you brought it in the first place.'

'I didn't trust anyone at the fort to look after her properly,' Trystan said. He exchanged a few words with his two remaining men, then watched as Corwynal tied the dog to the central post that held up the roof. 'But I trust you.'

The change in Trystan's voice should have warned him, but his head was aching too badly for thought, and, when his arms were grabbed from behind, all he felt was relief. Marc had sent someone after all, and, instead of ordering Trystan not to go, they'd chosen a simpler way of stopping him from leaving. So Corwynal barely struggled as he was tied to the same post as the dog, who was yelping with excitement, thinking this was all a game. But, far from being tied up himself, Trystan just stood there, his arms folded across his chest, then nodded for the two men who'd tied Corwynal up – not Marc's but his own – to leave.

'I'm sorry, Corwynal. I trust you to look after the dog, but that's all. I've been thinking about it all the way from the fort, and I don't think I can trust you not to break your promise. Oh, I know you'd try very hard to watch and not interfere, but it's not in your nature, and you're not sure you can. So how can I trust you if you can't trust yourself?' Then he grinned. 'Do you know, I'm almost grateful to whoever knocked you out and tied you up at the Mote because otherwise I wouldn't have thought of this. I expect it was Andrydd, and I never thought I'd be grateful to him for anything. But maybe it was Ferdiad. I liked him, didn't you? That music! I hadn't imagined such music could exist outside battle. It didn't affect me, but I saw the whole hall respond. One day I'll learn to play like that.' He smiled at Corwynal. 'I'm not going to die, you know. I'll live to play like Ferdiad, to fall in love with some beautiful and, for all our sakes, unattainable, woman. Have faith in me, Corwynal.'

'Please, Trys! Don't leave me behind. I beg you—'

'Don't!' Trystan crouched down beside him. 'Don't beg or plead because that isn't in your nature either. How can I let you come with me? You're concussed. I should have seen it before and not let you ride half-way across Galloway. Anyway, you know you'd be sick all the way to the Rock. So you'll stay here and I'll fight the better for knowing you aren't watching me and hating every moment. And I *will* win. I can't tell you how I know, but I do.'

He rose to his feet, raised one arm in the salute of one warrior to another, then turned, left the barn and barred the door from the outside. Corwynal called after him, cursing him by the name of all the gods he knew, and he cursed Arddu too for abandoning him when he needed him most. Then he wept, pleading and promising anything, if only Trystan would let him go. But all that answered him was silence.

'Row, you useless turds!'

Aelfric felt the muscles in his shoulders crack as he hauled on the oar. The Goose tilted to the waves as Maredydd, at the steering oar, angled the ship towards the shore, hoping to slip past the Scots warship that was coming straight for them.

'Row for your lives, you bastards!'

Bastard yourself! Aelfric thought, something he'd been thinking ever since the wind had backed into the south-east and, instead of seeking shelter in some port along the coast until the wind was favourable once more, Maredydd had ordered the sail hauled down and the oars manned, then had steered them right into the path of this warship. *Stupid greedy bastard!* Did Maredydd imagine Marc of Galloway was going to pay him for old news? Because it turned out there was no Scots fleet, no Strathclyde fleet, and even this news was almost a month old by then and therefore worthless. The only other piece of news, that the Scots tribute ship had set sail, would likely arrive long before they did, and so be worthless too. Nevertheless, Maredydd was determined to get to the Mote, regardless of the weather and the opinions of his crew, which, to his own surprise, still included Aelfric.

Bastard! he muttered, meaning Corwynal now, for he was still bitter about being given away. So what the fuck was he doing going back to Galloway, especially when the trip had proved, and was proving, so disastrous?

'A difficult harbour, Loch Gair,' Maredydd had said as they'd approached the narrows of the sea-loch that led to Dunadd's eastern port. Aelfric, eyeing the entrance, had thought it would be difficult enough in perfect conditions, but they'd been approaching with a fluky southerly wind behind them, and Thunor knew what sort of current under their keel. 'Maybe we should have headed for Crionan . . .' Maredydd was saying just as the Goose struck the rock. They could all have drowned, but, though the blow had breached the hull and dislodged their mast, the rising tide had swept them to safety and, in the end, bailing like mad and half-submerged, they'd made it to the shore. Only one man had died, crushed beneath the falling mast, but quite a few were hurt, Aelfric among them, his arm slashed open by a huge splinter of wood. He could feel the wound twinge as he pulled on the oar, but the stitches seemed to be holding.

'I want you to rest that arm for at least a month,' the woman who'd sown it up in the priests' place near Dunadd had said. She was some sort of priestess of their god, but a nice woman all the same. Not his type, being quite elderly, but she seemed to know what she was doing. Except resting his arm hadn't turned out to be an option.

'Come on, you useless cretins, put your backs into it!'

Aelfric craned his neck around on the return stroke. The warship was closer now, its sail bellied in the rising wind, and he could make out the symbol of a black ship.

'Row, curse you!' The Goose was coursing along now, cutting through the breaking waves. Maredydd heaved the steering oar over until they were heading dangerously close to the shore, but the Scots ship didn't alter its course to cut them off, even though it had the wind, and they watched, open-mouthed, as it carried on north, surging past them as if they were invisible.

'Well, fuck me!' Maredydd said, speaking for them all and

signalling for the drummer to slow the oar-beat until they were barely making way. 'They're heading for The Rock!'

They'd passed The Rock earlier that day, an island they'd seen in a squall, fringed with breakers. It seemed to rise straight out of the sea-bed, though it must have holding ground, for a big ship had been anchored below the northern cliffs in the island's lee.

'That must have been the tribute ship!' Maredydd exclaimed. 'And that warship's gone to meet it. The sodding Scots have taken their tribute to The Rock!' His eyes were gleaming with avarice because this news would be worth a great deal. 'Row, you fuckers! We'll make for Loch Ryan and send word from there . . .'

And so, soaked and exhausted, they finally reached the shelter of the deep sea-loch that was the base for the Galloway fleet, only to see a ship, a trader from the lines of its hull, pass them as the Goose rowed down the loch to the harbour at the southern end. The trader was heading north, riding light, and therefore empty – which meant Galloway already knew where the tribute was, and that ship was going to collect it. Which meant their journey had all been for nothing.

Aelfric exchanged a few explicit words with Maredydd before heading for the nearest tavern. *What am I doing here?* he wondered, as he made inroads into a flagon of ale and a double portion of stewed mutton. Why hadn't he found a ship heading east from the Scots' lands, then made his way overland to Lothian? Why, in Thunor's name, had he sworn that stupid fucking oath? *Bring him back to me.* But he *had* sworn it, so, now he was back in Galloway, he intended to do just that, whether the Caledonian liked it or not. Except it seemed he'd missed the bloody man, for the talk in the tavern was that he and Trystan had been sailing north on that trader.

'A Challenge!' Everyone was talking about it. Trystan of Galloway – of *Galloway* now, Aelfric noticed – had challenged some Scots warrior for the tribute. And they were to fight on The Rock.

Fuck! Aelfric was aggrieved at missing the fun, but surprised too. Had Corwynal really let Trystan accept this challenge? Being of a suspicious mind, Aelfric made further enquiries at the dock, and learned that people had seen the Caledonian arrive with Trystan but no-one had seen him leave. Indeed, his horse was still in the stable, apparently, and, when Aelfric went to check, he found the man's weapons still strapped to the beast's saddle. *He's still here*, Aelfric concluded, but didn't see what – or why – he should do anything about it, so he made his way back to the tavern, passing, as he did so, a barn at the back of a yard, guarded by two men. What, Aelfric wondered idly, were they guarding? Might it be a man? One who otherwise might have tried to prevent a certain challenge?

Aelfric shrugged and returned to the tavern where he had another flagon of ale and resigned himself to a long wait in reasonable comfort. Sooner or later, Trystan would be back, and then the Caledonian would be set free. There was no reason for Aelfric to get involved. No reason whatsoever.

20

THE BLACK SHIP

He's dreaming of the island. He hasn't been there, but now he knows where it is – Carraig Ealasaid, the island with the narrow beach of shingle where the sea crashes in long booming rolls. He smells weed rotting along the high tide mark, hears the grief of a snowstorm of gulls. He doesn't know the man who'll be waiting there, though now he knows his name: The Morholt. But knowing makes no difference. He still stands there, watching and watching and doing nothing...

Corwynal woke with a gasp that turned into a sob when he realised he was dreaming and that, far from being on the island to witness his dream of Trystan's fight and death, he was imprisoned in a barn in Loch Ryan. He'd been tied to a post because Trystan knew him too well. Despite his promise not to interfere, he wouldn't be able to prevent himself from trying to change his dream. But how could he change anything now?

'Curse you! Let me out!' He banged on the door with fists already bloodied from doing just that. His voice was hoarse from shouting, but the men guarding the door didn't reply.

They'd orders to let him out in the morning, they'd told him the previous evening. 'It'll be too late by then!' But that, of course, was the point.

It hadn't taken him long to untie the knots, but getting out of the barn proved impossible. The building was a substantial one, its single door barred and well-guarded, the roof supported by tall planed uprights that gave no purchase, so there was no possibility of reaching the thatch to see if he could force his way through. His only hope had been to persuade the men to let him go, but his persuasions had been as successful as his curses, and, after a time, he wasn't even sure the guards were still there. So he took to speaking to the dog – if it was a dog. He hadn't forgotten how he'd seen Arddu looking out of the animal's eyes.

'Why have you abandoned me? Why now, when I need you?'

You abandoned me. You forgot me and were glad never to hear my voice – until you needed me. Now you need me once more, but why should I help you when you are so inconstant?

'I'll do anything, give you anything. *Anything!*' He'd promised that once before.

To free you?

'To save Trystan, of course!'

To save him for what? To live the life you want him to lead?

'To do anything.' It was the promise he'd made to Trystan. 'It doesn't matter, as long as he's alive to do it.'

Like Trystan, the God wasn't convinced, and Arddu fell silent once more, withdrawing himself until he was no more than an odd half-beat in Corwynal's pulse. He slid down the door and dropped his face into his hands. The dog settled her chin on his thigh, sighed and closed her eyes, and weariness overwhelmed him. *I mustn't fall asleep*, he told himself. For if he slept, he might miss the moment, the moment when . . .

Surely he'd recognise the moment? Even if he wasn't on the Island, impotently watching, surely he'd know?

The dog sat up abruptly, gave a single bark, and got to her feet. There were voices outside, his guards speaking and laughing, then an exclamation and a cry, and the dog began to bark in earnest. The door-bar slid up, the door swung open and a single, very big man stood there.

'Well?' Aelfric asked crossly. 'Are you coming or not?'

⁂

It had been stupidly easy. For a start, the guards were so bored that when Aelfric had sauntered out with a jug and a couple of beakers, they hadn't even been suspicious. Yet why should they be? The Caledonian didn't have any friends who were likely to try and free him. Not that Aelfric was the man's friend. Or that he really needed to be rescued. Trystan was going to win, wasn't he? This Morholt bloke didn't stand a chance. Did he? *Did he?*

It was only a little doubt, but it had been enough. So, after chatting with the men guarding the barn, Aelfric grabbed one by the tunic and send him sprawling into a woodpile. A satisfying uppercut lifted the other man off his feet and felled him like a baulk of timber. Then Aelfric hauled up the bar and pulled open the door to find not only the Caledonian but – if Aelfric could believe his eyes – a little white dog.

'Arddu?' the man muttered at him, blinking in the torchlight. 'Aelfric?'

'Who the fuck did you think it was?' He grabbed Corwynal by the arm and yanked him out of the building. 'Quickly!' The guard by the woodpile was struggling to his feet, and the other man was groaning and feeling his jaw. 'This way!' Aelfric dragged the Caledonian down the narrow alley that ran between the barn and the tavern, kicked over a couple of barrels to block the way, then jinked around the back to where, earlier, he'd stashed both his and Corwynal's gear. 'Catch!' he said, throwing the man his bundle. 'Now run!'

They pounded their way north, through the outskirts of the village and along the track that wound its way up the eastern side of the loch. Aelfric had noticed the place earlier when the Goose had rowed into harbour – a huddle of houses with nets spread out on the rocks, barrels of fish stacked above the tide line, racks of drying herrings, and several fishing skiffs drawn up at the top of the beach.

Men were running down the track after them; it was going to be close. 'This one!' He chose a skiff at random, threw his bundle into the bilges and grabbed hold of the gunwale. 'Come on, man! Help me.'

Corwynal took hold of the other side, and together they dragged the little boat down to the water. 'Can we catch up with the ship?' he asked.

The skiff was little more than a rowing boat, with a mast and furled sail, and a canvas shelter over the bows. So, no, it couldn't catch up with the Galloway ship. Nevertheless, the skiff was light, and, with the wind behind them, and if they weren't swamped on the way, they might just make it to the Rock. Not in time, of course, but since Trystan was going to win, that wouldn't matter. Then Aelfric's little doubt resurfaced. If he lost then, yes, they'd be too late. Now, however, wasn't the time to tell the Caledonian that.

'With me at the helm?' Aelfric boasted as they reached the edge of the surf. And not a moment too soon, for their pursuers, five of them now, had reached the village and were heading for the beach. Ahead of them, barking furiously as if this was all a great game, was the little white dog.

'Wait!' Corwynal insisted.

'Don't be an idiot!' Aelfric jumped in as the boat lifted to the first wave, then grabbed Corwynal's gear from him and threw it into the bilge. 'Get in, man!'

But still the Caledonian waited as the dog skidded down the shingle and threw itself, still barking, into the surf. He seized it by the collar, tossed it into the skiff and sprawled in after it, half-swamping the boat in the process.

'She's Trystan's,' he said, as if this explained everything.

'Fucking idiot!' Aelfric yelled at him as the boat ground on the shingle and the men pounded towards them, but the next wave lifted them free and, with one strong sweep of the oars, they were in deeper water and out of reach.

'You're mad,' Aelfric said feelingly, as he pulled on the oars to drive them out into the channel where they could raise the sail. 'We're both mad.'

Corwynal spent the rest of the night huddled beneath the canvas shelter, alternately throwing up and shuddering with the cold. The dog, equally sick, whined miserably beside him. Aelfric was humming some dirge in his own tongue and crying out to the boat as a man will encourage a horse. The rain was streaming from his face and beard, but he looked more alive than Corwynal had ever seen him. He was a man in his element, as Corwynal was out of his, but he thanked the gods for it for, by his skills, Aelfric drove them on through the wind-torn night with only fleeting glimpses of the stars to show the way.

He must have fallen asleep eventually because when Aelfric shook him awake, there was a little light in the sky. The waves were higher now, their white caps creaming all around them and occasionally spilling over the sides. But still the boat surged on, the sail cracking and straining on the crest of each wave, then hissing down the face of the breaker, only to wallow in the trough as the sail fell slack, before rising slowly, oh so slowly, as the next swell lifted the stern.

'Bail.' Aelfric thrust a leather bucket at him and nodded at the water sloshing about the bilge. 'Or we'll all drown.'

The wind was keening like a grieving widow by then and was no longer the ally that had driven them north in pursuit of Trystan's ship. Rather, it was an enemy determined to prevent them from reaching the Rock. For the first time, Corwynal was afraid they might not make it.

'Here.' Aelfric thrust a piece of bread at him. 'Eat it, or you'll be useless.'

Corwynal already knew he'd be useless because he was struggling against the will of the gods themselves. Yet he had to try, so he took the bread and chewed it reluctantly. Swallowing, however, proved to be impossible, and he gave the rest to the dog.

Aelfric tutted disapprovingly. 'What the fuck did you bring that animal for?'

'I told you. She's Trystan's dog.'

'Got a name?'

'Trystan will give her a name,' he insisted, determined Trystan would live to give the dog a name, if for no other reason. Aelfric rolled his eyes and, just then, a larger than usual wave lifted the boat up, and Corwynal peered ahead, hoping to see Trystan's ship in the distance. He saw nothing. Had they overtaken the heavier ship in the night? Or had the weather swept it off course? Perhaps the wind had driven the Scots warship away from the island. Maybe he could still get there before Trystan.

'How much further?' he asked as the boat slipped down into the trough.

Aelfric shrugged. 'It should be around here somewhere, but in this murk we could sail straight past it. Wind's easing though,' he added, measuring some subtlety in the air of which Corwynal was unaware. 'Which means it'll clear, thanks be to Thunor, since I don't want to run into it without warning. Saw it on the way south, a bloody great rock, steep cliffs, deep water. Precious little holding ground, I'll wager.'

'There's a bay,' Corwynal said. 'A shingle beach and a grassy place below a cliff.'

'You've been there?'

'I've dreamt it.'

A year before, Aelfric might have scoffed at that, but he'd been in the lands of the Britons for too long. He opened his mouth to ask a question, but thought better of it. Then he lifted his eyes to the horizon and gave a grunt of satisfaction.

'There!' He pointed north. 'Dead ahead!'

Corwynal wiped the spray out of his eyes, followed Aelfric's finger and saw something emerge from the blurred horizon and grow gradually more substantial – a dark grey mass lying between the white-streaked grey of the sea and grey-streaked white of the sky. It was the Rock, Carraig Ealasaid, the place of Challenge, the place of Ending.

They were too late.

As they approached the island the little bay opened out and the ships came into view – first the Scots warship with the black ship sign on a pennant flying from the mast-head, then a second, a bigger trading vessel bearing the swan sign of

Dalriada. Even then Corwynal still had hope, for the two ships, anchored uneasily behind a spit of rock that lay at the southern end of that grassy place beneath the cliffs, seemed to be alone. Then, as the current drew the little skiff closer to the island, he saw a third ship anchored further away, this one flying the raven of Galloway.

'You knew we'd be too late!' he accused Aelfric.

The Angle leant towards him and put a hand on his arm. 'Listen, man, I said I'd bring you here. I didn't say when. It's not my fault the wind dropped. Hey! What are you doing?!'

Corwynal had slid aft to the rowing bench and made a grab for the oars. 'It can't be too late. Come on, help me make this thing go faster! I have to get there . . .'

Aelfric looked at him with the same compassion Corwynal had seen in Lot's eyes long ago in a glade in Lothian, but Lot had been wrong then, and Aelfric was wrong now. He had to be.

The Angle scowled at him, but he hauled down the sail, lashed the steering oar and took his place on the rowing bench. As they rowed towards the island, the tide took the skiff west of the bay and grounded them on a little scoop of shingle among the rocks, out of sight of the main anchorage. Corwynal abandoned his oar and plunged into the water, up to his waist, and struggled for the shore.

'Wait, you stupid Caledonian!' Aelfric jumped after him and pushed him down into the shallows. Waves broke over him until he was choking and spluttering. Only once he'd stopped struggling did Aelfric let him go.

'Wait!' The Angle dragged him out of the sea and up the tiny beach. 'Do you want to get us both killed? They'll see us!'

With an effort, Corwynal calmed himself and crawled up the rocks to look down into the main bay. A rib of rock obscured most of the beach, but he could see men posted on outcrops and along the top of the cliffs, Galloway men and Dalriad men, all of them armed with bows and ready to see that neither side interfered with the challenge. No-one had noticed the little skiff approach the Rock, because everyone's attention was on the grassy glade that lay out of sight above the steep shingle bank. Corwynal couldn't see what they were watching, but, between the crash and rumble of each wave, he heard the sound of blades clashing together. *I'm not too late!* He began to scramble over the rocks that lay between him and the bay, but Aelfric dragged him back.

'You have a plan?'

A plan? Corwynal stared at him.

'We need a plan,' Aelfric insisted. 'You say you dreamt this?'

'I didn't dream those men.'

'Did you imagine there wouldn't be witnesses? Someone to stop some mad half-Caledonian bastard with a death-wish from interfering? *Think!*' Aelfric's pale blue eyes bored into Corwynal's as he struggled to do just that. 'They haven't seen us,' Aelfric pointed out. 'So we'll go back to the boat, tie up that fucking dog, and collect the weapons you seem to have forgotten about. Although I don't know what we can do with them. That's up to you. But there has to be a plan.'

Corwynal let Aelfric lead him back to the skiff and he tied up the dog and gave her the rest of the bread to keep her quiet, then buckled on his sword. But he still couldn't think.

In his dream, he'd seen the end of the fight, but never the beginning. Now, however, hearing the clash of sword on shield, he knew it had barely begun. There were pauses while each combatant took the measure of the other, followed by the swift exchanges of men not yet exhausted. Trystan would be dancing out of reach, swerving as Corwynal had taught him. The

Morholt was a big man, but Trystan had sparred with Aelfric who was bigger than anyone Corwynal had ever met, and that would give Trystan an edge, one Corwynal had almost denied him by advising him to kill the Angle back in Lothian. Now he closed his eyes at the thought. He'd been so certain, and so wrong, because, right then, there was no-one else he'd rather have at his side than Aelfric.

'Over there,' the Angle whispered, nodding at a place on the cliffs where a low bluff ran out into the water and marked the western end of the bay. 'We'll have to keep low. Careful now. Slowly.' He was gentling Corwynal as if he was a nervous horse, as if he knew that all Corwynal wanted to do was charge through the cordon of men, screaming Caledonian curses at them all, and throw himself between Trystan and the Morholt. 'This way.' Aelfric slithered down the rocks, and Corwynal crawled after him through shingle and boulders and fly-infested seaweed, through the decomposing carcass of a seal, slimy rock-pools, and channels where the waves surged and tried to tear him from the rocks. By the time they reached the edge of the bay, he was aching and bloody, but he had a plan at last. It wasn't much of a plan, but it would do. It was a simple plan, yet sometimes those are the best. He remembered the day he and Trystan had fought Aelfric – the battle by the river when their swords had sung in harmony, their hearts beating as one, the same music ringing in their ears. They'd been one soul then, one man, fighting a giant. And Corwynal remembered a promise made to a god. *Anything!* Now, with a pulse of certainty, he knew what that promise really meant. It meant *everything*.

He took a deep breath and stood up, in full view of the men watching the fight. Behind him, Aelfric swore viciously. Corwynal felt eyes fall on him, sensed weapons being raised, but he had eyes only for the two men in the circle of grass and moss fighting to the sound of gulls. The smell of kelp was strong, and he felt sick. There was a foul taste of bile in his throat, and fear throbbed all through his body as he watched the two men fighting the fight he'd seen in his dream. No, that wasn't true. There was only one man worth watching, the boy with the grace and power, the one with the bright golden promise. Corwynal's heart swelled up in his throat as it hadn't in the dream, and his fear vanished, in spite of the watching men with arrows nocked to strings drawn tight and pointed at his chest, ready to loose if he moved.

'What the fuck are you doing?' Aelfric hissed from below him, out of sight of the bowmen.

'Just watching,' he replied, his voice unnaturally calm. 'Can't a man watch his son die?'

'Watch his—!? You mad bastard, you—!'

Corwynal was no longer listening. *Arddu!* he breathed as he stepped forward. He didn't draw his sword because it wasn't necessary. All he had to do was step forward and keep moving. All he had to do was act.

He was grabbed from behind, and a big hand clamped across his mouth. Corwynal kicked out and bit the hand, and, though Aelfric swore, he didn't let him go until he'd dragged him down the slope. Then he swung him around and struck him hard across the face, knocking him to the ground, and dived on top of him to smash him into the shingle. His knee was in Corwynal's stomach, his hands pinning his shoulders to the sand, his eyes snapping with fury.

'You fucking idiot! He might have seen you!'

'I wanted him to see me!' Corwynal was almost sobbing with frustration. 'I wanted them all to see me!'

'You'd have been dead in two strides.'

'More. I reckoned on more. I just need the Morholt to see

me. A moment's distraction, that's all Trystan needs. Let me go, Aelfric. Please! I have to do something!'

'No! Trystan thinks you're safe in Galloway. If he sees you, it will be the end for him, because he'll not watch you walk to your death. And nor will I.'

Corwynal began to weep then, because Aelfric was right, because fate can't be changed, because the gods might make bargains, but they don't keep them. He'd offered Arddu his life in exchange for Trystan's, but the God had turned him down. Now all he could do was watch, because that's all the gods do. They watch men struggle against their fate. They tempt them to make empty bargains and cross thresholds of life and death that don't truly exist. Corwynal had come to the Rock determined to act, but in the end he could do nothing. Nothing but watch Trystan be cut down, then be with him at the end, and tell him . . . tell him everything.

Aelfric let him go and turned away, shaking his head at the depths of Corwynal's despair. 'Pull yourself together, man,' he growled. 'It's not over yet.'

All he can do is crawl up the shingle bank until he can see what's happening. All he can do is watch and watch and do nothing. The past disappears because the past doesn't matter. So too does the future, because he can't face it. All that matters is the present, taking shape moment by moment as if he hadn't already dreamt it. He sees each blow as if he's seeing it for the first time. He sees them blocked, or not. He hears metal clang against metal or, sickeningly, slide into flesh. He hears the grunts of effort and the cries of pain. He watches blood flow, sees the Morholt's black ship symbol vanish as his tunic reddens from a slash in his neck below his helmet. They're tiring now, Trystan limping, favouring his left leg, and there's a shallow gash in his sword-arm that's bleeding freely. It isn't a bad wound, and it's not enough to kill him, because there's no future anymore, nothing to contain a death. But it's that wound that cracks open the present, for it slicks Trystan's hand with so much blood that the Morholt's next thunderous backhand tears the sword from his grip.

There's nothing now between Trystan and the next absurdly fast return, the down-sweep of the Morholt's sword that Corwynal knows will tear into Trystan's side and bite deep into the muscles, veins and guts, and finally shatter into his backbone. Because there's a past after all, and it holds the future in his dream. So there's a future too. Corwynal closes his eyes. In the dream he'd watched and watched, but now, in the present, he finds he can't. So he doesn't see the blow, but nothing can prevent him from hearing the crunch of steel on bone, the shattering of metal, or Trystan's cry. Nothing can stop his eyes flying open to see Trystan fall, his shield slipping from his left arm, his right hand gripping at the wound, the blood pulsing between his fingers.

Then, impossibly, a little white dog comes running across the grass, barking joyfully because she's finally found her master. That's all it takes, a moment's distraction, a hesitation on the part of the Morholt. Yet why shouldn't he hesitate when he has all the time in the world? Time to pick up Trystan's discarded sword and raise it over the fallen body of a man who has neither sword nor shield and who's kneeling at his feet. The Morholt can afford the luxury of distraction.

And so he dies. The Morholt should have acted, but he's savouring the moment. And Trystan, who's fallen to one knee – hadn't it been both in the dream? – grips the knife he'd dropped his shield to reach and drives it deep into the Morholt's chest.

The past blurs, and the present opens out into the future because, with the Morholt's moment of miscalculation, there's still a future.

The sea ceased to beat against the rock and the wind dropped away to nothing. Corwynal's old dream and this new reality meshed like the sea-eagles of the coast when they lock their claws and tumble on the air. For a moment, poised between the past and the present, there was nothing but silence. Then, in that silence, Corwynal heard Arddu laughing. Out of the corner of his eye, he saw a bird take flight, a gull or a raven or an eagle, and wing its way north, even as the Morholt fell like a great stone, slowly and gracefully, into that heart-stopping silence. Then everything was sound and movement once more, voices crying, men running, Corwynal ahead of them all. The dog was barking and licking at Trystan's face as he lay on the ground, his lifeblood pulsing into the moss.

'I wondered if you'd show up,' Trystan murmured, as Corwynal threw himself on his knees beside him. 'Did you see? I turned aside at the last moment. You warned me, so I turned aside. I had my knife ready. Is he dead?'

'Yes, Trys. He's dead. You won.'

'I turned aside,' Trystan repeated. 'If you hadn't warned me, hadn't told me about the dream, I'd be the one who was dead. I turned aside . . .' His eyes sought Corwynal's, and he tried to raise himself, but Corwynal pressed him back. '. . . but not far enough.'

The wound was as bad as Corwynal had feared it would be – the rib shattered, white fragments of bone glinting in the wet red ruin of flesh and pulsing blood, pale intestines showing through a rent in the muscle wall.

'Your dream was right,' Trystan whispered, and closed his eyes. 'How typical of you to be right.'

'You're not going to die!' Corwynal shook him until he opened his eyes again. 'I didn't come here to watch you die!'

Trystan smiled up at him. 'I expect you were sick all the way.'

'Of course I was. So was the dog.' Corwynal was weeping now.

'The dog...' Trystan murmured, still smiling. 'The dog was a masterstroke.'

Someone tugged at Corwynal's shoulder. 'Out of the way and let me look!'

A little man with a partly shaven head crouched down beside them. His once-white habit was a dirty grey, but his hands seemed clean enough. Some of the priests of Chrystos who lived on the islands of the west had healing skills.

'It's bad enough,' the priest said, having probed the wound, making Trystan cry out. 'But it might not kill him. So if you want me to help him, you'll have to get out of the way. And I'll need a strong man to lift him. You there!' The priest beckoned Aelfric over and Corwynal began to get up, but Trystan reached out a hand.

'Don't leave me!'

'I'll not be far away. Let Aelfric help you.' He stepped back to let the Angle take his place.

'Good fight?' Aelfric asked lightly, as he put an arm under Trystan's shoulders.

'Good enough,' he replied, wincing. 'I might have known you'd set him free. I suppose you'll be wanting your own freedom now?'

Aelfric bent forward to slip a hand under Trystan's knees.

'It's not yours to grant, lad.' He lifted him carefully, but Trystan, after one strangled cry, lost consciousness.

Corwynal's legs gave way as Aelfric carried Trystan away, and he fell to his knees, his head dropping into his hands. Tears spurted between his fingers as fast as the blood had spurted between Trystan's, and he bowed his head to the ground, wracked by sobs and keening like a woman.

Everyone left him alone. Men disappeared in the direction of the shore, their voices fading as they did so. There was, he remembered, the question of the tribute and who had the right to collect it. All that was required for the matter to be resolved was a single body lying on the grass, and that body was the Morholt's.

'He's not dead, you know,' said a familiar voice.

'I know.' Corwynal wiped his face and looked up. Ferdiad knelt beside the Morholt's body, his face haggard, his green eyes rimmed with red.

'Not him!' The Scot jerked his chin at the cliff face. Aelfric was carrying Trystan up a narrow track that wound through outcrops, followed by the little priest and the white dog. Another of the priests was hurrying down towards them from a cluster of beehive huts that crowned the summit of the island. 'Not him,' Ferdiad repeated. 'I know he's not dead. Not yet.' He dragged a shaking hand over his face. 'It shouldn't have happened like this. I didn't see *this!*'

'Neither did I. I thought the black ship was Feargus' sign.'

'His wife's,' Ferdiad said curtly. 'The Morholt was her brother. Feargus believed it would bring him luck at the battle last summer, but it didn't. The Morholt was determined to prove him wrong. He's . . . He *was* stubborn like that, but to no purpose, for it brought them both ill luck. Or the gods did.' He grinned with all the humour of a skull. 'You see how they play with us?' Then he threw his head back. 'Are you playing with us?!' he shouted to the wind, to the gulls, to any god who might be listening. There was no answer from any of them, and eventually Ferdiad lowered his head once more.

'He isn't dead, you know.' He nodded at the Morholt and at Trystan's knife that jutted horribly from the man's chest. '*That's* not death.' He knelt down and, with an effort, pulled the knife free. It came loose with an obscene sucking of flesh on steel, crimson in the sunlight. Ferdiad shook it at Corwynal, his face contorted with something far beyond grief. 'This isn't death!' And then, under Corwynal's appalled gaze, Ferdiad, not taking his eyes from his, licked the blood from the blade.

'I would cut out and eat his heart if I could, but it might be . . . misinterpreted.' The Scot wiped his lips with the back of a shaking hand, and his voice was empty of everything now. 'The boy was good, though,' he added. 'Better than I expected. Your brother?'

'Yes.'

'No!' Ferdiad leapt over the corpse and threw himself at Corwynal. The knife stopped just short of his throat and quivered with the magnitude of the Fili's emotion. 'That has to be a lie! I won't have lies, not here, not now, not after this!' His eyes were no longer the coldly measured blue-green of sea-ice. His gold-shot gaze was as feral as a hawk's and had the same inhuman ferocity.

'Shall I tell you my truth?' The knife shook in Ferdiad's hand and his eyes glittered with danger, but after a harsh intake of breath the Fili dropped his eyes and laid the knife down, and when he spoke his voice was empty once more. 'I loved the Morholt beyond reason, but never told him, and now it's too late. Can you imagine what that feels like?'

Corwynal shuddered, knowing how close he'd come to facing Ferdiad's anguish. He looked down at the Morholt and saw him properly for the first time. He was a big man, but far from being a giant. Without his helmet he was no longer a featureless monster, but a man with a pleasant, if not handsome, face. In life, he'd been terrifying. In death, he was unremarkable. Corwynal reached out a hand and laid it tentatively on Ferdiad's shoulder. 'Yes. I can imagine it.'

'Don't touch me!' Ferdiad flinched away. 'You're to blame for his death. You distracted him. But I'll have my revenge.' His unearthly eyes glittered with tears and something worse than tears. 'You've stolen something from me today, as you once stole everything else, but one day I'll take everything from you – everything you care about!'

Corwynal didn't know what he was talking about, but he understood how easily grief could turn to fury and so said nothing. Eventually, the glitter in Ferdiad's eyes dulled, and he looked away.

'You were ready to die for that boy, just to let him have a chance,' he said bitterly. 'The Morholt died because it didn't occur to me to do the same.' He dropped his ravaged face into his shaking hands, and his voice was thick with tears. 'It seems I didn't love the Morholt quite enough.'

He got up and walked away, stumbling as he went. Corwynal let him go. In his dream, at the ending he'd always imagined, it was he who'd walked away, lost, despairing and broken.

But Trystan lived. The fate Corwynal had dreamt had passed him by, and he'd played his part in that, if not in the way he'd expected. He still believed in fate, still believed what shaped a man was the struggle against it, but he no longer believed it could be foreseen, or that it was wise to try. He was free of his dreams, and, in the future, he'd be subject only to the promptings of his heart or his soul, or whatever part of him was ruled by the gods. Perhaps, in time, he'd even be free of the gods themselves.

There on the edge of Galloway, on a rocky outcrop surrounded by the sea he hated, Corwynal felt the weight of the future lift from his shoulders.

EPILOGUE

The Rock, Carraig Ealasaid

Summer 486

A DREAM OF A WHITE RAVEN

'Corwynal?'

It was little more than a breath of sound, but he woke immediately. He was lying beside Trystan in one of the priest's beehive huts on the Rock, shielding him from the draught. The place was crudely built, and when the wind blew – which it did constantly – it howled through the walls and it was impossible to keep warm. Even the dog was shivering.

'You were moaning,' Trystan murmured.

'I was dreaming,' Corwynal replied, getting up to rearrange the cloak he'd hung across the windward wall in an attempt to block the worst of the draughts. The fire had burned low while he'd slept, so he thrust another piece of driftwood into the embers. It flared blue with salt, briefly brightening the place, and showed him how pale and gaunt Trystan had become since he'd fought the Morholt. He'd won that battle, but his fight wasn't over. Now he was battling the poison in the wound he'd taken – and he was losing.

'A nightmare?' In spite of his own problems, Trystan's concern for him was written on his face.

'No.' *This is the nightmare.* 'It was a fair enough dream,' he lied. 'I was dreaming about a woman.'

'You? A woman?' Trystan raised an eyebrow, and a faint smile lit up his face. 'Was she beautiful?'

Corwynal forced himself to smile in reply. 'No, not really,' he said, thinking back to the dream. He'd been lying on a battlefield, a great wound in his chest, a raven hopping closer and closer. Except it hadn't been a raven. It had been Arddu. Corwynal had tried to give the God his life on the Rock, but Arddu had refused to take it. Now, in his dream, the God came to claim it after all, and his wicked beak darted into the wound in his chest and plucked out Corwynal's heart. Then another raven had come, a white raven.

'Leave him alone! Get away, you foul thing!' it shouted and turned into a woman who flapped her arms to drive off the bird. It croaked its displeasure and dropped its morsel of flesh into the mud as the woman bent towards him. 'It's a bad wound,' she said. 'But I've seen worse.'

She picked up Corwynal's heart and held it out to him. It lay motionless in her palm, but when she slid her hand into the cavity in his chest, his heart began to beat once more. 'Live, Talorc!' she said. 'Live!' She'd put her lips to his and then . . . Then Trystan had woken him.

The woman in his dream had been neither beautiful nor young. She was perhaps his own age, for there were silver streaks in her dark brown hair. A frown etched into her forehead made her look stern. Her eyes were an indeterminate greyish-brown and looked as if they'd seen too much in her lifetime. Her mouth was too wide for beauty, her nose too pronounced, and she was shorter and thinner than was fashionable. But, in Corwynal's dream, none of these things had mattered.

Trystan sighed. 'Do you remember telling me you wanted me to fall in love with a beautiful woman? I would like to have known what it's like to fall in love.'

'You will,' Corwynal said fiercely. 'One day you will.' A shadow crossed Trystan's face, followed by a spasm of pain as he moved. The stench rising from the wound would have made anyone gag, but Corwynal refused to give up hope, even though he was the only one to cling to it.

'You don't have to pretend for my sake,' Trystan said. 'What will happen will happen. Accept it and—'

'No! There must be something those priests can do!'

'They're doing their best,' Trystan murmured, and closed his eyes. Corwynal was about to make some savage response when the door was pushed open and one of the priests came in. At the sight of his expression – concern, sorrow and pity – Corwynal's anger drowned itself in gut-wrenching terror. Trystan was right. The priest *was* doing his best, but his best wasn't good enough.

Corwynal left them together and went down to the beach, the dog trotting at his heels. The priest would change the stinking bandages on Trystan's side, then dose him with poppy so he'd be able to sleep. From time to time the wound would erupt, its foulness flowing like milk, and Trystan would have some respite from the pain for a while. At other times, more often now, he'd fall into a fever from which he'd emerge weaker than before. But he wasn't dying. Corwynal clung to that conviction even though everyone pitied him for it.

Aelfric was waiting for him but said nothing when he came to stand next to him at the edge of the beach, and just picked up a stone and hefted it in his hand. Corwynal bent down, selected one of much the same size and flung it hard out into the waves, helplessness and fury giving such power to his arm that his stone sailed out well beyond the breakers. Aelfric grunted in approval, then threw his own stone which, as usual, went further than Corwynal's. It wasn't much of a contest, but there was little else to do on the island, and so they continued to throw stones at the sea until Corwynal's shoulders ached and Aelfric had won as decisively as he always did.

'He's not dying,' he said eventually, watching the dog, bored now the game had ended, nose her way along the tideline. Aelfric didn't reply, but met his eyes for a moment before letting his own slide away. 'He's weak, but he's not dying,' Corwynal insisted, then picked up another stone and threw it hard. 'Curse this island! If only we'd gone back to Galloway after the fight. We could have got him to Iuddeu from there, or Meldon.'

But the priests had advised against moving Trystan until his wound began to heal, so Corwynal had let the ship bearing the tribute sail back to the Mote without them. It had since returned, bringing much needed supplies, but then the wind had blown up into a southerly gale. The ship had dragged its mooring on the poor holding ground and so had left once more, heading for shelter and promising to return when it could. But the wind had barely abated since then and there was no telling when the ship would come back – or when Trystan's wound would heal.

'Is he worse today?'

'Not worse. He's lucid, if weaker than before. But he's not dying.'

Aelfric picked up another stone, but instead of throwing it he let it fall and turned to face him. 'He *is* dying. Accept it, man.'

'No!'

'When the ship comes back, you can take him back to Galloway.'

'Not until he's recovered, or it's calmer.'

'You can take him back to Galloway because he'll be dead,' Aelfric said bluntly. 'Then you can take his body back to Lothian where he belongs.'

'Is that all that matters to you?' Corwynal caught Aelfric's wrist when he reached for another stone and forced the Angle to look him in the eyes. 'Returning to Lothian?'

'Don't be such a fool!' Aelfric wrenched his arm away. 'Yes, I want to go back to Lothian, but that doesn't mean I want Trystan dead. I *like* the boy! But no-one survives that sort of wound.'

Corwynal turned away and stared out to sea, crossing his arms over his chest. Aelfric let him stare for a while before putting his hand on his shoulder and squeezing it painfully. 'Don't try to comfort me,' Corwynal said irritably, but didn't shake off Aelfric's hand, for, oddly, he did take comfort from the pressure of his fingers.

'Listen, man. I know – I can guess – what you're feeling. You said something, the day of the fight . . .'

Can't a man watch his son die? He'd been wondering when Aelfric would bring that up.

'Not sure you meant it, or if I believed it,' Aelfric went on, shifting his feet awkwardly. 'And it's not something I'd care to repeat. But if it's true, you should tell him before . . . while you still can.'

Aelfric was right. It was, after all, one of the reasons Corwynal had come to the island. But he no longer knew if it was the right thing to do. *If I tell him, he'll know I've been lying to him for his whole life. He'll know he's not who he thought he was*. Why take everything from Trystan at the moment he had to pass beyond the veil? But none of that was the reason he couldn't say what he wanted to say. It was because it would mean accepting what everyone was trying to tell him. *He's dying*.

'He's not dying,' he insisted.

'Have it your own way,' Aelfric said, lifting his hand from Corwynal's shoulder.

'He's *not* dying,' he whispered, staring northwards, his vision blurring in the pulsing light, bright and dark, bright and dark, as clouds scudded across the sun. The murk of the last few days had cleared, and the low-lying coast of Galloway could be made out in the east. To the north-west, the mountains on the Scots island of Arainn were hard and sharp against the sky. Behind them, grey with distance, were the northern lands of Dalriada. 'Where's Dunadd?' he asked, squinting into the sun that was setting in a welter of gold and grey behind the bulk of Arainn.

'There,' Aelfric said, nodding at the sunset. 'On the mainland, beyond that island. Not far. But getting there's tricky. The Goose ran aground at the entrance to the sea-loch that serves as its port. Dunadd itself is inland, near the priests' place where they fixed my arm.'

'How long would it take to sail there?'

'From here?' Aelfric scratched his beard thoughtfully. 'With this wind? Two days, maybe less. Why?'

Because, suddenly, everything came together – the stories Ninian had told him when he'd been ill in Meldon, of a monastery close to Dunadd where he'd learned the healing arts, and Trystan's words in a Selgovian wood – *The Scots healers are famous!* Aelfric stood beside him, his left forearm bearing a healing, neatly stitched scar. One of the holy women of

Chrystos had treated him at that monastery near Dunadd. Even Corwynal's dream of a woman driving off a raven seemed to be of significance. The God, in his raven form, had also been in that dream, as he'd been absent in his blood, the God he'd last seen in a little white dog's eyes. Now the dog looked up and barked, as if in answer to a question. *I'm right, am I not?*

Aelfric must have seen the hope flicker in Corwynal's eyes and realised what he intended, for he took a step backwards in dismay.

'No! It's madness! Three of us in that little boat? In the tail of a gale with Thunor knows what weather behind it? Do you know how far it is? More than twice the distance from Loch Ryan. And even if we get there, Trys killed their Champion. It's not something they'll have forgotten.'

'They won't know who we are. We'll change our names, avoid Dunadd and go straight to the monastery.'

'They'd remember me there.'

'But you were just a sailor on a trading ship. So we'll be traders too. Why didn't I think of it before!?'

'Because it's insane! Have you thought about Trystan? The journey might kill him.'

'You just told me he's going to die anyway. If there's a chance, even a small one, I have to take it. I . . . I'm asking you to take us to Dalriada, Aelfric.'

'Asking, is it? Not telling?'

'I think we've gone beyond telling.'

The Angle grunted but didn't reply.

'You have a price?' Corwynal asked, knowing how much he needed him.

'You want to haggle?'

'Must you always answer one question with another?'

'Must you?'

Corwynal began to laugh, and once he'd started he couldn't stop. He laughed until his chest hurt. Eventually, however, he recovered and shook his head. 'I'm not going to haggle. I'll give you anything you want if you'll take us to Dalriada. Is that enough?'

Aelfric looked exasperated, and Corwynal was afraid he'd refuse. 'You shouldn't have said that! Because, one day ... Oh, curse your soul and your pride and everything about you, you fucking bloody Caledonian! I'll take you, but as to the price, let's leave that for the future. Because none of us are likely to get out of Dalriada alive – if we even get there in the first place.'

'No?' Corwynal felt the God stir in his veins as he made yet another choice in the twists and turns of his life. Across the water lay Dalriada, the land of Trystan's enemies, and his. But that was where they had to go.

AUTHOR'S NOTE

I very much hope you've enjoyed reading *The Wolf in Winter*.

If you have, I'd love you to **post a review on Amazon**. It needn't be an essay – a couple of lines would be fantastic. Reviews are particularly helpful for authors like me who're just setting out into the stormy waters of self-publishing. It would be great to know you've got my back!

If you've spotted any typos and would like to let me know about them, please contact me through my website. I do really want to know so I can fix them.

If you'd like to find out about the next book in *The Trystan Trilogy*, *The Swan in Summer*, see the next page, and/or:

Subscribe to my Newsletter

Not only will you receive exclusive extracts from *The Swan in Summer*, but free short stories, regular newsletters, and notifications of new blog posts about writing in general and the world of *The Trystan Trilogy* in particular.

Go to **barbaralennox.com/subscribe** or scan the QR code:

THE SWAN IN SUMMER

The story continues...

Seventeen years ago, Brangianne, the Dark Swan of Dalriada, sister to Feargus, King of Dalriada, had her future stolen by raiders from the neighbouring Kingdom of Galloway.

Now, once again, Galloway has ruined the life she'd painstakingly rebuilt. Defeat in a misguided war, a crippling tribute demand, and, most recently, the death of Dalriada's champion, The Morholt, have put Feargus in a difficult position. If he's to survive, he'll have to sacrifice the people closest to him – his sister Brangianne and his daughter, Yseult.

But Brangianne, forced to make a choice between two unpalatable alternatives, chooses instead to escape to her old lands of Carnadail, where, in her stolen summer of freedom, she meets three shipwrecked Britons – and so sets in train the tragedy that is the story of Trystan and Yseult.

But tragedy lies in wait for Brangianne herself when she's drawn to the half-Caledonian stranger from the sea, a man calling himself Talorc, a man with beasts on his skin and secrets in his heart...

THE SERPENT IN SPRING

The story concludes...

One day you'll have to stand by and watch the woman who's the other half of your soul marry someone else.

Corwynal's prediction comes true when Trystan is forced to watch the girl he loves, Yseult of Dalriada, marry his uncle, Marc, King of Galloway. Trystan isn't willing to give her up completely, however, and Corwynal has to stand by, helpless, as the lovers endanger everything he cares about. But when they risk their own lives he has to act. He helps them escape to the one place they'll be safe, the one place he doesn't want to go – Atholl in Caledonia.

There he'll not only have to face the judgement of the Druid Council for a crime he committed as a boy, but the long-planned revenge of Ferdiad, Fili of Dalriada, for a crime he doesn't remember committing at all.

Corwynal will have to decide where he belongs and what and who he loves the most, unaware that his decision will lead to the final tragedy that is the love story of Trystan and Yseult.

HISTORICAL NOTE

The mediaeval romance of Tristan and Isolde was compiled on the continent in the 12th century and later incorporated into Malory's 15th century Arthurian fantasy, *Le Morte D'Arthur*. But it was based on much earlier tales derived from Irish and possibly Pictish sources. These early tales acquired a Welsh flavour following the resettlement of Britons from Strathclyde in Gwynedd at the end of the 9th century. Subsequently the same stories were taken to the other Brythonic lands of Cornwall and Brittany where they absorbed local references, and the story is now thought of as being Cornish/Breton. But the original stories were probably set in Scotland/Ireland.

In *The Trystan Trilogy*, the legend has been reworked to include many of the familiar elements of the story, but not necessarily in the same order, and has been set against the 'historical' background of late 5th century 'Scotland'. Historical is a very loose term in this context. Virtually no texts survive from this period and location, so the settings and characters are an amalgam of the little that is know about earlier and later times. Galloway and Strathclyde, for example, are later names, given to the lands of the Novantae and Dumnonni tribes detailed by Ptolemy in his 1st century map of Britain. The Votadini tribe of the east coast gave their name to the later Kingdom of Gododdin. Lothian, a modern term, comes from a reference to

Tristan's traditional home being Loonois, which has been equated with Lothian. Dalriada was a real Irish Kingdom, existing both in Ireland and Scotland. It was supposedly founded by Fergus, Loarn and Oenghus, but they are probably mythical. The Caledonian, or Pictish, tribes are also mentioned by Ptolemy, and a list of their kingdoms appears in a 9th century text. The name Atholl probably derives from Alflotha, or new Ireland, a name given to it after the area became part of a Scots-controlled territory.

The character names were taken from the various versions of the Tristan and Isolde legend, and from the oldest Arthurian texts, but have been 'adjusted' to give them more of a 'welsh' look since the people of the Lands between the Walls (a made-up name) would have spoken Brythonic, a precursor of Welsh. Some names, such as Dumnagual and Ciniod, come from genealogies and king-lists of the period. They may even have been real people, although the historicity of genealogies is very dubious.

All Celtic nations would have celebrated the four fire-festivals of Imbolc, Beltein, Lughnasadh and Samhain, but these are the Gaelic names, since I was unable to find reliable 'British' names for them.

The Trystan Trilogy is a work of fiction, and my intention was to give the reader a flavour of the cultures of the period rather than sticking strictly to the known facts – or lack of them. I've researched as widely as I could on these matters but, inevitably, will have misinterpreted or simply missed available evidence, and for that I apologise.

For further information and a bibliography of sources, refer to my website:

(barbaralennox.com/resources/bibliography)

ABOUT THE AUTHOR

I was born, and still live, in Scotland on the shores of a river, between the mountains and the sea. I'm a retired scientist and science administrator, but have always been fascinated by the early history of Scotland, and I love fleshing out that history with the stories of fictional, and not-so-fictional, characters.

Find out more about me and my writing on my website:

Barbaralennox.com

Connect with me on the following:

- Twitter.com/barbaralennox4
- Instagram.com/barbaralennoxwriter
- Goodreads.com/author/show/19661962.Barbara_Lennox
- Pinterest.co.uk/barbaralennox58
- Amazon: viewauthor.at/authorprofile

ALSO BY BARBARA LENNOX

Song of a Red Morning, a short story which takes place in 6th century Scotland and is set at Dunpeldyr, was published by Amazon in 2019.

getbook.at/Songofaredmorning

'*Thoroughly absorbing and beautifully written.*'

The Man who Loved Landscape, a collection of 40 short stories, many of which are set in Scotland, was published by Amazon in 2021.

getbook.at/Manwholovedlandscape

'*Simply the best book of short stories I have read in years.*'

The Ghost in the Machine, *poems of love, loss, life and death*, a collection of 69 poems, was published by Amazon in 2021.

getbook.at/theghostinthemachine

'*This is an excellent book, nuanced, accessible, human.*'

Forthcoming novels:

The Swan in Summer, second volume of *The Trystan Trilogy*, will be published in 2022.

The Serpent in Spring, third volume of *The Trystan Trilogy*, will be published in 2023.

ACKNOWLEDGEMENTS

I would never have written anything if I hadn't attended the 'Continuing as a Writer' classes, part of the University of Dundee's Continuing Education Programme. These classes were tutored by Esther Read, whose support and encouragement has been unstinting and invaluable. Esther, I can't thank you enough, not only for your help and advice as I mastered the art of short story writing, but for manfully reading through not one but two early (and much longer) drafts of *The Wolf in Winter*.

I'd like to thank my beta-reading team at The History Quill for reading the almost final manuscript. Their comments were so encouraging and helpful.

I have to give a shout-out to all my Instagram pals from whom I learned such an immense amount about the process of self-publishing, and who were always there for inspiration, support and encouragement. Thanks, guys and gals!

At home, my writing buddies, Harry, Rambo and Oscar, the best cats in the world, were with me all the way, usually asleep.

Almost finally, but not least, I have to thank my husband, Will, for putting up with all the scribbling and not asking any awkward questions.

My biggest thank you, however, goes to all my readers, especially my ARC team – you know who you are – without whom this book would just be a footnote in my own imagination.

Printed in Great Britain
by Amazon